The New Kingmakers

The New Kingmakers

David Chagall

Harcourt Brace Jovanovich, Publishers
New York and London

Requests for permission to make copies of any part of the work should
be mailed to: Permissions, Harcourt Brace Jovanovich, Inc. 757 Third
Avenue, New York, NY 10017.

Library of Congress Cataloging in Publication Data

Chagall, David.
The new kingmakers.
Includes index.
1. Presidents—United States—Election.
2. Political consultants—United States.
I. Title.
JK524.C45   324.973′092   80-7932
ISBN 0-15-165203-1   AACR2

Printed in the United States of America

B C D E

Contents

Acknowledgments

This book was researched and written over a six-year span. It concerns the most significant development in modern politics —the coming of age of campaign consultants.

Today these specialists wield great power, yet they are content to divert fame and glory to the politicians who pay their fees. They derive satisfaction from knowing that they, not their clients, determine the outcome of an election.

I talked to hundreds of these consultants. They call themselves "political consultants," "campaign specialists," or "communications consultants." Most speak for themselves in the chapters that follow.

Others, who do not speak for themselves here, helped shape this book, and I am grateful for the chance to mention them.

Gladys Alsin of Mercer Island, Washington, gave encouragement and support at crucial times during the writing of this book. My wife Juneau typed, proofread, and criticized the work at every stage, and took the photographs that appear on the book jacket.

Finally, special thanks to Hal Evry for opening my eyes to the consultant phenomenon, the full impact of which is yet to be seen.

David Chagall
Agoura, California
May, 1981

The New King- makers

Playing the White House Circuit

Ronald Reagan was having a cup of morning coffee with his political consultant, Stuart Spencer. New to politics, Reagan had been running around California for seven months making speeches, shaking hands, and charming voters in his drive to replace the incumbent Pat Brown as governor. Spencer was outlining a special point he wanted his candidate to stress in his speeches that week. Bemused, Reagan suddenly said, "You know something, Stu? Politics is just like show business."

"What do you mean?" asked Spencer, puzzled.

"Well, you begin with a hell of an opening, you coast for a while, and you end with a hell of a closing." The ex-actor grinned, dispelling any irritation Spencer might feel over such a flippant evaluation of the political process he valued so highly.

"I didn't like what he said at the time," Spencer told me a few weeks after helping Reagan win the White House in 1980. "But you know something? He was absolutely right!"

On that morning fourteen years ago the newcomer Ronald Reagan had zeroed in on a simple truth that political analysts have only recently begun to acknowledge: the transformation of elective politics from a clash of words-and-ideas conveyed in print to a contest of images-and-feelings broadcast on television.

In 1960 the first decade of the new game was launched by the candidacy of John F. Kennedy. That year Americans chose the image of optimistic youth over that of surly competence; television style overpowered political savvy, and media fakery became an essential of campaign strategy. Kennedy used a standard ploy at all his airport arrivals. He stationed a pair of accomplices below the walkway to hold a rope against the surging crowd as the candidate descended from the aircraft. At the crucial moment, a Kennedy aide gave the signal for the "rope drop." Released, a flood of humanity crowded around the grinning hero, who embraced the admiring multitude while television cameras recorded dramatic scenes to feature on the evening news.

Richard Nixon made sure he had a comforting middle-class crowd at all his televised rallies by yanking out all undesirable types, including blacks with Afro hairstyles, shabbily dressed workingmen, and bearded Hasidic rabbis. Jimmy Carter exploited his "populist" image by slinging an empty garment bag over his shoulder for the benefit of cameramen, while his real luggage was quietly removed from the aircraft by sweating porters.

Ronald Reagan cultivated the opposite image. So as not to remind voters of Reagan's former incarnation as George Gip of Notre Dame, Stu Spencer insisted that all his television material be underproduced, using plain backgrounds and a talking head instead of the drums, thunder, and marching bands of traditional political commercials. Reagan himself, no slouch at discerning the small touch that makes the big difference, discovered early how to make his conservative ideas acceptable to a larger segment of American voters. "Reagan says the same things Barry Goldwater said," Stu Spencer noted. "Only he says them better."

Reagan knew instinctively how to sell a controversial idea.

"Barry Goldwater was never defeated on the basis of his philosophy," Reagan once explained. "What people really voted against was the false image of a dangerous radical, a great big thumb over the nuclear button. And it traces back to the fact that Barry has a blunt, forthright way of speaking. People who know him love him for it. But during the election Barry had a way of saying the blunt thing first, and nobody stuck around to hear his qualifying remarks. For example, look at what he was trying to tell us about Social Security. By actuarial standards, the system is several trillion dollars out of alignment. Barry had no intention of dismantling it, but when he said, 'I don't mean to take social security away from anyone now getting it,' and, 'We must fix the program so these people will be secure,' he had already lost most of his listeners with his first scare line, the blunt statement."

"You say the qualifiers first," Reagan advised. "You say, 'Let's make it plain that our first priority must be that no one who depends on Social Security during their nonearning years should have that endangered or taken away. Today it is endangered by the shape the entire program is in.' Then you go on to say, 'The program is out of balance now; down the line can come the great tragedy of Americans' finding the cupboard bare. Before that happens, let's fix Social Security.'

"Always say the qualifier first," Reagan concluded.

It's not what you say but how you say it. It's not what it is but how it looks. In the new politics, appearance *is* reality. No serious political candidate can hope to win high office today without his own campaign consultant calling the shots. These consultants are high-powered professionals versed in the skills of polling, communications, and computer planning. They plot the strategies, set the stages, choose the themes, and mastermind the interplay of candidate and media in the kleig lights of today's electioneering carnivals. Reagan was right. Modern politics is indeed like show business.

Over the past two years I met and talked extensively with the top campaign consultants of America. Without exception they are bright, likeable, and hard-working, though sometimes brash and defensive. Naturally, they do not view the democratic process as the rest of us do. From the consultant's viewpoint, a campaign is something very different from the "issues," gaffes, and rhetoric delivered on the evening news or reported in the morning papers. It is an orchestrated clash of images, feelings, and perceptions, an "all-out war without bullets waged in the hearts and minds of voters, monitored by polls."

I have concentrated on the most recent Presidential elections as the prototypes of modern campaigns. In America no position is more exalted than the Presidency. The President is the closest thing we have to a monarch, and his influence on our national character is crucial. Inspirational, mediocre, or destructive as his administration may be, the President pervades our national psyche. Other nations judge us on the quality of our leader's looks, brains, spirit, and vision—just as we judge them. Like it or not, our Presidents represent the American Ideal to others; they are totems of the American soul. How we choose them is therefore very important.

Between the Presidencies of John F. Kennedy and Ronald Reagan, a brigade of consultant superstars developed and assumed positions of unparalleled power and influence in the political structure of America. These men behind the Presidents are the "new political bosses of America" and they have changed, for good or ill, our evolving democratic ideal.

2

Joe Napolitan

Joe Napolitan's star began to rise in 1960. As John F. Kennedy's "secret weapon," he helped win upset primaries—in New Hampshire, Wisconsin, and West Virginia—that launched the Bostonian's historical drive to become the first Catholic president in United States history. Later Napolitan helped win senatorial campaigns for the Kennedy brothers Bob and Ted, and earned the tag "Kennedy man." At the end of the decade, Napolitan gained superstar status when he took Hubert Humphrey to within a hair's breadth of beating Richard Nixon in what would have been the biggest campaign upset since Truman beat Dewey.

Today, at fifty-two, Napolitan is the quintessential field general and acknowledged dean of modern consultants. Adviser to presidents, kings, and prime ministers all over the world, he is the founder of his profession's two major societies—the American and the International Associations of Political Consultants. His bearing is reminiscent of old-world royalty: slim elegance, cool restraint. Behind tinted lenses, his eyes are always watchful.

In the United States, Napolitan works only for liberal Democrats although, as he is quick to point out, his reasons have less to do with party loyalty than with professional credibility.

"Suppose I did Senate races in Illinois and Indiana, one Democrat and the other Republican," he conjectures. "Can I go one place and brag how good the administration has been for the people, then travel fifty miles south and complain how the administration has screwed everything up? I'd lose all credibility. That's why most counselors work for one party or the other. On the other hand, technicians, guys who do automated telephone campaigns, or pollsters who don't decide strategy can work for both sides."

"But why liberal Democrats?" I asked Napolitan.

"I wouldn't feel comfortable with anyone else," he replied. "I couldn't work for somebody who doesn't have a Democratic philosophy. It would be hypocritical and I couldn't do a good job."

Napolitan's background has a lot to do with his ideological leanings. The only son of an Italian immigrant, a Prohibition bootlegger who opened a restaurant after booze became legal, Joe became the man of the household when his father died suddenly of a heart attack. Joe was seven, his sister five. His mother found work in a factory, so the kids were raised by a large clan of aunts, uncles, cousins, and grandparents. Franklin Delano Roosevelt was the family's savior and saint. Joe grew up in the Depression. Underdog ethics were his natural inheritance.

From those early days of hand-to-mouth struggle, Napolitan has come a long way. We talked in the offices of a company called Public Affairs Analysts, of which Napolitan is co-owner, on the eighteenth floor of a posh office complex near the United Nations in midtown Manhattan. Public Affairs Analysts has nothing to do with electing people. It is devoted strictly to communications, to advising governments and big businesses, both American and foreign, on how to send messages to the people they serve, and then to measuring the impact that these messages have on the public mind. In 1972 Nixon's burglars broke into the offices of Public Affairs Analysts, looking for dirt to use against Napolitan's partner Larry O'Brien in their campaign.

Joe Napolitan's election business still operates out of Springfield, Massachusetts, where Napolitan was born, raised, and educated, and where he married his home-town sweetheart, worked on local papers, and brought up his children. In an age of widespread mobility, Napolitan never left his hometown. Instead he made it a terminal for constant world travel. Not imposing physically, Napolitan nevertheless subtly radiates power. He speaks softly and precisely, handling phrases as if running them past a ticker-tape censor, a man who has been in all the tight spots and survived.

"A political consultant is a specialist in political communication," he explains with characteristic modesty. "That's all there is to it—it's not very Machiavellian."

Accordingly, Napolitan also maintains that "the best consultants always try to remain in the background." That willingness to let the candidate hog the glory goes with the territory. Politicians are notorious for their bloated egos, so it pays to sponsor the illusion that the consultant is only mildly responsible for the outcome of an election. Ever sensitive to cries of "manipulator" by the press, consultants have learned from sad experience to play down their real role.

Napolitan has a numerical mind. He is always listing things and counting them off, one, two, three. He has even distilled all his political skills and experience into a three-step, twenty-five-word formula for winning any election, American or foreign:

1. Decide how you want the voter to feel or react.
2. Decide what to do to make him react that way.
3. Do it.

What Napolitan does himself, he does brilliantly. What he can't do, he gets talented specialists to do. Of the more than 200 campaigns he has handled so far, he's won 170. Considering that he gets many long shots as clients, his 85-percent win rate speaks for itself.

Napolitan bases all his moves in a campaign on what he learns from the mouths of voters, so the first thing he does is extensive polling. While most consultants hire out their research work, Napolitan has his own polling firm, which is even used by his competitors. He enjoys a reputation as an intuitive pollster who can get to the heart of the public anxieties that become the issues of a campaign. He began to sharpen his own polling skills when he discovered that big-name survey research companies didn't know what questions to ask. Academic pollsters typically make assumptions about the campaign and test them on a sample of voters. Napolitan takes a different approach. He sees survey research as half a conversation with people. His questionnaires have a few yes/no questions but lots of open-ended ones that encourage people to say what's on their minds.

"A poll is the absolute first thing to do in any campaign," he stressed. "It's invaluable to media strategy. If you isolate an issue with special appeal for blacks or women or old people, you can zero in on that group. You reach blacks through black radio stations, newspapers, or by circularizing black neighborhoods. You hit the elderly with time buys next to television shows that appeal to old people. You hit young people through rock radio stations. Polls tell us people vote for people, not issues. They care more whether the candidate is honest and compassionate than if he agrees with them on issues. Issues score very low on polls. You don't worry so much about the candidate's positions as his perceived character."

Napolitan flew down to West Virginia in 1976, where Jay Rockefeller was running a second time for governor. Rockefeller had lost badly in 1972 and Napolitan knew why: Rockefeller had been outcampaigned and outspent.

"Rockefeller was so conscious of his wealth, he ran a low-cost campaign to prove he wasn't buying the office. He hired second- and third-rate people to do his films and they made the worst television spots I'd ever seen. Meanwhile consultant Bobby Goodwin did a fine job for Archie Moore with superb television material. So in 1976 we went out and got the best people available. Our polls showed West Virginians wanted more jobs, better roads, and they were mad as hell over a tax on food and groceries. That was our whole campaign—create more jobs, rebuild back roads, and abolish the food tax. And we had the man who would do it—Jay Rockefeller."

Now governor of West Virginia.

At Springfield Tech High in the forties, Joe Napolitan played first-string guard on a winning football team. At 156 pounds, he was the smallest lineman in the league, but he earned respect as a tough competitor, substituting brains, quickness, and courage for bulk—traits that serve him well in the free-for-all of a campaign. He doubled as sports editor for the school paper, and the day after he graduated he went to work as a sports reporter for the *Springfield Evening Union.*

After ten years as a political reporter and foreign correspondent in Europe, Joe came home, quit journalism, and opened his own public relations office in Springfield, Massachusetts. The year was 1957. He had just turned twenty-eight. One day a man in his early thirties walked in off the street and introduced himself.

"I'm Tom O'Connor, I want to be mayor of Springfield, and I need help."

O'Connor's sheer gall appealed to Napolitan. The incumbent mayor was a six-term politician deemed unbeatable by the experts and local newspapers. The challenge was more than Napolitan could resist. Despite the fact that O'Connor didn't have much money, he became his first candidate.

To save money, Napolitan did his own polling. He picked up the needed skills by reading books and professional polling reports. Those early polls he did in Springfield showed that voters thought the mayor was "entrenched, a public servant going stale." The mayor's big asset was that everyone knew him; nobody knew O'Connor.

Napolitan, among the first wave of political pros who understood the magical power of television, designed a ten-second commercial for the campaign, making it simple to keep costs down. The film showed a bowling-ball "bomb" with attached fuse sizzling for six seconds before exploding into fragments that formed the words: NEW LEADERSHIP . . . TOM O'CONNOR. That was it. Napolitan ran it regularly at cheap local rates and soon everyone in town knew about Tom O'Connor. In the primary O'Connor beat the mayor in every one of the city's sixty-four precincts and moved into city hall after the general election.

Four years later Napolitan ran a new candidate against O'Connor and licked him badly. That convinced him that the man who mapped the moves and controlled television was often the man who determined the winner.

In 1959 he became associated with Larry O'Brien, a rising

power in the Democratic Party network. Together they won a referendum that reformed the Springfield city charter, then went on in 1960 to win key primaries for John F. Kennedy. After Kennedy became President, O'Brien took a job in Washington as director of congressional relations. Joe Napolitan, who prized his free-lancer's independence, stayed in Springfield and helped elect a small army of Democratic candidates over the next two decades.

One of Napolitan's strengths is his knowledge of the reporter's life and the predilections of assignment editors. He can arrange campaign events for maximum effect on what he calls "uncontrolled media"—news, talk shows, and panel shows like *Meet the Press*. But his real concern is controlled media—commercials, films, literature—which can be targeted for specific audiences at the critical moment in a campaign.

Napolitan is his own media director, hiring film and sound people to turn his research findings into advertising that wins hearts and votes. He choreographs his ballet of media events to fill the time frame of a campaign, which is weeks, months, sometimes years in the execution but is resolved in twelve hours on election day.

Tony Schwartz, a legend in the world of creative sound, is a media specialist who works closely with Joe Napolitan. Schwartz has handled many Presidential campaigns and hundreds of lesser ones, and has created winning commercials for Coca-Cola and other top name brands, as well as public-service messages for the government. He gives Napolitan high marks for managing talent. "Joe gives you information and suggestions, then leaves you alone," Schwartz told me. "He has the ability to look at what you've done and say yea or nay. He's no nitpicker."

Most of what Schwartz turns out gets a loud yea. His most famous political commercial is the classic that featured a little girl picking daisy petals and counting them down into a nuclear mushroom blast. In 1964 this commercial helped push Lyndon Johnson to a massive victory over Barry Goldwater, who was labeled a hawk.

"My way of working with sound and Joe's way of interpreting research data are a great combination," Schwartz explained. "People best understand things they've heard before. I bet you can fill in the next word of this phrase: for the rest of your—"

"Life," I replied.

"You could have said 'days,' " Schwartz said. "Or the rest of your 'time' But what you did say was 'life.' And so will most other people. That's why Joe does research to determine the way people feel about a candidate. Then we can predict what they'll hear, how they'll respond to commercials.

"McLuhan talks about the electrical environment as a software world of information. It's totally invisible, nobody knows where his ideas come from. People are just beginning to realize they live in nonvisual space. Politically, sociologically, psychologically, they take inner trips instead of outer trips. We did research for Patrick Moynihan's 1976 campaign for senator and found out people best remembered him as a toughie at the United Nations. So we evoked that connection."

Schwartz turned on a tape of the radio commercial:

MOYNIHAN (voice-over): "When I was at the U.N., I fought for America. And in the Senate, I'll fight for New York. And *you'll . . . know . . . I'm . . . there!*"

The effect was staccato, strong. The research said the voters were hungry for someone firm and tough. Moynihan was elected.

"Napolitan and I proceed on the same premise," Schwartz summed up. "The research indicates the effect. The content of any commercial is not in the commercial itself. It's the interaction between what's in the listener and what's in the spot," Schwartz emphasized.

Napolitan explained his media strategy: "I use television every election I can. Sometimes I start early when my candidate isn't very well known and we're far behind. Sometimes I lull my opponent, if he has a good lead in the polls, by holding back television until late in the campaign and hitting him with a blitz the last ten days. Three weeks before the blitz I run some radio. I like radio. It's an invisible medium that sets the stage for television. When you run television spots, everybody screams, 'He's spending too much money! He's buying the election!' But you can spend the same amount of money on radio and nobody knows it. Even when they hear lots of your radio spots, they don't relate that to a big spender's campaign. But when you use television, everybody knows you're there.

"There's no secret formula for controlling emotions," Napolitan admitted. "But emotions control every campaign. Abortion, gun control, the Equal Rights Amendment are all emotional questions. The Right to Life people and the National Rifle Association play on emotions and they're successful. For example, every poll shows most Americans are in favor of handgun control, but we've never gotten a federal law because of the powerful lobbying of the NRA. Sometimes you can make an absence of emotion work for you. Take our 1978 campaign in Hawaii for George Ariyoshi, the least emotional guy you ever saw. Quiet, reserved, absolutely no charisma. On the other hand, his opponent was a volatile man who sparked strong feelings in his followers but turned other people off."

Those strong feelings were ethnic. The opponent, Honolulu mayor Frank Fasi, appealed to old, bitter antagonisms between Japanese and Caucasians. Napolitan's strategy against Fasi's huge lead in the polls was to let him hang himself in his own emotional noose.

"People in Hawaii may not have been too impressed with Ariyoshi," he recalled, "but nobody hated him. Even though the polls showed Ariyoshi was thirty-one points behind, they also showed that Hawaiians were totally ignorant of his considerable accomplishments. So our first wave of material concentrated strictly on what he had done his first four years. We developed a campaign theme: 'quiet and effective.' We used it in our literature, in a jingle, as a tag line for our ads—'working quietly and effectively.'"

Napolitan made sure every Hawaiian saw the contrast between his candidate and his candidate's emotional opponent. Quiet-and-effective Ariyoshi won his second term for governor in a very close election.

Joe Napolitan does not solicit business. He sits and waits for the phone to ring. When it does, it often means hopping a plane to a campaign in any part of three continents. For the past ten years he has averaged 200,000 air miles. In an eleven-month stretch he made seven trips to Europe, two to Asia, five to Alaska, ten to Hawaii, and one to the Caribbean, all on political work. Invariably, Napolitan is called by candidates in trouble. "Guys who know they're going to win don't need me," he explained. "The good people in this business are like doctors. What they do costs money, and they see people who are sick."

Before he takes on a client, Napolitan makes certain they agree about how the campaign should be run, the value of research, and the need for top-quality television material. Control is the bottom line. The client must acknowledge that Napolitan knows more about political campaigns than he does. He winds up taking a little less than half of those who come to him. "It's not always because I'm unhappy with them," he said. "Sometimes they find another consultant they like better. Or after I talk about what it costs to run for Congress, they realize they can't afford the kind of campaign I run."

In the United States Napolitan works only in statewide races, usually for the Senate or the House. His fees range from $30,000 to $50,000, depending on whether only the primary will be a hard fight with the general election a shoo-in (as in the one-party states of the South), or whether there are two hard races to run. He never asks a client to sign a contract. But in a business where credit given to losing candidates is traditionally not paid, Napolitan makes sure his labors are rewarded.

"I make them pay a three- or four-month installment in advance," he said. "If they fall behind and are weeks overdue paying me, I tell them they must want me to stop working. Hell, if I can't trust a guy, how can I get half a million voters in his state to trust him?"

One client a few years back did refuse to pay. Blair Lee, who was running for governor of Maryland, started out with a big lead in the polls. "He felt he was invincible," Napolitan later recalled. Nevertheless, four weeks before the election,

Napolitan sent Lee a crucial memo that explained in detail why, despite the big lead, he would lose.

"My polls showed me Lee's vote was soft. There was no movement on his part and the other candidates were campaigning hard. Lee had given control for the campaign to his thirty-one-year-old son, a bright guy with absolutely no political experience. He wouldn't approve my television films, wouldn't use any negative stuff, botched one thing after another. That's exactly what I told Lee. The memo obviously irritated him."

Lee lost. He still owes Napolitan $6,000, but Napolitan won't sue to collect it. "He knows he owes it and that's enough," he said.

Napolitan prefers to work alone. But when he lacks the tools or the time, he uses the top specialists in the business. "I wouldn't hesitate taking over immediate control of any campaign," he said without a trace of bluster. "I've done everything from referendums to Presidential campaigns and I know who the good people are. I know the quirks of pollsters, producers, and other specialists. I match them to a candidate who will work well with them. My time is spent more with production people than with candidates. As the campaign progresses, I hardly see the candidate at all and deal instead with his manager and media people. The candidate should travel, make speeches, get exposure. His main job is not to screw up."

Unlike journalists, who view elections as morality plays, political professionals view them as games. They are intrigued by tactics, images, messages, and energy; they are absorbed in scouting, in digging out information, in probing soft spots in their opponent's moves and in the public mind. Polls substitute for yard markers in the election ball game; at stake are 160 million votes.

I spoke with Michael Rowan, a thirty-seven-year-old consultant with one hundred campaigns behind him. He did his first ten under Joe Napolitan. Now he owns Media Group, a business in Mill Valley, California, that counsels, polls, and runs campaigns. He is a firm believer in Napolitan's genius.

"Napolitan is in a class by himself," Rowan said. "He's the

only one in this business who's a personal consultant to foreign heads of state. Journalists miss the whole point of an election. They write about the wrong people. The press thinks everything depends on what Carter says or Kennedy says or Reagan says. But it's Napolitan who's quietly using research to identify the things people need to know about the candidates and then getting the candidates to say the right thing on television. If you take a pencil and chart the Gallup and Harris polls against time buys of television pieces in a Napolitan campaign, you end up with a straight line; the relationship is absolutely clear."

A Napolitan hallmark is his trick of stepping up a campaign late and hitting hard unexpectedly. "One of his great talents is the ability to pull surprises," another well-known consultant told me. "An election is a cybernetic thing anyway. It hinges on the expectations and outlook of the opposition. One thing Joe does is to anticipate the entire campaign of the opposition. When the opponent tries for an effect or takes a position, Joe lets him do it and then makes it work for him instead of fighting it directly. His psychology is usually more complicated than his opponent's. The traditional campaign wisdom says come out swinging, get out in front, and try to stay there as long as possible. But everybody knows what happens to front-runners in this country—they're undermined by criticism. Joe holds back a good campaign, instead of dissipating early or giving his opponent the chance to analyze what he's doing."

That tactic has won Napolitan lots of upset victories as the press would read it, or simply come-from-behind wins as fellow professionals understand it. Once Napolitan's research discovers what becomes the logic of the campaign, he has the cool courage of the poker player to sit tight and do nothing. This drives most candidates up the wall, since the typical office seeker is a doer who wants to get out and solve a problem the moment he learns of it. But only one day counts in Napolitan's scheme—election day. That's the day he aims to have everybody convinced. The next most important day is the day before election day, with each preceding day fading in importance. Good consultants work backward, not forward.

If you see an emotion-packed half-hour biography about a political candidate which doesn't insult your intelligence but is warm, engaging, and artfully done, you're probably watching a campaign that Napolitan has his hand in. In the 1960s most candidate biographies were hard-sell propaganda pieces. Napolitan was the first to use top political film makers like Shelby Storck, Charles Guggenheim, David Sawyer, and Eli Bleich— stylists who evoke atmosphere, subtle emotions, and a soft, nearly invisible sell. Napolitan's influence is seen in the lighter touch of today's better campaign films.

Napolitan had a unique chance to measure the power of one of his half-hour biographies. During Mike Gravel's 1968 Senate race, Shelby Storck made a film called *Man for Alaska*. The film traced Gravel's career from his early days of poverty through his jobs in railroading, military intelligence, and the Alaskan legislature. One warm forty-five-second segment showed Gravel's beauty-queen wife pinning the forty-ninth star on the flag during the statehood ceremony.

During the last twelve days of the campaign, Napolitan polled every day. The numbers had been consistent for weeks, showing the incumbent Senator Gruening leading Gravel 2 to 1. The ninth day before election day, a Sunday, he didn't poll. That night Napolitan premiered *Man for Alaska* on all three Anchorage channels. When Napolitan polled that Monday, Gravel led Gruening 55 to 45. The only thing that had happened between Saturday's Gruening runaway and Monday's turnaround was the half-hour film. "I played the hell out of that film the last eight days," Napolitan recalled. Gravel went to Washington instead of Gruening.

Napolitan is the man who more than any other has helped political consultants to gain acceptance. Professional consultants have traditionally been characterized as hustlers and vote merchants, and have been held in low regard by some politicians and many news people. Even when not scapegoated as "manipulators" or "image makers," consultants are diminished more subtly by famous byline reporters who would sooner credit party arm-twisters for a campaign victory than the less-colorful strategist who really won the day.

Napolitan shrugs it off, seeing benefits in having the glory go to others. "As long as I get to call the plays and control the execution," is his attitude.

The superbowl for a campaign consultant is a Presidential race. It involves a complex interplay of personalities and events that demands skill, endurance, and raw nerve unmatched anywhere outside this special arena. It is an experience given to no more than ten consultants in each generation. It came to Napolitan in 1968.

3

How Nixon Almost Lost

The year 1968 was a dark one in American history. Fear and doubt assailed the national spirit. Revolution was openly urged. It was a year when Black Panthers and Weathermen hoarded weapons for use against the American government, when underground papers were the only news source people under thirty trusted, when mind-blowing drugs were celebrated as the solution to it all.

On January 1 Vietnamese Communist troops launched the victorious Tet Offensive against the Americans. On March 15 Robert Kennedy announced he was running for President with a plan to wind down the Vietnam War. Later that month Lyndon Johnson learned just how unpopular he was and tearfully dropped out of the running. On April 1 Dr. Martin Luther King, Jr., was assassinated by a hired gunman on the balcony of a Memphis motel. "Burn, baby, burn!" became a rallying cry for black rage. Arson, looting, and sniping brought the battlefields to the inner cities of the land. Bob Kennedy appealed to an anguished black conscience, and it responded to the white man who shared the pain of an assassin's bullet. Faint hope stirred in young Americans. But in early June that dream exploded in a Los Angeles hotel pantry, when a Palestinian misfit shot Bobby point-blank in the head. The nation was numb.

In July, at a traditionally dull convention in Miami, the Republicans nominated Richard Nixon for President. Then in the last week of August the Democrats named Hubert Horatio Humphrey their candidate in Chicago, while outside in the streets the police and state troopers clubbed war protesters in full view of national television. By early September Nixon enjoyed a sixteen-point lead over Humphrey, who had only eight weeks to change things. Most experts agreed that the lead was insurmountable, but somebody forgot to tell Joe Napolitan.

Napolitan had turned thirty-nine that year and business was hot. He was working hard on a half dozen Senate and House races, having declined twice that number. *Newsweek* and the *New York Times* were calling him a "genius of strategy" and the Democrat's "secret weapon." Napolitan's children were blooming, his marriage was rock solid, and life was sweet and full. He watched the ebb and flow of the Presidential primaries from a safe distance.

"Presidential campaigns are the most chaotic operations known to man, except possibly war," he told me. "We have no true national election, we have a series of state elections."

A Presidential prospect must leap three hurdles. He must first become famous enough and trusted enough so voters in the states holding Presidential primaries will give him their vote. He must convince news people whose stories promote the flow of money that he is a potential winner. And he must convince party machine delegates who influence the nominating process that he is best able to lead the party to victory.

The nominating convention poses a totally different challenge. Today it is a marketplace buzzing with symbolic speech-making and with bargaining for platform planks and for support in the general election. This is the last bastion of the legendary smoky-room negotiating and arm-twisting. Political consultants do not get involved in nominating battles, in which their special abilities are lost.

Larry O'Brien, a master of the nomination game, was up to his ears in Presidential intrigue that year. He worked to re-elect Lyndon Johnson until March 31, when Johnson, his popularity at a record low, announced over national television that he would not try for a second term. Four hopefuls jumped at the opportunity: peace candidate Eugene McCarthy, the most radical; Robert Kennedy, who was less so; segregationist George Wallace; and Vice-President Hubert Humphrey, who was unsure just how to position himself.

The moment Johnson dropped out, Kennedy-man O'Brien took over Bobby's campaign. Two weeks after Bobby was assassinated, Humphrey summoned O'Brien to a meeting and begged him to manage his campaign. O'Brien was reluctant in the face of the Vice-President's low poll readings, and so insisted on two prior conditions: first, Humphrey had to announce a plan to stop all bombing of Vietnam and follow that with a call for negotiated peace; second, he had to give O'Brien absolute control of all campaign decisions.

"Done," said Humphrey.

So O'Brien took on his third Presidential candidate in six months, a record unlikely to be broken. He took one look at the aides inherited from Humphrey's primary contests and blanched. As a party powerhouse, O'Brien was sure he could control enough delegates to get Humphrey nominated; the problem was winning the general election. Humphrey's people had blown their energies in the primaries, exhausting money and imagination to prove that Hubert could pull votes in the boondocks. Now that he was a certain candidate, they had no clue how to get him from there to the White House. As strategists, they were wet behind the ears. O'Brien knew what he had to do.

It was a Monday. Joe Napolitan was holed up studying the latest polls from Alaska where his man Mike Gravel was pushing to upset incumbent Senator Ernest Gruening; Napolitan felt good about the way things were going. The phone rang. It was Larry O'Brien's secretary, asking him to come to Washington and discuss the upcoming race for President. Two days later he sat in the impressive office of Postmaster General Larry O'Brien, with O'Brien himself and O'Brien's aide Ira Kapenstein across from him.

"How's it going?" Napolitan asked.

"Horrible," replied Kapenstein.

O'Brien painted the gloomy picture. Humphrey was having problems breaking with Johnson's hawkish war policy. Ten days before the convention and only ten weeks to election day there was no research, no campaign plan, no media schedule. The only written thoughts were bits and pieces sent in from Humphrey citizen groups scattered around the country, and none of that was worth much. The campaign treasury was so broke it owed several hundred thousand dollars to suppliers and ad agencies. And because Humphrey was so far behind in the polls, the money would be even harder to get.

"I already told Hubert he hasn't a snowball's chance in hell," O'Brien said glumly.

"So what do you want from me?" asked Napolitan, equally glum.

"Come to the convention and help me," O'Brien pleaded.

"I can't. I promised Mike Gravel I'd be with him in Alaska."

"Is he in trouble?"

"Not seriously."

"Well, I am. You can't do him any good in Alaska, win or lose. But you can do us all kinds of good in Chicago."

"For example?"

"Take a look at our media, give us your thoughts on post-convention strategy. The ad agency will have some stuff to show and I need you to look at it—I don't trust anybody else. Will you do it, Joe?"

Chicago, Napolitan thought. He held back a sigh and nodded. "Okay. Can you get me a room somewhere?"

"It's all arranged," O'Brien said, grinning.

August 23, Chicago. Author Theodore White, digging up material for his book *The Making of the President, 1968,* wandered around the sixth floor of the Conrad Hilton Hotel, where the Democrats were staying. He spotted an open door, stuck his head in, and saw Joe Napolitan hunched over a typewriter, pounding furiously.

"Writing a speech?" asked White.

"No, the campaign plan," Napolitan replied, launching another series of rat-tat-tats.

"You mean there's no formal campaign plan? Tomorrow's the nominating ballot, for God's sake!"

"If there's a plan anywhere, I haven't seen it," Napolitan said.

Rat-tat-tat.

August 25, Chicago. Napolitan and Ira Kapenstein attended a meeting with Doyle Dane Bernbach admen at the Hotel Conrad-Hilton. A top national agency, DDB had a reputation for trendy ideas, flashy graphics, and witty headlines. Its clever campaigns for Volkswagen, El Al Airlines, and other name companies had won many industry awards, so the agency had been hired to do President Johnson's run for a second term. When Johnson dropped out, Humphrey inherited DDB. Aware of the agency's credits, Napolitan sat at the conference table. Agency founder Bill Bernbach had flown in from New York to make a personal presentation.

To show the flow of any proposed television commercial, ad agencies use a money-saving shortcut. Their artists draw a series of panels in sequence, much like cartoon strips. The panels are bound with a ring and flipped over as the presenter goes on to explain the next panel. A typical commercial idea consists of five or six panels that together form a "storyboard."

The first storyboard presented by Bernbach set the morning's tone. It opened with a close-up of an elephant wearing an embroidered "GOP" on its head. The camera followed the pachyderm as it walked backward and disappeared, while a narrator recited a list of statistics downgrading the Republicans. The final panel was a blank screen with three small letters: HHH, for Hubert Horatio Humphrey. This commercial, Bernbach announced, was budgeted at only $57,000.

Napolitan did some quick mental arithmetic. Renting an elephant would cost at most $1,000. Draping an embroidered GOP over its head, about $500. Filming it would be simple, just a matter of shooting the beast walking toward the camera, then running the film backward. Insert the narration, a disclaimer, and that was it. But for $57,000? To Napolitan, it wasn't worth a tenth the price.

When he flipped the last panel over, Bernbach looked at the two Humphrey men for reaction. Napolitan spoke first.

"That's a terrible use of television," he said, and went on to explain that using lots of numbers to make political points turned television viewers off. It was best to go for warm, easy-to-grasp messages. "You can't fight emotion with logic," Napolitan told Bernbach. "It may sound good, but it just doesn't work."

Enthusiasm waning, Bernbach went on with the presentation. In all he showed about a dozen storyboards. Napolitan felt only two or three were good enough to go into production.

Immediately after the meeting, Napolitan wrote a memo to Larry O'Brien describing the "disappointing showing." "The spots lacked conviction and the approach was typically Madison Avenue," he reported. "There were twenty people there all set 'to go to work,' but none of them had the vaguest notion of what the hell they were supposed to do. I doubt there were three Humphrey votes in the whole crowd. The agency conceded they were unaware of any campaign nuances. Two of their spots, for example, had Negroes as narrators—an insane thing to do." All the polls, public and private, showed widespread fear and anger toward blacks among suburban, small-town, and blue-collar whites. Following on the heels of the spring arson and riots, any candidate who wanted the votes of middle America had to put space between himself and black militants.

Napolitan decided on drastic action. Just nine weeks before election day he replaced Doyle Dane Bernbach with Lennen & Newell, a more conservative agency. The experts thought he was mad, starting over from scratch with no money and little time to catch up. The Doyle Dane people were angered by the dismissal. Some even charged Napolitan with racism. "Napolitan's polls said the majority of the country think the Negro has had too many handouts," one DDBer claimed. "So Napolitan had Humphrey stop talking about federal aid to the cities and switch to law-and-order stuff. We were told not to show a black man in our commercials."

As a professional pragmatist, Napolitan does not afford himself the luxury of personal bias. As a human being apart from politics, he abhors racism and his reply was pointed:

"That's pure bullshit. The first Humphrey spot after the convention had black faces in it. So did the second and so did many others. Our three-minute films had black faces; so did the Q-and-A programs and the election eve telethon. It wasn't black faces I objected to but simply two spots that Doyle Dane showed us that day. Both would have outraged the Black Panthers and the Ku Klux Klan at the same time—a hell of an accomplishment in just sixty seconds!"

Black outrage and white reaction played a major role in campaign strategy that year. From the start, Nixon locked black voters out of his plans. "I'm not going to alienate the suburbs by going after black votes," Nixon admitted. "If I win, I won't owe a thing to blacks."

Nixon's campaign showcases were his festive indoor rallies, populated by friendly lily-white audiences suitable for display over national television and in newspaper photos. To guarantee a "proper crowd," Nixon's advance men scheduled events in midafternoon when manual workers could not attend. White high-school students were bussed in from the suburbs and rally tickets went out only to solid-citizen types, providing the desired color for his Norman Rockwell tableaux. If "wrong types" showed up, they were yanked out of line by his security people. At one Nixon rally in New York's Madison Square Garden, the undesirables weeded out included scores of blacks in Afro dress, hairy and bearded youths, men without ties, and three bearded Hasidic rabbis.

August 30, Chicago. Larry O'Brien was officially named Hubert Humphrey's campaign manager, and Joe Napolitan director of advertising. Napolitan was given absolute control of all paid media; he would receive no salary or fee, only expenses.

The delegates passed a Minority Rules Report they didn't fully understand, one that would revolutionize Presidential elections. First, it abolished the old "unit rule," whereby state delegates voted in blocs and old-style horse-trading dominated the nominating process. Then, through an "outreach" rule, it insisted that a jumble of races, sexes, and special interests make up every state delegation in the name of "full participation." These mutations would bring forth bizarre offspring in the presidential races that followed.

It was the weekend before Labor Day, the traditional campaign kickoff. On Saturday morning, at a meeting of the Democratic National Committee in the Conrad Hilton Hotel, the appointments were officially confirmed. After a lunch accompanied by speeches of empty optimism, the convention broke up and everyone scattered.

Napolitan went back to Springfield for what was left of the weekend. Having no heart for family activities, he went to his den, closed the door, sat at his desk, and brooded about the situation. There was no media plan, no television commercials or even raw film in the can, no spots from before the convention that were worth a damn. There were no radio spots on hand or being produced, no polls in the field, and not one dime in the treasury.

The Democrats, Humphrey, and his chances had been clobbered by that disastrous convention. Those scenes of Chicago cops bloodying protesters in living color, interspersed with television images of the nominating foolery, balloons, and party hats, hurt badly. They cut off contributions, froze morale, and triggered a huge Humphrey drop in the polls. Gallup would release its poll on Labor Day, showing Nixon ahead by sixteen points. A weight grew in Napolitan's chest. He sighed, pushed away from his desk, and went out to join the kids.

September 2, Labor Day. That morning Napolitan attended a family picnic, his mind far removed from the high spirits, hot dogs, and potato salad. In the early afternoon he caught a plane to LaGuardia Airport in New York, where Humphrey's chartered jet waited on the runway. Napolitan climbed on board. O'Brien and Humphrey hadn't returned from a rally in Manhattan, so he sat down, pulled a yellow legal pad from his case, and started to write. Nine hundred words later he had outlined what was to be the entire media plan for the 1968 Presidential campaign.

First Napolitan named three men crucial to his attack: Tony

Schwartz, Charles Guggenheim, and Shelby Storck. He proposed that Guggenheim and Storck do the longer television material, from five-minute pieces to half-hour documentaries. Most would focus on Humphrey, his accomplishments, and his family, with a few concentrating on Vice-Presidential running mate Edmund Muskie. Schwartz would do all the issues-oriented television and radio spots. "This guy is a true genius," Napolitan wrote in that memo. "He works best by giving him a problem—Vietnam, crime, racial tension—and letting him go." Napolitan planned two kinds of newspaper ads—fund-raising pitches and promotions to boost the audience for scheduled television films.

That was it, the entire media plan.

After Humphrey, O'Brien, and their aides breezed in from the rally, the plane took off for Humphrey's home in Minnesota. Napolitan slipped the draft media plan to O'Brien, who read it quickly and passed it across the aisle to the candidate. Humphrey read it, smiled, scrawled "OK—HH—GO!" across the bottom, then gave it back to O'Brien. Napolitan had his license to operate.

In Minnesota the candidate holed up with a small army of advisers and aides. While O'Brien was on one phone making promises and veiled threats to state party chairmen, union heads, and minority leaders, Napolitan was on another putting together his media team. Besides Schwartz and Storck, Napolitan's gang included Bob Squier to coach Humphrey for "live" television encounters with *Meet the Press* and Johnny Carson; Bill Wilson for short films; Harry Muheim to write radio spots; and Sid Aronson and Charles Guggenheim for short and long documentaries. While everyone around him babbled about endorsements, unions, and black ministers, Napolitan saw the entire election reduced to one factor—the effect of media messages on voters.

Few of us "know" candidates in any real sense. Our impressions about them come from things we've seen, read, or heard secondhand. In modern political campaigns each side builds a cardboard mockup of their candidate based on a frame of poll findings and an equally unreal portrait of the opposition; the

most positive image wins. Richard Nixon, as Vice-President
under Eisenhower, still enjoyed a mild halo effect gained from
his connection to a popular war general hailed as the "Peace
President." Humphrey, on the other hand, was tied to Johnson's
hard-nosed stance on the Vietnam War. Nixon's pollsters discovered early on that his best vote-getter was not an appeal to
"law and order" sentiments, but an appeal to Americans' hun-
ger for peace. Many months before the convention he had
drawn standing ovations in speech after speech with one terse
declaration: "After four years of war in Asia, after 25,000 dead,
200,000 casualties, America needs new leadership!"

Vietnam and lack of money were to plague Napolitan all the
way. In the end, the Humphrey campaign scraped together $3
million for television, whereas Nixon spent $5.2 million. Had
the labor unions not come up with $500,000 plus lots of free
labor, and had Humphrey's personal friends not lent him $3
million, there would have been no campaign at all. As things
stood, Napolitan had no choice. He had to rely on his finishing
kick and hope for the best. Since he had no money at all to
spend in September, he worked on polls and films, and
watched Nixon run unopposed on the airwaves.

Napolitan planned to hold back any resources that did come
in for the last few weeks. Maybe by then, he hoped, Nixon's
media campaign would have become boring and predictable.
That would magnify whatever emotional jolts Napolitan
could get on the screen.

In political campaigns, everybody pays cash. The tradition is
as true for buying network air time as it is for paying the
downtown printer for position papers and bumper stickers.
The supplier's first lesson in survival is: *You don't collect from
a loser.* So everybody demands payment up front, Joe Napolitan included.

Things were so bad for Humphrey that in September even
his campaign manager tried to shield him from the truth. On
one swing through West Virginia, Humphrey was pleased
about the way his speeches were going. The crowds were large
and friendly, the usual antiwar hecklers hadn't been showing
up, and applause was more frequent. But one thing bothered
the old campaigner.

"Where're the Humphrey signs?" he asked Larry O'Brien. "I don't see any literature or buttons. I'm out breaking my butt, and there's no campaign activity to back me up."

"We can't get those materials, Hubert," O'Brien replied. "We have no money and we can't get credit. We're dead broke."

It wasn't until September 23 that his fund-raisers scraped together the first $100,000 for buttons and bumper stickers. More sorely missed were the commercials Napolitan couldn't air and the pollsters who wouldn't deliver their reports.

On Labor Day weekend, Napolitan had commissioned studies from five polling firms to measure seventeen key states. Though results were in and tabulated, several key pollsters refused to deliver their reports until they were paid. Things looked so bad in mid-September that Napolitan sat down and wrote a desperation memo. Dated September 14, it numbered key points in his terse style:

1. If we continue as we are, we will lose.
2. If we try some bold plans and they backfire, we still lose.
3. If we try some bold plans and they work, we may win. We have nothing to lose, and the Presidency to gain, by being bold. Three things are necessary to put the Vice-President in contention. One, a sharp break with Lyndon Johnson. Two, an independent Vietnam policy that will win back votes that should be Humphrey's but are wavering. Three, a policy on law-and-order that separates him from Nixon/Wallace, advocating federal spending and making a strong emotional appeal to the conscience of America.

O'Brien's plan to stop bombing Vietnam had nothing to do with his own antiwar feelings. It was pure political strategy backed by research.

"Our research showed that lots of people didn't really trust Nixon or care for him that much," Napolitan recalled. "But everybody wanted the war over. So in all his television spots Nixon said, 'I'll end the war,' while he waved the flag a little and talked about the glowing future of America under a Republican President. He had a big lead, he knew it, and he was sitting on it, so he did nothing. In his television films he avoided people. Everything was carefully staged. But his films were well done and fooled a lot of people. As for Humphrey, people saw him too closely merged with Lyndon Johnson's war policies. We needed something explosive. The war was the logical forum and Humphrey just waffled on it."

Napolitan sent his "bold moves" memo to O'Brien, but got no reply. He assumed it was dead, until September 30 when, during a speech in Salt Lake City, Humphrey hemmed and hawed his way to a peace position a half-degree to the left of President Johnson. Weak as his words were, Americans were so starved for crumbs of hope that over $300,000 in small contributions poured into Humphrey's headquarters after that one appearance.

Napolitan feels that Humphrey didn't go far enough. In a memo to the candidate at the time, he wrote: "If it comes to a choice between electing a President or getting a President angry, I know what I would do. This is a time for boldness."

But Humphrey couldn't make the break. He was afraid to offend Johnson, who had warned through his aide Marvin Watson, "We may not be able to elect Hubert Humphrey President, but we sure as hell can stop him from being elected."

Humphrey couldn't be persuaded to boldness, so Napolitan had to use other information coming back from his polls. "We found that lots of people didn't know anything about Humphrey," he explained. "Young blacks, for example, had no idea that this was the guy who had spearheaded the fight for civil rights and fought for blacks before they were born. So our media campaign concentrated on showing what Humphrey had done."

September 30, Washington. Good material had been delivered by Napolitan's media team to his office in the Democratic National Headquarters at the Watergate Hotel. All of it—films, print ads, radio tapes—was stacked on a side table. When Teddy White visited that afternoon, he found the usually affable Napolitan in a dark mood.

"We have such beautiful material," he said sadly. "Here, listen to this, Teddy." He put a spool on the tape player. "I want you to hear our wonderful radio spots. This'll be your only chance, because we'll never get the money to put them on the air."

Polls still showed Humphrey losing badly. Since donations don't come to losers, those early polls were self-fulfilling. Napolitan's private polls showed Humphrey to be much stronger than either Gallup or Harris did, however, so Napolitan sent out a special report to media editors and party chairmen titled "Humphrey on the Upswing, Gallup or Not!" The press remained unimpressed. Most editors were skeptical, and some even accused Napolitan of faking the figures and twisting the truth for his own advantage. But party brokers were not so cynical and money began to come in. Napolitan's polls convinced them that Humphrey was far from finished. In the end, his private polls proved more reliable than the highly touted published polls.

Early in October, Napolitan got his first radio and television commercials on the air. Created by Tony Schwartz and filmed by Hal Tulchin, they exploited the respectability gap between the opposing Vice-Presidential nominees; Democrat Edmund Muskie, who had a fine track record as senator, and his Republican counterpart, Maryland Governor Spiro Agnew, the champion of the rednecks. One commercial was called the "Twenty-Second Laughter Spot." It opened with a close-up of a white card that said, "Agnew for Vice-President." The only sound was of a man laughing uncontrollably until at last he gasped, "Agnew for Vice-President?" The piece ended with a tight shot on a second white card: "This would be funny if it weren't so serious." Another Schwartz/Tulchin classic showed a medical oscilloscope with zigzag tracings accompanied by the "bleep bleep" sound of a human heartbeat, repeated until a narrator's voice cut through the electronics: "Muskie . . . Agnew . . . who is your choice to be a heartbeat away from the Presidency?"

Meanwhile Nixon's television commercials were noncontroversial but plentiful. Because the Republican time-buyers had lots of cash on hand, they were able to arrange a heavy schedule of regional and local stations, buying the most heads for every $1,000 spent.

With just five weeks to go, time was of the essence for Napolitan. His first buys were for expensive network time, a counterattack consisting of the anti-Agnew spots and a thirty-minute montage on the Democratic Party. The latter, a film produced by Sid Aronson, highlighted speeches by Democrats Franklin D. Roosevelt, Harry Truman, John F. Kennedy, Robert and Ted Kennedy, Eugene McCarthy, Lyndon Johnson, George McGovern, Humphrey, and Muskie—juxtaposed with cuts of speeches by Richard Nixon, George Wallace, Benito Mussolini, and Adolf Hitler. The film was aired before Napolitan spotted a major flaw: it lacked the happy ending it needed in order to win votes and contributions. Later research showed that the film had appealed mostly to young people—few of whom came out to vote for Humphrey.

More effective was a five-minute film by the Schwartz/ Tulchin team which featured television actor E. G. Marshall, known for his starring role in a law-and-order television series. Marshall was shown standing beneath a huge blowup of George Wallace's face. After speaking in low-key phrases about Wallace's boyhood in the South and his career as a segregationist politician, Marshall moved to a blowup of Nixon to talk of his early days as an anticommunist congressman. The approach was informative, flat, and brilliantly paced. The last blowup was of Humphrey, under whom Marshall pulled his points together and asked the viewer to make his own choice. The sell was subtle; it implied, but never demanded.

From Humphrey's late-September fifteen-point deficit in the polls, by mid-October the gap had closed to twelve. On October 14 Napolitan found cash to put his radio commercials on the air. There were now three weeks to go. He counted on a secret weapon to make things closer, a half-hour biography of Humphrey by St. Louis film maker Shelby Storck. Storck had done biographies for other Napolitan campaigns and the impact had been sensational. Even now Storck had two camera crews stalking Humphrey everywhere he went, shooting thousands of film feet for a few seconds of footage that would justify the discards.

October 20, Washington, D.C. Sixteen days before the election, Storck's film was delivered to Napolitan's office. Napolitan quickly ran it through and knew Storck had hit a home run. "It was a masterpiece," Napolitan later recalled. "This one film did more to help Humphrey climb the polls than anything else we did in the campaign. No other incident, speech, program, film, or statement had such an impact on the American public." The Humphrey biography was shown more than any other political documentary in history—fourteen hundred times.

Napolitan had asked Storck to do two things. First, to show a warm, friendly "Hubert the Man," to contrast with the cold efficiency of Nixon. Second, to refresh public memory of Humphrey's legislative achievements. The film opened with Jimmy Durante singing "Young at Heart," then shifted to a pair of middle-aged couples bowling. They were ordinary Americans—the men in shirtsleeves, the women in skirts and blouses. The camera zoomed in. The couples were Hubert and Muriel Humphrey and running mates Ed and Jane Muskie.

Storck had dug up old film of the 1948 convention when young Senator Humphrey led the fight for a strong civil-rights plank in the Democratic platform. Humphrey had made a passionate speech calling for the party "to walk out of the shadow of states rights into the sunshine of human rights," sparking a near riot among Dixiecrat delegates, who finally walked out of the hall. Another cut dramatized his work for a nuclear test–ban treaty, featuring Humphrey and John F. Kennedy linking arms at the ceremonial signing of the pact.

But the most effective segment of the biography was the result of patient digging. Storck had lots of footage showing Humphrey playing with his grandchildren at his Minnesota ranch. Later, during a question-and-answer session in San Francisco, the candidate talked movingly about his love and affection for his retarded granddaughter, "this special little girl who taught me the meaning of true love." The segment warmed the hearts of those who had been indifferent to Humphrey's political accomplishments.

Gallup's poll for October 21 showed the gap at eight points, 44 percent to 36 percent for Nixon. But Napolitan's media machine was running on open throttle and the flow of money responded. During the last two weeks of the campaign Napolitan was able to match Nixon's media spending, and his whip was flailing hard. Newspapers reported turnarounds in key states like Massachusetts, New York, and Washington.

Napolitan was spared having to spend precious money fighting Wallace, even when his polls found the Alabaman taking away Democratic blue-collar votes. The press became a temporary ally, attacking Wallace as an incendiary racist demagogue. All the major television newscasters and big-city newspapers outside the South joined the anti-Wallace blitz. Many blue-collar votes returned to the Humphrey fold.

Nixon held fast to his noncampaign and played statesman. He started with twenty-one "safe" states (117 electoral votes) that the campaign could ignore and leave for state committees to hold. These included New England and most of the Midwest and the Pacific coast. Of these states, only Washington with 9 electoral votes went to the Democrats, and those just barely. The usually Democratic solid South belonged to Wallace. Nixon targeted only fourteen states for personal appearances and heavy advertising. California, New York, Texas, Ohio, and Pennsylvania were among them. These amounted to 298 electoral votes. He needed 152 of them to add to his safe bloc and pass the 270 votes required to win.

Nixon used an elaborate polling system devised by Indiana University Professor David Derge and carried out by the Opinion Research Corporation of Princeton, New Jersey. Part of that system was a repeating poll of voter panels, used to measure the effects of advertising and other campaign events. When the research showed that Nixon scored higher as "statesman" than Humphrey, he froze in that role like a broken record. Nixon's elaborate computer campaign was too ponderous and clumsy to self-correct when the tide began to turn. As early as the end of September, Republican pollster Walter DeVries saw the danger and dashed off a memo to John Mitchell.

"It bugs me that Nixon's vote has stayed the same, about 40 percent, for five or six months now," he warned. "The 60 percent divided between Humphrey, Wallace, and the Undecideds is volatile. If Wallace and the Undecideds start to break for Humphrey, a change in strategy will be in order. Appeal to independents and alienated Democrats; tell them Nixon offers the chance for change that Humphrey doesn't offer. Add specifics to back it up—reduced commitment in Vietnam, more and better-trained police, joint private/government efforts in the cities. There should be a plan in the tank in case events or voter movement overtakes you the last few weeks."

Mitchell didn't even acknowledge the letter. When the voters began to move, there was nothing else in the tank. Nixon kept flashing his V-fingered victory signs, praising America, and sweating it out. The Nixon campaign was the most controlled one in modern history, making use of a library of computer printouts, phone banks, targeted computer letters, and literature handsomely financed by state networks. Nixon's inability to act against Napolitan's blitz was a harbinger of his later problem in dealing with the discovery of the Watergate burglars. In the White House as in the campaign, he sat tight and did nothing.

During the final weeks Napolitan ran his thirty-minute question-and-answer programs, which showed Humphrey fielding tough questions from young antagonists. This was the strategist's substitute for the debate that Nixon refused to wage. War protesters, blacks, and Republicans were encouraged to attack Humphrey and pull no punches. The passionate exchanges made Humphrey angry; he responded like the rugged campaigner he was. After careful editing, the sessions were shown all over America.

On November 2, three days before the election, both Harris and Gallup agreed on their readings: Nixon was ahead, 42 to 40.

The last big media event of the election matched the two sides in competing telethons. Each party produced a two-hour show that was held in Los Angeles on November 4, election eve. The Republicans' format was cool, efficient, safe, and very dull. Spiro Agnew was banished from the set. Nixon shared center stage with football coach Bud Wilkinson and chatted about Green Bay's chances. Nixon's only show-business attraction was a ninety-second cameo by comedian Jackie Gleason. The Democrats ran a loose show. People moved on and off camera without pattern or design—"organized chaos," Bob Squier called it. Paul Newman moderated, while Joanne Woodward and other Hollywood stars praised Humphrey.

The election everyone had called "no contest" had turned into a last-minute cliffhanger. After the Monday night telethon, Joe Napolitan joined the other Democrat warriors for a party in Beverly Hills. Booze was plentiful, hope ran high, and the spirit of camaraderie pushed it even higher.

Election day, Minnesota. Napolitan watched the returns on television, packed in a fourteenth-floor room of the Leamington Hotel in Marysville with Humphrey, O'Brien, and the other campaign generals. He stayed up until five o'clock Wednesday morning, the outcome still doubtful. Once inside his own hotel room, he undressed, went to bed, and spent two hours staring wide-eyed at the ceiling. Finally he got out of bed, shaved, showered, and turned on the television set. It was 7:30 and the numbers told a clear story. Even if nobody was admitting it officially, Napolitan knew it was all over.

In the hallway outside his room he ran into Humphrey, who told him he was on his way to break the news personally to his old friend Fred Gates before making Nixon's victory official. Humphrey's smile held tight but his eyes were moist. He was about to say something but it didn't come out; he shrugged instead and went on his way.

On November 5, 1968, some 75 million Americans went to the polls. Wallace got 13.5 percent of the vote, Humphrey 42.7 percent, and Richard Nixon 43.4 percent. Nixon had won by less than 500,000 votes, the second-closest election in the twentieth century. The closest squeak of all happened eight years earlier when John Kennedy edged Nixon by a mere 110,000 popular votes.

Had he pulled it off, Joe Napolitan would have changed the

shape of history. There would have been no Watergate. An election that close generates lots of second guessing. Now, Napolitan wistfully raises the customary *ifs*. If he had spent his limited funds more wisely, buying television time by state or region instead of top-dollar network rates, states like California or Illinois might have gone for Humphrey; either one would have thrown the election into the House of Representatives, where Humphrey was the certain choice. If Humphrey had shown more guts and split from Johnson in any clear-cut way . . . If Johnson had scheduled the convention in July instead of August, so he would have had four extra weeks to campaign . . .

"If I'd have had a few extra weeks, Humphrey would have won by three or four points," Napolitan says matter-of-factly. But he soon wearies of the game. "A miss is as good as 1.6 kilometers. More people voted for Nixon than for Humphrey, so they got what they deserved."

In that election the American people also changed the way they chose their candidates, trading the old boss system of party structure for the free-for-all dogfights of open primaries. In this way Democrat George McGovern got the nomination in 1972, and Jimmy Carter in 1976 and 1980. Without realizing it, we passed into a new era of prophetic pollsters, mystic mediamen, and career candidates. The old checks and balances of organization had yielded to the political soulmates of Vince Lombardi. Winning was everything and Presidential pretenders were measured by nothing more than their skill at manipulating mass sentiment.

4

Gerald Rafshoon and the Disciples

In 1976 Jimmy Carter was attuned to the winds of popular sentiment that followed Vietnam and Watergate. Disillusioned with Presidents Johnson and Nixon—men who were highly qualified but whose veracity was suspect—America elected a self-proclaimed "honest man" with dubious qualifications. Carter's ignorance of American history, law, and social movements was not really important, insisted President Carter's in-house image shaper; what really counted were his good intentions.

"I'd feel more secure knowing there's a decent man in office than an expert," said Gerald Rafshoon, an advertising man turned Carter propagandist.

We talked in the Executive Office Building, adjoining the west wing of the White House. Rafshoon's spacious eighteen-foot-high office, once Vice-President Hubert Humphrey's office and Richard Nixon's hideaway workroom, was furnished with restraint: a white overstuffed sofa, antique end tables, modern upholstered chairs, and a carved wooden desk. Several large contemporary paintings enlivened the stark white walls. Rafshoon has been immortalized by Gary Trudeau in the comic strip *Doonesbury*. Trudeau coined the word "Rafshoonery" to depict image and symbol manipulation in the pursuit of votes.

Beginning in 1966, when Rafshoon first joined Jimmy Carter, he was a key cog in the Georgian's electioneering machine and was instrumental in Carter's rise from obscurity. Rafshoon is not a political consultant in the same sense as the other professionals. He is a one-candidate phenomenon. He could not effectively hire out to other political bidders what he had learned under Carter. His magic worked for only one man.

In 1977 Rafshoon and Pat Caddell, the pollster Carter inherited from George McGovern, flew to New York, where they did media work and polling for a mayoralty candidate. Mario Cuomo, former secretary of state for New York, was the client. His chief rival in the primary was state representative Ed Koch, whose campaign was being run by consultant David Garth. The big concerns at the time were a soaring crime rate, blackout looting, and the Son of Sam murders. The two liberal candidates, former Congresswoman Bella Abzug and incumbent Mayor Abraham Beame, were slaughtered in the primaries. Ed Koch had the hardest position, advocating the death penalty and the use of National Guard troops to control looters.

Rafshoon positioned Cuomo between the extremes. He appealed to the fears of embattled white New Yorkers, but not so nakedly as Garth did with Koch. Each side spent about half a million dollars. Cuomo lost badly. When I spoke to Cuomo, he accepted the blame. "I regarded flexibility as a weakness," he said. "I was naive." In the language of the new politics, Cuomo was troubled by believing one thing and saying another. By 1978 he had learned his lesson and was easily elected lieutenant governor of New York State.

To understand how Jimmy Carter gained power, it is necessary to analyze the special bond between the candidate and his younger confidants. That bond was a shared faith in the goodness of one man. Members of religious cults share a similar bond. They become devoted to a charismatic leader upon *experiencing* him. They are dizzy in his presence, weak in the knees. They see a light around the avatar or messenger.

Kandy Stroud, a reporter for the *Washington Star*, recalled the time when Carter described his prayer habits to her. Suddenly she was transfixed. "Carter's eyes flooded with light and I felt an overwhelming sense of his prayerfulness." Pollster Pat Caddell talks of Carter's "finished" quality, and others mention his "sincere look." However the charm is rationalized, it works best on a one-to-one basis.

"I knew if I could get anyone to spend five minutes alone with Jimmy Carter, we'd have his vote," Rafshoon told me.

"Is that the way he won you, in five minutes alone?" I asked.

"Yeah, yeah," he admitted.

Despite Rafshoon's unwillingness to elaborate on his devotion to Jimmy Carter, I could sense the loyal disciple. "I was in the advertising business, had an interest in politics, and then met a very unique man named Jimmy Carter."

Like two of the other three disciples, he made the first move. It was 1966 and Jimmy Carter was running for governor of Georgia. "I had just opened the agency," Rafshoon recalled, glossing over the years he struggled to establish himself among Atlanta advertisers. "I heard some of his advertising and was struck by how bad it was, a jingle singing, 'Jimmy Carter is his name.' " So he picked up the phone and called a go-between, Hal Gulliver of the *Atlanta Constitution*.

"Your friend Carter needs help," he said.

"I'll set up a meeting," said Gulliver.

Rafshoon put together a presentation—"one hundred twenty pages of bullshit," he called it—and presented it to Carter and some friends at a motel. One Rafshoon idea was a montage of film clips showing the candidate traveling around the state, speaking with farmers and factory workers while a narrator said: "Jimmy Carter. They say he can't win. You're the only person who can decide. Meet him, talk to him. If you like what you see, vote for him."

Rafshoon had focused on the candidate's most powerful weapon: one-on-one, eye-to-eye confrontation. But that morning in Atlanta, most of Carter's friends were not impressed with Rafshoon and said so openly. Rafshoon was devastated, until he felt a kick under the table. When he looked up, Carter smiled at him meaningfully. Later, when the others had gone, Carter told Rafshoon he liked his ideas and wanted him to develop those commercials.

"That started me liking him," Rafshoon said. "He asked me out to Plains that weekend and I got to know him then. He was one of the few politicians who seemed to give a damn about what I had to say." From that weekend on, Rafshoon was a true believer.

All four of the inner ring were believers: Hamilton Jordan, Gerald Rafshoon, Jody Powell, and Stuart Eizenstat. Except for Eizenstat, they were political amateurs until Jimmy Carter chose them to express their own ambitions through his. Carter picked his people carefully, preferring dedicated amateurs to more dispassionate experts. For one thing, he could teach them his philosophy of campaigning. For another, they came a lot cheaper. Carter formed a circle of charismatic power. Loyal disciples, as any preacher knows, are worth their weight in the collection plate. As one aide put it, "Jimmy Carter has God, and Hamilton Jordan has Jimmy." The same could be said of the other three.

Hamilton Jordan was the first to latch on—in 1966, when Jimmy Carter tried to become governor of Georgia, using the same low-budget campaign that had won him a seat in the state senate six years before. Jordan, studying political science at the University of Georgia, heard Carter talk and was so impressed by his "sincerity and moderate race views" that he offered himself as a volunteer. Carter put him to work under Rosalynn on what became a standard feature of all future campaigns, writing "I so much enjoyed meeting you" letters over Jimmy's name. Carter would go out and make speeches, then come back with piles of business cards and scraps of paper bearing the names and addresses of people whose hands he had shaken and whose eyes he had looked into. The letter reminded them who he was and planted seeds for later harvest.

Though Carter's communications were amateurish until Rafshoon entered his life, Carter already had a mania for planning, which he picked up from his Navy commander, the then Captain Hyman Rickover. Carter has an engineer's mind. He always makes detailed plans and follows them rigidly. In Ham Jordan he found a willing protégé. Jordan became so adept that, when the campaign ended, Carter awarded him the title of campaign manager. Jordan acknowledged his debt to Carter: "I learned from Jimmy how to plan. I look six or seven months down the road and try to stay one step ahead."

Hamilton Jordan was the strategist for Carter's Gang of

Four; he wrote the campaign plan that the others and Jimmy Carter himself would follow. The youngest of the group, he was jaunty, playful, and talkative, but fiercely competitive, with a passion for winning.

Carter made Ham Jordan feel good about himself. The two met when Jordan was renouncing the rabid racism of his parents' generation for a moderate outlook inspired by John Kennedy. Jimmy Carter became his idol, and his insurance-agent father faded from his mind, along with his fanatic uncle. "Hamilton is like a son to me," Carter once told a meeting of his Cabinet.

When Carter made Jordan angry by criticizing him, the short, stocky aide compensated by drinking too much, eating too much, partying too much, and reportedly using unauthorized substances in the presence of outsiders. In 1977 Jordan got bombed at a party thrown by television queen Barbara Walters, pulled at the bodice of the Egyptian ambassador's wife, and said, "I always wanted to see the twin pyramids of the Nile." After a flood of publicity about the incident, which came at a delicate point in the Middle East talks, Jordan cracked to reporters, "You should have heard what I said about Menachem Begin's wife." So when Jordan, early in 1980, resigned as chief of staff in order to run the reelection campaign, a collective sigh of relief went up from Washington.

Stuart Eizenstat was Carter's "issues man." The only child of a Chicago shoe jobber, he remembers his childhood as bleak, with his father away selling all the time. Spurred by loneliness, Stuart became a superachiever at school, earning top grades at the University of North Carolina.

As "issues adviser," Eizenstat was Carter's bridge to the thinkers of the country. He evaluated ideas and people, scouring the pool of talent for those who could be useful as speech writers or policy researchers. Eizenstat joined the Carter clan in 1968, after serving as a paid speech writer during the last two years of Lyndon Johnson's administration. Of the four disciples, only Eizenstat was not lean, hungry, and on the make when he ran into Carter. Unlike the others, he was sought out by Carter, who arranged a meeting through a mutual contact. At first Eizenstat was not overly impressed. He refused to join the club, skeptical about the chances of a peanut jobber—even one "so bright and attractive" as Carter. But Carter persisted, called him a few more times, got those five minutes alone behind closed doors, and Eizenstat became a believer.

Jody Powell was closest to Carter in the most important way. Where the others came from humble families, he was of the same social class as Carter—rural landowners. Both families had owned slaves, and both men grew up with blacks on their lands. "Outside of Rosalynn, Jody understands me best," Carter has said.

First-born sons, both Powell and Carter had poorly read segregationist fathers and strong-willed, well-educated mothers. Both went to college on political pull and both attended service academies. Carter graduated fifty-ninth in his class at Annapolis; Powell was thrown out of the Air Force Academy for cheating on a final exam. Until then, Powell had been a good Baptist boy who went to church every Sunday and taught Bible classes, just like Carter. Unlike his mentor, he was a star athlete in both football and baseball. After being expelled from the Academy, Powell returned to Georgia and got his B.A. degree from Georgia State University—a "receptacle for rejects," as he described it.

While researching his Master's thesis on Southern politics at Emory University, Powell came across a speech from Carter's unsuccessful gubernatorial race. The year was 1969, Powell was twenty-six. He wrote Carter a letter, explaining that he understood the populist movement, supported what Carter stood for, and wanted to help. Carter invited him to Plains, talked for more than five minutes, and found his right-hand man. During the 1970 gubernatorial race, Powell served as Carter's aide-de-camp, valet, and spokesman. He chauffeured the candidate around the state, slept in the same hotel room to keep down expenses, grew closer than family, and learned politicking from the inside. Soon Powell was contributing his own ideas and writing some of the candidate's speeches.

Where Ham Jordan was the tactician, Rafshoon the propagandist, and Eizenstat the theorist, Jody Powell was Carter's inspiration and support. Though Carter claimed no favorite among "the boys," Jody was reportedly a little more equal than the others. He was the only one secure enough to show annoyance publicly when Carter asked him to do something that he, Powell, didn't feel like doing. But ultimately Jody always did what he was told. Carter's authority was absolute. All four aides, in fact, feared Carter's displeasure and worked mightily to avoid it. What they had in common was an unhappy relationship with their own fathers, a lack filled by Jimmy Carter.

Rafshoon was born in Brooklyn during the Depression. His childhood was miserable. "My father was a mean man," he admitted. "We had lots of arguments and he left us." Shy, awkward, and undersized, he became a reader, a young, literate loner. Rafshoon received a degree in journalism from the University of Texas in 1955. Then, instead of seeking a newspaper job, he decided to "make more money" and entered advertising. His first job was at Lyndon Johnson's radio station in Dallas, where he made fifty dollars a week writing ad copy. Going nowhere fast, Rafshoon joined the navy, did three years on a tanker, and when he got out, found a job writing ad copy for an Atlanta department store. He later got a taste of the big time with a job at Twentieth Century Fox in New York, where he promoted feature films.

In 1963 Rafshoon returned to Atlanta and opened a small ad agency. In 1966, when he heard that awful Jimmy Carter jingle, Rafshoon Advertising was still small-time. Its biggest accounts were the Atlanta Sears Roebuck, a few supermarkets, and some local muffler shops. Ten years later, the company had grown from a two-man shop into a business that billed $22 million in 1976, netting $2 million.

Money was not a dirty word in the Carter inner circle. Everyone, Carter included, benefited handsomely from the spoils of winning political office. In the time-honored Southern manner, they didn't talk about it or flaunt it; they just did it and kept quiet about it. The Georgians proved masters at the game of payoffs and twist-arm politics, more grasping and vicious than the previous Presidents they publicly deplored. The big difference was the Carter style, which blended professed piety and ruthless singlemindedness.

That style carried Jimmy Carter into the White House at a time when Americans hungered for honesty and humility in their top man. Carter's style was a combination of moral superiority and down-home slyness—the attitude of a Southern backwoods preacher. It is no coincidence that he gained his experience in public speaking by talking to Sunday School children about the Bible. Carter went after people in one-to-one encounters the way missionaries go after potential converts. He astounded people by playing back a bit of exotic information he had memorized to convince them he knew more than he did. Characteristically, he always needed a single rival to energize him. From his earliest days in grammar school, he found he did best when vying with one another person.

In politics, he was impressed by the Kennedys and dreamed of one day beating one to prove his superiority. In the 1970 gubernatorial election in Georgia, the target was Carl Sanders, a white liberal who was vulnerable on the black issue. By then Jimmy Carter and his band were tough adversaries.

Rafshoon had spent the past few years setting up letterhead "citizen commissions" with Jimmy Carter as their president. As spokesman for these dummy action groups, Carter lobbied for reorganization of state government. Carter kept his name before the voters by promoting safe, noncontroversial issues. Lots of free newspaper and television coverage came as a result, and they lost no opportunity to set up meetings where Carter could eyeball people into becoming supporters.

After adding Jody Powell to his campaign team, Carter began his drive for governor. Using volunteers from the last election, he ordered a painstaking analysis of voting patterns in Georgia. Charts were compiled for all 139 counties, showing how people voted on campaign issues. "A general impression of voter motivations began to form," Carter explained in the *Washington Post*. Carter was evolving his modus operandi: find out how voters think and feel, then play it back to them;

it will echo at the ballot box. In effect, opinion blocs vote for themselves.

A year before the election, he hired William Hamilton to poll for him. The research showed that Carter and his main competitor, Carl Sanders, were both considered "a little more liberal than the bulk of the electorate." But Carter had one huge advantage: he was still "Jimmy Who?"—known to far fewer Georgians than the former governor. The pollster's report made a strong suggestion: "Over the next twelve months, the candidate can emphasize a conservative tone in his campaign and thus put himself between Sanders and the electorate."

That premise became the soul of the campaign. Taking stands consistently more hard-nosed and redneck than his rival, Carter courted the segregationist voting bloc. Rafshoon concentrated on literature and advertising. Carter stumped the state, spieling safe, bland themes: "I promise to serve all Georgians, not just a powerful few"; "I'll make appointments based on qualifications"; and "I'll strengthen local control"—in the code language of Dixie, a classic, down-the-middle segregationist stance.

Sanders was stuck with his liberal image, being too well known in that role to make any swing to the right credible to white Georgians. "I was frozen in," Sanders observed. "Everybody knew what I stood for, so I couldn't very well start yelling, 'Hooray for George Wallace!' It wouldn't have worked." Rafshoon's media painted Sanders as a corrupt big-city slicker who had grown rich in office from dirty dealings. In fact, Sanders was no richer than Carter, and by Georgian standards he had run a clean shop.

Emphasizing the populist theme, Rafshoon created a television commercial that appealed to working people: Carter was shown with his sleeves rolled up, elbow-deep in a bin of peanuts pouring out of a conveyor. "Jimmy Carter knows what it's like to work for a living," intoned a resonant voice. "Can you imagine any of the other candidates for governor working in the hot August sun? Vote for Jimmy Carter. Isn't it time somebody spoke up for you?"

Carter's strategy was to ignore blacks, but he didn't want his opponent to get them by default. Instead, to erode Sanders' black base, Rafshoon developed a series of radio commercials promoting votes for a third primary candidate, C. B. King, a black attorney who could be counted on to attract "ethnic clusters" or "soul brother" votes. Carter's campaign paid to air King's radio commercials, and by election day a substantial bloc of black Sanders supporters had been diverted to King's candidacy. "I can win without a single black vote," Carter said then, as he said later about the Jewish vote.

He almost did, taking 49 percent of the vote. But the lack of a majority required a runoff election between Sanders and himself. In the weeks before the second contest, Carter openly courted support from the region's most notorious segregationists—George Wallace, Lester Maddox, Roy Harris. He was photographed shaking hands, embracing, and grinning warmly at his new allies. In symbol-sensitive Dixie, he was making all the right moves.

"I'll invite George Wallace to Georgia when I'm governor to discuss mutual problems," Carter promised. "Lester Maddox is the embodiment of the Democratic Party!" he proclaimed in his speeches. "The peanut farmer is the right man," Maddox reciprocated. Meanwhile Rafshoon produced a leaflet showing a photo of Sanders with a bunch of basketball players, dousing each other with champagne in a victory celebration. The players were Atlanta Hawks; all were blacks. The text painted Sanders as sympathetic to blacks, and the leaflets circulated in white neighborhoods with devastating effect.

This time Carter won easily. Carter and the boys knew what they had to do and they did it. They had scaled another rung of his impossible dream. Though Carter's jubilant communications man didn't know it at the time, his candidate was already plotting for the Presidency.

No sooner was Carter sworn in as governor than he began working to change his address to 1600 Pennsylvania Avenue. In his quest for the Georgia state house, Carter had taken a course in speed reading, which enabled him to crib phrases for his "symbol-projecting" speeches. He had an Atlanta hair stylist, Gloria Swinn, cut his hair in imitation of John F. Kennedy. He took a crash course from the Florida "Memory Man," who taught him to mentally fix names, faces, and biographical details of people he aimed to impress. Carter began a regular practice of sending flowers to Democratic Party power brokers all over the land, using national holidays, family anniversaries, weddings, and funerals as his pretext.

Joining the Trilateral Commission, an international group of businessmen, educators, and politicians, the governor traveled abroad, ostensibly to promote trade for Georgia but primarily to meet foreign leaders, so that when he returned home he could drop impressive phrases into his speeches—"when I last spoke to my friend Golda Meir" or "in my long talks with Japan's Prime Minister Fukada"—allusions that implied considerable international expertise.

One summer day in 1971 Carter let one of his aides, Peter Bourne, know that he lusted after the White House. That day Carter and Bourne went to a hearing in Washington chaired by Sen. Ed Muskie, who was then considered a hot Presidential prospect. Carter looked into Muskie's eyes, sized him up, and judged himself superior. On the way back to the hotel, he let Bourne know how he felt.

"If that guy can get to be President," he said, "it's not far-fetched for me to go after it."

"Have you thought about running?" Bourne asked, wide-eyed.

"No. But if I did, I'd run the way I ran for governor—four years and all out."

The seed was planted. That set the target date—1976.

A year later Carter and his crew were in Miami for the Democratic National Convention. Rafshoon had obtained copies of a poll which not surprisingly showed that McGovern would do better in Georgia with Jimmy Carter as his running mate than with several Northerners already proposed. Rafshoon showed the poll figures to Carter during a party in Miami Beach.

"Would you be interested in Vice-President?" he asked his boss.

"Why not?" Carter replied coyly.

Rafshoon and Hamilton Jordan went to the Doral Hotel, where McGovern's people were lodged. They asked for pollster Pat Caddell, hoping their presentation of the Georgia findings would sell him on Carter as a Vice-Presidential choice. It didn't take long to find how they rated on the party power scale. "They kept us waiting for an hour in the holding room where they put the turkeys," Rafshoon recalled.

The pair were able to see Caddell only by appealing to an old friend they discovered working in the McGovern campaign. Ushered into Caddell's room, they got all of three minutes to argue their case for a Carter Vice-Presidency before the harried pollster cut them short.

"Yeah, yeah, looks good," Caddell muttered as he led them out of the room. "I'll make a recommendation."

He recommended someone else. "He thought we were crazy," Rafshoon observed. Rafshoon and Jordan licked their wounded egos. They would exact their pound of flesh later, when Caddell would join the team as a brilliant but "not quite equal" member.

Caddell, a Harvard graduate who lives in Massachusetts, was the most literate and intellectual mind in the Carter entourage. Precisely for those qualities, he was distrusted by the clan, and was often the target of insults, which he accepted with good humor. He felt grateful just to be part of Jimmy Carter's cosmos. Ever since first visiting Carter in Plains, he had been converted and marked for future service in the siege for the Presidency.

Except for Pat Caddell, the team had been trained, tested, and fine-tuned through two grueling campaigns, losing one and winning one, self-correcting mistakes like lab mice solving a maze. Now, with their eyes raised on the vision of the Presidency, the crew included Rosalynn Carter, Hamilton Jordan, Gerald Rafshoon, Jody Powell, Stu Eizenstat, and Peter Bourne —with Jimmy Carter at the helm.

In their journey from the obscurity of Georgia to the majesty of the White House, they fought many big-name consultants in the primaries. In both major contests—the Presidential elections against Gerald Ford in 1976 and Ronald Reagan in 1980 —they would match their collective wits against the best all-round professional the Republicans had to offer: a Californian who learned his politics from the streets up, and who came to maturity in the computer and television age—Stuart Spencer of Newport Beach.

5

Stu Spencer, Street Fighter

Stuart Spencer took Ronald Reagan from picket-line battles as head of the Screen Actors Guild and a faltering television acting career to eight consecutive years as governor of California, a reign that launched Reagan's triumphant push for the Presidency. He is the man who almost got Gerald Ford a full four years in the White House after Ford's pardon of Richard Nixon prompted most political pros to call him unelectable. Two years later, Spencer gave Texas its first Republican governor in over one hundred years by putting Bill Clements in office.

Some strategists learn their politics from books. They study statistics, accounts, and reports until they absorb an intellectual understanding of the elective process. For example, Doug Bailey spent four years as Henry Kissinger's aide at Harvard, and John Deardourff worked as Nelson Rockefeller's research director, before the two joined forces to form the highly successful Bailey & Deardourff consulting team. Word orientation gives such consultants a feel for print, an ease with management details, and a reputation for being able to fine-tune a campaign to meet a limited budget.

Others come to books secondarily, calling on gut skills culled from "going through the political chairs." Men like Matt Reese and Sanford Weiner started sharpening their wits in the precincts, developing from doorbell-ringing, petition-carrying volunteers into consultants whose advice is eagerly solicited by senators, governors, and Presidents. These are the street fighters of the business. They view voters less abstractly and know the value of hard, face-to-face persuasion. They use polls and film makers, too, but spend more energy and money recruiting volunteers to run telephone banks and knock on doors. To promote their candidates, they make personal contact as often as possible. Combining communications skills with street savvy, the street fighters bridge the gap between electronic campaigning and the dissolving party organizational structure.

Stu Spencer represents a diminishing clan of campaign consultants who feel equally at home with media maps, computer printouts, and precinct walking teams. He works out of a modern suite on the ground floor of a smoke-glassed complex in Irvine, California, just north of posh Newport Beach. Photos and busts of famous Republicans adorn the wood-and-leather comfort of his office—Abraham Lincoln, Nelson Rockefeller, Gerald Ford, and Ronald Reagan.

At fifty-three, Spencer looks like a street fighter. He has a tough-set jaw, a burly chest and shoulders, and sky-blue eyes that spark quickly at a challenge. He grew up during the Depression with the tough Mexican kids of the San Gabriel Valley.

"I was always in a fight," he recalled. "It helped form me, toughen me up for politics. Things get really brutal in a campaign—emotionally, physically, and every other way. You see all kinds of strange things come out of people when the pressure's on. They fold, they disappear, they get sick. Some people don't like controversy or tough decisions; they want to be loved. Other people thrive on stress and I'm one of them."

Spencer freely admits that he's a "gut politician." "I've been around long enough that much of our research only confirms what I already know. No doubt about it, even with our polls, computers, and communication explosions, intuition is important in this business. It's an art form, not a science."

He admires and uses media expertise wherever and as much as he can. But the days of big-spending campaigns are ending. The survivors in the 1980s, Spencer feels, will be the consultants who understand precinct politics as well as they do computerized mailing lists and ten-second ID spots.

"Sometimes you create an issue before it shows in any research," he explained. "Take Ronald Reagan's first campaign for governor in 1966. In the early months he ran around California giving his number-one speech, set for twenty minutes and a question-and-answer period. The purpose was to show the press he wasn't just a dumb actor, but a man who could think on his feet and answer questions credibly and knowledgeably.

"Up to then, none of the research showed campus unrest as particularly upsetting to voters. But everywhere we went in the boondocks, somebody got up to ask: 'What are you going to do about those bastards at Berkeley?' The question came up over and over again, so I knew we had something. We slipped a two-minute insert into his set speech, slashing away at students trying to burn Berkeley down. Boy, did we get a reaction! Two weeks later it started showing up in the research and kept growing. We had created the issue and it was wild, emotional as hell!"

Spencer regards emotions as 75 percent of the turf he plays on. "People make value judgments because of what they see on television. They come away from the tube and say 'this is an honest person' or 'this is a thief' or 'this is an idiot,' just because of his eyes or smile or cut of clothes. Strictly emotional—no basis in fact or sense. It's simply their personal *feelings*. Those feelings are what you have to deal with. How people perceive a candidate is the whole ball game. Three forces shape the voters' perceptions. What our side does, what the opposition does, and what the Great Mediator—the press—says about it. Everything we do is aimed to shape that perception—organization, media, how we raise money, volunteers. The voters' final perceptions of the candidates decide the election."

Today the coalition of 51 percent tyrannizes our electoral process. More than ever before in U.S. history, as party loyalty wanes, smaller pockets of special-interest groups rush in to fill the power void. In place of the ward heelers who could fix a citizen's parking tickets or get him or her a twenty-five-dollar check as an election official, we have a proliferation of groups who trade off votes for legislative backing of their cause. Surrounding themselves with halos of morality, such diverse cliques as the profeminist, antiabortion, progun, antinuclear, and proecology lobbies can deliver large blocs of adherents. They are available to the candidate who will do the most for their cause, regardless of party affiliation.

"When you talk about people not active in the political process, single issues are dynamite," Spencer noted. "These are people who vote every four years instead of every two, or they stay away four elections in a row. If you can get them excited over single-issue things, they really come out for you. They can be an important part of your 51-percent coalition."

Human prejudice as a factor in elections is vastly underrated, says Spencer. "Voter bias is the whole decider for many people. Lots of people vote only against things, never for anything. How many times have you heard how folks don't like the choices, so they'll vote for the least of the evils? Every prejudice you find in everyday life is reflected in a campaign.

"You get racial prejudices, economic, sexual, intellectual prejudices—you name it. In the Carter-Ford race, Jewish people in the Northeast had a very hard time accepting Jimmy Carter because of the way he talks. They had an even harder time in 1980, but for other reasons. In fact, the whole Northeast felt that way about Carter's being a Southerner. He had to overcome the prejudice against Southern politicians to become President the way John Kennedy had to overcome the prejudice against Catholicism. We're a diverse nation and many parts still don't understand one another. People in the East have no understanding of the farm problems in California or the battles over water reclamation. Westerners have no feel for the coal-mining struggles in West Virginia or Pennsylvania. Neither can appreciate the Indian problems of South Dakota."

Both parties approach an election the same way. They study the electorate, decide they need x number of votes to win and ask where they may reasonably find them. The regions and districts are mapped, and evaluated according to past voting history, then research uncovers issues within each region. Spencer calls his technique of mapping out potential pockets of support "prioritizing the precincts."

"You approach voting blocs the same way," Spencer explained. "They have leaders and issues they're involved in. You meet with them and they tell you what they want. They are very demanding. The toughest bloc I ever had to deal with was the gun people. Man, were they uncompromising! So, depending on your candidate, you come out with a hard position, a waffling stance, or a soft stand. Some ethnic groups are regional. Chicano Americans are the deciding factor in California, Texas, New Mexico, Arizona, and parts of Colorado. If Illinois is on your map, you've got a tremendous East European bloc around Chicago."

A traditional tool for picking up votes from minority blocs is "street money." A candidate simply hands a packet of greenbacks to brokers who merchandise and deliver bloc votes. In the South the brokers are white men, usually local car dealers or lawyers connected with the state Democratic Party. There the customary payoffs are to black schoolteachers and ministers, who in turn distribute ten- or twenty-dollar bills to voters they claim to represent.

Street money is by no means confined to Dixie. In the 1976 Presidential election, black ministers in Oakland freely admitted being paid by the Carter campaign. The same thing occurred in the poorer wards of Philadelphia and in the Mexican barrios of Texas. It isn't one of the prettier aspects of American politics, but it is one which any politician seeking national office disregards at his peril, particularly if he is a Democrat. Consultants don't like to talk about street money— it embarrasses them. Still, if it means winning, they pay it.

"My job is to do what I have to do and get the job done," Spencer explained. "We didn't use any in the Ford Presidential campaign, but Carter used it in Louisiana and Mississippi. It's distasteful, but I've done it. In 1964 we registered fifty thousand blacks in Los Angeles so they could vote for Nelson Rockefeller in the Republican primary. They were all Democrats, but pro-Rockefeller because every black family who's sent a son to a black college knows how the Rockefeller family has supported them for years. This was their chance to do something for him, so they changed their registration to vote for Rockefeller in that primary against Barry Goldwater. That

almost won it for us, but it wasn't very idealistic. We paid out
a lot of street money—over a million dollars—and had a lot of
ministers to deal with."

Democrats use street money much more than Republicans,
not because they are more corrupt but simply because their
natural constituency needs it more and is used to getting it.
The poor sections of industrialized cities contain the biggest
concentrations of apathetic voters, so that is where Democrats
go with their street money. By the time a twenty-dollar payoff
reaches a retired domestic on social security, however, it may
be watered down to a free ride to the polls and a five-dollar
bill.

A huge advantage Democrats have is rooted in the power
they seized during the Depression. In the twenty-five Con-
gresses that have convened since the days of Franklin Delano
Roosevelt, only two had more Republicans than Democrats.
Not only do Democrats usually monopolize the two houses,
they also hold more political jobs all over the country and have
more political favors to dole out. From appointments as
judges and commissioners down to the fee for poll officials, the
party in power can spread around a more respectable form of
payola.

In 1980, the California Republican Party sued the U.S. government, claiming that the hiring of temporary workers for the
1980 census discriminated against Republicans since it was
based on political affiliation. Over 300,000 of these workers,
openly chosen by the party in power, represented almost 1 percent of the nearly 41 million votes the Democrats won in 1976
—votes of gratitude that were claimed in 1980. Of course in the
1970 census, which Richard Nixon administered, the preferred
choices for enumerators and clerks were good Republicans.

Black votes have traditionally belonged to Democrats, except for a span of years after Lincoln. Republicans feel uneasy
about the paucity of blacks in their party, but they tend to
ignore campaign charges of racism. Most Americans do not
understand the hard realities involved in putting together a
coalition of 51 percent. They wrongly interpret the Republican
appeal to the white suburbs as a rejection of the inner cities,

when in fact the Republicans would prefer to have them both.

Stuart Spencer started life as a Democrat. An adopted only child, he was raised as a Roosevelt New-Dealer by a dentist father and activist mother. In 1948 he became a leader of the young Democrats at East Los Angeles City College.

"I was a moderate then, trying to keep things together," Spencer recalled. "And I used to have vicious fights with Communists who were running wild, disrupting anything they could. One night the Commies rigged a meeting and stacked a vote to destroy campus rules. It would have turned the campus upside down so nobody could learn anything. So I put together a coalition, used parliamentary rules to control the Commies, passed around booze for endurance, and beat them. I was for most of what they wanted, but we were on different planets when it came to methods for getting there. That turned me away from the Young Democrats, who gave too much support to those crazies."

After laying low a few years, Spencer and boyhood friend Johnny Rousselot (now a congressman) met Republican Congressman Pat Hillings, who asked them to help in his re-election campaign. Though it was unpaid volunteer work, it was a way for the young men to get back into political action. They rang doorbells, handed out literature, phoned people, and talked incessantly about their major passion: politics.

"I was never that issues-oriented," Spencer admits. "It was power that interested me." His path to power came through the Young Republicans. In two years he ran the organization for all of California and a few months later the nation. Meanwhile Spencer's daytime job as a recreation director in an Alhambra playground was boring him to death. His only bright moments came from outside coaching for junior high football and track teams. The recreation job confirmed his instinctual distaste and fear of government. "I don't like government," Spencer says. "They drove me nuts for eight years telling me I couldn't do this or **that** and had to do the other thing. When I got a job offer from the Republican county committee, I grabbed it."

He and Bill Roberts, a television salesman, went to work for

the party at the same time. Inside the organization they got to
see firsthand how elections were waged, and watched top political pros do their magic. Spencer worked his first assignments
with Whitaker & Baxter, the firm that had started the whole
political-engineering business thirty-five years earlier.

Clem Whitaker and Leona Baxter began working in 1930 as
public relations mouthpieces for big corporations. Soon they
branched off into managing the business side of initiative campaigns. From there it was an easy jump to handling politicians.
In those days, electioneering techniques were much more
heavy-handed. "Whitaker and Baxter were propagandists pure
and simple," Spencer recalled. "It worked in the thirties and
forties, but the whole communications structure has changed
since their time. Hell, you could own reporters then. You play
with fire trying to own a writer today."

The two embryo kingmakers, Spencer and Roberts, watched
the two pioneers working the vote arena, analyzed precinct
statistics, and absorbed strategic lessons. One night over beer,
they decided to try their own wings. "We made a pact that the
first chance we had, we'd run with it. A year later we put up
five hundred dollars apiece and started Spencer-Roberts. It
was 1960. We had three clients, high hopes, and heavy bills. I
told myself if things went bad I could always go back to the
playgrounds. But they haven't caught up to me yet."

In the course of keeping ahead of the pack, Spencer has
pulled the strings for over two hundred candidates, putting his
man in office three out of every four tries. For a strategist who
works only Republican campaigns, his record is remarkable.
Every time he goes into battle, Spencer gives away a fifteen-
point handicap. In the United States, less than 20 percent call
themselves Republicans. About one-third say they are Democrats. The remaining half have, in spirit if not conscious intention, opted out of the two-party system. That reservoir of
skeptical, disenchanted, surly, bored, or just plain lazy citizens
is where Stu Spencer and other Republican masterminds have
to make up most of their point spread.

How they do that comes down to background and personal
style. Washington, D.C.–based Bailey & Deardourff use exten-

sive studies of voter dissatisfactions and produce media campaigns that feature subtle use of television. Californian Hal Evry likes to use media blatantly, opting for huge shock headlines and deliberately sentimental television commercials aimed at the unconverted masses. New Yorker David Garth uses his commercials as news vehicles, packing all the information and statistics he can into them, forgoing mood and symbols.

Issues are totally predictable to top consultants. These men have seen cycles come and go, have studied thousands of research reports, and know what to expect.

"I can sit here today in Newport Beach and tell you what people around the country will tell you when you ask them, 'What is the single most important problem facing the nation?'" says Spencer. "These problems don't change, only their priority. Today the big issues are jobs, taxes, and inflation." He struck the desk emphatically with his fist. "National defense is way up, energy is way up, and street security is always big. You can watch the calendar and match some issues to the month. In late winter—tax-paying time—the tax issue shoots way up, and then goes down. In California you can plot a curve for the worst smog times of the year, July and August—the smog issue peaks over the summer and dips way down in December. In the cold belt and the Northeastern states, you can do the same thing with energy over the winter months."

Research is where the real action is today. Polling and interviewing methods are becoming more sophisticated. Such exotic techniques as eyescans, voice-pitch analysis, and skin testing are now common practice.

In 1970, Spencer introduced a research wrinkle never before applied to political campaigns. Called "tracking research," it has a long history in marketing, where it is used to measure the effects of advertising or promotions on product sales. By taking frequent measurements, a computer can quickly isolate specific cause-and-effect relationships. In politics, tracking research involves running continuous polls to measure the impact of campaign events. Once he has pinpointed people's reactions to the political propaganda aimed at them, the strategist can fine-tune his media.

Spencer used tracking to win a 1978 election in Texas. His
client was Republican William Clements, a home-grown millionaire, now governor and a future Presidential prospect. At
the time, although $3 million of his own money was ear-
marked for the campaign, Clements was considered the underdog. His home town, Dallas, had never had a native son in the
governor's mansion. The state of Texas had not had a Republican governor in 103 years. Most distressing of all, nobody outside of a handful of businessmen knew who Bill Clements was.

Nine months before the election, the polls showed Clements
thirty-five points behind the pack. Spencer credits tracking for
turning things around. "We tracked the last four weeks," he
recalled. "We watched how we were doing by regions and by
population segments so we could fine-tune for the Clements
media. We polled by telephone every night and laid out the
curves for what was happening in Dallas or what our opponent did last week in Houston. If we hadn't been tracking,
we could never have pulled it off. Clements had done everything wrong. He got up one morning, called the papers, and
told them he was running for governor. He had asked no one's
advice, didn't talk to his friends, had no chairman or the
vaguest idea what to do next—the best way to lose. I'd known
Bill a while so he phoned me and asked me to help. Bill is
Texan to his boots, down-home style, not suave like George
Bush. Texas politics fits my style—it's swinging, wide open,
played for keeps. It sounded like fun so I agreed to go down
there."

Since most Texans had never heard of Bill Clements, Spencer had to promote instant fame. So he had his media man put
together a series of simple ten-second commercials. They featured a one-color backdrop and upbeat music playing as a
ticker tape ran his client's name across the screen and into the
memory banks of Texans: BILL CLEMENTS . . . BILL CLEMENTS . . .
with a tag line at the end featuring Clements himself or an
announcer's voice-over spieling a one-liner—"Bill Clements
stands tough on *energy*," or "Bill Clements will make a great
governor."

With money to burn, Spencer saturated Texas television stations with the spots, and inside a week most Texans knew that Bill Clements was running for governor. "Name identification is easy to handle," Spencer noted. "With saturation buys, your name ID rises in a steep upward curve. But you have to reinforce it, stay with it. If you don't, it will drop off."

A big problem for Texas Republicans is winning the rural areas of the state, where conservative white Sam Rayburn Democrats reign. Though Republicans in the past had managed to do fairly well in Dallas, Houston, and the big cities, they inevitably were destroyed in the hinterlands. To counter that rural power, Spencer launched his "260 Program." In July and August, he sent the candidate barnstorming through 260 rural communities, then followed with a few weeks of media blitz. By September, whatever rural base Clements had built was allowed to stand on its own.

"We told them who Clements was and where he stood on some issues, but more importantly we showed them what his personality is like. Personality is crucial everywhere, but in Texas it's the biggest factor in the whole race. Our strategy was to neutralize the boondocks and win the cities. From September on, we spent all our time, energy, and money in the big population centers."

The final vote spread was 18,000 in favor of Clements, with 3 million votes cast. When an election is that close, it is hard for even the strategist to point to the one thing that won it. Ten different moves may have contributed to the outcome, plus a few things the other side did badly.

Spencer loses, too. His defeats can almost always be blamed on one of two things: a major issue that is too tough to handle, or one that is just badly managed. In 1974 Spencer met an issue too tough to overcome when he ran Houston Fluornoy's campaign for governor against Jerry Brown. "In pre-Watergate days we'd have won that race," he noted. "Watergate destroyed us because it cut off the flow of money. There was a direct correlation between our being able to buy television time and our rise in the polls. But we got too little too late and never enough to do the job."

In Nelson Rockefeller's first try for the Presidency in 1964, an issue Spencer had handled successfully came back to haunt him. When Spencer took over the Rockefeller campaign, polls showed Rockefeller with only 29-percent support against Barry Goldwater's 57 percent. He had less than five months to close a twenty-eight-point spread. The big obstacle was Rockefeller's messy divorce and imminent remarriage. After thirty-two years of marriage, Rockefeller divorced Mary Todhunter Clark. Only a year later he married "Happy" Fitler Murphy, a divorced mother-of-four. It was just the kind of scandal the news media loved to exploit.

"The press kept calling him a womanizer and it was destroying us," Spencer recalled. "So we fought back by totally confusing the issue. Instead of defending Rockefeller's right to a love life we just attacked Barry Goldwater: 'He's crazy, you can't trust him. What's he gonna do with the hydrogen bomb?' We got everybody thinking about all those scary things instead of the divorce. In the end, nature did us in. We had quieted things down and managed to make our polls look good, but then, on the Saturday before the primary, Happy delivered a baby boy. It made headlines in all the papers and was all over television. The Rockefellers themselves reopened a wound we spent over $2 million to heal. The Goldwater people did a good job of keeping the baby issue big those last few days, so we were finished. By one point Rockefeller lost his best shot at the White House. If that baby had been born five days later, we'd have won the primary for sure."

Stu Spencer and other professional electioneers have been tagged by the press "dirty tricksters who pollute our political system." There is a widely held notion that he and his colleagues play the game dishonestly, sneaking around looking for dirt to throw or payoffs to arrange. It's a notion that dies hard, even if it doesn't square with the reality of the consultant's role.

"It's a carryover from political history," Spencer observes ruefully. "Party bosses did some pretty rotten things over the years. They really were cigar-smoking, wheeling-dealing bagmen—I met a few of them. What people don't realize is that consultants are not very close to political parties. They may work with them, but they don't belong. I go down to my local bar and people start bitching to me about what the Republicans are doing and how they should change things. I used to say to them, 'Hey, I'm not even part of the Republican Party, so what the hell are you guys complaining to me for?' But they never heard a word I said. They identify you with the process and you pay that price."

Money is not the main inducement for Spencer and most of the others. Media directors make much more from each campaign than do the consultants who manage the whole thing. What fame consultants achieve is strictly among fellow professionals. You are not likely to see Stu Spencer or most other consultants on *Good Morning, America* or the *Today Show.* Honors rarely come their way. Of the top consultants, only Spencer is listed in a major *Who's Who.* Newspaper accounts of campaigns rarely include consultants' analyses and comments. Why do they do it?

As Spencer admits openly, and others suggest more obliquely, it's power—the game itself, the thrill of victory, and the ultimate freedom of calling all the plays. American politics is still a form of warfare and these men, its field generals, love every moment on the battlefield.

"Campaigns are living entities," Spencer explains. "Like the human beings involved in them, every campaign develops its own character. No two are alike, not even two campaigns by the same candidate going after the same job." The easiest candidate for any consultant is the "virgin"—a person running for his first political office. "Once politicians get in office, they become pains in the ass," he observed. "Suddenly they become experts—they stick their noses into the ball game. That's when you get big problems."

Spencer had those problems his second time around with Ronald Reagan. In 1966, however, when he managed the ex-actor's successful first try for the governorship of California, the lines of communication were strongly drawn. Reagan knew Spencer was the expert, and was happy to follow instructions to the letter. "Because of his movie training, he knew how to take direction," Spencer explained. "Once you decided on a direction and spelled out the program, Ron never asked any questions. You did your end, he implemented it, and it all worked beautifully."

First, Spencer and Bill Roberts had to tone down a right-wing image that Reagan had acquired in the fifties, when he spoke against progressive income taxes, civil rights, and biased Supreme Court justices. They had the candidate agree to censor such sentiments and stick to the basics spelled out in "The Speech," a twenty-minute orator's stew consisting of small-town, Protestant-safe jokes, bursts of passion against harmless targets, and lots of appeals to down-home patriotism. After a lifetime of memorizing scripts, Reagan was the perfect television candidate. In all his commercials and set pieces, his studied sincerity made each line sound fresh, spontaneous, and believable. By contrast, Democratic incumbent Pat Brown looked the office-weary old pol reeling after eight years of running the volatile Golden State.

The "just an actor" tag was a big negative, however. Voters had to be shown that Reagan was smart and could think for himself. When Spencer persuaded Brown to appear on camera with Reagan in three televised news shows, he had the break he needed. Though Brown insisted on no one-to-one exchanges and the two rivals were simply questioned by a panel of reporters, the two faces were on view side by side. The beauty contest was no match.

On *Meet the Press*, Reagan sparked fireworks by accusing Brown's administration of being loaded with "left-wing radicals." Brown effectively retaliated by calling Reagan "an enemy of the people." But when Lyndon Johnson, already in low regard over the Vietnam War, called from the White House to congratulate Pat Brown on his showing, Californians moved closer to Reagan. A second show on KNBC-TV, a local Los Angeles station, took place at the end of a week which had seen rioting break out in San Francisco. Reagan railed against the "lack of leadership in Sacramento." The next day was the last match-up on ABC's *Issues and Answers*. Both candidates repeated their left/right countercharges, only Reagan knew when to smile.

After those appearances, Reagan's poll standing rose like a rocket. Brown's consultants, Baum & Ross, had been running Brown on his accomplishments while ridiculing Reagan's conservative stands. Now, with the election just weeks away and their man behind, they were desperate. They decided to hit hard on the opponent's Hollywood past. Baum & Ross hired Charles Guggenheim, who flew in from Washington to produce a last-hour media blitz. Commercials featured famous actors saying "I'm a cowboy and I play Western roles but I couldn't play governor." Another warned, "Remember, it was an actor who shot Abraham Lincoln." In the final two weeks forty-five hundred radio spots and four hundred one-minute television commercials played across the state. A half-hour film biography called *Man vs. Actor* ran many times while Governor Brown gave a five-minute television appeal every night during those last fourteen days.

Spencer countered by cutting out the longer television pieces and running more exposures of his twenty-second and one-minute commercials, sticking with the basic themes that got them the lead—campus unrest, violence in the cities, and runaway government spending. When the furor died down and the votes were counted, Ronald Reagan won by a record one million plurality out of 4.5 million cast.

"Then he became governor," Spencer noted. "And he got himself experts, guys I called 'the Palace Guard.' When he came up for reelection in 1970, I spent half my time fighting those turkeys over what should or should not be done. They second-guessed me all the time and it wasn't fun any more. We won, but maybe in some ways he lost something, too."

Those "experts," the public relations team of Peter Hannaford and Mike Deaver, replaced Spencer after the 1970 victory as Ronald Reagan's political masterminds. Unlike Spencer, they were fundamentalist conservatives who would rather have their candidate preach unwavering doctrine than win office. Following the advice of the Palace Guard, Reagan spent the 1970s confirming a popular conception of his right-wing rigidity, an image he would later fight hard to soften.

But political cycles often turn last election's outcast into the

next one's golden boy. Stuart Spencer's destiny would remain
linked to that of Ronald Reagan's in the coming years, as
Reagan aimed at the Presidency. Reagan was Gerald Ford's
chief rival for the 1976 Republican nomination. Spencer,
Ford's strategist, used his knowledge of Reagan's weaknesses
to edge him out in the primaries.

In 1980 Spencer got an unprecedented second shot at the
Carter gang, this time working *for* Ronald Reagan, who had
decided early in the primaries to reject unbending ideology for
a real chance to capture the White House. It had been unheard-of for the same professional consultant to represent two
different Presidential candidates in successive elections. But
Stuart Spencer got that opportunity, one which tested his own
predictions of his political ability.

"I'm an action guy," he told me, long before he ever
dreamed he would be doing Reagan's 1980 campaign. "I can
take a challenger and dump the incumbent almost as naturally
as breathing. That's my style, that's the way I work. But if I
have the sitting incumbent, I could end up doing something
totally unnecessary and screw up the campaign."

In 1976 Gerald Ford was the incumbent and Stu Spencer
had him.

6

How Carter Won

When U.S. Congressman Gerald Ford was vaulted by the Watergate purge of 1974 into the first unelected Presidency in the nation's history, the Republicans knew they would have a hard time holding power. Four weeks after taking his oath of office, President Ford pardoned Richard Nixon for any crimes he might have committed. By that one act, he lost an irretrievable chunk of public trust, and from that day on every Democratic politician with national name recognition licked his chops dreaming about the bicentennial election.

Getting the jump on everyone else, Carter's Georgians had begun running from the moment George McGovern was named the Democratic nominee for President in 1972. Walking back from the convention that night, Rafshoon had talked to Hamilton Jordan about "running Jimmy for President." Two days later Jordan spent an afternoon on the beach with Peter Bourne, discussing just how they would do it. Early the next week, Bourne mailed an eight-page memo to Carter. Dated July 25, 1972, the memo summarized his vision of political realities for the seventies.

"To seek the Presidency," it read, "you have to begin now and develop a carefully planned strategy to develop a base throughout the country. George Wallace proved that the South as a power base cannot be used to get you anything more than a protest vote, so to compete nationally you must take positions that will alienate a lot of people in the South."

Carter was advised to hire a ghostwriter for a political auto-
biography that would give him national stature. (*Why Not
the Best?* by Jimmy Carter was subsequently published in
1974.) Bourne recommended that Carter hire people to travel
the country pushing Carter's candidacy to wealthy donors and
party people. (Bourne himself was one of those hired for this
task.)

"Two years from now," the memo advised, "you should
capitalize on the image created by the book and go on a nationwide speaking tour, fund-raising for the Party. That way
you can exploit your greatest asset—your personal charm." (In
1974, Robert Strauss gave Carter and Jordan jobs with the
Democratic National Committee, touring to raise funds, thus
enabling Carter to shake lots of influential hands.) "If the
McGovern ticket loses, the field will be wide open in 1976." (It
did and it was.) "Kennedy appears to have diminished ambition for national office, has repeatedly handled stress poorly,
and has never been tested by a knock-down drag-out campaign." (Kennedy decided not to run, opening the Democratic
nomination for a mob of hopefuls to rush in and fill his liberal
void.)

Early in September, as McGovern launched his ill-fated
campaign, Rafshoon, Jordan, and Bourne met with Jimmy
Carter in the governor's mansion. For five hours they traded
ideas about how Carter could win the Presidency in 1976, and
then the governor ordered Jordan to summarize the main
points. Hamilton Jordan's ensuing memo became both battle
plan and inspiration for their four-year steeplechase, a blueprint Carter followed religiously.

A few days later, Rafshoon wrote his own memo to Carter
about his public image. "It talked about negatives and positives," Rafshoon explained. "I made negatives into positives; I
turned it around." Through public relations alchemy, Rafshoon
found the right words to transform base metal into gold. A
negative like Carter's shyness emerged as sincerity. Lack of
culture became populist simplicity. Peanut wholesaling became
blue-collar farming. Carter's evangelical background, normally
a negative, during the "born-again" zeal of the 1970s became a

sure vote-winner among millions of fundamentalist Christians. Even his candidate's segregationist background was transformed into New South moderation simply by wooing highly publicized support from famous black leaders. Blacks, Southerners, and evangelical Christians would be the bedrock of Carter's coalition of 51 percent.

"Positioning" was the soul of Rafshoon's strategy. In advertising, positioning means finding a unique slot for your product among its competitors, one that offers distinct marketing advantages. A cold tablet that fights coughs, fever, pain, inflammation, and runny nose is positioned as "all-purpose," compared to others that fight only two or three symptoms. Adding vitamin C would add another dimension. The idea is to play off perceptions that already exist in the public mind for a quick "image fix."

Jimmy Carter was positioned as a nonracist populist with farm-boy honesty, a Mr. Smith of the South aiming to clean up a corrupt Washington. That would be his public stance come hell or high water, the image Rafshoon and the rest of the Carter team would sell to the nation. It was the picture they would repeat over and over again, to burn it into the mass imagination.

Rafshoon gave Carter a book to read, *The Boys on the Bus*. In it reporter Timothy Crouse explains how journalists assigned to candidates influence how the public sees their champion. Since the candidate's fate is tied to their own—a reporter who covers the winning entry gets automatic promotion to the White House press corps—many writers openly begin to root in print for their great hope.

After speed-reading the book twice, Carter ordered everyone who worked in his campaign to read it. His aides drew up a list of influential political writers; all received personal invitations to visit the governor's mansion in Atlanta. "The strategy was to get to know the press," Rafshoon noted. "We knew your names even if you didn't know ours." But they knew more than just names. Rafshoon had little biographies drawn up describing each of his press targets, so that when they arrived Carter could drop a few targeted lines to astound them. Over the next two years, hundreds of big-name press and television journalists came to dine, talk, and be wooed. Among the frequent visitors to Atlanta were Bill Moyers, Barbara Walters, and columnist David Broder. Carter's courtship of the media was the springboard to everything else he would do.

Rafshoon knew that the press and most big-time politicians saw Carter as just another Southern politician growing bigger than his britches, not to be taken seriously as a national figure. To the true believers, that was just another negative that needed transforming.

Gerald Ford had never in his life run for even a statewide office, let alone a coast-to-coast marathon like the Presidency. His congressional district in Michigan counted fewer than 500,000 people, and his campaigns had always been short, easy, and cheap. Research showed that Ford's pardon of Nixon cost him an 8-percent bloc of voters who would not support him come hell or high water, strictly because of that act. In 1974, the Democrats nationally held a 12-percent lead in registrations over the Republicans, so before our thirty-eighth President ever thought about running to keep his office, he faced a 20-percent deficit, no matter whom the Democrats threw against him.

While the campaigns of his rivals were already operational, Ford hadn't even begun to put together a campaign team, mostly because he had no idea how to go about it. Instead, he concentrated on battling Congress and working on government business. Politically, he was an ostrich with his head in sand.

Two weeks before Christmas 1974, Jimmy Carter spoke to the National Press Club in Washington and proclaimed himself a candidate for the Presidency of the United States. In that opening speech Carter preached his unvarying doctrine: malaise stalked the land—gloomy mistrust and skepticism that could only be healed by a virtuous President. The "spiritual malaise" theme, borrowed from Pat Caddell's national readings of mass America since 1968, became a litany echoed in a hundred speeches.

Carter's cure for our national malaise? "I'll never lie to you."
It was a refrain that challenged reporters who covered him.
They looked for lies and found lots of them, but still Carter
murmured, "Trust me, I'll never lie to you." Thus he made
"trust" his issue merely by claiming it.

In the spring of 1975, with the first state caucuses only
months away, Ford began to stir. His party advisers, mirroring
the Eastern establishment view, told him there would be no
one seriously competing against him for the nomination at next
year's convention. A few more perceptive souls whispered that
Ronald Reagan had been traveling the country making can-
didate-like statements. When the whispers persisted, Ford
finally moved.

It was late May. Southern California skies were clear, except
for little low-hanging cloud wisps. Perfect sailing weather,
thought Stu Spencer, looking out his Newport Beach office
window toward the nearby harbor. He sighed and forced his
concentration back on the computer printouts spread across his
desk. Suddenly the phone rang. It was Leon Parmer, a California Ford supporter, with a job offer: putting together a
"California for Ford" organization from steering committee to
phone banks. Spencer was ready for a new challenge and
grabbed the assignment.

Fingering through his Rolodex file, he began calling Republican likelies to plead his case. In a few weeks he had a
mushrooming organization going that built through the summer by chain outreach. With half a dozen other campaigns to
oversee, Spencer had no ambitions for more responsibility, assuming that Ford's Presidential campaign team had long been
assembled.

He was wrong. What was really going on back in Washington was a labyrinthine power struggle among party regulars.
As a sop to the conservatives, former Secretary of the Army Bo
Callaway became Ford's first campaign manager and he
proved a disaster. Callaway made tactical blunders at press
conferences, triggering negative headlines on the evening
news. With his penchant for Machiavellian power struggles, he

instigated purges that caused one staff resignation after another, until his own was demanded.

On July 8 Gerald Ford spoke over national television from the Oval Office to announce his candidacy for a second term. He named industrialist David Packard, a former Nixon aide, as his finance chairman. Packard promised to raise $10 million by the end of the year, but he barely made 10 percent of his goal. Most of Ford's early choices were ill-advised, but Bo Callaway groped through his network of contacts to bring Ford the few heavyweight campaign professionals who would give him a sporting chance for victory. One was Bob Teeter, a veteran pollster and analyst with Market Opinion Research in Detroit. Teeter had been George Romney's pollster in the 1960s and directed research for Nixon's 1972 slaughter of McGovern.

Callaway's next right move took him to California. Stu Spencer attended a central committee meeting in downtown San Diego in early September and Bo Callaway, a surprise observer, had flown in for the meeting. Halfway through the wordfest, Callaway came over and sat down next to Spencer.

"We could sure use you back in Washington," he said softly.

"I can't get away just now," Spencer countered.

"It would only be for a little while," the chairman drawled. "Two, three weeks, no more. Come on up, take a look at what's going on in New Hampshire, in Florida, give us your assessments, and you're on your way home. Things are tight, Stuart. We could really use you."

"Got to think about it," Spencer replied.

By the time the meeting broke, Spencer left with Callaway and flew to Washington carrying only his overnight bag. Three weeks later he returned to Newport Beach to pick up his clothes, kiss his wife goodbye, and fly back east. The Ford team had its third and most important permanent member.

In Atlanta the Carter team was busy building support for the opening rounds. For the obscure, long-shot ex-governor, the first caucuses and primary elections were crucial. The handful of delegates meant little. But the banner headlines,

TV news reports, and syndicated columns ballyhooing those early results could promote Jimmy Carter to national prominence virtually overnight.

Carter's 1975 travel schedule had him on the road 260 days. Most of those days were spent in Iowa, Oklahoma, and Mississippi, where the first caucuses would be held, and in New Hampshire and Florida, the first primary states. He had enlisted six hundred Georgians who chartered their own planes to blitz those states with leaflets, complimentary peanuts, and purring Southern charm in a memorized doorstoop spiel:"Hi, I'm from Americus, Georgia. I'm a friend of Jimmy Carter, I know him real well, and I'd be glad to tell you the truth about him, answer any questions you might have about him." A few weeks before each voting date, the "peanut brigade" switched gears from doorbells to mass media, booking themselves on talk shows, interviews, and call-in programs.

Meanwhile Carter played the role of revivalist preacher, speaking incessantly about truth, trust, and traditional Christian values. He built state organizations, using a card-file technique learned from the Baptist crusade he joined after his gubernatorial defeat. According to speech writer Robert Shrum, the success Carter had with that revivalist role prompted him to remark, "I don't need the Jews, I have the Christians." Carter's "born again" plank was a naked appeal to 40 million evangelical voters, a calculated exploitation of their fierce religious emotions. While nonevangelical Americans were simply promised love, concern, and no lies, dedicated "propagators of the Faith" heard other tunes. Advertisements in Christian magazines called Carter "the Evangelical's Candidate." "Carter has faced head on that America's problems are the result of a spiritual crisis," they boasted. "Carter will bring the Christian perspective to the American people." The candidate spoke at hundreds of churches, Christian seminars, and evangelical conventions, where he constantly invoked the name of Jesus and declared himself "twice born" and "washed in the blood of the Lamb" to standing ovations.

In 1960 John F. Kennedy found his religion a campaign liability, so he vowed to be a President for all Americans. Fifteen years later Jimmy Carter's religion was a huge asset. Before a vote had been cast and while few Americans even knew his name, Jimmy Carter had already gathered a big chunk of his 51-percent coalition.

The theme Carter used in his speeches and interviews was the same "spiritual malaise" that pollster Caddell had found haunting America in the 1960s. It formed the focus for all of Rafshoon's careful image-defining. The one thing Carter avoided like the plague was taking a stand on anything. He double-talked every idea into mashed grits, made every statement so ambiguous it could be taken any way anyone wanted. So skilled was he at this game that conservatives and liberals, union leaders and corporate managers, whites and blacks, the Ku Klux Klan and the ACLU, Jews and anti-Semites, all felt he would champion them once he took office.

"The voters can't distinguish any substantive difference among the Democratic candidates," Carter explained. "What the voters look for is someone who understands their problems and tells them the truth. That is the American political consciousness now. If I could shake the hand of every voter, just sit down and talk with them all a little bit, I'd get every damned one of them."

In President Ford's camp there was open dismay. Stu Spencer found no one in charge who knew where the campaign was or had even done detailed planning. With the crucial first primaries only months away, they had a media team with an absentee leader, no organization at all in New Hampshire, and an inept chairman in Florida. Moreover, no one realized it would be a dogfight for Ford to get the nomination.

"What really shocked me when I got to Washington," Stu Spencer recalled, "was that none of those guys around the President expected Ronald Reagan to run. Considering this was an incumbent President, they were miles behind where they should have been in their thinking and planning. Of course I knew Reagan was running and I told them so in no uncertain terms. It was their turn to be shocked."

The first bright spot came from Bob Teeter's November polls

in New Hampshire and Florida: both states were winnable. Even more interesting, though, were Republican perceptions of Gerald Ford and Ronald Reagan in the two states. "The assumption," Teeter noted, "was that the more core Republican you were, the more conservative you were and therefore pro Reagan. But contrary to this conventional wisdom, Ford did best among people who were most rock-ribbed Republican. Reagan did best with independent types. Reagan has a kind of populist, maverick appeal." Another finding was that Ford was perceived as much more liberal than either his voting record or his reputation among members of Congress would have suggested. That meant broader appeal.

Teeter unveiled his new technique to read the public mind—"Perceptual Mapping." Using statistics to project the images of competing candidates side by side, it pinpointed the kinds of voters attracted to each candidate, the issues that candidates were identified with, and the feelings that people had for them. "It places candidates in space exactly the way voters place them in space," Teeter explained.

From thousands of probing interviews, Teeter charted a two-dimensional map of the Presidential heavens. On that map Jimmy Carter occupied a space slightly above center-left of the chart. Surrounding Carter were little dots indicating blue-collar workers and intellectuals, blacks and Chicanos, liberal women, conservative women, and environmentalists. Below Carter, a little to the right, was Gerald Ford with dots of farmers, suburban Catholics, hard-core Republicans, women age eighteen to thirty-four, and not much else. Above Ford and to his right, a bigger, more varied group hovered around Ronald Reagan, most of them antis: antiabortion, anti–gun control, antiblack, and antipoor. The same kinds of dots hung around George Wallace on the map.

The job of the primary campaign, according to Teeter, was not to move people to their candidate but to move their candidate to where the people were thickest—the center position. Perceptions of Ford needed to be changed by speeches, advertising, and media events, so as to shift him into that central zone while nudging Reagan farther to the right.

Easier said than done. In those months before the first primaries, Stu Spencer had a hard time getting Callaway, Ford,
or anyone else to move on anything. Finally he took things into
his own hands. He flew to New Hampshire, looked at what
was going on, and found nothing to build on. So he hired
local people to enlist Ford workers and volunteers, installed
phone banks for outreach, and got things rolling.

The next stop was Florida, where things were even more
hopeless. Ford had hired a friend, Lou Frey, to manage his
campaign there. Frey in turn appointed incompetents and
often blundered badly himself when he spoke in Ford's name.
Spencer wasted no time. He fired Frey, phoned ex-partner Bill
Roberts in Los Angeles, and persuaded him to take over Frey's
job. It was the middle of December, with the vote only two
months away. Polls showed Reagan far in front in New Hampshire and leading comfortably in Florida. But Spencer had a
few surprises up his sleeve.

While the New Hampshire primary in late February was
important to Carter's strategy, Florida, two weeks later, was
crucial. Florida marked the first real confrontation between
Carter, segregationist George Wallace, and military hardliner
Sen. Henry Jackson. If Carter couldn't beat Wallace in the
most liberal state in Dixie, his hopes for Solid South backing
were down the drain along with his candidacy.

Early in December 1975 Pat Caddell put his studies into the
field. When the numbers came back to Atlanta headquarters,
they told him George Wallace had 35-percent support, Carter
22, and Jackson 14, with 29 percent undecided. The Florida
issues list mirrored the rest of the country—distrust of government, spiritual malaise, and fear of crime. Floridians were
more upset over inflation than most other Americans, but less
worried about unemployment.

Campaigning in Florida on thirty-five separate trips between
December and the March vote, Carter amended his standard
speech to include promises of vigorous action against "ram-
pant, crippling price rises." Carter was weakest in southern
Florida, with only 13-percent support, while running strongest

in the north—Wallace country—with almost 50; in the center of the state he had about 30. Jackson had strong Jewish backing in the south because of his ardent support of Israel, while Wallace scored heavily among workers everywhere. Besides Carter's sure Baptist vote, Catholics and blacks were two groups the research identified as potential Carter voters. Carter stumped the south part of Florida sixteen of the twenty-one days he spent there, hitting Miami, West Palm Beach, and the string of wealthy cities in between. The other five days he spent in central Florida and Tampa; he did nothing in the north.

Rafshoon targeted his advertising in the same pattern— heavy down south, light in central counties, and none at all in the north. "We did an early media blitz," he explained. "Four five-minute programs showed Carter on the road, going to factories and state fairs. We also did a biography and commercials, then begged and borrowed all the money we could and let it all run over a three-week period in January. When it was over, we polled again. Carter had gained to 50 percent in southern Florida, held his own in middle Florida, and dropped a little in the north because we didn't do anything there. When the interviewers asked people why they liked Jimmy Carter, they said things like 'He's a farmer' or 'He works with his hands' or 'He's the first member of his family to finish college, just like me.' They were throwing back things they had seen on the commercials and five-minute programs. And when the interviewers asked, 'Where did you hear this?' most of them said, 'On the evening news.'"

After the blitz, Carter had gained 34-percent support statewide, a twelve-point rise that nosed him ahead of Wallace. All they had to do was hold the lead for another five weeks. Then late in January Carter's drive spurted. He won three small caucus states: Iowa, Maine, and Oklahoma. The victories yielded him few delegates, but they sparked big media headlines that launched his public image as a winner. But he also lost caucus votes to George Wallace in Mississippi and South Carolina, thereby raising the dangerous question as to whether Carter was a quixotic Dixiecrat who couldn't win in his own region. The contest in Florida now loomed bigger and bigger.

As February 24 approached, the New Hampshire poll readings looked good. Since there is no statewide television there, the personal touch makes the difference. Handshakes, streetcorner talks, factory stakeouts, peanut-brigade blitzes, Carter family stumping, and expensive banks of professional telephone persuaders all paid off. Carter got 30 percent, exactly as Caddell's polls had indicated for weeks, while Udall took 24, Bayh 16, and Harris 11. "JIMMY CARTER IS HIS NAME," read newspaper headlines. National magazines ran folksy stories about Carter and his family.

But in Massachusetts, the Carter machine tasted defeat. Caddell's polls showed Carter leading the pack a few weeks before primary day. It also showed a lot of Yankee prejudice against a Southern President. Rafshoon hit it head-on with advertising. "We did one commercial out on the Concord Bridge," he recalled. "There was snow all around and we had Carter look into the camera saying, 'There are a lot of people who feel that a Southerner can never be elected up North. That reminds me of 1960 when a New Englander and a Catholic was running for President and they said he would never get votes in the South. But when the votes were counted, John Kennedy got the second largest percentage of any state in my home state of Georgia. I know the people of New England will also accept somebody who is different.' We thought people would feel guilty over their bias."

A week before the vote Carter took a stand, something he didn't do again. The issue involved homeowner taxes, and the usually wily Carter admitted he favored raising them. After that, his patronizing Sunday-school-teacher speechmaking didn't charm the politically wise, hard-nosed Catholics. Days before the vote, Caddell's polls showed Carter still ahead, but with Jackson "really coming on." The final count gave Jackson 23 percent, Morris Udall 18, and Carter's down-home rival George Wallace 17; Carter had attracted only 14 percent of the vote.

Caddell recalled how "stunned" Carter was by the defeat. The candidate stuttered, came unglued, and fell into a depression. "He wasn't angry though," Caddell insisted. "That defies everything I know about politics," Carter moaned. "I don't see how Jackson could win." For the first time since Caddell joined the team in September, his research magic had not brought victory. With the Florida election now only eight days away, Carter and his band had the sinking feeling that "we face the crisis of our lives."

Six weeks before the New Hampshire primary, Reagan led Ford by a big twelve percentage points. That would have worried Spencer a lot, were it not for the hole card he had been saving for this occasion. Two months before announcing his candidacy, Reagan had made a speech in Chicago promising to cut the federal budget by $90 billion. This neat 25-percent off-the-top trimming, Reagan claimed, would come simply by turning federal tax money back to local authorities, who would spend more frugally. His speech writer threw in the $90-billion figure merely for dramatics.

The speech got very little attention; *Newsday* and the *Washington Post* ran a few paragraphs buried deep inside the paper. But Stu Spencer read the item and saw its potential at once. He got a copy of the speech and found to his delight that Reagan had advocated changing tax structures long in place, without any Presidential authority to back such radical reforms. If effected, his proposals would cause widespread job layoffs, bankrupt scores of local governments, and push business taxes sky-high.

When Reagan flew into New Hampshire on January 5, he found a hornet's nest waiting. A few hours before his arrival, two prominent New Hampshire Ford supporters held a press conference to chop down Reagan's $90-billion plan. If enacted, they warned, it would cost the people of New Hampshire many millions, eliminate needed social programs, and necessitate higher property taxes and a new sales tax.

Reagan was stuck with defending himself. He argued his case to reporters wherever he went and in question-and-answer sessions after his speeches. Reagan strategist John Sears thought that the $90-billion furor was helping his candidate, since Reagan's poll numbers showed no dropoff, so he did nothing to end the public argument. "We wanted to disguise the fact it wasn't hurting us," he explained. "What we really feared was that Ford would attack Reagan as an inexperienced warmonger, so we let this go on." Answering daily questions about the $90 billion kept Reagan on the defensive—exactly what Spencer had intended. He had created the issue and now it was bottling up his opponent's energy and attention.

Bob Teeter explained the dynamics of such a ploy. "If you don't point out defects in the other campaign, nobody will do it for you. So you create the issue, and it affects the public's perception of your opponent and puts his campaign under pressure. They've got to spend time and effort figuring out how to react to what you're doing and when they're under that pressure, they begin making mistakes."

While Reagan continued to battle the $90-billion distraction in New Hampshire and Florida during his frequent visits there, Ford did little active campaigning. A week before the vote, polls showed Reagan as much as eleven points ahead in New Hampshire. But Spencer was grinning over Ford's prospects. Inflation and unemployment rates had just dropped again, and his telephone banks were bearing fruit. Teeter's last reading before election day showed the race too close to call. His figures were on target.

Out of 109,000 votes cast in New Hampshire, the candidates ended with a difference of only 1,300 between them. Ford trailed all night, but found himself the winner next morning. However slim the victory, its effects loomed mightily in the next big contest in Florida. A few days after the New Hampshire win, momentum carried Ford to a huge seventeen-point lead in the Florida polling.

Reagan's camp needed a shot in the arm, and fast. Reagan's researcher, Richard Wirthlin of Decision Making Information in Santa Ana, California, surveyed Florida voters to see how they would react to criticism of the President's foreign policy. The numbers showed it would help the challenger, so Reagan added new cards to his deck of three-by-fives. His first chance to test live reaction came at a retirement community. Early in the speech he deplored "giving away the Panama Canal because of blackmail," and even he was shocked by the raucous applause rattling the rafters. Each time he hit the theme, he got the same reaction, so he played it hard and the numbers began to close. Wirthlin polled regularly to measure the effects of the attack. In the last twelve days of the Florida campaign, he chopped fourteen percentage points from the President's lead.

Spencer got the same news from Bob Teeter and kept working the biggest advantage he had—the Presidency itself. "We'd fly Ford all over the state in *Air Force One*," he recalled. "He'd be met with sleek, black cars and secret service guys all over the place. That's impressive as hell and it makes for great visuals." The President also used another traditional weapon of incumbency, political payoffs. He promised disabled veterans a new hospital, awarded a $33-million missile contract to an Orlando facility, provided Miami with an $18-million transit program, and gave a highway construction grant to Fort Myers.

By election day, Reagan's attacks had cut the lead—but not enough. Final tally: Ford 53 percent, Reagan 47. The President had gained credibility and Reagan's can't-miss candidacy had lost some luster.

In Florida Carter sold himself as the stop-Wallace candidate. He got union endorsement, volunteers, and money, and even convinced Andrew Young, then a Udall backer, to come down and campaign heavily among Florida blacks for him. Carter's brochures injected a note of fear: "I need your help now to end the threat Wallace represents to our country."

George Wallace complained: "I don't know how a man like Carter could claim he never supported me. When he was running for governor of Georgia, my name was on his tongue in every speech he made. He even recommended me for Vice-President in 1972 and made a speech about it!"

Carter worked the race issue hard so as to squeeze out every liberal vote. He accused Jackson of racist appeals to antibusing suburbanites in Massachusetts, claiming he lost that primary because he refused to take advantage of racist emotional issues. Research found Wallace's support frozen, but Jackson, campaigning hard in southern Florida, was closing fast. Carter got meaner, calling Jackson a manipulator of racist feelings whose ambition had made him a liar. He made his attacks in northern Florida to impress blacks in the southern part of the state. Segregationists knew it was only strategy, while the blacks took him at face value.

On March 9 Florida voted. Carter took 34 percent, Wallace 31, Jackson 24. Carter was now the clear favorite to win the nomination.

Stu Spencer was Ford's front man after Callaway resigned. He wore two caps, strategist and mouthpiece, and worked under three different campaign chairmen before the battle ended. He was the man who held the campaign together and gave it the leadership it needed. Meanwhile the North Carolina primary looked like an easy win, so the President did not do much stumping there. "We felt Reagan was beaten so there was no sense mauling him," Teeter recalled.

When North Carolina went to Reagan, 52 to 46 percent, even the winner was surprised. His foreign-policy attacks had turned it around for him, so he kept the heat on elsewhere. He spent his money in states like Texas, where the Republican organization was virtually nonexistent, and ran a heavy schedule of media attacks. In places like New York and Pennsylvania, where local politicians committed to Ford held a firm grip, he did little because it was too expensive to build a Reagan base from scratch.

Spencer decided to put big money—$800,000—into the battle for Texas. "Our thesis was simple," he explained. "If we could stop Reagan in Texas, he was finished. But he had the right issues for that state—oil, the Panama Canal, and Kissinger."

Texas also had voting rules favoring Reagan. They ran a wide-open primary where voters could cast their ballots for any candidate regardless of party affiliation. By April, Wallace supporters who didn't want to waste their vote on sentiment looked around for a new champion. Reagan's media appealed to these alienated Democrats in TV and radio commercials starring well-known Wallaceites urging a cross-over vote. "Wallace can't be nominated, but Reagan can," they argued. "He's right on the issues and he speaks right out about them. That's why I'm going to do something I've never done before —vote in the Republican primary. And I'm going to vote for Ronald Reagan!"

On May 1 a record turnout for a Texas Republican primary told the story. Reagan took all twenty-four Congressional districts and swept all ninety-six delegates as 100,000 Democrats fattened the Californian's total. Ford now led by only forty-nine delegates. Reagan took the next three primaries, sweeping Georgia's and Alabama's eighty-five delegates and taking forty-five of Indiana's fifty-four. Now he was in the lead, with momentum clearly on his side.

Spencer decided Ford was too visible. By campaigning so much, Ford had put himself on a level with Reagan instead of relying on his biggest weapon, the Presidency. In the next two primary states, West Virginia and Nebraska, Ford was scheduled for two short visits each. Then he returned to the White House and acted Presidential by attending briefings, discussing defense with the Joint Chiefs of Staff, meeting with heads of state and members of Congress, and taking care of national business twenty-four hours a day. Meanwhile Ford's radio and television commercials defended his stand on the Panama Canal. They featured spokesmen like Barry Goldwater, who praised him and blasted Ronald Reagan's irresponsibility.

Ford won West Virginia, Reagan took Nebraska. Ford won big in his home state of Michigan and traded victories with Reagan right up to the last big primaries on June 8—California, Ohio, and New Jersey. The polls showed Reagan unbeatable in his home state, so Ford concentrated on New Jersey and Ohio. He visited California only twice, but Spencer ran a heavy TV schedule to keep Reagan tied up there. The new spots were designed by BBD&O's president Jim Jordan, brought in to create a fresh Ford who exuded "more warmth and humanity."

The older material, put together by Los Angeles adman Pete

Dailey, had been strictly Presidential—Ford addressing Congress, signing bills, greeting dignitaries. But the new commercials were slice-of-life vignettes, designed to dramatize Ford's domestic achievements. They starred professional actors acclaiming Ford. Thus two housewives were seen stopping in front of a supermarket to look in the window.

"Notice anything different about the prices of fruit lately?" one asks.

"Now that you mention it, yes," her companion replies. "They don't seem to be going up the way they used to."

"President Ford has cut inflation in half," beams the first.

"In half?" her friend replies. "Wow!"

Other commercials featured actors dressed as hardhat workers boasting how Ford had cut unemployment, and a father advising his son to grow up to be as fine a man as President Ford.

The commercials did little for Ford's poll readings, but an offhand remark by Reagan gave Spencer an unexpected break. Answering a press-conference question about Zimbabwe (then Rhodesia), Reagan admitted that he would send troops to that African country if its government officials asked for them. Spencer jumped in, scrapped the dreadful slice-of-life advertising, and rushed out a batch of simply produced commercials that were strong on punch.

"Last Wednesday Ronald Reagan said he would send American troops to Rhodesia," the narrator said. "On Thursday he clarified that—he said they could be advisers. What does he think happened in Vietnam? When you vote Tuesday, remember—Governor Ronald Reagan could not start a war, President Ronald Reagan could."

Spencer explained why he ran the spots in California. "We knew we were going to lose the California primary, but we had these other big ones in Ohio and New Jersey plus all those state conventions in the East. That commercial was run for those other states, not California. Fact was, they hurt us in California—we got the reputation of being too ornery. But California was winner-take-all, so who cared if we lost by 35 percent or by 10 percent? The night those ads ran, we took a lot of heat. But the commercial made national news, they even ran it on the network news shows. When Reagan went to Columbus, some reporter asked him about the troops and he lost his cool. I know his character—I knew he'd do that."

As expected, Reagan routed Ford in California, but Ford won New Jersey and Ohio. By nightfall Reagan had added 176 delegates to his column, while Ford had 155. The primaries ended with neither candidate holding the 1,130 delegates needed to nominate. Ford was shy 170 and Reagan 270 of the magic number. There were 400 delegates left to woo in states awarding delegates by convention. In the next sixty days there was heavy romancing of party members great and small, voices reaching across networks of friends and contacts for a favor owed here, a debt to be called in there. It would be smoky-room infighting all the rest of the way.

Wallace lost badly to Carter in Illinois and North Carolina, and was forced to drop his campaign professionals when contributions dried up. From then on, Jimmy Carter spoke with one voice for the South. Outside Dixie, however, bias against Southerners was a major problem. Gerald Rafshoon explained how they made that negative work for them.

"For a hundred twenty years Southern politicians were seen as folks to bring the vote North and help the Democrat win. If you behaved yourself, they might let you on the ticket as a Vice-President. Our research told us there was big antipathy toward a Southerner. Fifty-five percent of Northerners wouldn't vote for a Southern President, no matter what. Why? Because they thought all Southerners were racists like George Wallace. Wherever we went, they expected a Lester Maddox or a George Wallace and they'd get a hell of a lot more. So they'd exaggerate, they said Carter was fantastic and made him bigger than life. We also had a lot of expatriate Southerners around the country, guys on newspapers and television going for us. I remember in Sacramento, Calilfornia, there was this news director who kept laying on half-hour interviews and gave us far more coverage than we deserved. I asked him why and he said, 'I've lived out here twenty years and gotten all kinds of crap for being a Southerner, so I'm going to shove this guy Carter down their throats!' "

In the Wisconsin, New York, and Pennsylvania primaries Carter beat out challengers Udall and Jackson and talked of "unifying the Party." Carter kept building up his delegate total by pushing his basic theme—honesty, trust, and a homey grin. Reinforcing that image was a five-minute Rafshoon biography that mixed film and still photos in a fast-moving montage of Carter driving in a parade, cuddling a baby, speaking to the National Press Club, inspecting peanuts in a denim jacket, all interspersed with childhood snapshots and segments where mother Lillian spoke of a family "bound together by love."

June 8 was the last primary day. Over a third of the total delegates were dispersed that day in Ohio, New Jersey, and California. If Carter won but 200 of the 540 delegates up for grabs, the nomination was his. Caddell's polls showed Jerry Brown leading Carter in California 2½ to 1, so the Carter team decided to concentrate on New Jersey and Ohio.

All during the campaign Rafshoon's commercials had featured Carter in blue-collar settings—elbow-deep in peanuts at his warehouse, standing near a storage shed, talking to factory workers in his shirtsleeves. Voice-overs drove home the point: "Jimmy Carter is a working man himself, a nonlawyer who works with his hands." Then the candidate suddenly became "Presidential." He wore dark suits and ties, and was showcased by authoritative head shots as he spoke into the camera about his vision "for a better America where we turn away from scandals with pride in the past and future." And when research showed people beginning to believe the charges about Carter's "waffling on the issues," Rafshoon countered with a series of issues spots. Each began with a printed title—"Jimmy Carter on the Issue of Arab Oil," "Jimmy Carter on the Issue of Secrecy"—showing the candidate in impressive settings like a faked news conference or at an airport runway. Though the rhetoric walked both sides of the ideological line, the headline "On the Issues" was effective.

On June 8 California went to Brown, 59 to 21 percent—but Carter netted twenty-five delegates. In Ohio, where Caddell's polls showed Carter strongest and where they spent the most time and money, it was no contest: Carter grabbed 52 percent, Udall 21, and Church 14, which translated into 126 delegates and a last-day total of 218. Carter's primary steeplechase was over. The only question left was who would be his running mate.

On July 12 the Democrats held their convention in New York. The Bicentennial celebration was fresh in everyone's mind and New Yorkers bent over backward to prove their city was the friendliest in the land. Carter and his team ultimately chose Senator Walter Mondale of Minnesota as running mate. Political logic and poll readings agreed that Mondale was the right man. When the convention broke up, the Georgians returned to Atlanta, where they spent the next two months planning for the general-election slugfest.

President Ford, Stu Spencer, and Bob Teeter had no such luxury. Throughout June and July, Ford and Reagan each picked up handfuls of delegates. On July 16 the last set of convention states voted. Ford got Connecticut's 35 delegates and Reagan took Utah's 20. The final delegate count now read Ford 1,102—28 shy of nomination. Reagan had 1,063, lacking 67—with 94 delegates still uncommitted.

Jim Baker, Ford's "head hunter," was responsible for holding delegates already won and for persuading uncommitted people to commit. After much work and argument, victory still hung in the balance. That was when Gerald Ford took off his Presidential pinstripes to do some arm-wrestling of his own. He invited entire state delegations to the White House for lunch, dinner, a drink, or a chat. Patronage and Congressional influence baited his hook. He talked of federal money available as trade-offs. He telephoned delegates he couldn't meet personally. Ford had no intention of becoming the first President in office since Chester Arthur to be denied his party's nomination. Baker got the closet commitments he needed from available delegates, who held off announcing their support for Ford so they could use the upcoming convention to milk national television attention.

Kansas City, August 16. Reagan's strategists proposed rule

challenges and plank demands they prayed would set off a chain reaction of emotional changes of heart among delegates. But the desperation moves only provided mild diversion for what had already been privately decided. Ford calmly accepted Reagan's nonbinding plank recommendations and waited patiently as the roll call began. Thirty minutes later West Virginia's 20 delegates pushed him over the top, and he ended with 1,187 delegates. Ronald Reagan's 1,061 supporters gave him a passionate ovation for a stirring closing speech. Reagan would have four years to correct the mistakes of the campaign just concluded, thereby giving him a big jump on the rest of the Republican pack for 1980.

After the traditional agonizing, Ford named as his running mate Senator Bob Dole, a conservative acceptable to Reagan people. The grueling second round was over. For the first time in Ford's troubled campaign, his strategy team was set. Spencer replaced the old advertising group with Doug Bailey and John Deardourff, top strategists and consultants. The final Republican brain trust that would fight Carter's team in the general election consisted of Stu Spencer, Dick Cheney, Jim Baker, Bob Teeter, Deardourff, and Bailey.

Prospects had looked impossible a month before, when Gallup reported Carter crushing Ford, 62 to 37 percent. Following television coverage of the Republican convention, a new Gallup reading showed the gap had narrowed to 10 percent. When the postconvention pendulum finally came to rest, polls showed Carter with a fifteen-point lead—still formidable, but by no means invincible.

During the eight weeks between Labor Day and election day of 1976, the two candidates and their support troops attacked the bastions of public opinion through paid media and press manipulations in a propaganda war typical of elections at the time.

A week before the Republican convention, Stu Spencer slipped out of Washington and flew back to California. On the sands of Newport Beach, the sun soaked his body while in his head danced a thousand bits of polling data, insights into regional quirks, ethnic affinities, and social-class peculiarities, and the whorl of gut intuition that tries to make sense of it all. By late afternoon, ideas began to flow. He took a ballpoint pen and yellow legal pad from a canvas tote bag and started to write. In a few hours he had filled dozens of pages. It took two more days to pull his ideas together. Then he headed for Kansas City, carrying in his briefcase the strategy for the general election. "I fed that outline to Cheney and Teeter," Spencer recalled. "We kicked it around, refined it, added ideas, and had it typed up."

The document was a 120-page "Plan for the General Election," a blueprint of assumptions and tactics that the Ford campaign would follow from start to finish. It began by setting forth the problem: "No President has ever overcome the obstacles you will face following our convention this August. President Truman trailed Dewey in August 1948 by eleven points, but we expect to be trailing Carter by about twenty points after our convention. Although the point spread will begin to close fairly quickly until Carter is five to ten points ahead, the remaining distance to victory will be very difficult to bridge."

Polling revealed how the American people saw Ford: "Boring . . . not decisive . . . an honest man who tries hard . . . always bumping into things." Then Teeter's analyses uncovered another dismaying fact. "Ford was, to put it kindly, a lousy campaigner," Spencer pointed out. "We had a direct correlation from data compiled from 1974 through 1976 that every time Gerald Ford went out to campaign, he dropped in the polls. He had a propensity for shooting himself in the foot while on the road. It all tied into his personality, into not being the greatest orator in the world, into getting tired and irritable. It told us one thing. We were going to stick him in the White House, keep him off the campaign trail, and take advantage of the seven o'clock and eleven o'clock news where we had a captive audience. Now that's hard to tell anybody, especially the President of the United States. But it had to be done."

Spencer broke the news with characteristic bluntness when he presented the plan to Ford in the Oval Office: "Mister President, as a campaigner, you're no fucking good." Faced with Teeter's findings, the President reluctantly agreed and the "Rose Garden Strategy" was launched.

The plan went on to detail what Ford had to do if he were to have any chance of winning: "If past is prologue, you will lose November 2," it cheerily observed. "To win, you must do what has never been done, close a gap of twenty points in seventy-three days, from the base of a minority party, while spending approximately the same amount of money as your opponent. You cannot overcome the Carter lead on your own. Carter's position must be changed by a strong attack launched by the Vice-Presidential nominee and others.

"To win we must persuade about ten million people to change their opinions. This will require very aggressive media-oriented efforts. For the general election, Presidential campaign events are not significant in terms of impact on the people who attend. These people are merely backdrops for the television viewer. All Presidential travel must be planned for impact on those who learn about it through the media. It is vital to plan, prepare, and execute *all* on-camera appearances carefully. The President should be seen on television as in control, decisive, open, and candid.

"Carter's campaign must be linked to Nixon's 1968 and 1972 campaigns—very slick, media-oriented; a candidate who takes positions on polls, not principles. Carter must be seen as a devious man whose thirst for power dominates, a man who uses religion for political purposes, who doesn't know why he wants the Presidency or what he will do with it. We must mount an attack against him on economic and social conservative issues. If we succeed we can keep him busy holding the South, which he takes for granted. By occupying him, we free the President and his advocates to concentrate on the swing states. The attack in the South must be on issues and not on a personal level, since this would cause a backlash of regional pride."

Spencer's state-by-state planning was based on a cluster approach. "We assumed we were not going to take the South," he recalled. "So we had to carry the West and five of the 'Big Eight,' the big industrial states—California, Texas, Illinois,

Indiana, Michigan, Ohio, Pennsylvania, and New York. If we didn't get all of those five, then we had to pick up electoral votes in bits and pieces."

Spencer teamed his experience and political intuition with Bob Teeter's polls to rank all the states on a priority scale, one through four. Priority Four states were those judged as already won or lost—Georgia and Massachusetts were in this category. Priority Ones included the important, winnable states where the campaign would spend most of its time, money, and energy. These were states where Nixon won overwhelmingly in 1972—California, Illinois, Michigan, New Jersey, Ohio, Pennsylvania, and New York. Priority Twos were states where they would allocate a little less of their resources but still make a good fight—Texas, Missouri, Wisconsin, Maryland, Washington, Connecticut, Virginia, Iowa, Florida, Kentucky, and Tennessee. Priority Threes included small states with few electoral votes, many of which tilted toward the Democrats—states of the Old Confederacy, border states like West Virginia, and Democratic strongholds like the District of Columbia.

The focus would be on the eighteen Priority One and Two states, for which some $5 million of the advertising budget was targeted. The other thirty-two states would be reached through network television, which goes everywhere, plus whatever small amounts local state organizations were allowed to spend under the new campaign laws.

"That was our state-by-state framework," Spencer explained. "Then we had to look at issues within each state. In the West Carter was on the other side of gun control, which is important to lots of Westerners. Carter never understood the California farm problems or, for that matter, California itself—and he still doesn't. So we played off that."

The Ford men met with special-interest groups and their lobbyists to negotiate stands and look for support. Ethnic voting blocs were handled similarly. "Lots of groups are concentrated regionally," Spencer said. "In areas with strong Catholic populations and church ties, you're looking at the abortion thing—Ohio, Massachusetts, and such places. In New York you've got the Jewish vote. You have labor problems in various communities, right-to-work disputes So you tie them together and you orchestrate them, aiming for your coalition of 51 percent."

Spencer and his media assaults would have only eight weeks to change the minds of one out of every six Americans.

In Atlanta, with the luxury of two full months to plan, Carter's strategy team knocked ideas around in a series of meetings. Hamilton Jordan's summary memo was in many ways a mirror image of Spencer's plan:

"The Southern states provide a base of support that cannot be taken for granted. The Republicans cannot win if they write off the South, and I believe they will challenge us in larger Southern and border states they view as contestable—Texas, Florida, Maryland, and Missouri. It would be harmful nationally if we were perceived as having a Southern strategy. To the extent that regional bias exists in this country, and it does, there would be negative reaction to a candidate perceived as a captive of the Southern states and people. Southern regional pride can be used to great advantage without alienating potential anti-South voters."

Jordan warned that dealing with the personality of President Ford would be sensitive and tricky. "Americans consider Gerald Ford a well-intentioned man who inherited a job bigger than he can handle," he observed. "They see many of the same attractive qualities in you [Carter] but have made the tentative judgment that you are more capable of leading the country than Ford. I do not worry in the weeks ahead that we can clearly demonstrate you are better qualified to manage the government. I do worry that our campaign rhetoric might undermine the favorable image you have with American voters. Any statements perceived as being personal attacks on Gerald Ford will hurt us and help him. Discontinue using the term 'Nixon-Ford administration.' This phrase suggests a conscious effort on your part to equate Ford the man with Nixon the man. This will not wash with the American people, and will be taken as a personal attack on the integrity of Gerald Ford."

However, Carter continued to connect Ford and Nixon in the weeks ahead, disregarding the advice of his young aides for the "give 'em hell" encouragement of Charles Kirbo, a Georgia country lawyer and long-time adviser. This tendency to hit below the belt was to cause difficulties later.

Jordan's memo also stressed one great advantage Carter had over the unelected President: "Ford lacks any base of support. There is not one region of the country or political grouping of states he can count on in November. Consequently he lacks a mathematical base on which to build a majority of electoral votes. Without a base, he lacks a strategy. By campaigning early in traditionally Republican states, we can put Ford on the defensive, making him spend time and money in states he should carry. More importantly, we can prevent the Republicans from developing a clear strategy for winning. The Southern and border states are our base of support. The only way we can lose in November is to have this base fragmented. So we need to spend early time campaigning in the South and key border states. If our solid lead holds here, we can cut back time in October and simply show the flag regularly."

While the Republican plan detailed state-by-state allocations for time and money, Jordan's memo systemized the process into mathematical values. Each of the fifty states were scored on Jordan's rating scale. A state got one point for every electoral vote it carried, for a U.S. total of 538 points. Then 269 points were divided among states likely to vote Democratic— a state got one point for each Democratic U.S. senator or governor, one point if it had more Democratic than Republican congressmen, another point if both state houses were Democratic, one point if it had given 35 percent or better of its popular vote to George McGovern in 1972, and two points if it had given 40 percent or more to McGovern.

The seven-point maximum according to this system was assigned to only five states—California, Minnesota, Montana, Rhode Island, and Wisconsin. Seven other states scored six points—Connecticut, Delaware, Illinois, Iowa, Kentucky, Massachusetts, and Nevada, along with the District of Columbia. States requiring the most intensive campaign efforts made up another group. These were states Carter had either lost or barely won in the primaries, or states where polls showed Ford ahead or contending. Eleven states were so classified: California, Maryland, Missouri, New York, New Jersey, Washington, Wisconsin, Michigan, Connecticut, Indiana, and Illinois. Another batch included states where the Republicans were expected to campaign heavily—Texas, Florida, Ohio, Pennsylvania, and nine Plains, Mountain, and Western states. Jordan then combined all these factors and assigned each state a "percent of total effort" figure, which was used to allocate money, manpower, and resources. California scored highest at 5.9 percent, Alaska and Wyoming lowest with 0.6 percent each.

A mathematical approach was devised to schedule the Carter campaigners. A day of Jimmy Carter's time was assigned 7 points, Walter Mondale's 5 points, Rosalynn Carter's four points, Joan Mondale's three points, and each Carter son or daughter's 1 point. The designated value was multiplied by the number of days a campaigner would work the circuit. For example, Jimmy Carter planned forty-three days on the road: this, multiplied by his 7 points per day, gave 301 total points for the candidate. Rosalynn had 140 points to be scheduled, and so on for each campaigner.

According to these calculations Oregon, a state worth 1.7 percent of total effort, got 1.7 percent of the 941 campaigning points available, or 16 points to be spread among the speakers. Jimmy Carter spent half a day in Oregon (3.5 points), Mondale one day (5), Rosalynn one day (4), Joan Mondale half a day (1.5), and Jack and Judy Carter one day each (2), for the sixteen-point total.

Jordan's strategy aimed at winning the minimum 270 electoral votes needed for victory. He projected that 96 would come from the ten Southern and border states—Alabama, Arkansas, Georgia, Kentucky, Louisiana, Mississippi, North and South Carolina, Tennessee, and Virginia. Another 43 were expected from Florida and Texas, though not without a fight. Four other strongly Democratic areas were added to the Carter column—the District of Columbia, Massachusetts, Minnesota, and Wisconsin—bringing 38 more electoral votes. Two border states, Maryland and Missouri, added 22 more for a total of

199. The balance needed for victory was to come from the six largest industrial states—any combination of California (45), New York (41), Illinois (26), Ohio (25), Pennsylvania (27), and New Jersey (17) that would add up to 71 electoral votes.

"Our clear and simple goal must be simply to win 270 votes," Jordan's memo warned. "In trying to win 400 votes, we could easily fall short of the 270. Never forget that in 1968, in six weeks, Hubert Humphrey closed twenty points on Richard Nixon and almost won the Presidency." But this caution, too, went unheeded. Cocky after his easy victory in the primaries, Carter spoke of winning a "broad mandate among the electorate" that would pressure a stubborn Congress to support his programs. But in fact Carter's bravado only helped Ford.

Labor Day, September 6. Gallup's latest reading showed a fifteen-point lead for Carter.

In the next fifty-seven days Carter and Ford pitted their public images against each other, images carried in the minds and hearts of American voters, built bit by bit on a montage of news headlines, television roundups, and political commercials. Their strategists and media teams attacked those composite pictures with speeches, visuals, debates, and press releases, which were in turn colored by the reporters who screened them for public consumption. Controlled media—television commercials, print advertising, and literature—reinforced the "good aspects of the candidates' image" wherever research showed a tactical advantage. It downplayed or simply ignored negatives. The uncontrolled media—press and television news —presented favorable views about the candidate they supported and negative ones about his opponent.

The candidates recited scripts written by others. Their job was to stick to the format, cling to strategy, and most important, not "screw up." Every word of every speech would be scrutinized for shading and innuendo, then compared to past statements for consistency. Every slip of the tongue would be magnified a thousand times, every stumble on an airport ramp blown into a major disaster on the evening news.

Television decided this election—television news, television commercials, televised talk shows and panel shows, and televised political films. The candidates were matched in three televised *Meet the Press* extravaganzas masquerading as "debates." While viewers were not treated to a true battle of spontaneous wit and oratory, they at least had a chance to size up the two pretenders to America's highest office at the same time.

On Labor Day itself—September 6—Americans were bombarded with impressions—headlines in the morning paper, thirty-second film clips on the *Today Show*, ten-second snippets over their car radios, ninety-second reports on the evening news. President Ford spent the holiday working at the White House, poking his head out from the burrow of state affairs only long enough to tell television cameramen how tough it was fighting a hostile Congress while seeking solutions to the problems of the land.

Although traditionally the Democratic candidate kicks the campaign off at Detroit's Cadillac Square, paying homage to the auto industry, Jimmy Carter drove ninety miles from his home in Plains to Warm Springs, Georgia, where he spoke from the front porch of Franklin D. Roosevelt's summer house, hoping to win by association some of the public's devotion to FDR. Rafshoon pasted a large poster of Roosevelt at Yalta on the front of Carter's podium, where the cameras had to pick it up. Roosevelt's sons, FDR Jr. and Jimmy, sat on a platform behind the candidate, and black accordionist Graham Jackson played FDR's theme song, "Happy Days Are Here Again."

The next morning Ford invited cameras and reporters to the Rose Garden and signed a bill to aid day-care centers. He then gave a short talk explaining how concerned he was not to waste the taxpayer's money. That afternoon he called a press conference in the west wing of the White House to denounce the government of Vietnam for not accounting for all 550 U.S. servicemen listed as missing in action.

Toward the end of the first campaign week, the *New York Times* broke a story of corruption high in the Ford administration. FBI Director Clarence Kelley had asked a man from the Bureau's carpentry shop to install a window sash in his apartment. At prevailing rates the work would have cost $335, but Kelley paid nothing.

Carter immediately attacked Ford in a New York speech for promoting such thievery. He slashed away in Philadelphia the following day: "When young people see Nixon cheating, lying, and leaving office in disgrace, when they see the head of the FBI break a law and keep his job, it tells everybody crime must be okay."

That afternoon Ford called reporters to the south lawn to reply. Kelley's wife had been dying of cancer at the time of the incident, he explained. The director was under tremendous stress and unwittingly asked a friend in the shop to do him a small favor. By howling for Kelley's blood, Carter showed himself to be "a man who lacks compassion."

Carter countered that since Kelley was now planning to remarry, he could not have been that upset. Soon even the reporters got bored and the issue died. But Carter had accomplished his goal by tying Ford, however groundlessly, to Nixon-era "corruption."

September 9. Poll readings showed Carter needed a boost among conservative, blue-collar, Catholic, big-city ethnics. So Carter's entire first week of travel was dedicated to ethnic media events in big Eastern cities. Adorned with a white T-shirt with big red letters spelling "Polish Hill," he visited Pittsburgh's Polish Hill section. The parish priest led several hundred parochial school children to greet him. Carter beamed as the priest kissed both his cheeks, the cameras whirled, and flashbulbs flared.

Rafshoon, meanwhile, resurrected some of the "Southern pride" spots used with such effect in the primaries, appealing to blacks and whites of the Old Confederacy to elect one of their own as Top Man. He ran new commercials using film shot at the convention, emphasizing party unity and Carter's newly won stature as its candidate. The theme lines remained unchanged: "Trust me, I'll never lie to you . . . a man who works with his hands . . . owing nothing to the special interests but everything to the American people."

Carter flew from city to city, adhering tightly to his script. Appealing to populist emotions, he called for tax reforms that would take more from the rich and less from the poor. Then, before a group of Associated Press editors in Washington, D.C., he made his first slip. When one editor asked Carter where he would draw the line between rich and poor, Carter hedged. When the questioner pressed him, he replied the best cutoff would be the "median income line." If he were President, he would raise taxes for those over the line and lower them for those under.

Next morning the headlines screamed, "CARTER FAVORS TAX RISE FOR FAMILIES OVER $14,000," and both sides took action. Republicans assailed the reform as an "insult to hard-working middle-class families," while Carter charged his foes with distortion: "I never implied I would raise taxes for families making over $14,000. I mean only to eliminate loopholes for the very rich, the corporations." The fuss filled the evening news two days running.

Ford, true to his strategy, hid in the White House and waited for the first debate where, as underdog, he had everything to gain. His first television commercials would not be ready to show for a month. But his campaign received unexpected publicity in Binghamton, New York. Incumbent Vice-President Nelson Rockefeller shared a platform with Ford's running mate, Robert Dole. Hecklers kept interrupting Dole's speech until Rockefeller could stand it no more. Rocky glared at the troublemakers and gave them the finger in a widely circulated photo of aristocratic contempt. Another two days on the evening news celebrated the gesture.

As Americans were absorbing these indications of Presidential worthiness, *Playboy* published an interview with Jimmy Carter. In it he discussed his Baptist beliefs, admitted "lusting in his heart" after women, and used two slang expressions, "screw" and "shack up," to emphasize that Christians are not to sit in judgment of their fellow sinners. The interview made headlines and news reports through many weeks of the campaign.

September 20. Three days before the first debate, Carter abandoned a whistle-stop train tour designed to reinforce his image as a Democratic populist and returned to Plains, where he prepared for the confrontation with Ford. Carter brain trusters had prepared a volume called "the Book" for their candidate—a massive compendium of facts and figures, sample questions, and suggested answers on the nation's economy and social conditions. Carter applied himself diligently, speed-reading the material incessantly over a seventy-two-hour period. He would not allow any of his staff to question or rehearse him. Then on September 23 he flew to Philadelphia. That afternoon he visited the Walnut Street Theater downtown, studied podium locations and other stage details, then returned to his hotel and napped. He spent the last three hours before the big event eating with Rosalynn and being reassured.

Ford, on the other hand, approached the encounter as he would a football game. A week before the debate he had the family theater at the White House transformed into a replica of the set in Philadelphia. The rostrums were identical, dummy television cameras were mounted, and aides held up cards reading "1 MIN," "30 SECS," and "CUT." His advisers took turns portraying the news panelists, firing questions and challenges at the President. Cameras recorded every session for playback, criticism, and refinement. They ran tapes of Carter appearances on panel shows, screening his replies to key questions so Ford could get used to his style.

The only time Ford got upset was when his advisers worked his weak spot: implying in their questions that he lacked compassion for ordinary people. The heat grew so intense that his aides simply avoided pushing in that direction. Another deficiency they uncovered was one they could not correct: the President was not blessed with natural political instinct. "Ford's mind just didn't work to take political advantage of his opportunity," one aide explained. "He didn't deal easily with ideas. And if you don't think in conceptual terms, you don't think in strategic terms either."

In politics as in horse trading, the opportunist is more blessed than the saint. Ignoring what he couldn't change, Ford trained as hard as he could and then flew to Philadelphia the morning of the debate. He briefly examined the theater set, and spent the rest of the day with Cheney, Bailey, and Spencer, going over fine points. After a stimulating dinner with his key people, he left for the theater.

Going into the debate, Gallup showed Carter ahead 54 to 36 percent.

Carter arrived first, wearing a dark blue suit and a red tie with a crooked knot. He licked his lips nervously until the President entered a few minutes later. Ford played executive to Carter's populist. He too wore a dark blue suit, but unlike the challenger he wore a vest. There was a gold pin on his subdued tie.

Carter won the coin toss and received the first question. His reply was too long, full of statistics and dates, and ultimately boring. His voice was high-pitched and he seemed intimidated. As Carter spoke, Ford gripped the lectern and stared at him, unnerving him even more. When Ford's turn came, he attacked Carter as a big spender "who would raise taxes on half the working people of America."

The attack snapped Carter out of his stage fright. He accused Ford of insensitivity to the pain of the poor and unemployed. Ford's neck reddened, and soon they were trading punches. Then, just as Carter launched a hard-hitting assault on CIA and FBI abuses, the sound system blew. Both men stood mute for twenty minutes, the network cameras still focused on their heads. Finally the stage director ordered the cameras turned off. Carter sat down; Ford remained standing an extra seven minutes until the system was repaired. Only enough time remained for each man to make a final statement.

After the debate, Gallup polled again. This time Carter got 50 to Ford's 42 percent. An eighteen-point lead had shrunk to eight.

Polls showed that Ford had a chance to win in Louisiana and Mississippi. Stu Spencer hired the *Natchez Steamer*, a big paddleboat, to sail down the Mississippi River from St. Louis to New Orleans with stops along the way. While a Dixie band played and cameras whirled to record the scenic splendor and hoopla, Ford assailed Walter Mondale as "the biggest spender in the Senate," exploiting the antifederalist sentiments of the South.

The trip produced good copy and warm feelings. But then United Press International stepped in, reporting that U.S. Steel had sponsored three golfing trips to New Jersey for then Congressman Ford. The *Wall Street Journal* followed with a story that Watergate Special Prosecutor Charles Ruff was investigating campaign contribution irregularities against Ford. Finally John Dean, pushing his book *Blind Ambition* on talk shows, hinted that as a congressman Ford had helped stymie the Watergate investigation.

Carter, campaigning in Oregon, grabbed the news lead with both hands. His writers inserted references in his speeches to Ford's free golfing holidays and his close ties to cronies around the "old Nixon-Ford administration." One of Carter's stones was hurled from a glass house, however: news reports surfaced that as governor of Georgia Carter himself had been treated to three hunting trips paid for by timber companies doing business with the state.

Carter waited until September 30, when he returned home to Plains, to strike his hardest blow: calling a press conference, he challenged Ford to explain those questionable campaign contributions. Ford then called reporters to the Oval Office, where he insisted he had never taken a dime of campaign money for personal use. The next day both the *New York Times* and the Associated Press reported that the FBI and Special Prosecutor Ruff had finished their investigations: Ford was innocent on all counts.

But Ford's problems weren't over. Earl Butz, Secretary of Agriculture, told a racial "joke" on a plane carrying John Dean. Dean reported it in *Rolling Stone*, identifying the source only as a "high administration official." A few days later Butz was named as the man who had posed a riddle: "What are three things that keep a colored man happy? Answer: All coloreds want is a tight pussy, loose shoes, and a warm place to shit."

When Ford heard about it, he called Butz to the White House and gave him hell. Butz said he was sorry and promised to apologize publicly, which he did at once. But the joke had become a campaign issue. Republicans and Democrats alike urged Ford to fire Butz, but Ford stalled, for he liked Butz personally. Butz was popular in important farm states, and neither blacks nor white liberals were very big factors in his targeted 51-percent coalition. Maybe it would all blow over, he reasoned. But the pressure against Butz grew fiercer. Finally on October 4—three days after he had first heard about the "joke"—Ford called Butz in and asked for his job. Butz resigned immediately, but Teeter's polls found that the President's hesitancy over firing him had raised doubts about Ford's leadership.

Meanwhile Carter toured the East, wooing support from big-city politicos so as to attract some of their popularity to his cause. In Boston, escorted by Mayor Kevin White and Senator Ted Kennedy, he deplored Ford's callousness toward unemployed workers: "He is even worse than Nixon. The spirit of this country has been damaged by Nixon and Ford." Caddell's readings found that some voters, particularly independents, were turned off by the stridency of Carter's rhetoric. But other advisers told him how well his "giving Ford hell" was going over with the public, so Carter kept up the pressure.

As October 7, the date of the second debate, approached, Carter stopped traveling in order to prepare. This time he was not so cocky. After studying a new version of the Book dealing with foreign relations, he fielded rehearsal questions from Jordan, Rafshoon, Powell, and Caddell. Rafshoon played videotapes of the first debate, and they took turns picking it to pieces. Now that the poll numbers had tightened, Jimmy Carter was willing to listen.

Ford also reviewed tapes of the first encounter, but his analysis included marketing research touches added by Bob Teeter. Using a theater audience equipped with a dial device, Teeter screened the entire first debate. As the film ran, the audience twisted the dial clockwise to indicate favorable feelings and counterclockwise for negatives. Reports from all 275 seats were fed back to a computer, which printed a continuous record of how the audience responded to the replies made. The research showed that people were turned off whenever Ford became visibly angry, so he agreed to restrain himself.

Ford was instructed to repeat two basic ideas. One, the country was at peace. Two, Carter had absolutely no experience in defense or foreign affairs. No matter what question he was asked, he was to bring the discussion back to these two points. During the rehearsal, Ford fielded questions about the Soviet oppression of Eastern Europe and handled them well. He seemed ready.

The debate was held at San Francisco's Palace of Fine Arts. Carter bored in from the start, hitting Ford's administration: "All style and no substance . . . not respected abroad . . . tried to buy success from our enemies and excluded our allies . . . an absence of leadership." Ford retaliated by charging Carter with waffling, with first advocating a $15-billion defense cutback and then, after feeling political pressure, reducing the sum to $7 billion and now $5 billion. "Carter's program means a weakened defense," he concluded.

Panelist Max Frankel asked Ford about the Helsinki Agreements and human rights. Ford outlined the situation and then ended his otherwise authoritative statement with what sounded like a slip of the tongue: "There is no Soviet domination of Eastern Europe, and under the Ford administration there will never be."

Frankel looked puzzled and asked him to clarify. Surely the President had not meant to imply that the Soviets did not militarily control those countries? Instead of easing out of the misstatement, Ford dug a deeper hole. "The Yugoslavians don't consider themselves dominated by the Soviet Union," he replied. "The people of Poland don't consider themselves dominated."

Carter barely hid his excitement as he waited to drive the stake in more deeply. "I'd like to see Mr. Ford convince Polish-Americans and Hungarian-Americans in this country," he said grimly, "that those countries don't live under the domination of the Soviet Union!"

The panelists moved on to another subject and the debate

settled into boring point-counterpoint exchanges. The Ford camp didn't realize at the time how much impact the Eastern European statement would generate in the media. But after the debate Ford's press secretary Ron Nessen rode back to the hotel with other reporters on the press bus. All they talked about was "Eastern Europe." The moment he got to the Holiday Inn, Nessen went to Stu Spencer's room, where the consultant was conferring with Cheney, Teeter, and the others. "You've got a real problem with Eastern Europe," Nessen told them. Spencer called an impromptu press conference and tried to talk his way out of the comment, but news-hungry reporters were not about to soften their leads. Headlines the next morning read, "FORD MAKES MAJOR BLUNDER." Television news spread the word swiftly and the "blooper" was certified.

Evidence indicates that if the press had not blown the story up, it would have died at birth. Right after the debate, Teeter took a poll of people who had watched the debate, and discovered that Ford had "won" by eleven points. Readings taken the next day, after news reports began appearing, showed progressive declines for Ford until, two days later, polls had Carter winning the debate by as much as forty-five points.

"The average guy in his living room watching the debate didn't see the Eastern European comment as a monumental mistake," Nessen explained. "But after twenty-four hours of being told how bad a mistake it was, people changed their minds."

Spencer tried to convince Ford to admit the error publicly, cut his loss, and go on to other things, but the President stubbornly resisted. Finally he relented in a speech at the University of Southern California and "clarified" his understanding about the reality of Soviet domination. The next morning, however, at a breakfast meeting with Burbank businessmen, he "reclarified" and got his foot back into his mouth. After explaining that the captive nations were indeed under the Soviet yoke, he added, incredibly: "The Polish people are not going to be dominated forever, *if they are*, by the Soviet Union." Those three extra words dramatized a streak of ego common to politicians, a deep-seated reluctance to admit a mistake.

"The Eastern European matter resurrected our worst negative," Teeter noted, unwilling to specify what that was. Another aide identified it off the record: "It was the 'dumb' issue all over again."

Carter stormed the Midwest, railing at Ford's blunder. In Cleveland, Indianapolis, and Chicago, where many Eastern Europeans live, he hammered away and made headlines and television news stories. Carter's people in Buffalo, where there is a large Polish population, reported they had been losing the ethnic vote until Ford and the media turned things around. Ford fought back, hitting at Carter's defense cutbacks and the *Playboy* interview, but the media gave only minor attention to his attacks. Finally, back at the White House, he met with a group of ethnic leaders and recanted clearly. "The mistake about Eastern Europe was mine," he admitted. "I did not express myself clearly."

The tempest finally ended. Teeter's polls found the flap had not cost Ford so much in actual votes as it halted momentum and wasted precious time. With just two weeks left and still chasing a big lead, they could not afford another such debacle.

The unreported campaign—paid media—had been working its subliminal effects on the electorate for weeks. Political television and radio commercials merged into game shows, sitcoms, soap operas, news programs, ball games, and the hodgepodge of ordinary product pitches, until the viewer couldn't tell where one began and the other ended. Here the real propaganda war assaulted American minds with symbol, sound, and sight. Each side spent $10 million for its advertising—$7 million of that on television. Commercials saturated 480 local television stations and 1,800 radio outlets around the country, while a hundred different thirty- and sixty-second spots played the three networks and their affiliates.

Down-home Carter commercials showed Carter in work shirts, sleeves rolled up, walking through peanut fields to the beat of a guitar. Rafshoon made the film move, using jump cuts, pans to faces in the crowds, and cutaways to new shots of the candidate pressing flesh, kissing cheeks, rolling his fingers in peanut bins, and grinning incessantly.

"Executive" commercials showed the candidate on the campaign trail, his face in three-quarter profile, speaking intently to off-camera audiences of reporters or well-wishers: "Listen to me carefully. Watch television, listen to the radio. If you hear me tell a lie or make a misleading statement or avoid a controversial issue—if I ever do any of those things—don't support me."

A five-minute biography centered on home, family, mother, and country, pushing old-fashioned virtues with unabashed sentimentality. In the space of three hundred seconds, Rafshoon's copy repeated the words "hard work," "family," "home," "land," and "love" a minimum of six times each. Though the narration was static, the images constantly moved to give the impression of action and variety.

Rafshoon's fascination with moving images led one media expert to call him a "film tripper."

"I just wanted to show Carter the Man," he replied.

While the Democratic media campaign was in full swing, Ford was nowhere to be found. The absence was not due to strategy but to circumstance. Not until the Republican convention was Stu Spencer able to replace the media people who had struggled through the primaries, by bringing in John Deardourff and Doug Bailey. Using Teeter's research findings and Spencer's plan, they came up with their own media strategy. Ford's commercials stressed two basic ideas: the decency of Gerald Ford, and the progress the country had made since Nixon's resignation. Television and radio would have to do most of the work, since Spencer planned to keep the candidate away from live encounters whenever possible, to avoid blunders.

Deardourff hired a Boston advertising man, Malcolm Mac-Dougall, to translate media goals into film and commercials. MacDougall screened the material inherited from Ford's primary efforts and found nothing, not even one thirty-second spot, he could put on the air against Carter. Rather than rush out a panicked reply to counter Rafshoon's early scheduling, Deardourff decided to hold back, do no media at all for five weeks, and then shoot the works on one roll of the dice—a three-week blitz during the last part of the campaign.

MacDougall and his technicians plugged away, working on six packages of commercials. The first was a quintet of five-minute shows: "The Ford Family," "A Ford Biography," "The President's Accomplishments," "Ford as Leader," and "Feelin' Good," a free-wheeling montage of film and upbeat music aimed at sparking momentum to end the campaign. "He's Making Us Proud Again" was the theme line on all these positive spots.

A second group consisted of thirty- and sixty-second spots showing Ford with old people, workers, women, and children. A third batch used snippets of man-on-the-street interviews to air on radio and television. A fourth, targeted for regional markets, tackled specific local problems, aimed at ethnic Mexicans in the Southwest, Cubans in Florida, and Puerto Ricans in New York; other versions starred popular state figures like John Connally in Texas and Gov. Robert Ray in Iowa. A fifth package was a hodgepodge of anti-Carter and pro-Ford commercials. Finally the *pièce de résistance*, a thirty-minute campaign wrap-up to be played election eve, starred Joe Garagiola, Pearl Bailey, and Cab Calloway. The Democrats would run a similar film, marking the last official media event for both sides.

October 15: Gallup showed the spread at six points—Carter 48 percent, Ford 42 percent.

Ford's man-in-the-street spots had been on the airwaves only one week and early feedback found them having a strong effect on young voters and independents. One spot showed an attractive woman standing on an Atlanta street speaking earnestly at the camera: "My friends here in Georgia don't understand when I tell them I'm going to vote for President Ford. It would be nice to have a President from Georgia—but not Jimmy Carter."

The productions were contemporary, well crafted, and subtle, leaving the viewer with a feeling instead of a message. By contrast, Rafshoon's commercials were old-fashioned—a throwback to the sentimental political advertising of the 1960s.

In 1976 they were not doing the job of holding his candidate's lead.

Pat Caddell's polls showed bad slippage in the big states. If there was low turnout and the almost automatic Democratic votes of the inner-city poor didn't show up, Ford might edge in to win them. Just as worrisome was the fact that Carter scored weak in masculinity with women, particularly housewives, who felt safer with Ford. On October 18 a crisis meeting was called at the Atlanta office of Bob Lipshutz. Attending were the original brain trusters—Jordan, Powell, Rafshoon, Kirbo, and Caddell. They decided the advertising needed "refocusing," to soothe the nervous feelings women had about Carter. Despite Carter's repeated entreaties, women just "didn't trust him."

The next day Carter and Rafshoon flew to New York for a fund-raising dinner. At nine o'clock that night they slipped away and made a pilgrimage to a converted church in Manhattan which houses the studios of advertising genius Tony Schwartz. Schwartz had won his political spurs with his hard-hitting work for Lyndon Johnson, Hubert Humphrey, Ted Kennedy, and other Democratic notables. He sat Carter in front of a camera and had him talk about himself, his ideas for the country, and his beliefs. After a few hours, the candidate left for his next campaign stop. Rafshoon stayed on five days as Schwartz and his wife Reenah wrote copy, spliced film, and edited a batch of twenty-five commercials. One was inspired by a media event that had been televised October 15.

That night in Houston, Vice-Presidential rivals Walter Mondale and Bob Dole met for a one-shot debate. Mondale was all business, grimly attacking the Ford administration for the country's mounting unemployment, "raging inflation," and its failure to solve energy problems. Dole, on the other hand, played the evening for laughs. "Carter has three positions on everything," he jested. "That's why he and the President are having three debates." He jocularly accused the Democrats of starting the last four wars, but insisted that he and Mondale would resume their friendship "once this is over and Fritz is back in the Senate."

After the debate Caddell did research and found that half

his sample believed Dole unqualified to be President. When he ran Carter in a dry run against Ford head to head, Carter led by six points. But when he matched the Carter-Mondale ticket against Ford-Dole, the margin jumped to nine points. So Tony Schwartz prepared a "Mondale" commercial, shown everywhere except in the South, where Mondale was widely despised as a big-spending liberal. The film showed blowups of Dole and Mondale while a narrator asked: "Have you thought about the Vice-Presidential candidates? What do you think of Mondale? What do you think of Dole? What kind of men are they? When you know that four out of the last six Vice-Presidents wound up being President, whom would you like to see a heartbeat away from the Presidency?"

Some of the Schwartz spots featured Carter dressed in a dark Presidential suit and tie, looking straight into the camera and talking earnestly about what was wrong with America and about its need for leadership. One strongly symbolic commercial used E. G. Marshall's voice talking over still photos of FDR, John Kennedy, and Jimmy Carter, emphasizing the candidate's ties to greatness and national destiny. It was aimed at reassuring those uneasy women. "Lots of people felt they didn't know Carter," Schwartz explained. "So we brought him in close, right into their living rooms, and let the people *feel* him."

Of twenty-five commercials churned out that week, Rafshoon ran seventeen. The ones he never let out of the can were the tough spots, attacks on Ford that Schwartz designed to counter what the other side's man-in-the-street spots were doing. As the race tightened during the last two weeks, nerves frayed and Rafshoon lashed out publicly against Tony Schwartz. "He came up with such crap," Rafshoon griped. "He had these Jewish New York characters saying why they were against Gerald Ford and for Jimmy Carter. One he called 'The Résumé' said 'against Medicare, against this, against that.' They were too heavy-handed. People seeing them said, 'You're goddam right to be against them; I'm going to vote for Ford.'"

Schwartz felt Rafshoon's reaction came from his advertising background. "Rafshoon was reacting in terms of a print ethic," he explained. "If you *read* about Ford's rejection of expensive programs, you might agree with Ford. But hearing it is different. In sound, you *feel* what you hear."

What started as a difference of opinion ended in animosity. "Rafshoon came to me at a time when Carter was losing a point a day," Schwartz noted. "When a story ran in the *New York Times* about my doing the Carter commercials, he felt insulted. From that day on, he started bad-mouthing me. When he doesn't like someone, he turns nasty and lies. He told people I took his money and ran. The fact is I had to send him a lawyer's letter months later just to get paid for my work. He said he didn't use more than two or three of my commercials—he used seventeen. Rafshoon is a person who plays it cool, but in terms of media he is old-fashioned. He had never even heard of a line-of-sight teleprompter that lets you see right through the lens, and he spurned advice from some of the great media people in the world, people like Joe Napolitan, who offered to help without charge."

A fellow professional who knows both men ascribed the feud to Rafshoon's advertising mentality. "Rafshoon asked for my advice when things were going bad," he recalled. "So I promised to introduce him to some big people, people who had their own egos but who could help him if he learned how to listen to them. At the time he was losing a point a day in the polls. I told him from an ass-covering point of view, he could bring these people in and if he won he could take the credit, but if he lost he could blame it on them."

While the two consultants traded barbs in the press, the opposing media teams slashed away on behalf of their candidates through television and radio, and the main men sought headlines in press events. Carter pushed the Ford-Nixon connection, charging, "Ford is even worse than his predecessor." Ford fought back at Carter's doubletalking: "He sounds like Bella Abzug in New York, and like a little ole peanut farmer in Illinois. He wavers, he wiggles, he wanders, and he waffles—and he shouldn't be President of the United States."

October 20. Two days before the final debate, Gallup showed Carter holding his six-point edge, 47 to 41 percent, with a bigger chunk of the electorate undecided.

A surprise issue reappeared the last weeks of the campaign —Watergate. Though Watergate had been in the news the first few weeks of the campaign, it died quickly. Then, abruptly in October, it began showing up in the polls again. Contributing to the renewed interest was a movie produced by Robert Redford and distributed by Warner Brothers—*All the President's Men.*

The film dramatized the Watergate cover-up and the downfall of the Nixon White House. Redford's Wildwood Enterprises had finished most of the filming in September 1974. Normally a movie can be edited and advertising schedules set for release six months or less from that time. In this case Warner's waited a full eighteen months before putting it into theaters. The move made good business sense, since a political movie has its greatest popular appeal in a political year, but it also helped Carter. In April 1976 the film went into limited release and played at select theaters for top box-office prices. In late September it went into "general and multiple release," showing at movie houses and drive-ins everywhere. To catalyze the mass-market push, Warner's launched a major television and newspaper campaign, and stars Dustin Hoffman and Robert Redford appeared on talk shows to discuss those dark hours of modern Republicanism. By mid-October Teeter's polls showed the Watergate issues again a red-hot problem, seriously damaging to Ford. It was to plague him right to the end.

About this time a big argument began among Carter strategists over whether to openly identify Ford with Nixon and Watergate. One reason Spencer had pushed Ford's man-in-the-street attacks was in the hope that the other side would be provoked into such a counterattack, since research showed it would hurt Carter more than Ford. The ploy almost worked, for Rafshoon prepared a cruncher of a commercial, a roughly produced effort that looked as though it had been done by small-town amateurs. There was nothing on it to link it to the Carter organization. A disclaimer identified the film's producers as the "Marion County Democratic Committee." Rafshoon ran it in Indiana to measure its effects.

The spot opened with a long shot of the White House, as a

countrified narrator proclaimed, "Here's a message from the man who picked Gerald Ford to be President of the United States." A blowup of Richard Nixon filled the screen, with a legend reading "Checkers Speech, 1952." Nixon castigated Harry Truman for dumping problems on the nation and then picking Adlai Stevenson to succeed him. "You wouldn't elect the man who created the problems," Nixon argued. "So why should you turn around and elect the man he picked to solve the problems?" And the folksy voice-over added, "We couldn't have said it better ourselves."

The commercial ran in Indianapolis before the third debate. Caddell's research showed it was risky, so Rafshoon held it back as an insurance policy. If Ford developed momentum going into the final week, Carter would have nothing to lose going for the jugular with the Ford-Nixon link on national television. But if the race were still close, it might backfire by arousing feelings of foul play to spark a sympathy vote for Ford. They kept their finger on the trigger, but never pulled it.

One behind-the-scenes factor working for Carter was the traditional Democratic support of the labor unions. COPE, the political-action wing of the AFL-CIO, provided 120,000 volunteers for his campaign. They manned thousands of phone banks around the country, made 10 million calls, registered voters, and delivered people to the polls on election day. Union volunteers distributed some 80 million pieces of literature to members and families, a pool of about 30 million potential votes. This hurt Gerald Ford, particularly in the crucial big industrial states of the North.

October 22. Eleven days to go. The contenders met at Williamsburg, Virginia, for the third debate, held in the College of William and Mary. Going in, Caddell found many people, particularly independents, turned off by the "stridency" of Carter's attacks on "nice guy" Jerry Ford, so Carter was advised to tone down for this last encounter. Ford, on the other hand, had developed a deep contempt for Carter, resenting his character and style. During the second debate Ford's face had reddened visibly under his opponent's attacks, and on several occasions the anger came through in his replies. His advisers counseled him to stay cool, no matter what.

The President began the exchange by listing his accomplishments in office. Carter came back implying he was a liar: "You should be ashamed of yourself for saying you've led the country out of a recession." Ford was bogged down most of the evening defending his record and answering panelists' questions on the ghosts of Watergate. One reporter asked him point-blank if he had helped Nixon stymie a preelection investigation by Congressman Wright Patman. Ford refused to answer, insisting "the matter was closed and best left behind us."

Carter got his chance to reassure dubious women voters. Answering a question no one asked, he admitted the *Playboy* interview had been a mistake. He justified it by pointing out that such luminaries as Walter Cronkite, Albert Schweitzer, and Ford's own Secretary of the Treasury, William Simon, had also sat for the magazine's interviewers. He closed the subject by waving the evangelical flag: "If in the future I decide to discuss my deep Christian beliefs, I'll use another forum besides *Playboy*."

Polls showed the final debate did little for the fortunes of either candidate. With ten days to go and six points to make up, Ford needed some media magic, and fast. Teeter and Deardourff came up with the idea of a traveling talk show starring the President, where he could answer questions in a relaxed setting. Research had shown that Ford was perceived as a controlled remote man, when in fact he is a warm, back-slapping sort. First they considered hiring a Hollywood actor to host the show. Then Ford suggested ex–St. Louis Cardinal, television personality Joe Garagiola, a relaxed, likable man with a self-deprecatory sense of humor. MacDougall phoned Garagiola, who agreed to do six thirty-minute political shows around the country.

Using *Air Force One*, Ford and Garagiola barnstormed in flashy limousines with motorcycle escorts, hordes of dark-suited Secret Service agents, and a small army of production people. A typical show began with a short introductory comment by Garagiola. Ford delivered a brief set speech and then answered questions posed by his host. The "Joe & Jerry Show" played to millions of people in the big industrial states, and Ford used the format to meet the suspicions of his involvement in Watergate head-on.

"People say you just took over where President Nixon left off," Garagiola began.

"That's totally wrong," Ford replied. "You see, Joe, under me there's no imperial Presidency, no imperial White House, no pomp, no ceremony. The average guy in the street knows that on August 9, 1974, there was a distinct break between the previous administration and my administration."

As they traveled the country, Ford and Garagiola used sports terms to appeal to the average American: "We're in the last quarter now, Joe," the President said, hitting his palm with his fist. "We're in the ninth inning and that's when Jerry Ford is going to win the ball game!" Most people watching the pair felt good because they honestly liked both Joe and Jerry.

October 28. Five days to go.

Headlines read "ECONOMY FALLS AGAIN" as the Commerce Department released its index of leading economic indicators, showing decline for the second straight month. Carter earned space on the evening news with a speech in Philadelphia proclaiming that "the average worker could not depend on those who created the economic mess to clean it up"—another steal from Nixon's "Checkers" speech.

Gallup released its last preelection poll, based on interviews taken a week earlier. It found Ford at 47 and Carter at 46 percent, with 4 percent undecided; too close to call, concluded the pollster. The weekend before election day, the Roper Poll found Carter ahead by four points, with a three-point margin of error. Whichever way it went, it would be close.

Each camp had produced a batch of hard-hitting television commercials assaulting the character and record of the opponent, but because of the tight finish, neither side dared risk blowing it by a misstep. Among the commercials Americans never got to see was one where Jimmy Carter talked over a picture of the New York skyline and asked, "How could anyone say to this great city of New York—*drop dead?*" Another showed Russian tanks on the streets of Hungary and Czechoslovakia while a narrator asked incredulously, "Can the President of the United States be ignorant of this?"

On the Ford side, two negative spots were ready for a last-minute assault. The first, called "Map Zoom," opened with a close-up of a television set showing the end of an actual Carter commercial. The narrator repeated Carter's tag line—"What Jimmy Carter did as governor of Georgia, he will do as President of the United States." A map of the United States filled the screen, and the camera zoomed in on a blowup of Georgia where legends read "Government spending up 58 percent," "Government employees up 27 percent," "Bonded indebtedness up 20 percent." The camera pulled back to the U.S. map again, where a larger legend read "More Big Government" as the announcer urged, "Don't let him do as President what he did as governor."

A second spot, called "Personal Taxes," implied Carter was a hypocrite for denouncing tax loopholes for millionaires. It showed a 1976 income tax return indicating that Carter took advantage of those same loopholes to pay only $1,375 on an adjusted income of over $120,000.

Teeter and other media staffers took tapes of the commercials to a Cleveland motel and screened them before a group of typical voters. There was no consensus. The people there couldn't understand the point of the tax commercial because of its legal complexity. Neither commercial was shown.

The last week of the campaign, Spencer and Deardourff decided to eliminate *all* negative advertising, including the highly potent man-on-the-street spots. "We wanted to close on a positive note," Stu Spencer told me. "We felt the negative advertising had served its purpose. At the end we wanted to show who the President was and what he stood for."

Rafshoon and Caddell felt the same way. They stopped their strident assertions of Carter's honesty and freedom from the

taint of corruption, and cooled down their campaign's emotional intensity.

On the Sunday before election day black minister Clennon
King, accompanied by two black women and a child, tried to
worship at the Plains Baptist Church. They were turned away
at the door. Carter issued a statement that he wouldn't quit the
church but would work within it "to change an attitude I
abhor." Ford's campaign committee sent telegrams to hundreds of black ministers around the country, hoping to erode
some of Carter's massive black support. But the Georgian's
hold on black America was unshakable.

Andrew Young took the lead in calming the black community, branding the incident a "Republican trick." Rev. Jesse
L. Jackson spoke in Boston to discredit Clennon King, as did
"Daddy" King—Dr. Martin Luther King, Sr.—in a recorded
statement circulated by the Democrats. Walter Cronkite reported on the evening news the allegation of a "set up." Thus
the impact of the event was blunted and even reversed.

On Monday night, election eve, each side ran a thirty-
minute film on all three networks, scheduled at half-hour in-
tervals across a three-hour span. Film maker Robert Squier
produced the Democratic show. He sat Carter behind his desk
in Plains, and had him look into the camera and answer questions from common people filmed on streets, shopping centers,
and farms around the country. The questions chosen dealt with
issues on which Caddell's readings found Carter "fuzzy."

Deardourff put more production into the Ford half-hour.
Starting with an introduction by Joe Garagiola aboard *Air
Force One*, it featured an unscripted endorsement by Pearl
Bailey and some biographical snips of Ford and his family.
The film ended with the President in vest and shirtsleeves
pleading, "I want your prayers as you gave them to me two
years ago, but this time I hope you confirm me with your bal-
lots."

It was all over, except for the voting.

Turnout in 1976 was the lowest since 1948: only 54 percent
of all Americans eighteen or older showed up at the polls, so

actually fewer than 81 million people decided the issue. Carter got 50 percent and Ford 48 percent of the ballots. Carter won the Presidency by a plurality of only 1.7 million. The electoral college totals were even closer: 297 for Carter, 241 for Ford. This was the slimmest electoral-vote margin since Woodrow Wilson squeaked past Charles Hughes in 1916 by 23 votes. Had a mere 9,250 popular votes shifted in Hawaii and Ohio, Ford would have had four more years in the White House.

In the end, black Americans tipped the scales. An unprecedented 93 percent of the black ballot went into Carter's column—7 million out of his 40.8 million votes. They tipped the balance of victory in the eleven once Confederate states and provided heavy margins in the big cities, helping to carry contested states like Ohio, Texas, Pennsylvania, and New York.

"We made one major mistake," Stu Spencer admitted. "We spent too much time in New York the last days of the campaign—days we should have been in Ohio. Polls always show a Republican doing better in New York than he ends up doing, and we had pressure from Nelson Rockefeller to keep campaigning there, so we stayed. We assumed we were within striking distance and reasoned that if we put the man in there heavily, we could turn it around. Boy, were we wrong! We lost New York by 288,000 votes, Ohio by only 7,000."

Bob Teeter saw other ways the Ford campaign could have been improved. "Maryland was one state we overestimated our chances of carrying. We could have won it if we had paid it a little more attention. We might have kept our anti-Carter advertising on a little longer instead of pulling it the last five days. When it's very close at the end, you want to get off the negative kick and build momentum. When you win or lose by a percent, anything worth one percent could have turned it around. But the campaign was well run and we didn't make many mistakes. Carter was a mile ahead and we almost caught him. Carter's campaign had a fundamental weakness they could never satisfy: he wasn't really qualified. He didn't have much of a record of accomplishment, no experience in foreign affairs, and he was fuzzy on issues. He was intentionally fuzzy because they wanted to make sure they didn't turn off any wing of the Democratic Party, from liberals to Wallaceites."

"How about 1980?" I asked Teeter to prophesy, ten months before the Iowa caucus.

"Now Carter has a record," he replied. "He's an incumbent President, so his advertising has to be more specific, based more on his record than what a trustworthy person he is. His record will also be his biggest problem."

7

How Kennedy Lost

In December 1976, after Jimmy Carter had been elected President and Ted Kennedy senator, it seemed a time for both politicians to rest. Christmas was two weeks away, the candidates were weary of campaigning, and holiday lights already glittered in the main streets of Boston, Atlanta, and Washington, D.C. But as the Kennedys planned family dinner parties and touch-football matches on the lawns of suburban Boston, the Carter scheme machine was working overtime. Pat Caddell sat down and drafted a forty-page memo explaining how Carter could exploit his victory to ensure reelection in 1980. The memo was titled "Initial Working Paper on Political Strategy, December 10, 1976." In it Caddell outlined a policy of governing by poll.

"Governing with public approval requires a continuing political campaign," he wrote. "Pessimism still reigns in this country. Trust in government remains at an all-time low. Voters are not willing to grant authority to leadership. Too many good people have been defeated because they tried to substitute substance for style. They forgot to give the public the visible signals it needs."

Caddell recommended a series of symbolic acts to create a Presidential image that was "nonideological, open, compassionate, and different." He advised Carter to cut back on "frills and perks," use fireside chats to build intimacy with the public, schedule town meetings for dramatic impact, and make os-

tentatious use of big-name celebrities such as Bob Dylan and
Martin Luther King, Sr. Caddell also suggested the Democratic National Committee set up a low-profile electioneering
group to begin the 1980 campaign in 1977. "Jerry Rafshoon
and I should participate in this group from the beginning," he
urged.

What Caddell suggested, Carter did. Carter made the news
by wiping visible "frills and perks" from White House cere-
monies. He eliminated the playing of "Ruffles and Flourishes"
and "Hail to the Chief" when he entered rooms. He retired
the yacht-sized Presidential limousine, replacing it with a less
showy vehicle. He wore a cardigan sweater during his one
"fireside chat" soon after taking office; went to town meetings
in Mississippi and Massachusetts, where˙ he answered questions in shirtsleeves; slept in the houses of ordinary Americans;
and spent one Saturday afternoon at the White House answering phone calls over a national radio hookup, calls that had
been carefully screened by his media friend Walter Cronkite.

All these public relations stunts were blown up into "media
events," heavily photographed, televised, and reported across
the country as serious news. As Pat Caddell put it, "If you
want to be President, you've got to be consistently reinforcing
people. You've got to keep the signal-sending process going."
Symbols were everything. Behind them lay a web of cynicism rooted in the patronizing view of American democracy as
practiced in the South. It was an inheritance Carter never
outgrew.

Abraham Lincoln maintained that you can't fool all of the
people all of the time. Jimmy Carter's approval quotient, as
measured by the Gallup poll, seemed to confirm that thesis.
From a high one month after he took office of 66 percent who
lauded his Presidential performance, Carter's ratings fell steadily. Contributing to his decline were the Bert Lance banking
scandal, a deteriorating economy, price-gouging by OPEC, and
a loss of American power overseas. In early 1978, when Carter's popularity sank to 38 percent, a worried Rosalynn Carter
called a breakfast meeting with Pat Caddell.

Caddell was aware that Americans were not thrilled with
their new President. Once hopes for new leadership had been

dashed, pessimism afflicted the nation again; the feeling was that this weak but well-meaning man in the White House was making things worse. For them, the future looked bleak. Caddell's remedy? A change of signals, which would be followed by a change in image, and soon people would feel better.

Rosalynn saw the handwriting on the wall. After breakfast with Caddell, she cornered her husband and told him what she had learned.

"Jimmy, we need help," she said.

"What kind of help?"

"Get Jerry Rafshoon back here."

The President picked up the phone, got Rafshoon on the line, and asked him to come back to work full-time. Rafshoon, making money faster than he could spend it and newly remarried on the heels of a divorce, was reluctant. But when Jimmy put on pressure, Jerry could not refuse. He put his agency stock in trust, turned his projects over to his associates, and rushed back to the White House. There Carter assigned him an Old Executive Building office in the west wing, a $60,000 federal salary, and the title of Communications Adviser.

Assuming control over the flow of information coming out of the White House, Rafshoon insisted every idea be "coordinated" and "proper themes" laid out in press handouts, position papers, issues statements, speeches, government brochures, and every other channel through which the American people learn from its government what is going on. Former Carter speech writer Robert Shrum saw Rafshoon's role as twisting truth to advantage: "His job was to make Carter appear as competent as possible."

"I'm here to save the President's ass," Rafshoon boasted.

Rafshoon wasted no time laying down the law. Abandoning dozens of proposed Carter projects, he compressed all statements that the country received from the White House into just three subjects—inflation, bureaucratic reform, and foreign affairs. Caddell's polls revealed that Carter was deemed most ineffective in these areas, and as an advertising man, Rafshoon knew that people get confused by too many ideas. Rafshoon saw his job at the White House as just another selling problem: "Developing a marketing program for issues is like putting together an ad campaign. In the ad business, you don't do twelve campaigns a year for a client. You stay with just a few." Soon all administration mouthpieces—Cabinet members, aides, and even Carter's family—were spouting unified themes orchestrated by Rafshoon: inflation, bureaucratic reform, and foreign affairs, those three and no more. Every position paper, speech, and press release mirrored the narrowed focus.

Since Carter was seen as a weak leader, wishy-washy and nonpresidential, Rafshoon scheduled a rafting and camping trip for Carter which was heavily covered by the national press. Rafshoon made sure he controlled what the press heard and saw. He insisted that reporters sleep in tents out of sight and earshot of the Presidential campsite. Rafshoon also arranged for Jimmy to pitch in softball games to build a macho image, and after the camping trip sent him out to perform visual Presidential acts such as signing New York's aid bill on the streets of Manhattan.

Rafshoon resurrected the pomp of "Ruffles and Flourishes" and "Hail to the Chief." Urging the President to fire Bella Abzug from the Council on Women, Rafshoon painted a new image of a tough, hard-hitting chief executive. Two years later he explained: "In 1976 we had a country that was disgusted with politicians. People felt we had lost our direction and moral values. So Carter spoke about patriotism and old-fashioned virtues. Today, the times demand a conservative thrust."

When Sadat and Begin met at Camp David in October 1978 to ratify a peace process begun during Nixon's administration —a ratification which earned Henry Kissinger a Nobel Peace Prize—Rafshoon and Carter were quick to claim credit. Carter paraded his achievement before the American electorate. "Jimmy Carter, Man of Peace" was Rafshoon's message, one he would lean on heavily in the two years preceding the 1980 election.

A few months after Rafshoon's return to the Carter scheme machine, Carter's fall in the polls was halted.

Everyone knew that some day, when he decided it was time, Edward Kennedy would run for President of the United States.

His own Massachusetts clan knew it, all the Eastern Democratic politicians knew it, and even the band of scheming, dreaming Georgians knew it. The only question was when.

Jimmy Carter and his disciples feared Kennedy would make his bid in 1976, and were prepared at that time to fight him. Hamilton Jordan's memo of 1972 bravely argued that Kennedy was not a viable candidate then, citing research done by Caddell and others. "I believe it would be very difficult for Senator Kennedy to win a national election," he wrote. "The unanswered questions of Chappaquiddick run contrary to the national desire for trust and morality in government. Time solves a lot of problems, but the memory of the Chappaquiddick incident is still fresh in the minds of a majority of American people as indicated in recent polls."

Still, Carter's group hedged their bet by considering a 1976 ticket that would star Ted Kennedy as President and Jimmy Carter as his Southern running mate. The face-off was postponed when Kennedy himself, reading those same polls and being preoccupied with family troubles, decided to stay in the Senate.

In the following years Kennedy helped end poll taxes, gained voting rights for eighteen-year-olds, deregulated the airlines, and worked to do the same for the trucking industry. When Hubert Humphrey died in January 1978, Kennedy assumed his role as champion of the Senate liberals. Educating Americans to the need for a comprehensive national health service, he worked hard to enlarge social welfare programs at a time when the nation's mood was growing more conservative, and in so doing disregarded the advice of political advisers and national pollsters. Kennedy now had every reason to believe that Americans would not hold Chappaquiddick against him. More than nine years had passed since the incident, he had proven himself in government, and polls seemed to indicate the country was ready for his leadership.

Christmas 1978. A national survey by the *Los Angeles Times* showed that Americans were disenchanted with Carter's economic and foreign policies. They preferred Kennedy over Carter for President by 42 to 33 percent. Jerry Brown had 15 percent of their support. By May 1979 a follow-up survey showed Kennedy's lead as 46 percent versus 28 percent for Carter, with 17 percent for Brown.

The word went out to the Kennedy people—this was the year. But there was no need to rush things. If Kennedy simply waited long enough, the decision to challenge an incumbent for the nomination would seem less like a power play and more like a draft by desperate Democrats hoping to save their party from certain defeat in 1980.

Meanwhile Carter took hope from Caddell's research, which revealed that Kennedy's support was soft. Still, as long as Kennedy remained an unannounced rival, the President was running against "an image of perfection, tied to two martyred brothers." If Kennedy could be persuaded to declare his intentions, voters would have to choose between two "flesh and blood candidates," a comparison the Carterites believed would benefit them because of the Chappaquiddick affair.

In May 1979, oil shortages caused block-long lines at filling stations.

In June, Carter gave a speech to a group of congressmen and goaded Kennedy: "If Kennedy decides to run, I'll whip his ass!" The statement was intended as a ploy to get Kennedy mad enough to grab the challenge. Once Kennedy showed himself as a rival candidate, Carter could unleash his heavy guns and start chipping away at the Bostonian's "vision of perfection."

But Kennedy wisely kept his mouth shut, and the Carter ship of state continued sinking. The latest Harris poll showed the President not only far behind Ted Kennedy but, for the first time, even losing to a possible Republican opponent, Ronald Reagan, by four percentage points. At 25 percent, Carter's approval rating was lower than Richard Nixon's at the height of Watergate.

When Carter left for a state visit to Japan, his inner circle held a series of worried meetings. While Stu Eizenstat, Ham Jordan, and Jody Powell blamed the disastrous polls on inflation and OPEC, Pat Caddell looked elsewhere. It was Carter's image that needed fixing, Caddell argued, not his policies.

Symbol battled substance, resulting in two memos giving conflicting analyses and advice. The first, written by Stu Eizenstat, summarized an energy reform attack. Dated June 28, 1979, it summarized the reasons for a deteriorating fuel crisis and maintained that angry Americans blamed Carter for their troubles. Eizenstat's solution? Blame OPEC for inflation and long gas lines, announce a widely publicized "new approach" to energy, create a National Energy Board, and give lots of speeches to show commitment to solving the problem and defying OPEC.

Caddell knew this would be politically disastrous. By taking action Carter would in effect be admitting he was responsible for inflation and the energy crisis. Caddell's solution was to get off the defensive and attack. He advised Carter to turn the issue around and blame Americans for their own poverty of spirit. When Carter returned from his trip to Japan on July 1, he was greeted by aides Jordan, Powell, and Rafshoon, all pressuring him to make an energy speech based on the Eizenstat memo. Two days before Carter was scheduled to make a hastily written televised address to the nation, Caddell sent him a 107-page analysis explaining why he should not make this energy speech. Instead, he urged Carter to be inspirational and "transform" the nation.

Carter digested Caddell's memo, called off his scheduled speech, and retreated to Camp David. For ten days Carter hid from the public while an assortment of lawmakers, union leaders, writers, black ministers, economists, and feminists told the President what they thought was wrong with the country. Carter listened, made voluminous notes on a yellow legal pad, and smiled enigmatically.

On July 15 he emerged and presented his conclusions to the American people. In a national televised speech, he told them it was not he who had failed but they. There was a "crisis of confidence" stalking the land, a malaise that threatened to destroy America. Listing such causes as the assassinations of John and Robert Kennedy and Martin Luther King, the Watergate scandal, and the Vietnam War, he harangued the people for their selfishness, using phrases borrowed virtually word for word from a four-year-old speech written by Pat Caddell.

Carter spoke loudly, with unaccustomed emphasis, banging his fist into his palm. Rafshoon had convinced him his image needed toughening and had spent long hours rehearsing with him for the speech. Although Carter appeared a bit mechanical, the image-shaper was pleased. "From now on you'll be seeing a tough Jimmy Carter," he told reporters. After the address, Carter's approval rating rose by 11 percent.

Two days later, following Rafshoon's advice, Carter asked for the resignations of his entire cabinet and accepted a third of them, including Health, Education, and Welfare Secretary Joseph Califano's. It was a bravado attempt to counter a growing perception of Jimmy Carter as a weak leader, a barking dog with no bite. "You've got to break eggs to make an omelette," Rafshoon said of the mass firings. "Camp David was a catharsis. From now on you'll be seeing a President who's tough and who makes changes when he finds it necessary."

But two weeks later, once the dust from the cabinet shakeup had settled, Carter's approval rating came to rest at an even lower level than before his Camp David retreat. The public relations shuffle had failed, the leopard still had his spots, and Jimmy Carter's abdication to Ted Kennedy seemed inevitable.

For a long time *CBS Reports* had been negotiating for a television show starring Sen. Ted Kennedy. Roger Mudd and two of his producers visited Kennedy's Washington office and hashed out ground rules with his press secretary, Tom Southwick. In March 1979 they told Southwick the show would run for one hour and would not air until February 1980. It would be called "Edward M. Kennedy, a Profile," would be a sympathetic personality piece, a week in the life of the only surviving heir to a political dynasty. "They wanted to spend a lot of time with him," Southwick recalled. "They wanted to follow him to committee hearings, staff briefings, and meetings, have access to family events, and do some interviews. It was to be a portrait of Kennedy, personally and professionally." Andy Lacks, the CBS producer, pursued Kennedy that summer with his film crew. He spent several days from breakfast to nightfall following the senator wherever he went, shooting forty to fifty hours of film.

Then, as Southwick put it, early in September "things began to heat up." A front-page story in the September 8 *Washington Post* announced "FAMILY BACKS KENNEDY RACE," explaining that Kennedy's mother and wife had urged Ted's candidacy despite ever-present assassination worries and Joan's highly publicized drinking problem. The following week an interview with Kennedy was published in the *New York Times* with the headline, "LEADERSHIP NOT ECONOMIC POLICY IS AT ISSUE, SAYS KENNEDY."

In the interview Kennedy stressed that though he substantially agreed with President Carter's economic programs, Carter lacked the leadership to "make them work"—leadership Kennedy could provide. The senator "scoffed at the suggestion the Chappaquiddick incident" would be a factor in the campaign. As corroboration, Sen. Howard Baker was widely quoted as insisting that Chappaquiddick was not "a legitimate issue." Neither he nor "anyone else working in my campaign will be allowed to mention it."

Roger Mudd and CBS News began to get jittery. Arguing that they wanted to finish their filming before Kennedy announced his candidacy, they pressured Southwick for access to Kennedy. Their requests came at a time when Kennedy was getting conflicting advice about whether to run and, if he did, how he should do it. So Southwick refused the CBS request until Mudd made it a personal matter.

Mudd, a long time "Kennedy family friend" who had been close to Robert Kennedy and was still friendly with Robert's widow, Ethel, got Ted Kennedy on the line and virtually begged for time to finish filming and interviewing on the show. Kennedy finally agreed to let Mudd's film crew accompany him and Kennedy family nieces and nephews on their annual camping trip in western Massachusetts.

Mudd persuaded Kennedy to let him visit Hyannisport the last weekend in September to "get some footage of the senator walking along the beach and talk briefly." The real interviewing, Mudd assured Kennedy, would take place four days later at the senator's Washington office. Mudd described the session in Hyannisport as a "softball thing"—no embarrassing questions. When Mudd and his film crew arrived at Kennedy's summer home, Ted met him on the front porch. He had no advisers present, no press secretary to protect him, no staffers of any kind, according to Tom Southwick. Southwick recalled the incident:

As soon as the cameras began rolling, Mudd set the tone.

"Do you think your preoccupation with politics contributed to nephew David's becoming a drug addict?"

Puzzled, Kennedy fumbled. Mudd followed up more strongly:

"Do your children also take drugs? . . . Is Joan's drinking under control? . . . What about your marriage?"

Kennedy reddened with anger. Though these segments would not survive the final editing, they succeeded in upsetting him and throwing him off stride. His replies to later questions about his candidacy and Chappaquiddick were halting, inarticulate, and distracted. Kennedy was furious at Mudd for ambushing him.

Such is the power of media stars who shape public perceptions of national heroes. Behind the scenes, where judgments are made on how to slant a story or even whether to show it at all, factors other than balanced reporting and fair play often tip the scales. During the summer and winter of 1979, Roger Mudd was in a heated competition with colleague Dan Rather over who would inherit Walter Cronkite's anchor spot when Cronkite stepped down in 1981—the top job in American television news. Rather had a reputation as an objective, tough, even ruthless reporter who had taken on Richard Nixon and stuck it to him. Mudd, on the other hand, was known as a friend of the Kennedy family with a more relaxed reportorial style. The question being asked in journalistic circles was whether Roger would be soft on Kennedy in his CBS profile. Would he go after him or would he produce a puff piece?

Mudd filmed a second interview in the senator's Washington office, a session that lasted several hours. In television even more than the printed media, the message and images that go out depend heavily on the editing process. If Mudd chose the frames that showed Kennedy at his worst, it could be disastrous for Kennedy. If, on the other hand, the film made Kennedy look heroic, his run for the White House might take off so decisively Carter could never catch up. Kennedy had to wait another five weeks to find out.

Kennedy had never run in a national election before. His campaign experience consisted of helping his brothers as a young man, and four cakewalks to the Senate from Massachusetts, where the Kennedy name was enough to win him office. Now he faced the task of assembling an electioneering unit skilled enough to do what has been done only once before in American history—to take his party's nomination away from its incumbent President. Moreover, Carter's team had proven skilled in waging a modern election.

From the start, Kennedy made the wrong moves. Instead of hiring a top professional to run his campaign, Kennedy turned to his brother-in-law Steve Smith. Smith, an acknowledged expert in finance and organizational skills, was something less than a brilliant political strategist. Smith staffed Kennedy's campaign team with young unknowns: liberals like lawyer Paul Kirck, labor organizer Carl Wagner, prosecutor Richard Stearns, and former Kennedy press secretary Dick Drayne. Most of these men worked for Kennedy's Senate office or one of the committees he headed.

Waiting in the wings was Joe Napolitan, the "Kennedy man" who had done so much for John F. Kennedy in 1960 and had been ready to do the same for Robert in 1968. When Steven Smith didn't invite him in, Napolitan swallowed his pride and sent extensive memos to Smith without charge, outlining what had to be done to win the nomination. As one insider noted, "Nobody paid any attention to Joe's memos at the time." Smith lived to regret it.

Smith brought in Herb Schmertz, the public-affairs head at Mobil Oil, as media strategist, despite the fact that Schmertz was credited with "losing Oregon for Bobby" in 1968 and had done nothing since then to salvage his political reputation. But Schmertz's friendship with Smith and his fine institutional ads for Mobil were judged reason enough to assign him the most sensitive job in the Presidential effort. Schmertz took a six-week leave of absence to "set up" Kennedy's media.

Even Jerry Rafshoon, acknowledging the Kennedy handicap, could not resist commenting on the six-week wonder boy: "I know and like Herb Schmertz. I think he does a fine job at Mobil. But I can't believe he can set up a campaign so quickly. If I thought it could be done in six weeks, I'd be doing something else this winter."

Dick Drayne, a Kennedy speech writer and longtime aide, explained why Schmertz, a volunteer, was used instead of a top pro: "They wanted to keep important media decisions within the campaign among people the senator knew personally. A person like David Garth, for instance, wants total control. Maybe you need that to work effectively, I don't know. But we were not willing to cede control to somebody who did not have a history with the Kennedys. So Herbie Schmertz was called in to do it piecemeal. When he left, media fell back into the hands of Steve Smith. We did no polling because polling is vastly expensive and at the outset there was the feeling we didn't need it."

Schmertz interviewed some top political media people, intending to farm out work to a half dozen stars, rewrite their copy, and use the best of the lot. One of those called in was David Garth, who ended up running John Anderson's independent campaign. "They didn't understand media," Garth recalled, "and they didn't understand the modern use of polls. They thought in terms of moving Teddy around. But today's campaigns don't need a barnstorming tour, just one press conference and one media event a day. What amazed me most was that they weren't prepared."

Another professional explained that Herb Schmertz believed he didn't need to conduct research, since he felt he knew instinctively what the political climate and voter perceptions were. In this election, with an electorate turning conservative, he decided to gloss over the ideological differences between Carter's right-leaning philosophy and Kennedy's New Deal liberalism. Instead, he emphasized that Carter's policies were not the problem so much as Carter's inability to execute them. Leadership was lacking, and it was leadership that Kennedy could supply in abundance. As a concept, it sounded good.

Translating it into effective campaign advertising and speech
writing proved harder to achieve.

Among the media experts Schmertz interviewed were David
Sawyer, Charles Guggenheim, and Tony Schwartz, all of
whom would make abortive contributions to the beleaguered
campaign. Schwartz was the first hired and the first to resign,
though he returned late in the race when the die was all but
cast. "I came in during October," he recalled. "And I found
myself working with a twenty-headed monster. Whatever I did,
they'd call in twenty people who had to go over everything
and decide what they should run. Each one said something
different, so what the hell can you do? These twenty may have
been skilled in their own fields, but they knew nothing about
campaigning. Now I'd worked Kennedy's Senate campaigns
where you didn't need strategy, all you had to do was tell a
little of what he'd done. He'd have won even without media.
But for a Presidential campaign, that approach was disastrous.
There was no media strategy, no instructions, absolutely the
worst run campaign in the history of politics."

But the polls still showed Ted Kennedy demolishing Jimmy
Carter. A Gallup survey published October 12 had it Kennedy
over Carter by 60 to 30 percent. But the Chappaquiddick bomb
had not yet exploded. Although Kennedy had been interviewed in July by the *Washington Post*, the *New York Times*,
and the networks, and had insisted there was nothing new to
be said on the subject, Kennedy aide Tim Hanan knew the
relative calm of the media was illusory.

"I knew from the beginning that Chappaquiddick would be a
dominant issue if he ran," Hanan explained. "I told the senator
and the people around him, 'If you believe polls saying 79
percent of all Americans believe it should not be an issue, you
don't understand politics. If it doesn't rise by itself, you can bet
those guys from Georgia will raise it every chance they get. So
you'd better be able to deal with it. Running for President is
different from running for senator from Massachusetts. You'd
better have your ducks in a row before you start, because the
press is going to pick you to ribbons. Every reporter has to

have something to distinguish his line of patter from everybody else's, and he'll get attention only by being negative, not
positive.' The campaign got started before Kennedy's people
were prepared. They failed to realize how important it was to
have precise answers to obvious questions, number one of
which was, how are you going to deal with Chappaquiddick?"

President Carter decided to help the press along, even before
Kennedy was a declared rival. During the last few weeks in
September, he began dropping oblique references to Chappaquiddick in town meetings and news conferences. "I have
never panicked in a crisis," Carter proclaimed to reporters and
cameras. "I have the ability to remain calm in a crisis."

While newspapers and television reporters quoted the President, and aptly pointed out that he was referring to Kennedy's
inability to stay calm ten years before, Carter moved in to fan
the flames. He wrote a personal note to Kennedy, assuring him
that he had intended no veiled references to Chappaquiddick,
that the news stories implying he had were "not correct." Kennedy had reason to suspect the President's sincerity when Jody
Powell called in the networks and print reporters, gave them
copies of the note, and elaborated on the theme. The next
morning headlines read: "NO CHAPPAQUIDDICK INTENT, CARTER
SAYS." Most press accounts summarized the events at Chappaquiddick Island.

When Kennedy tried to shift focus away from his "character" to his compassion for suffering people, the power of the
Presidency upstaged him. The last week in October, when
hundreds of thousands of Cambodians were threatened by
starvation, Kennedy made an impassioned plea for immediate
aid. Within hours, Carter announced that plans were underway for stepping up U.S. aid to Cambodia. Carter got front-
page headlines for his proposal, while Kennedy earned one
paragraph deep inside the newspapers and a single sentence
on the evening news.

Monday, October 29. Hurrying to a meeting, Roger Mudd
bumped into Steve Smith on a downtown Washington street.
When Smith told him Kennedy would officially announce for
President on November 7, Mudd hurried back to his office and

called CBS in New York. His show *Teddy* was scheduled for November 7 and the network was anxious to show it before Kennedy made his move. With no time to change television listings, they switched the air date to November 4, a Sunday.

Wednesday, October 31. Kennedy's people were deluged with questions from reporters about the Mudd interview. That was curious, because the last the Kennedy people had heard, it would not be shown for another week. "Copies of the show's transcript had been leaked by CBS," Tom Southwick noted. "Marty Nolan of the *Boston Globe* had a big story on it that Wednesday. Other papers and news shows followed. Every reporter in town had a transcript, but CBS never let us see one. I finally got a copy from a reporter friend."

CBS held a "press preview" of the show, where they gave out transcripts and offered refreshments to reporters. "When you watch something and then read a transcript, you get very different impressions," Southwick explained. "There were all kinds of inserts in the transcript to make it obvious Kennedy was halting. The effect of reading the phrase 'uh-uh-uh' four times in a row is much worse than watching it on television, where you can see by the expression of the face why the person is pausing." Long before the program aired, Ted Kennedy was being branded "indecisive . . . inarticulate . . . a Kennedy without star quality . . . who raised more questions than he answered about the Chappaquiddick incident."

By Sunday evening when *Teddy* was telecast, two things had happened. First, every American who read newspapers or watched television news had been informed that this Kennedy was not of the same quality as his brothers, but was a slower, less confident man who tended to "panic in a crisis." Second, on Sunday afternoon, hours before the Mudd telecast, Iranian terrorists took over the American embassy in Teheran and imprisoned fifty-three Americans. So as Americans sat in their living rooms to watch the *Teddy* show, images of Iranian mobs trampling on Yankee pride still burned in their hearts and minds. The President and the country were under fire, and Americans began to close ranks. The overriding question was, who was best able to lead the country to safety?

Roger Mudd's profile made it clear the youngest Kennedy brother was not that man. The show barely mentioned Ted's seventeen years in the Senate or his legislative achievements. Instead, viewers saw a shaken, inarticulate Kennedy claim that there was nothing new to say about the drowning of Mary Jo Kopechne. A full third of the broadcast time was spent rehashing the tragedy; it included a devastating reenactment from inside the death car, on its drive from the party on Martha's Vineyard to its fatal destination at Eyke Bridge.

"The style of questioning, the editing techniques, and the voice-overs on that show were highly questionable," Tom Southwick charged. He cited the technique of showing a camera's-eye view through the windshield of a late model car of the same make the senator had been driving, and the facts that the road's white center line didn't exist in 1969, and that the dense, overhanging shrubbery had been cut back since then. For the television reenactment, a special camera lens made the road's surface clearly visible, though it was actually dark and misty at the time of the accident. The film's unmistakable message was that there was no way Kennedy could have made a wrong turn.

There was other evidence of malicious intent on the part of CBS. "Take the camping trip sequence," Southwick said. "Every year the senator takes his nieces and nephews on a camping trip. They usually set aside half a day for the press to take pictures and do stories, so they'll then be left in peace. But CBS insisted on meeting the campers in Hyannis and covering the whole trip. Then, when they showed film of it on *Teddy*, the voice-over said, 'Even a simple camping trip turns into a media circus.' Who turned it into a media circus? The senator didn't want them along at all, but Mudd begged for access.

"In another segment, set in Kennedy's Senate office, Kennedy's administrative assistant handed him the phone and said, 'Ed Markey,' who's a Massachusetts congressman. The voice-over said, 'Kennedy is known as a good politician, even though he sometimes forgets the names of congressmen in his own delegation.' It's standard procedure for a senator's aide to tell him who's on the line when he hands him the phone. Aides have to keep track of all the phone conversations a senator has, but that does not imply that the senator doesn't remember people's names. Presumably the show was designed to educate the public. But a voter who tuned into the CBS special on Edward Kennedy would get absolutely no idea where Kennedy stood on any issue. Even many journalists questioned the program's validity."

Whatever its validity, *Teddy* won a Peabody award for Roger Mudd. But in February 1980 he lost his fight for Cronkite's job to Dan Rather anyway, and left CBS soon thereafter.

Five days after the hostage takeover and the telecast of *Teddy*, Kennedy officially announced his candidacy for President of the United States. Among his campaign staff there was a feeling that the Mudd show had dealt Kennedy's chances a mortal blow.

Payola always works on the side of an incumbent President. There is an endless variety of grants, jobs, appointments, contracts, and favors he can dangle before reluctant noses. When a President is in trouble with the voters, payoffs become his chief weapon. In the 1980 elections Carter used that weapon to an extent that has not been seen in this century, making the modest carrot-and-stick efforts of Gerald Ford in 1976 seem child's play by comparison.

On October 19, 1979, Carter invited two hundred mayors, governors, and legislators to the White House, ostensibly to celebrate the second birthday of the Urban Development Action Grant program. After feeding his guests pastry and coffee, Carter reminded them who holds the federal purse strings. By the end of that week, Carter aides boasted they had received pledges of endorsement from over forty mayors, more than a hundred congressmen, and twenty-one out of thirty-two Democratic governors. As a delegate of Mayor Ed Koch of New York put it: "It was the greatest trading post since New Amsterdam. It means a hell of a lot to a mayor or the head of a local machine to get word the White House is calling, especially when he's responsible for a local economy. The Kennedy mystique does not put cash in the drawer."

With the 1980 census looming, the White House was handing out jobs to 275,000 Americans ranging from $3.55-an-hour clerks to $20,000-a-year district managers. Though the jobs were budgeted strictly for census-related duties, workers who were hired revealed that they had to agree to work for the Carter-Mondale campaign before they would be accepted. Local census employees in Massachusetts, Oklahoma, and Michigan were put to work at Carter campaign headquarters addressing envelopes and making telephone calls to reluctant voters, urging them to support Carter—all paid for by tax money allocated strictly for the national head count. Inside government, anyone whose job was not protected by the Civil Service was thrown out if he favored Ted Kennedy over Jimmy Carter. A Carter spokesman made no apology for the blatant use of force: "If they are not loyal to the President, they can go to work for Kennedy. We don't want them on the federal payroll anymore."

In a largely symbolic test on October 13, Carter showed his payola power in the Florida Democratic caucuses, where he won a majority of delegates to December's state convention. In the weeks just before the caucuses met, Carter announced he was awarding federal grants for housing, transportation, health, and public works amounting to over a billion dollars. An electric cooperative in the Sunshine State was given a $2-billion loan just weeks after they had filed an application, though that process usually takes a year or more to complete. A $100-million "people mover," federally financed and already under construction in Miami, was threatened with having its funding cut off. Carter approved federal aid to Los Angeles, where Mayor Tom Bradley vigorously endorsed Carter's candidacy in return for a $150-million "people mover." Carter threatened to withhold similar grants from Chicago, where Mayor Jane Byrne supported Kennedy. And the first primary was still three months away.

Gallup interviewed Americans between November 16 and 19, and found that Kennedy's thirty-point lead of October had diminished to nineteen. He was now ahead 55 to 36 percent. A survey by NBC and the Associated Press at that time summarized the effects of the Mudd interview: "One third of all

Democrats polled said Chappaquiddick and Kennedy's explanation had lowered their opinion of Kennedy's Presidential stature. It also raised questions about how he would react in a crisis."

Yet the Kennedy magic retained enough luster that another big media "mistake" was required to bring Teddy down to earth. On Sunday, December 2, Kennedy visited the studios of KRON-TV in the *Chronicle* building in downtown San Francisco. During an interview with a local newscaster, he was asked about the Iranian crisis and the current hostage situation. "The Shah had one of the most violent regimes in the history of mankind," Kennedy replied. "He took umpteen million dollars from his country, and he should never have been invited to this country."

That statement was edited out by a producer who felt it was too inflammatory, so it never got to the screen. But the tape found its way into the hands of a newspaper reporter who turned it into a lead story in Monday's *San Francisco Chronicle*. That night the story was on the wires and the evening news. By December 4, newspapers all over the country were headlining the "major goof" by Kennedy. Stories called Kennedy's comment "inexcusable," "a cynical campaign ploy," "irresponsible," and "not very smart." In one voice, the media trumpeted support for the President and assailed the rival who had dared to question his foreign policy.

Carter quickly went in for the kill. He told a congressional group on December 6: "I don't give a damn what crimes the Shah may have committed. The crucial thing now is to get the hostages back. We can talk later about the Shah and where he's going to live." Carter's comments made headlines for the next two days.

Overseas war crises always boost Presidential popularity. When North Korea invaded the South in 1950, Truman's approval rating shot up nine points. When Eisenhower sent Marines to Lebanon in 1958, he gained six points, and the 1962 Cuban missile crisis pushed John Kennedy's popularity up by twelve. More recently, Gerald Ford was given a lift of eleven points in 1975 when the Cambodians seized an American ship, the *Mayaguez*. Even a military failure can do the trick: after the 1961 Bay of Pigs invasion in Cuba ended in disaster, Kennedy's approval rating rose 5 percent.

Dick Drayne later criticized the press for allowing Carter to hide his defects behind the flag: "We were trying to get out from under the cloud Iran had put on all political debate. With the nation preoccupied with Iran and the President encouraging that preoccupation constantly, it was very difficult to get anything started. The press did an inadequate job. The press never focused on the fact the President was using the situation as a very handy device to stifle the issues. People's emotions got so involved, it put a damper on reasonable debate. The way that whole hostage situation was treated by the press would have made me critical, even if Kennedy hadn't been running. It wasn't only what effect it had on us—it had an unfortunate effect on the entire political climate of the times."

When Gallup went out to the people again on December 7–9, he found the race turned around. Carter had 48-percent support, Ted Kennedy 40 percent. A *Time* magazine poll conducted a few days later found Carter's lead lengthening to twenty points, 53 to 33 percent. Voters gave three overriding reasons for their change of heart: Carter's pacifist handling of the Iran crisis, Kennedy's waffling on Chappaquiddick, and Kennedy's "misstep" of denouncing the deposed Shah while Americans were being held hostage.

Tactically, it was a bind that Joe Napolitan would have foreseen long before the campaign got underway. When Kennedy's strategists decided to deemphasize his policy differences from Carter, afraid of being locked into a left-of-center position where only a minority of Democratic voters could be found, many people wondered why Kennedy was running in the first place. Once they were reminded of Chappaquiddick and heard his views on the Shah of Iran, the only place for moderate Democrats to go was back into Carter's fold. By the time Smith and his advisers decided to shift strategy in late December, Kennedy had assumed a handicap he would strive in vain to overcome.

In the ninety-nine days between February 26 and June 3, the Democrats held primary elections in thirty-five states and the Commonwealth of Puerto Rico. The remaining fifteen states selected their delegates at local caucuses or statewide conventions. While primaries call for the whole arsenal of electioneering weapons—advertising, organizing by precincts, candidate-stumping, and media manipulation—caucus and convention states demand a lot more organizing muscle. Kennedy stood a better chance in primaries than in caucuses, because through media he could partially offset the organizational advantage enjoyed by the Carter machine. "We did this nitty-gritty organizing in 1975 and 1976," Hamilton Jordan observed. "This is the first time Kennedy or any of his people will get involved in any real trench warfare."

Jordan's primary strategy was based on results from 1976, plus new Caddell polls in key states. It aimed to grab a big lead from Carter's Southern base, win Illinois, and concede Kennedy's New England home territory. Then, just matching delegates in the Northeast industrial states, Carter could put Kennedy away with big victories in the remaining Southern states, the Midwest, and the West.

Kennedy's plan was to take Iowa and launch his winning posture, sweep New England, then beat Carter in his own backyard by taking Florida. By scoring heavily in the industrial states from Illinois and New York through Pennsylvania, Indiana, and Michigan, Kennedy hoped to wrap it up June 3 with victories in Ohio, New Jersey, and California.

The first test was in Iowa on January 21. When Kennedy operatives began organizing efforts in November, they found the territory already claimed by Carter's network, who offered substantial rewards for supporting their man. For those who hesitated, Carter minions warned of what would happen to them after Jimmy won. The highlight was to be a debate scheduled for January 7 among the Presidential candidates. But when the Iranians imprisoned the U.S. embassy staff, Carter's enthusiasm for open discussion decreased in direct proportion to his rising poll readings. He canceled all public appearances, giving the impression that he was locked in the Cabinet Room day and night working with generals, diplomats, and State Department officials to "solve the hostage crisis." An army of stand-ins roamed Iowa, including his wife Rosalynn, his son Chip, Vice-President Mondale, and a bevy of Cabinet members all pushing the Rafshoon line.

Rosalynn led the "rally round the flag" and imputed treason to those who disagreed—including Senator Kennedy, who accused Carter of bringing on the crisis himself. A Rafshoon television commercial that ran incessantly in Iowa showed Carter perusing papers in the Oval Office. A narrator asked: "Do we or do we not support the President as he makes the hard decisions in response to the challenges from Iran and Soviet aggression in Afghanistan?"

Whenever Carter could sneak away from his "perpetual meetings on the hostage crisis," he sat down at a telephone and made fifty calls a night to key Democrats in Iowa, Maine, and New Hampshire. On the desk beside his phone were a pile of 5 × 7 cards filled with typed notes describing the background of every person he called, along with the best approach for assuring support.

Iowa farmers had enjoyed a very good 1979 harvest and price supports remained healthy, so Kennedy's attacks on the economy and his criticism of Carter's Russian grain embargo over the Afghanistan invasion had no real impact. Conversely, the Iranian situation stirred up sympathy for Carter, emotion that was milked by a series of television commercials.

In 1976, about 45,000 Democrats had voted in the primaries. Kennedy hoped for the same kind of turnout, because his organizers had isolated about 30,000 Iowans who promised him their caucus votes. But television worked against him. Whereas in 1976, all five Democratic candidates had spent only $35,000 combined for Iowa television and radio advertising, in 1980 the Carter campaign alone spent $60,000, whereas Kennedy spent $15,000. Rafshoon produced a multifaceted flock of commercials that used Iowa as a test market for various themes.

One commercial series was designed to question Kennedy's honesty, using a standard tag line following Carter speech excerpts on the economy, energy, or defense to drive home the point: "President Carter—he tells you the truth." Others used a variation: "You may not always agree with everything he does, but President Carter is telling the simple truth." Another batch of thirty-second, sixty-second, and five-minute spots featured Carter at the White House, discussing policy with his Cabinet and other officials. Geared to make Carter look hard-working and decisive, one typical commercial showed the President ending a foreign policy discussion with the comment, "I'll make a decision on it today." A third set, created to drum up "continuity of support" for Carter, showcased man-in-the-street interviews with locals who backed Carter in 1976 and proclaimed they would do so again.

Kennedy's advertising was pale by comparison to Rafshoon's barrage. Media specialist Charles Guggenheim had taken over Tony Schwartz's position in mid-December and had few things ready to show. Guggenheim, who had worked three previous Presidential campaigns—for Lyndon Johnson, Hubert Humphrey, and Robert Kennedy—found himself on the defensive from the start. He cited the interview Kennedy gave to KRON-TV in San Francisco as the real backbreaker. One poll found that two out of every three Democrats agreed with the President that Senator Kennedy's statement about the Shah "damaged the country abroad." Explained Guggenheim: "Senator Kennedy's character became the issue then. Television shows like *Face the Nation* focused on that and we were on the defensive."

Carter poked his nose out of hiding only to look Presidential and manipulate free media. On January 20, the day before Iowans went to the polls, Jody Powell set up an appearance on *Meet the Press*, where Carter did not encounter any tough questions about Iran. The net effect was like a paid question-and-answer session.

A record 110,000 Iowa Democrats showed up at the polls on January 21. They chose Carter over Kennedy by almost 2 to 1, 59 to 31 percent. Though the number of delegates tied to each man was negligible—30 for Carter and 15 for Kennedy, with 1,666 needed to win nomination, the press already painted Kennedy as a desperate loser. "Kennedy is up against the ropes and Carter can deliver a knockout blow in New Hampshire," wrote the *Los Angeles Times.* The same message went out over network news and in newspapers all over the land. Campaign contributions dried up. "It's going to be tough now to raise dough," admitted press aide Tom Southwick two days after Iowa.

Kennedy and his advisers went back to the drawing board. With three primaries and a caucus looming in his New England home base over the next few weeks, the press called it do-or-die time for Kennedy.

Forsaking traditional tactics, Kennedy's team also saw New England as do-or-die time and put unholy pressure on themselves to win. The usual strategy is to insist that no single primary or caucus state is crucial, so if you lose you have not decreed your own death knell. In this case, Kennedy painted himself into a corner.

On February 10, Maine Democrats would hold state caucuses. On February 26, New Hampshire would hold the first statewide primary, followed by two more in Vermont and Massachusetts on March 4. Since the Carter team was attacking Steve Smith's candidate mercilessly on "character," family problems, and Chappaquiddick, Smith abandoned his gentlemanly "lack of leadership" theme and decided to play hardball. A major policy speech was scheduled at Georgetown University on January 28. That talk marked the beginning of Kennedy's gloves-off stage. He railed against Carter's handling of the Afghanistan invasion, and broke cleanly from Carter to advocate wage and price controls, profit and interest ceilings, and the rationing of gasoline to combat inflation.

Before leaving the beleaguered campaign, Herb Schmertz decided the best way to handle Chappaquiddick and the character slurs was to meet them head on. "We fought back with personal material," Charles Guggenheim recalled. "We had people talk about Kennedy as a human being, the trials and tragedies he had been through." A half-hour speech filmed in Kennedy's Washington office attacked Carter administration policies. It opened with Kennedy looking directly into the camera, saying, "While I know many will never believe the facts of the tragic events at Chappaquiddick, those facts are the only truth I can tell because that is the way it happened, and I ask only that I be judged on the basic American standards of fairness."

Carter aides Rafshoon and Jordan reportedly chortled over Kennedy's raising the "character" issue himself, magnifying it at a time when it was beginning to fade. Other professional strategists agreed it was an unwise move, as events later in the campaign proved. "Trying to answer something unanswerable is dumb," one said. "They should have let it die by itself." Instead, Guggenheim produced several Chappaquiddick commercials for the Maine caucuses and the New Hampshire primary. Buying $200,000 worth of television time, Smith saturated the airwaves with them.

Ted Kennedy stumped Maine vigorously. A volunteer army of a thousand rang doorbells and manned telephones in a last-ditch effort for the senator. Allard Lowenstein, the New York liberal who drove Lyndon Johnson into retirement and was a key cog in Bobby Kennedy's Presidential try, came to Maine on Ted's behalf. A Carter victory in Maine, Lowenstein warned, could finish the Democratic contest "without a single vote being cast in a single primary." Lowenstein foresaw the potential impact of Maine on the heels of Iowa.

A statewide poll published February 8 in the *Bangor Daily News* showed Carter leading Kennedy 52 to 33 percent. Caddell's polls showed the same split. Complicating Kennedy's efforts was the presence of Jerry Brown, campaigning in Maine as an admitted "spoiler" for Jimmy Carter. Brown's campaign manager, Tom Quinn, predicted that the California governor would pull enough votes from Kennedy to embarrass him and force his early withdrawal from the race, if Brown campaigned hard against draft registration and nuclear power, two Kennedy issues. Carter's campaign staff gave Brown their list of three thousand key party members to call on in a joint effort to defeat Kennedy.

Carter hid at Camp David while Rosalynn, Walter Mondale, and other surrogates worked the state, and Gerald Rafshoon's commercials made Ted Kennedy the issue instead of President

Carter's governing. "You'll never find yourself wondering whether President Carter is telling you the truth," proclaimed a television voice-over. Others boasted that Carter "never panics in a crisis," and several worked the "family" issue: "Jimmy Carter—father, husband, President. He does each job with distinction." A radio commercial urged voters to "stand up for Maine and America by supporting Jimmy Carter," implying that those—like Kennedy—who challenged his policy were less than patriotic. It was vintage Rafshoonery.

When the votes were counted, Carter took 44 percent of the 35,000 who attended the caucuses. Kennedy got 40 percent, and spoiler Brown 14. What should have been a morale-building victory for Kennedy ended in a second defeat as headlines February 11 blazoned: "CARTER WINS IN MAINE."

Ted Kennedy tried to be optimistic: "Four days ago we were nineteen points behind President Carter. Tonight we're in a virtual dead heat with him." But Jody Powell made the most of Kennedy's defeat and at the same time publicly complimented Brown's showing. "If Kennedy can't win in his own backyard, where can he win?" he gloated. "It's a boost for Brown. He got something here and he started from nothing."

Pressure mounted for Kennedy to take New Hampshire on February 26. He made subtle changes in his appearance, cutting his hair short, and giving up the half-rim spectacles that, according to advisers, "made him look like a patriarch." He tried to modulate his booming speaking style, with some success. As polls showed Carter ahead by nearly 2 to 1, Steve Smith pulled campaign workers out of other states and brought them to New Hampshire. According to researchers, continuing doubts about Chappaquiddick accounted for about half the President's lead.

His back to the wall, Kennedy attacked the Iranian hostage issue: "It is a crisis that never should have happened. President Carter has assumed a posture of the high priest of patriotism. The price of war in the Persian Gulf will be a nightly body count of America's children." Carter replied that Kennedy's statements "have not been true, have not been accurate, have not been responsible, and they have not helped our country. Everything I am trying to do is to take peaceful action . . . to prevent the Soviets' taking further steps that might lead to a war."

Kennedy hit at Carter for refusing to debate: "No President who refuses to explain his record and to run on it should regain the office by a base on balls." Carter pledged to stay in the White House: "I am not going to resume business as usual as a partisan campaigner on the campaign trail until our hostages are free and back at home." And Jody Powell made headlines when he called Kennedy "irresponsible, obnoxious, and cynical . . . a spoiled, fat rich kid."

Though Carter enjoyed a public image as a meek, cheek-turning pacifist—and reinforced that picture with timid foreign policy and bumbling forays into international disputes—his pugnacity in political campaigns was undisputed. He was as ruthless a word-slinger as ever occupied the Oval Office. Even top aide Jody Powell noted his mentor's hair-pulling, groin-kicking style by boasting, "He's a mean little son of a bitch, isn't he?"

As anti-Soviet feeling grew on the heels of the Afghanistan invasion, Gerald Rafshoon projected his boss as a born-again hawk, attacking Kennedy for supporting Carter's own military budget cuts. As polls showed Americans growing more militant, Carter commercials emphasized "a strong defense at the top of my priority list."

Other Rafshoon spots quietly probed Kennedy's weak spots with a "doublebacking" approach. Instead of openly charging Kennedy with lying about Chappaquiddick, he used tag lines that made the point by endowing Carter with the opposite, positive trait. The same approach was used to attack Kennedy's home life. One spot showed Carter with his daughter Amy and his wife Rosalynn, all seated in the White House upper floor, while the announcer intoned, "President Carter believes a close-knit family is the greatest asset to the future of America."

Kennedy, meanwhile, was continuing to fight with one hand tied behind him. With money drying up, Steve Smith produced television and radio commercials using in-house volunteers to write copy and an advertising agency to put film together. The results were a disconnected batch of scatter-gun assaults, none up to professional standards. One showed Kennedy on camera attacking Carter for asking the nation to rally around his overseas failures. Another charged that New Hampshire voters paid while oil companies profited, because Jimmy Carter decontrolled the price of oil. In a third, Kennedy explained his stand on handgun control: "I know personally the kind of loss a handgun can inflict."

To counter Carter's criticisms of Kennedy's troubled family life, Smith used film showing scenes of Kennedy's family in Boston and Hyannis. Teddy, Jr., the senator's nineteen-year-old son, appeared before small groups, raising the Chappaquiddick question before it was asked and describing his father's closeness to his wife and children. Kara, his twenty-year-old daughter, spoke of her mother's battle against a drinking problem, and Joan herself appeared on television, giving interviews and making speeches.

Ten days before the vote, Pat Caddell discovered a shift to Kennedy by "doves" worried about Carter's new militant stance. After conferring with Rafshoon, he replaced tough radio spots with softer commercials describing Carter as a "man of peace." A television spot in the making was rushed through production to get it on the New Hampshire airwaves. Called "The Peacemaker," it conjured up the ghost of Abraham Lincoln, recalling his words about America's being "the last, best hope on earth." The next scene showed Jimmy Carter standing between a smiling Anwar Sadat and Menachem Begin, saying, "I would like to say to these two friends of mine, blessed are the peacemakers for they shall be the children of God"—a slight misquote. In a typically heavy-handed Rafshoon touch, the voice-over reminded viewers who may not have gotten the message first time out: "President Jimmy Carter—peacemaker."

Caddell and Rafshoon had outflanked Kennedy by being "flexible," ready to shift position the moment the public mood shifted. In New Hampshire it stopped the erosion of Carter's dove votes, so that on February 26 Carter pulled 49 percent against Kennedy's 38 percent. Jerry Brown, still spoiling things for Kennedy with his antinuke lobby, took 10 percent. Headlines on the evening news trumpeted, "KENNEDY LOSER IN NEW ENGLAND." Newspaper headlines underlined his "loser" status and reporters began wondering in print when Kennedy would drop out. That "loser" tag haunted his efforts and affected his fund-raising fortunes until the New York primary, at the end of March. Until then, he would suffer the indignities of the politically damned.

In the Wyoming caucus on March 1 and the Vermont primary on March 4, Carter overwhelmed Kennedy by 3-to-1 margins. So when Kennedy won his first big victory in his home state, Massachusetts, by 65 to 29 percent, the press was unimpressed. Stories noted he had won reelection to the Senate in 1976 by over a million votes. "The real point," they wrote, "was that President Carter pulled so well in Kennedy's own backyard. Maybe it's time for the youngest Kennedy to call it quits."

March 11. Carter's Solid South began voting with primaries in Alabama, Georgia, and Florida. Alabama and Georgia gave him 82 and 88 percent of their delegates, respectively. Many Florida Democrats decided they would vote for Carter, particularly the black bloc and upstate rednecks. Dade County Jews, on the other hand, supported Kennedy almost 2 to 1 because of his liberal philosophy and strong stand on Israel.

Tim Hanan, who ran Kennedy's campaign in Florida, recalled the brutal pressures there: "The Carter people coopted almost all the recognized black leaders. There was a great deal of political muscle used—promises, favors, threats. I met with black leaders who told me point blank, 'My heart is with Kennedy, but politically I can't afford to risk coming out for you. Either I endorse Carter or I sit on my hands.'"

White House payola was a big factor. "In Miami, a $100-million people mover was held dangling," Hanan said. "Mindful that Chicago Mayor Byrne's calls were not being answered because she supported Kennedy, the Miami politicians were not about to come out for Kennedy and risk blowing their people mover. The same thing happened in Tampa, where the mayor endorsed Carter after the federal government made significant monies available to the city. This happened all over the state. The grand master of political manipulation was Lyndon Johnson, but I never saw anything in Texas, Kansas, Indiana, Pennsylvania, or California to compare with Carter's blatant threats in Florida in 1980."

Hanan tried to combat the machine votes with a media plan he assembled himself. He used volunteers for a telephone survey to get rough readings on which voting blocs were susceptible to a media blitz. "But we couldn't put our media plan into action," he recalled. "The priorities were not in Florida at that point, and the campaign staff wouldn't allocate any money."

One crucial problem he had hoped to solve was a perception about Iran that put Kennedy in a bad light with many south Florida Jews. "In all the Jewish areas—the Gold Coast, Palm Beach, Miami—most Jews saw the Shah as a stabilizing factor in the Middle East and a good friend of Israel," Hanan noted. "When Kennedy attacked the Shah, that was a perfidious act as far as they were concerned, one that put Carter on the right side by default."

Kennedy got only 50 percent of the Jewish vote, and Carter and Brown split the rest. Statewide it meant a big Carter victory, 61 percent to Kennedy's 23 percent, while Brown took 5 percent. Now Carter had 299 delegates to Kennedy's 153, with the big industrial states still to come. Certainly not an overwhelming lead, yet the networks and major newspapers already reported a "bandwagon effect" and wondered aloud when Kennedy would bow to the inevitable.

On March 18 Illinois, the first big industrial state, would allocate 198 Democratic delegates. Infighting had been going on for almost six months and it was brutal. The state's Democratic stronghold in Chicago's Cook County was splintered when Mayor Richard Daley died and was replaced by Jane

Byrne, a Kennedy supporter who antagonized what was left of Daley's machine. After flirting with the idea of supporting Carter, she announced her endorsement of Ted Kennedy in late October. Then she felt the Carter sting.

Carter's self-proclaimed "political arm," Transportation Secretary Neil Goldschmidt, threatened Byrne publicly: "We allocate funds where we have confidence in the local government. I don't feel confident with Mayor Byrne." Carter held back some $50 million in federal grants, froze funds for Chicago's new jetport, and ordered federal harassment at O'Hare International Airport, having inspectors constantly check for "potential hazards."

Byrne's inexperience hurt Kennedy badly. As Kennedy aide Gerrard Doherty described it, she made "an utter mess, foundering badly," of Kennedy's Illinois campaign. She angered old Daley operatives who broke with her openly. Some pledged to support Carter, while others vowed to sit on their hands election day and refused to bring in their votes.

Doherty flew to Chicago late in January and tried to piece together an effective organization in the time remaining. But, even putting the best light on them, prospects seemed gloomy. Early in March Steve Smith and his advisers realized they were in over their heads. If they dropped out, the "quitter" tag would haunt Kennedy the rest of his political career. If they continued blundering along, the humiliating image of a "loser" could easily produce the same result.

It was then that Steve Smith turned to Joe Napolitan for help. Napolitan immediately made several recommendations. He suggested that Smith rehire Tony Schwartz for radio and special communications, and let him work unhampered with a previous Napolitan choice, David Sawyer, retained to do television spots.

With polls showing Carter holding a 3-to-1 lead just twelve days before the vote, Illinois was a lost cause—but Kennedy could shorten the margin by hitting hard on bread-and-butter themes. So for twelve days Kennedy lived in Illinois, making speeches all over Chicago, pounding away at inflation, unemployment, interest rates: "The economy is the issue and Carter is accountable!" he roared. About that time Carter made his "mistake" in the U.N. vote over Israel and the West Bank. Kennedy criticized it strongly, but kept his biggest guns trained on the economy an dthe failures of the Carter administration.

The only commercials in the can were the "personal spots" put together by Herb Schmertz and low-paid technicians on a shoestring budget. With Carter all over the state on television, sniping at Kennedy's "untrustworthiness" and tendency "to panic in a crisis," Smith's only response was to go with what they had—a five-minute film about Kennedy's life sufferings as "the only survivor of four brothers," a sixty-second spot of Ethel praising Ted, and another with Ted and his wife Joan. All were soft and ineffective.

"They tried to produce their own stuff and it was terrible," Joe Napolitan noted. "It was some of the worst I've ever seen, certainly the worst anyone has ever produced for a Presidential candidate." Said another professional: "They raised the character issue themselves. Everybody knows Kennedy doesn't have a good relationship with his wife. Trying to fake it doesn't do it and trying to explain Chappaquiddick just made people think more about it."

While Illinois suffered from Herb Schmertz's "volunteer media," David Sawyer & Associates were signing contracts for the New York and Pennsylvania primaries a few weeks away. A spark of professionalism had finally entered the Kennedy campaign and the results would soon show. But on March 18 Illinois returned its verdict: Carter 65 percent, Kennedy 30 percent. The delegate split was even more painful: 165 for Carter, only 14 for Kennedy. "KENNEDY TO STAY IN DESPITE LOSING STREAK," headlines read. "CAMPAIGN ALMOST BROKE."

Months before the New York primary, Jimmy Carter spent long hours phoning key New York politicians, meeting delegations ranging from upstate assemblymen to Hasidic rabbis, and handing out batches of federal grants and jobs, including a $500,000 study looking into the construction of a third World Trade Center in Harlem and a $10-million "rescue plan" to save Brooklyn Jewish Hospital from bankruptcy.

New York Mayor Ed Koch, an early Carter supporter, sent representatives to the White House bearing a "wish list" of projects Koch wanted funded before the March 25 primary. In February, Carter invited *New York Post* owner Rupert Murdoch to lunch. Three days later Murdoch's paper, the third biggest in the state, formally endorsed Carter for reelection. Six days later the Export-Import Bank granted a Murdoch-owned Australian airline a $290-million low-interest loan.

Clearly, New York was one state Carter aimed to win big. But Charley Guggenheim, the media adviser to Steve Smith, later explained a turn in Kennedy's fortunes just before the New York primary: "As Kennedy hung in and held his head up, defeat after defeat, without folding, people began pulling off the character issue. It began to take second place to economic issues. Then Carter's foreign problems hit with great intensity during the New York and Connecticut primaries."

When Carter waffled over a U.N. vote condemning Israel and tried to save political face by claiming "a mistake in communications," Jewish voters were not the only ones offended. Peter Hart's polls showed large numbers of non-Jewish Americans recoiling from the weak image projected by such Presidential doubletalk. Pat Caddell saw those reactions and urged Rafshoon to fight back. Since Carter would not leave the White House to campaign in New York, Rafshoon called New York to the White House via television cameras.

Four days before New Yorkers voted, Carter appeared in the Map Room for a taped interview with WABC-TV anchorman Roger Sharp. Twenty minutes later Jack Cafferty of WNBC-TV entered for another "exclusive interview" on the U.N. snafu. Fifteen minutes after that Gabe Pressman of WNEW-TV did a third "exclusive," followed ten minutes later by Tim Malloy of WPIX-TV and fifteen minutes after him by Jim Jensen of WCBS-TV. In the space of eighty minutes, the President used "free media" to air his views unchallenged on the five biggest New York television stations, reaching a combined audience of 5 million viewers without setting foot outside the Map Room.

"Free media overwhelms paid media in a Presidential race,"

observed Guggenheim. "A day or two before every primary, Carter announced some news to affect those primaries and there was nothing we could do about it. It was only good for us when the public saw through it and perceived these as political ploys, which was not very often. A Presidential race is covered every night on the network news. By the time we got into a primary state like New York, people there had already been through seven primaries on the national news. Whatever perceptions, good or bad, the free media had established were already in motion. By the time we got there the crops were growing—all we could do was intensify things."

Six days before New Yorkers went to the polls, a Harris poll found Kennedy trailing Carter, 34 to 61 percent. The single most-asked question was, when would Kennedy drop out? His campaign treasury was so low that Kennedy aides were reduced to asking reporters traveling on the campaign bus to pay a ten-dollar fare, whereas two months earlier they had been winging through the skies on chartered jetliners.

Then David Sawyer's advertising began to have an impact. In the space of a forty-eight-hour period, Sawyer put together a series of four commercials focusing on growing public resentment of Carter uncovered by Peter Hart's research. One was called "Comparison." It began with a visual of Jimmy Carter grinning while a voice-over said, "This man has misled the American public into the worst economic crisis since the Depression. He's broken promises and cost New York a billion dollars a year. In his latest foreign policy blunder he betrayed Israel at the United Nations." Then a shot of Ted Kennedy appeared, smiling and shaking hands in a crowd, while the voice-over said: "This man has endured personal attacks in order to lead the fight for specific solutions to our problems, like mandatory wage and price controls to stop inflation, and programs to help the poor and elderly on fixed incomes. Let's fight back, let's join Ted Kennedy in stopping four years of failure."

Another pair of thirty- and sixty-second spots used Carroll O'Connor, television's Archie Bunker, to hit out at the Democratic incumbent. O'Connor, looking directly at the camera, exclaimed, "Friends, I've seen some oddities in my time, both onstage and off, but nothing so odd as Jimmy Carter running in a Democratic primary. He may be the most Republican President since Herbert Hoover. He is responsible for a foreign policy nobody understands, runaway inflation, a dollar that's hardly worth the paper it's printed on, and industrial layoffs all around the country. Meanwhile Jimmy sits in the White House making patriotic pronouncements and warmhearted speeches. I want you to support a man who's been out there facing the issues. I mean my friend Ted Kennedy, a strong leader with a solid record in the Senate of the United States. I trust Ted Kennedy, I believe in him in every way, folks. So let's get out there and support the man who calls for specific programs. Let's join Ted Kennedy and stop four years of failure."

A third spot hit hard at the United Nations foul-up. It showed Kennedy talking at the camera: "Never again should the United States betray its closest allies in the council of world powers. Never again should a President of the United States have to admit he didn't know what was happening in our United Nations votes."

Rafshoon spent over four times as much on television time in New York as Kennedy—$750,000 versus $175,000—and ran a heavy schedule of commercials for three full weeks before the March 25 vote. To mollify Jewish feelings, he prepared several versions of the Camp David accords film. "More than most Presidents, Jimmy Carter has been a peacemaker," one reminded voters. Another featured Mayor Ed Koch endorsing Carter and talking about the U.N. vote: "President Carter is a responsible man who, when he makes a mistake, admits it rather than covering it up." He also replayed his character spots to emphasize his candidate's "trustworthiness" and "truth telling," and used lots of local endorsers such as Connecticut Governor Ella Grasso and New York's Lieutenant Governor Mario Cuomo.

The day before the election, the Harris poll showed that the gap had closed to twenty percentage points. In Connecticut, which held its primary the same day as New York, Carter led by a comfortable twelve points. But the combined effects of advertising and voter antagonism had a startling effect on the outcome. When the votes were tallied the night of March 25, Kennedy had trounced Carter in New York, 59 to 41 percent. The sweep pulled in Connecticut, which gave Kennedy a 47 to 41 percent margin.

The double victory not only reestablished Kennedy as a viable candidate, but stopped the press from badgering him about "dropping out" and opened up contributions from people who had believed his candidacy finished. The fresh money attracted federal matching funds and gave Kennedy's campaign a chance to battle on less uneven terms in the remaining primaries. Still, because of the horrible start, Kennedy trailed Carter in the delegate race almost 1 to 2—385 against 746. Reporters pointed out that to stop Carter, Kennedy would need to win more than 60 percent of the remaining delegates. "Almost impossible," they argued—an assessment affecting the primaries still to come.

Kennedy's strategists had not given much attention to either Wisconsin or Kansas, two primaries scheduled just six days after New York. Early polls had shown them far behind in those states, but with the momentum of the big wins they decided to make a token try. No fresh commercials were cut, but David Sawyer made minor revisions on two spots for limited play in the two states. Stripping in a new tag line for the Carroll O'Connor commercial, they sent that plus the "Comparison" spot to Kennedy's campaign headquarters in Milwaukee and Kansas City. Despite a minuscule budget and sparse campaigning, polls found Kennedy making inroads on Carter's big lead.

Complicating the Wisconsin picture was Jerry Brown, who popped up again. Brown had a budget of $300,000 to spend in Wisconsin, ran half a dozen television commercials incessantly, and scheduled an election eve "television extravaganza" produced by film maker Francis Ford Coppola. Accompanying Brown on his Wisconsin meetings with union heads and farm workers was Cesar Chavez, the leader of the United Farm Workers.

But the Carter team took nothing for granted. At 7:20 a.m. April 1—forty minutes before the polls opened in Wisconsin and Kansas—Carter scheduled an extraordinary prebreakfast press briefing in the Oval Office, covered by all three networks. In it he hailed "as a positive step Iran's decision to consider transferring the American hostages to the Revolutionary Council." The movement, Carter said, indicated definite progress in freeing our embassy captives. It was not until just before the polls closed that night that the "dramatic movement" was found to be mythological. But the ploy had worked. Carter whipped Kennedy in Wisconsin, 56 to 30 percent, with Brown taking 12 percent. In Kansas it was Carter 57, Kennedy 32, and Brown 5 percent. Voters in both states cited "hostage progress" as a major factor in their choice. Kennedy complained bitterly about Carter's toying with the emotions of American voters, but the press maintained remarkable tolerance for the gimmickry that helped Jimmy Carter throughout his 1980 campaign.

Approaching the Pennsylvania primary, Carter held his 2-to-1 lead in delegates, 887 to 457. Reporters continued to focus on the "impossible Kennedy dream," pointing out that Kennedy needed to take 75 percent of the remaining delegates to beat the President. Even as the mathematics mocked Kennedy, popular sentiment began swinging his way. In mid-March Carter led Kennedy by 25 points, but ten days before the vote it was too close to call. Peter Broer of David Sawyer & Associates described the changing mood: "Both campaigns saw the same swing. Kennedy's positive was growing in the polls. After a long period of judging him on Chappaquiddick, people felt he had endured the fire, was a pretty plucky guy, and they believed in what he was doing."

A New York firm called Kennan Research did studies for Sawyer using Pennsylvania focus groups. This technique involves intense probing of twelve to fifteen voters in several geographic areas. Led by trained psychologists, the sessions uncover underlying feelings which are then used to structure campaign themes and advertising messages. In Pennsylvania the studies revealed two major concerns, one obvious, the other more subtle. Not surprisingly, people were scared to death over inflation, but paradoxically they had trouble blaming Jimmy Carter for their problems, because "he smiles a lot and is perceived as a nice, if incompetent, guy."

The image drawn by the focus participants drew a parallel between the nation and a grocery store. In this scenario Jimmy Carter was a store manager who smiled at the customers very sweetly on their way in and out the door. Inside, the shelves were not stocked, things were hard to find, and the prices were too high, but it was hard to get mad at him because of his smile that said, "here's a kind, foolish, but pleasant guy."

That perception had profound effects on campaign strategy. "That meant you couldn't come out and accuse Carter of lying or breaking promises," explained Kennedy's media man. "Even when you could document where he had not been up front, you couldn't come right out and say so. If you did, people would resent it."

Instead of focusing on Carter's broken promises and lies, Kennedy strategists decided to attack him simply as a President who couldn't govern. The paradox cut both ways: on the one hand, Kennedy was perceived as a man who could get things done but was not to be trusted; on the other, Carter was someone people trusted, but who couldn't get anything done. So Sawyer had Kennedy make a series of speeches detailing specific programs to solve problems in energy, inflation, and unemployment, while keeping the supersensitive hostage situation at arm's length. The strategy was to develop a clear sense of issues, so voters would have real reasons to back Kennedy. Lacking this kind of consensus, people would revert to the "trust" issue—even if Carter was ruining the economy, at least he was a "nice guy."

To go with the hard-hitting Carroll O'Connor and "Comparison" spots, the Sawyer people created a new commercial for Pennsylvania. It combined an attack against Carter's mismanagement with subtle mockery of his self-publicized piety and frequent references to "praying for the hostages." They called it "Fingers Crossed." The visual showed Jimmy Carter batting in a softball game. As the first pitch floated across the plate, Carter watched it go by without swinging. The narrator said, "When it came to the economy, this man's attitude was, 'I'll keep my fingers crossed.' And the result was inflation, the highest of any administration in American history." When another pitch floated across the plate, Carter watched without taking the bat off his shoulder. The voice-over continued, "On housing, interest rates, even foreign affairs, his attitude was, 'I'll keep my fingers crossed.'" Then a clip of Kennedy filled the screen. "We have a choice," the narrator concluded. "We can choose a man who will do the job—or we can keep our fingers crossed."

Caddell and other researchers found that most Americans believed Carter had been too soft in dealing with Iran and Russia, that in fact he was a weak leader. So on April 7 Carter called a press conference and announced that he was breaking off diplomatic relations and imposing sanctions against Iran— five months after they imprisoned the Americans. A top Carter campaign adviser told the *Los Angeles Times* that the move was made more to affect voters in upcoming primaries than in any real hope it would help the hostages.

The public had grown tired and cynical of Carter's repeated scolding of opponents who challenged his foreign policies. People no longer believed that such criticism either "endangered sensitive negotiations in progress" or "damaged America overseas." Pressure mounted inside his campaign for Carter to abandon the Rose Garden and campaign openly.

A few days before the election, Kennedy's chances got an unexpected boost. Gwendolyn Kopechne, mother of Mary Jo Kopechne, told a Pittsburgh reporter that she would vote for Ted Kennedy over Jimmy Carter in this primary. At a time when the "character" issue was fading, the highly publicized quote added a "forgiveness" factor to the equation.

In the final days Carter campaigned in Pennsylvania from the White House, claiming to radio and television reporters that Kennedy "is the biggest spender in the history of the United States Senate." With the tide turning, Rafshoon launched attacks rougher than anything he had done before. Most effective were man-in-the-street commercials using quotes from ordinary people to remind voters of what Caddell's research showed they liked least about Kennedy.

The technique used a series of quick cuts, from a housewife saying, "I don't think Kennedy has credibility," to a worker's "He's too liberal," then to a student complaining, "Kennedy would be a big spender of other people's money," then an old woman announcing, "I just don't believe him," and a family man saying, "I don't trust him." One version using four blacks to praise Carter was targeted for shows with large black audiences to shore up wavering support in black communities.

In an effort to knock Kennedy out by a decisive defeat in Pennsylvania, Rafshoon spent $750,000 there against Kennedy's $300,000. "They were counting on Kennedy's dropping out of the race earlier," Kennedy's media man explained. "They were anxious to stop him because Carter was approaching his spending limit. Having overspent the early primaries, they ran into problems in the later ones." Kennedy made up for his own lack of money by stumping the state for fourteen days, taunting Carter for hiding in the White House, and criticizing Carter's failures in the economy and foreign policy. Carter retaliated with payola, giving a $2.2-million grant to Philadelphia to establish an American shoe center.

The day before Pennsylvanians voted, Peter Hart's polls showed the race very close. The unusual factor was the large number of undecideds, about 25 percent. "I can't remember a vote with such a high percentage of undecideds," noted a Sawyer spokesman. "Carter put out some very tough ads, so you had a Democratic electorate saying, 'Jesus, it's a muscling match.' Lacking real, positive reasons to go for somebody, they stayed in the middle."

On April 22 the Pennsylvanians voted: 46 percent backed Kennedy and 45 percent Carter. Narrow though it was, Kennedy proclaimed victory and the taste was sweet. Overlooked in the hoopla, however, was the fact that Carter had quietly gained large blocs of delegates in caucus states between April 17 and 20. Carter had added 172 delegates from Iowa, Minnesota, Mississippi, Oklahoma, Virginia, and his share of the

Pennsylvania allotment. Kennedy had added only 120 delegates.

A Lou Harris poll released in mid-April confirmed Caddell's findings that Americans were fed up with nightly scenes of frenzied Iranians shaking their fists at Uncle Sam, while American citizens trembled fearfully in their embassy prison. On April 24 President Carter gave the go-ahead for a contingency rescue operation. It failed.

Predictably, the media treated the incumbent with sympathy. So did the viewing public. While Carter's image of incompetence was reinforced, his level of support increased, carrying him to victories. In May Indiana, Tennessee, North Carolina, Texas, and Oregon all rewarded him pluralities of 2 to 1 or better over Ted Kennedy in their primaries. Carter took Maryland 47 to 32 percent. His only loss came in Washington, D.C., where black voters gave Kennedy 62 percent to Carter's 37.

Approaching the final primary day, June 3, Carter had amassed over fifteen hundred delegates to Kennedy's eight hundred. Kennedy needed 86 percent of all votes cast in the eight-state extravaganza of "Super Tuesday" to keep Carter from locking up the nomination.

For his big final effort in New Jersey, Ohio, and California, Kennedy's media people produced new commercials accentuating the positive. A series of thirty-second television spots sold Ted Kennedy as a "positive alternative to Jimmy Carter"—a more compassionate man than Carter, with a better record of social reform. "It's up to you," the narrator pointed out. "With the country's future at stake, there's only one choice—Kennedy for President." In California they hit harder. Carroll O'Connor cut a new thirty-second television spot that reduced the Carter Presidency to a formula for disaster: "Carter equals Reagan equals Hoover equals depression."

A classic Tony Schwartz radio commercial measured Carter's performance by a multiple-choice test. A calm-voiced narrator began matter-of-factly:

"I'd like to ask you questions about Jimmy Carter. I'll ask

the questions and then I'll give you four possible answers. Okay? Let's begin. What kind of job do you think he's been doing as President? Excellent? Good? Fair? Poor? All right. Now how would you rate Jimmy Carter's handling of unemployment? Excellent? Good? Fair? Poor? How would you rate his handling of the economy? You know—inflation, prices, interest rates, things like that. Excellent? Good? Fair? Poor? Think of your answers, and if your answers are like most people's, how can you possibly think of voting for Jimmy Carter again?"

For the first time, Kennedy was able to outspend Carter in a big state primary, budgeting $200,000 for California against Carter's $150,000. Rafshoon created no new material for "Super Tuesday." Instead he replayed man-in-the-street spots hitting Kennedy as a "big spender," and town-meeting segments portraying Carter as a peacemaker and family man.

Caddell polls showed that Carter's best chance was in Ohio, so Rafshoon bought $150,000 in air time for the buckeye state. His candidate used federal funds to convince Ohio politicians he was their man. In a single day Carter awarded an $829,000 community block grant, three summer youth recreation awards, and a federal grant to a local college in Cleveland. He gave Cincinnati $1.4 million to convert the train depot into a shopping mall and gave $50 million for recession relief to hard-hit Youngstown, which had closed down its steel plants.

Even as Kennedy's fortunes turned, the mathematics strangled his chances. Reading the writing on the wall, the senator's backers substituted dreams for possibilities. "June 3 is not the goal line," Steve Smith said. "The goal line is the convention."

Theorizing that delegates pledged to Jimmy Carter could be persuaded to switch sides before the August convention, they argued that circumstances since the first February primaries had changed so markedly that Carter could not win the general election. The shadow of Ronald Reagan's quixotic 1976 convention fight began to loom over Ted Kennedy as voters cast ballots on June 3.

The results confirmed that the Democratic mood had indeed shifted since the Iowa caucus. Kennedy won resounding victories in California, New Jersey, New Mexico, Rhode Island, and South Dakota, capturing 383 delegates. Carter won only West Virginia, Montana, and Ohio, but with extra caucus delegates to buffer his losses, he added 381 delegates to his total. After eight months of battling through thirty-four state primaries, Carter had won twenty-four, Kennedy ten, and most of Kennedy's were won in the last two months. Carter had 1,764 delegates and Kennedy 1,139. The incumbent had gone over the top. His nomination was a mere formality.

But the popular vote showed a less clear-cut endorsement. Carter had attracted 10 million votes to Kennedy's 7.3 million. Many people had the distinct feeling that if the race could be run again, the outcome would be different. While Kennedy's people licked their wounds bitterly and complained of Carter's "groin punching" in the primaries, Kennedy vowed to fight Carter's renomination right down to the convention floor.

But the pros knew it was all over. Any Presidential dreams Kennedy still entertained would have to wait until 1984. Among the insiders who had watched his campaign closely, the consensus was that Kennedy had no one to blame but himself. Joe Napolitan, who had helped the other Kennedy brothers win office, had tried to do the same for Ted but was shunted aside early, when he would have made the most difference. In a dispassionate post-mortem, he discussed the tactical mistakes in Kennedy's ill-fated campaign.

"There were people around Ted Kennedy who, because early polls showed him way ahead, figured, 'We don't need the people who helped Bobby and Jack—we can do this one on our own and show our independence from those people.' Whether from ego or simply from inexperience, they did not do the things they should have done. Early on, I sent a series of memos to Steve Smith outlining things that should have been done. They weren't.

"First, he violated one of the cardinal rules of announcing: you don't announce until you're ready. And he wasn't ready. They hadn't done any research to find out just how damaging Chappaquiddick would be. They didn't hire a pollster until a full month after they announced. There was no reason to announce in November. If he had wanted to announce then, he should have started assembling his campaign team in July, done the research, and put it all together. If he had delayed, he would have avoided the trap on the hostage situation which broke a few days after he announced and really screwed things up.

"They had no real media direction and didn't hire a good film producer at the beginning. Early in the primary they tried to produce their own commercials and turned out the worst stuff I've ever seen. By the time they did get somebody in, they didn't allocate enough money for production or time-buying. They wasted lots of money early in the campaign on crazy chartered planes and stuff they didn't need, spending hundreds of thousands on frills. There was a hell of a lot of talent floating around who, because of friendship or family obligation, would have been glad to help. But they didn't get called in until it was too late. The whole campaign was just run poorly. By the time Kennedy recovered, he was so far behind he didn't have a chance to catch up.

"In the end, Kennedy lost because his campaign was ill-conceived, ill-planned, and ill-timed. It was pathetic."

8

How Reagan Won

A few months after Ronald Reagan lost the 1976 Republican nomination to Gerald Ford, there was a political seminar at Perino's Restaurant in Los Angeles. Long-time Reagan aide Lyn Nofziger cohosted. Established by veteran consultant Hal Evry, the annual get-together featured a discussion of recent elections and new campaign techniques. It was attended by a hundred would-be candidates, politicians reaching for higher office, and young consultants seeking new tools.

On this occasion Evry and Nofziger formulated for the first time in a public forum what Evry calls his "invisible" campaign ploy: setting up a public-action organization headed by a candidate several years before the target election. This maneuver gives the contender a seemingly legitimate platform from which to make public statements, and helps offset the incumbent who easily gets instant press coverage.

After the seminar, Evry and Nofziger sat down over a drink and talked about setting up such an organization for Ronald Reagan. Evry suggested a name: Citizens for the Republic. Inside a week, bankrolled by the one million dollars left over from Reagan's 1976 Presidential try, Nofziger had the association in place. He ordered letterhead and brochures, got prominent Reagan boosters to act as advisers, and began filling a speaking schedule for the newly chosen president of Citizens for the Republic. By 1978, the organization was so wealthy it gave more money to more candidates than any nonbusiness political-action committee in the nation. More important, it was Ronald Reagan's launching pad to the White House.

Nofziger, once a political writer for the Copley newspapers, was, besides Stu Spencer, the only aide who had been with Reagan from the start of his 1966 gubernatorial campaign. During Reagan's first years in Sacramento he served as press secretary. He later worked in the Nixon White House and ran Nixon's California campaign organization in 1972.

After years of devoted service, Nofziger fell victim to a power struggle, much as Stu Spencer had earlier with Reagan's Sacramento "Palace Guard," Mike Deaver and Peter Hannaford. The chief bone of contention was how to present Reagan's case to the electorate. When polls showed Reagan far ahead of all other GOP contenders, Reagan's chief strategist John Sears decided the time had come to moderate Reagan's conservative image and make it more palatable to other Republican factions. Nofziger disagreed vehemently, arguing that the climate of opinion would not favor compromise. Reagan, Nofziger insisted, had risen to prominence by speaking his mind forthrightly; to muzzle him now would only alienate loyal supporters. Sears's view, he contended, was a gross misreading of shifting public sentiment. Nofziger lost the argument and was dropped from the Reagan high command in the summer of 1979, just as planning for the 1980 campaign was entering its crucial phase.

So in 1979 Reagan began the process of softening his image. By "fuzzing over" Reagan's conservative beliefs, Sears hoped to move him closer to the ideological center where most Americans are generally found. Reagan stumped the early primary states, shuffling through a set of 3 x 5 cards that elaborated safe themes: "a strong family, a strong economy, a strong nation"—sentiments that even the most ardent liberal would find hard to fault.

Reagan's appeal was personal, enhanced by the movie-star charisma that had carried him to two runaway wins as governor and a near victory in the 1976 Republican primaries. He would turn sixty-nine in February 1980, but he didn't look it. Fixing fences around his Santa Barbara ranch and daily workouts on his Exercycle kept him trim and athletic.

In December the polls showed Reagan was the choice of some 50 percent of Iowa Republicans, the remainder spread safely across half a dozen also-rans. With a "cattle call" debate coming up in Des Moines January 5, Sears decided the best strategy was to stay away and not diminish Reagan's stature by having him show up with the others. This move proved a mistake. Although the debate did little to raise the level of political consciousness in Iowa, Reagan's absence made headlines and sparked resentment from hard-core Iowa Republicans, who felt the Californian didn't care about their votes. The press furor that followed compounded the injury, as pre-election readings showed.

Meanwhile, former CIA director George Bush, borrowing strategy from Jimmy Carter, began to organize his bid for Iowa ten months before the January 21 caucus. He visited the state fifty times, pumping hands and winning friends. He worked the first primary state of New Hampshire with equal intensity. His plan was to show early strength, steal some of Reagan's national media coverage, and ride momentum to a dark-horse victory.

Bush's strategist James Baker and media man Robert Goodman saw their candidate as a marriage of Kennedyesque spirit and moderated Reaganite views. "Our first commercials were uplifting and Presidential," Goodman explained. "Bush was the candidate of optimism, a buoyant decade-of-the-eighties spirit, a young man with solid credentials who could really get things done." Goodman pieced together commercials showing Bush surrounded by cheering crowds and promising, "We can turn this country around!" A short biography included snapshots of Bush during World War II, Bush playing baseball at Yale, and Bush as the U.S. Ambassador "who secured our China initiative." In all his paid media spots, a tag line attacked President Carter on the grounds of incompetence: "George Bush, a President we won't have to train."

Overconfident because of flattering polls and the experienced Reagan campaign machine, John Sears designed his media spots for "statesman" appeal. His main worry was countering the charge that his candidate was too old for the Presidency. His New York advertising agency, the Clyne Company, produced a series of television commercials aimed at refuting that charge. They projected a "fatherly" Reagan image, while ostensibly attacking other problems. A typical spot featured a gymnasium where a group of preteen children played. Reagan put his arms around a young boy and girl, then asked the camera somberly, "If inflation keeps growing the way it has the past three years, what will happen to our kids? If we go on as we are, these youngsters here will have to pay over seventy thousand dollars for a college education."

Bush spent $26,000 for Iowa television time. A cocky Sears spent only $6,000 for Reagan. On election eve George Bush was a guest on a talk show in Des Moines. Ronald Reagan was back home in Santa Barbara with friends, watching a private screening of *Kramer vs. Kramer*.

The election results were a shock for Reagan: George Bush got 31 percent of the vote, Reagan just 26 percent. Far behind in third place was Howard Baker at 13 percent, followed by four others, including John Anderson with an unimpressive 4 percent.

"This is the beginning of the end for Reagan," proclaimed a triumphant George Bush as he left to campaign in New Hampshire. Instead, it marked the beginning of the end for John Sears. Though it would not be announced for another month, Sears was on his way out, along with organizational director Charles Black and press secretary James Lake. As the New Hampshire primary approached, Reagan sought the campaign team of tried-and-true Californians that had brought him nothing but victories before John Sears. Out came the old 3 x 5 cards comprising "The Speech," a hard-hitting array of facts and case histories advocating tax cuts, a big military buildup, less bureaucracy in government, and the elimination of welfare abuse. The "new" Ronald Reagan died in Iowa, and the old was reborn. Come hell or high water, Ronald Reagan would stand or fall on the beliefs that had been his trademark for over two decades.

Reagan did not announce the changes in his campaign team until after the New Hampshire primary. The reorganization of his inner circle was quietly carried out with controlled urgency. Ed Meese, a San Diego lawyer who had worked in Sacramento as Governor Reagan's chief of staff, was promoted from backstage issues adviser to campaign administrator and media mouthpiece.

Meese was indirectly responsible for John Sears's fall from power. As chief strategist, Sears had forced out all but one of the old California Reaganites. He overstepped his bounds when he tried to fire Meese, a final indignity that Nancy Reagan found intolerable. Tapped to replace Sears as campaign manager was New York lawyer William J. Casey, former head of the Securities and Exchange Commission, a moderate Republican and a supporter of Ford in 1976.

A key addition to the Reagan team was Richard Wirthlin of Decision Making Information, based in Santa Ana, California. He was the researcher who had come to prominence as Stu Spencer's protégé during Reagan's first term as governor. In 1968 Dr. Wirthlin was a thirty-eight-year-old professor of economics and survey research at Brigham Young University and a respected Republican pollster. When Spencer called him to research Reagan's successful 1970 reelection campaign for governor, Wirthlin began accumulating the mass of correlations he calls PINS, or Political Information System. By storing voter traits and political-behavior patterns in a computer bank, Wirthlin extracts relationships that are not readily apparent, insights that prove useful in planning strategy and advertising assaults. For example, using this technique he discovered that people over sixty-five with incomes of $25,000 or more were heavy backers of Ronald Reagan and tended to vote in larger concentrations than other groups—87 percent versus the national average of just 54 percent in Presidential elections.

"It's not a lack of information that's a problem in a campaign," Wirthlin explained. "It's having too much information, usually in a form that doesn't make sense. A political data bank gives order, coherence, and accessibility to that information."

Wirthlin's information system enables him not only to pinpoint clusters of potentially favorable voters and to identify the opposition, but also to gauge trends in individual cities, states, and regions. It is also set up to run "simulation model-ing," that is, to predict voter reactions to various political, economic, or media events. Simulation tests were to play a key role late in the 1980 Presidential campaign.

Another Wirthlin contribution was a tool called "tracking," which involves taking frequent polls before and after cam-paign events or advertising to measure voter response. "Track-ing a campaign allows you to watch it almost the same way you watch a movie," Wirthlin said. First used in Reagan's 1970 effort, tracking has now become a standard part of most mod-ern campaigns.

Stu Spencer quickly recognized the genius of Wirthlin's research and established DMI in 1969 as a subsidiary of Datamatics, a research firm he already owned. Wirthlin man-aged the new polling company and in 1973, after a power struggle, bought Spencer's interest in it. Today DMI has fifty full-time employees and grosses $3 million a year. Much of their earnings come from nonpolitical clients such as Sears Roebuck, Standard Oil, and Coors Brewing, but Wirthlin's first love is campaigning. For him, joining Reagan's 1980 drive for the Presidency was a dream come true.

Another addition to the Reagan campaign team just before the New Hampshire primary was a young Philadelphia adman named Elliott Curson, who replaced Sears's Clyne Company. While the secret new brain trust agonized over tactics and polls, Curson went about his job independently. Without bene-fit of polling data, he visited the Reagan Library at Stanford, extracted quotes, and drafted short scripts for a batch of com-mercials. The next week he was in Los Angeles with Reagan, and in a single day cut eleven commercials that would run continuously through the Wisconsin primary—no mean ac-complishment.

Originally, Reagan had approached the primaries as a mere formality. After all, just four years earlier he had come within a hair's breadth of beating out incumbent President Gerald Ford as his party's standard-bearer. In the process, he had demonstrated his power to attract grass-roots votes. His popu-

larity had broadened considerably in his three years as spokesman for Citizens for the Republic.

That was why the Iowa defeat was so shocking—just the
kind of jolt needed to destroy complacency. Preparing for New
Hampshire, Reagan's advisory team left nothing to chance.
Back in 1976, research had uncovered the fact that Reagan's
appeal was more pronounced among independents and maverick Republicans than among hard-core party regulars. So
Reagan's New England coordinator, Gerald Carmen, organized a televised debate between Reagan and Bush sponsored by the *Nashua Telegraph*, to woo the support of hard-
core New Hampshire Republicans. Having learned his lesson
in Iowa, naturally Reagan would participate. This time Carmen planned a surprise for George Bush—the "solidarity
ploy."

When the sponsoring newspaper was prevented from paying
expenses for the debate because of a legal technicality, Reagan's treasury assumed the nominal two-hundred-dollar cost
—an investment that would prove its worth. Then a few hours
before the debate, Reagan invited the four other Republican
candidates to appear with him on the platform. When George
Bush arrived fifteen minutes before the scheduled start to find
the stage filled with the other contenders, he objected vigorously and with justification about the ground rules' being
changed in the middle of the game. Reagan argued just as
vehemently for the right of the others to participate. "I'm paying for this microphone, dammit," he yelled angrily. After a ten-
minute wrangle, the superfluous Republicans cleared the stage
and the moderator announced a compromise: they would be
allowed to address the audience once the two front-runners
had finished their encounter. So the Reagan-Bush debate went
on as scheduled, with no clear-cut winner or loser immediately
evident. But Carmen's ploy made Bush appear an "outsider,"
while Reagan played the insider role of good guy fighting for
party unity.

The week before the debate, most statewide polls showed
the race between Reagan and Bush as too close to call. New
Hampshire voters pronounced their verdict on the Tuesday

following the Saturday night debate. By a devastating 50 to 23 percent margin, they declared Ronald Reagan the winner. Virtually overnight Reagan regained a lead that he would not relinquish again.

Overshadowed by the debate was the impact of Elliott Curson's television commercials. Particularly effective in New Hampshire were those advocating tax cuts. When the voters of New Hampshire were asked why they supported Reagan, many mentioned his promised tax slashes. The effective Curson television spot on this issue began with cutaway newspaper headlines decrying rampaging inflation and mounting interest rates. A voice-over broke in: "It's a fact that whenever you tax something, you get less of it." Ronald Reagan's face then filled the screen. "I didn't always agree with President Kennedy," he said, "but when his 30-percent federal tax cut became law, the economy did so well that every group in the country came out ahead. Even the government gained $54 billion in unexpected revenues. If I become President, we're going to try that again."

Elliott Curson described his approach to the Reagan candidacy as a "nonbullshit" technique. "You know what they say about conservatives," he told me. "What they say is right, only they say it offensively. Well, I just presented it straight, without the bullshit. What Ronald Reagan supported for so many years is now fashionable. We didn't try to win any Academy Awards, hide him on his ranch, or do funny commercials with helicopters and fancy music. Our advertising was straightforward, all issues."

Stu Spencer calls Reagan "the greatest television candidate in American history." Without rehearsing, Reagan can make the most commonplace thought seem significant. He has a good ear for effective speech, and edits until phrases sound just right. Curson took full advantage of his candidate's natural stage presence.

There were eleven commercials in the entire primary package, all thirty-second spots using a repeating format: first a narrator made an opening statement, then Ronald Reagan came on to do the rest. Curson's "Leadership" spot had Reagan exclaim, "I'm tired of hearing the American people blamed for the failures of government. It's time Washington had a government that stopped complaining and started performing." Curson's "Foreign Policy" presentation was classic in its simplicity and power. A Moscow May Day parade was screened, showing Brezhnev saluting from a viewing platform while giant missiles rode past. A voice-over noted, "Ronald Reagan spoke out on the danger of the Soviet arms buildup long before it was fashionable." Cut to Reagan: "We've learned by now it isn't weakness that keeps the peace, it's strength. Our foreign policy has been based on the fear of not being liked. Well, it's nice to be liked—but it's more important to be respected."

One big question raised by the press and opponents alike was how Reagan's age might affect his potential Presidency. Curson didn't try to disguise Reagan's age on camera. Instead, he showed his candidate up close and in full face. "By being up front about it, we just obliterated any age issue. Once you see Reagan you're apt to say, how can that man be considered old?"

New England, March 4. Reagan was surprised by the strong showing of John Anderson. Though Anderson did not win either Massachusetts or Vermont, he came closer than anyone expected. In Massachusetts, Anderson lost to Bush by only a fraction of a percentage point, each pulling 31 percent of the vote while Reagan got only 29. In Vermont, Anderson took 30 percent, just behind Reagan's winning 31 percent and comfortably ahead of Bush's third-place 23 percent.

Anderson's showing attracted a new surge of contributions and raised hopes of winning big in his home state of Illinois on March 18. He bet all his money on one roll of the dice, earmarking $200,000 for radio, television, and newspaper advertising to blitz the state the week before Illinois voters went to the ballot box. "You've got to believe" became more than John Anderson's slogan—it was his prayer of affirmation.

In early March, television and newspaper reports hinted that Gerald Ford might enter the primary contests by April 1. As Reagan looked virtually unbeatable, the former President cautiously only floated trial balloons, soliciting "signals of support" from his party's moderate opinion leaders. Ford based his candidacy on the argument that moderates always use against conservatives—that Ronald Reagan could never prevail in the general election. He cited polls, including one by Pat Caddell, which showed that the toughest Republican for Jimmy Carter to beat would be Gerald Ford. The fact that Ford had been President himself would rob Carter of the incumbency advantage he had used to demolish Ted Kennedy and would presumably employ with equal ferocity against Ronald Reagan. Stu Spencer publicly announced that he was ready to run the new Ford campaign if it materialized.

The development created a media furor. Rumors flew that Ford's motives were less than noble. "He wants a grudge match," a former aide observed. "He'd like to nail Reagan because Reagan didn't campaign for him in the fall of 1976."

Spencer set March 19 as the last day a Ford entry would have any chance at all of carrying the nominating fight to the convention floor. Spencer emphasized that Ford needed public signals of support from party leaders all across the country before he would actually file. Such pronouncements would have to come from governors, U.S. senators, and Republican Presidential candidates who would offer to leave the race and back Ford. "The man's been around politics for thirty years," Spencer pointed out. "He knows the difference between cloakroom talk, quiet conversation, and public pronouncements of support."

Henry Kissinger visited Ford's Rancho Mirage home in California and emerged publicly urging Ford to throw his hat in the ring. John Sears, fresh from the Reagan camp, met with the former President and also urged him to challenge Reagan. But mathematics were against Ford, the number of outstanding delegates being too few for his last-minute candidacy to have any chance of succeeding. Ford abandoned the idea of seeking the nomination. But, forever the optimist, he didn't close all doors behind him—if the convention became deadlocked, he would be available.

The Reagan juggernaut rolled over George Bush in the next seven primaries. With "Reagan Country" primaries in Western,

Plains, and Mountain states still to come, even die-hard Republican moderates privately conceded that Ronald Reagan would head the ticket. By April 1 Reagan had 343 delegates, Bush 72, and John Anderson only 52. Anderson had lost his home state to Reagan 48 to 37 percent. For the first time Anderson began talking about mounting an independent campaign for the White House.

Reagan campaign strategists were already living in the future. A confidential memo from Richard Wirthlin, dated March 28, said it all: "With over a third of the 998 delegate votes needed to nominate now locked into the governor's column, and with his best primary states starting to come up on the primary calendar, the general election campaign, from our point of view, starts today."

In early April Stu Spencer got a call at his Newport Beach office from Mike Deaver. Deaver, one of Reagan's old Palace Guard, had been ousted from Reagan's inner circle by a Sears power play. Spencer and Deaver had made their peace in January, so it was no great surprise when Deaver phoned. What Deaver said, though, was altogether unexpected: Deaver had been asked to rejoin the Reagan campaign. The Reagans and Richard Wirthlin were determined to reassemble his old team in good time for the general election, and Deaver wondered how Spencer felt about working for the Reagans again. With his unhealed wounds still smarting, Spencer replied that he wasn't interested. When Deaver hung up, Spencer was sure he had heard the last of the reunion effort.

As Pennsylvanians prepared to vote in their primary April 22, Reagan already had 457 of his 998 required delegates, Bush 72, and Anderson 56. Despite his underdog role, Bush gamely observed the unspoken party injunction—not to speak ill of any Republican, particularly Ronald Reagan, with whom he wanted to maintain cordial relations. Though he denied it publicly, Bush recognized that the best he could hope for was the second spot on a Reagan ticket.

Just before the Pennsylvania vote, I spoke to Bush's media man, Bob Goodman. Goodman acknowledged the tough role his candidate had to play: pretend that the immediate enemy was Carter, when in fact his was Reagan. "Carter must be the issue," Goodman stressed. "Our new spots will show George outside the White House giving Carter hell about inflation, unemployment, and Iran."

Though Bush won a narrow victory in Pennsylvania—51 to 44 percent—Reagan added a large bloc of caucus delegates to his total. By the end of the day he had gained sixty-four more delegates to Bush's thirty-three and, even as the press bally-hooed Bush's "impressive win," most insiders expected the governor to have it all wrapped up before "Super Tuesday," June 3.

On April 24 two events took place almost simultaneously that would have considerable impact on the race for the 1980 Presidency. That morning eight helicopters rose from the decks of the carrier *Nimitz* in the Indian Ocean and headed toward Iran, in an attempt to free the American hostages in Teheran. Hours later two of the choppers crashed, another turned back disabled, a C-130 transport plane burned on the ground in Iran, and eight U.S. servicemen died before the mission was aborted. The following day President Carter went on television to tell Americans these sad particulars.

Then, on the evening of that same April 24, John Anderson announced he was giving up his struggle to win the Republican Presidential nomination. Instead, he would challenge history and both major parties by seeking the Presidency as an independent candidate. "This is not an assault on the system, it's a challenge," he declared. When asked whether he enjoyed the role of spoiler, he replied, "What's to spoil? Spoil the chances of two men at least half the country doesn't want?" He was pinning his hopes on the "Anderson difference," a factor that would scramble both Carter's and Reagan's strategies for the rest of the campaign.

Early May. Richard Wirthlin invited Spencer to his Santa Ana office for a meeting. Mike Deaver was there and the three men talked political strategy for a campaign plan that Wirthlin was putting together. Then Wirthlin and Deaver came to the point and asked Spencer to help run Reagan's campaign against Jimmy Carter. With the nomination locked up, Reagan was eager to arrange things for the general election.

Spencer asked tough questions about lines of responsibility and authority in the campaign management. "I wanted to know whether I would be responsible to an individual or a committee," he recalled. "I sure wasn't interested in working for a committee."

Wirthlin promised to pass the word and let Spencer know. The feedback from the new Reagan high command was equivocal. "Spencer has cleared some hurdles but not all," one insider reported. "The problem isn't with the governor. He'd be glad to have him back."

Without the independence he demanded, Spencer assumed this was one campaign he would watch from the outside. So he concentrated on work at hand and followed events in the newspapers. Then just before the last primary day, Mike Deaver approached Spencer again. "He seemed a lot more serious this time," Spencer noted. "I told him I'd think about it while I was in Oregon."

While setting up a campaign in the Pacific Northwest, Spencer got a call from William Casey, who also urged him to come aboard. Casey told him Lyn Nofziger was returning for the Presidential battle. Spencer would be the only holdout from Reagan's old brain trust. The pull was strong, but Spencer still had reservations. Then Bill Timmons, Reagan's new political director, put on the heat. If Spencer joined them, he would be answerable to only one man—Bill Timmons himself. His resolve weakening, Spencer put Timmons off, promising to think about it.

In the web of communications that decides what is news, particularly political news, big-name campaign consultants loom larger and larger. In mid-May John Anderson took a giant step toward changing his status from cantankerous loser and "spoiler" to serious independent challenging the candidates of both major parties, when he announced that management and strategic decisions for his campaign would henceforth be handled by David Garth. Though Garth had never worked on a Presidential campaign before, he was no novice at high-stakes electioneering. His winning clients included Mayors Tom Bradley of Los Angeles, John Lindsay and Ed Koch of New York, Governors Hugh Carey of New York and Brendan Byrne of New Jersey, U.S. Senators Adlai Stevenson of Illinois and H. John Heinz III of Pennsylvania, and President Luis Herrera Campis of Venezuela.

"In a political campaign, you fight all the way," Garth observed. "And the last thing you do is tear your leg off and hit the other guy over the head." Garth's professional style is characterized by similar ferocity. One of his clients described his sledgehammer approach: "Garth stands back, finds out where his guy or the other guy is most vulnerable—then hits like a ton of bricks."

Garth's television material shuns dramatic narrative, musical inspiration, arty film effects, and man-in-the-street scenes. Instead, a typical Garth television spot tends to overwhelm the viewer with a stream of information on issues, history, and statistics favoring his candidate. "In an era when voters are skeptical about politicians, facts are required," Garth explains. "When information commercials are shown over and over again, viewers discover something new every time they see them." Garth has his man look straight into the camera and talk while a running scrawl or legend fills the bottom of the screen with additional data. Garth doesn't mince words. If race is a campaign issue and Garth is managing a black candidate, a Garth script will likely begin: "There are some people who believe a black man should not run for mayor of a major city."

He manages, coaches, and often even dresses his candidates. He taught John Lindsay relaxation techniques; chose Hugh Carey's shirts and ties; put John Heinz on a strict diet and lectured him on the benefits of regular exercise. "In the process," Heinz said, "Garth builds up the confidence of his candidates." As third party challenger, John Anderson needed all the confidence and media magic Garth could muster. But by adding Garth to his team, Anderson made sure that, from here on in, the press and media would take him seriously.

By the beginning of June, Reagan had 969 pledged delegates, 29 short of clinching the nomination. Another 75 were promised but not publicly announced.

Conserving resources, Reagan did little media spending for "Super Tuesday." George Bush, already heavily in debt, decided to cut his losses short and go light on television time buys. So Reagan, Bush, and Anderson all relied on personal appearances, free media, and limited replays of commercials that had played heavily the past months.

On June 3 Ronald Reagan demolished Bush in all six states by margins ranging from 4 to 1 in Rhode Island to 20 to 1 in South Dakota, and scored a virtual sweep of the 423 delegates up for grabs, taking all except 7. Even Gerald Ford accepted the inevitable: after a Reagan visit to his Rancho Mirage home, Ford announced that he now believed Ronald Reagan to be "electable," vowing "to campaign wholeheartedly on his behalf." Looking ahead to the July convention in Detroit, the Republicans were more united behind a conservative leader than at any other time in modern history.

While Carter and Reagan were busy battling polls and challengers in the last batch of primaries, John Anderson spent his energies raising money, getting all the free media he could hustle to preach the "Anderson Difference," and pushing petition drives to get his name on the ballot in all fifty states. David Garth, being fully aware he had to broaden his candidate's appeal beyond the white suburbs, used the petition-signing pilgrimage to organize grass-roots networks across the country—safaris that would often take him into black ghettos and Latino barrios. As public sympathies mounted for Anderson, news reports called him a viable alternative and his standings in the polls responded. By mid-June Gallup showed Anderson with 24 percent voter support against 35 for Carter and 33 for Reagan. Garth was feeling good.

Carter's strategists were less joyous about Anderson's spurt in public affection. The Democratic hierarchy, under John White, publicly announced that they would work through state parties to keep Anderson off the ballot. White charged that Anderson was part of a Republican conspiracy to split Carter's support, distributing a press release titled "The Real John Anderson" that accused Anderson of being a closet conservative Republican play-acting independent liberal. The fifteen-page tract was circulated widely among government employees, despite protests from Anderson's people about the illegality of such activity. But if anything, these tactics only helped build more sympathy for Anderson.

Reagan's operatives continued to pressure Stu Spencer about joining the campaign. "Finally we had a meeting at Jimmy's restaurant in Beverly Hills," Spencer recalled. "The irony is that the place is owned by Charley Manatt, head of the state Democratic Party. We all had a good time and then Bill Casey, Ed Meese, and Mike Deaver put the screws to me. They said the Reagans really wanted me badly and they wouldn't take no for an answer. So I told them yes."

Spencer agreed to give the campaign 70 percent of his time, planning to apply the remaining 30 percent to other candidates. He was to work for Bill Timmons out of the Reagan headquarters in Arlington, Virginia, and answer to no one except Timmons. As overall campaign consultant, he would be available to provide counsel and direction for every aspect of the campaign, from issues to advertising and organization. On paper, it was ideal. At last, Ronald Reagan's original band of Californians was back together for the big one.

In the weeks before the convention, Dick Wirthlin put the finishing touches on the Black Book. Coauthored by Wirthlin and two fellow researchers—Vincent Breglio of DMI, and Richard Beal of Brigham Young University—the 176-page document served as "campaign Bible." Half its contents were based on surveys Wirthlin had done for Reagan over past years and during the 1980 primaries, a fourth was devoted to historical voting patterns, and the rest was a collection of practical advice. The Black Book set forth the strategy Reagan's cam-

paign team would follow; it would be up to the campaign
team to devise the best tactics to make it all work.

Completed in June, the book began with a list of "conditions
of victory" on which a Reagan success depended. Victory
could be achieved, wrote Wirthlin, only if:

—The conservative Republican Reagan base is expanded to
include enough moderates, independents, soft Republicans, and
soft Democrats to offset Carter's natural Democratic base and his
incumbency advantage.

—The impact of John Anderson stabilizes and he ends up
cutting more into Carter's electoral vote base than Reagan's.

—The campaign projects the image of Governor Reagan em-
bodying the values a majority of Americans currently think are
important in their President: strength, maturity, decisiveness,
resolve, determination, compassion, trustworthiness, and steadi-
ness.

—The candidate and/or campaign avoids fatal, self-inflicted
blunders.

—The attack against Carter reinforces his perceived weaknesses
as an ineffective and error-prone leader, not respected by our
allies or enemies.

—The campaign innoculates voters against Carter's personal
attacks by pointing out in early stages of the campaign that
Carter has in the past, and will in the future, practice piranha
politics.

—The campaign neutralizes any "October Surprise" staged by
Carter.

—The governor does not personally answer the Carter attacks;
that will be the job of the Vice-Presidential candidate and
other surrogates.

Reagan can win the easiest, least expensive minimum of
270 electoral votes with victories in California, Illinois, Texas,
Ohio, Pennsylvania, Indiana, Virginia, Tennessee, Florida, Maryland, Idaho, South Dakota, Wyoming, Vermont, Utah, Nebraska,
North Dakota, New Hampshire, Kansas, Montana, New Mexico,
Nevada, Arizona, Oregon, Alaska, Iowa, Colorado, Washington,
and Maine (totaling 320 electoral votes).

Anticipating a tough, close race, Wirthlin pointed out that
an elected incumbent historically wins two out of three
times when he runs for reelection. "Thus," he wrote, "unseat-

ing Jimmy Carter will be extremely difficult, even unlikely."
The Black Book went on to identify highly desirable voting
blocs: "Older voters are almost twice as likely to turn out as
are younger voters . . . the highly educated are two to three
times more likely to turn out as the poorly educated . . . 'Born
Again' Protestants and 'High Church' Protestants are very
likely to vote and vote Republican. . . . Voters in the Mountain, Pacific, farm-belt, and Great Lakes regions constitute almost half the population and also have the highest turnout
probability." Target groups were singled out for special attention.

"The campaign must convert into Reagan votes the disappointment felt by Southern white Protestants, blue-collar workers in industrial states, urban ethnics, and rural voters, especially in upstate New York, Ohio, and Pennsylvania. There is
a tendency in our increasingly complex and highly technologi-
cal society to forget that American democracy is less a form of
government than a romantic preference for a particular value
structure."

Wirthlin did an "issues" study in June that uncovered what
was really important to voters in 1980; among the highest-scor-
ing interests were government spending (75 percent), national
defense (72 percent), income tax policy (62 percent), the military draft (56 percent), and abortion (48 percent). More than
one voter in four (28 percent) were involved in single-issue
advocacy, an emotionally strong attachment that often becomes the sole basis for casting a vote. The most popular
causes Wirthlin found were national defense (27 percent),
government spending (25 percent), draft registration (11
percent), abortion (11 percent), and the income tax (10 percent). About 10 percent of the electorate were activists—letter
writers, contributors, and protesters; their main causes were
the ERA, gun control, and abortion.

A measure of "voter expectations" showed that Americans
found it easier to think of "good things" that might happen if
Ronald Reagan were elected than if Jimmy Carter won another term. Conversely, more people could itemize more "bad
things" that would result from a Carter victory than if Reagan

prevailed. Wirthlin concluded that if people voted according to their expectations, Reagan would win. The only chance Carter had, Wirthlin determined, was to change the electorate's vision of the future and make them believe in some positive things that would happen if he were to win.

Reagan's plan was contingent on certain geographic assumptions. For example, states west of the Missouri were taken for granted. The campaign needed to concentrate its research and communications efforts, along with most of its available money, on eight big electoral-vote states that could ultimately decide the election: Illinois, Ohio, Pennsylvania, Texas, Michigan, California, New Jersey, and Florida. A ninth state, New York, was considered too costly to turn around, as Stu Spencer had learned to his sorrow during Ford's narrow 1976 defeat by Carter. Though New York was not conceded, the amount of campaign resources spent there would be minimal.

The big question, of course, was how best to achieve the goals set out in the plan. Reagan's strategy committee—Bill Timmons, Dick Wirthlin, Ed Meese, and Stu Spencer—had to draw on the "plan," but at the same time be prepared to deviate from it.

"Wirthlin made a good campaign plan," Spencer noted. "As Eisenhower used to say, plans are important even if they are seldom used. Your plan gives you guideposts, but you've got to be flexible as you go. We knew the basic issue would be the economy. We knew it would be domestic more than foreign affairs. It was hard to target states early on because the research showed Reagan had at least a chance in every state.

"We made several key assumptions. The first was that Reagan was an outstanding media candidate and we had to use him to full advantage. Secondly, there was a correlation between the time he spent in a region, state, or community and his standings in the polls in those places. East of the Mississippi people knew who Ronald Reagan was, but they didn't know anything about him. This was not true in the West. In a sense, the situation in the East was a national replay of Reagan's first campaign for governor of California in 1966."

Reagan's campaign strategy was to put Jimmy Carter on the

defensive. "Our goal was to reinforce the impression that President Carter was ineffective and unable even to get his good programs through Congress," Wirthlin explained. "If the issue was Jimmy Carter, we would beat him. If Reagan became the issue, the outcome was problematical."

Taking advantage of a research budget of over $1.4 million, Wirthlin set up a program to monitor developments play by play. A four-wave barrage of nationwide telephone polls measured basic voting trends. Evolving "voter anticipation" readings would give direction to the campaign's communications. When positive Reagan perceptions were uncovered, the campaign reinforced them with advertising, speeches, and media events. When negative perceptions were uncovered, campaign communications focused on correcting them. Play-by-play monitoring pinpointed Carter vulnerabilities and strengths.

"Simulation modeling" programs gauged the effects of "what if" eventualities. For example, what if the Carter administration arranged a release of the hostages from Iran before the November 4 vote? What effect would that have on the election? Iran was a wild card that would haunt the outcome right up to its final days; if the hostage crisis broke, the Reagan strategy team knew it must have the right answers waiting.

"The research didn't tell us anything about an October Surprise," Stu Spencer explained. "We just expected they would use some power of the incumbency to deal with the hostages or some foreign event. We knew they had to do something by the fifteenth of October for their surprise to be effective. It would smack too much of politics if it happened any later and would backfire. We just had to wait and see what developed. A lot of our talk about an October Surprise was to warn the press of a last minute ploy by Carter."

By having Reagan mouthpieces George Bush, Ed Meese, and others discuss the "October Surprise" right from the start of the campaign, the Reagan strategists injected an element of skepticism toward any "hostage break" that might develop during the campaign, preempting the effects before they occurred, painting Carter into a corner. Meanwhile a "running mate" study found that Ronald Reagan scored higher pitted against

Carter by himself than when joined to any other Vice-Presidential possibility being considered, but with one notable exception: Jerry Ford added several points to the paired equation. With the Black Book as their guide, Reagan's top men waited for the convention in Detroit before putting the final touches on their blueprint.

Jimmy Carter and his aides had never run for reelection before. They opted to hold fast to the strategy that took them from Plains to the Atlanta governor's mansion and then the White House—the strategy that had just defeated Kennedy in the primary. It was the strategy which pollster William Hamilton had advised Carter to adopt in 1970: put yourself between your opponent and the electorate. Make your adversary the issue, yourself the solution. It was the strategy of a challenger, not an incumbent.

After a series of meetings with Pat Caddell, Jody Powell, Bob Strauss, Jerry Rafshoon, and the President, Hamilton Jordan summarized the conclusions in the Orange Book of election strategy. Logistically the plan seemed simple enough: all they had to do to win was hold on to the states they took against Jerry Ford in 1976. That meant they could concede the West, hold their Southern base, win most of the border states, and fight hard to repeat their victory in New York, Pennsylvania, Ohio, and New Jersey. Since Reagan was a conservative, they saw a good chance to take Michigan and Illinois, two states that narrowly went to Ford, a moderate, four years earlier.

In the Democratic scenario, they even had a chance for a breakthrough in the West, in Oregon and Washington. Though popularity polls in the early summer did not show any great affection for Jimmy Carter, they felt confident that the disgruntled liberals, Ted Kennedy's supporters, would soon return to the fold. Either of two developments could guarantee victory in November—an easing of the recession, or a break in the hostage crisis. Either, in conjunction with increased attacks on Ronald Reagan, would render Jimmy Carter unbeatable.

The mathematics were impeccable and the logic not too farfetched, but the major assumption was questionable. Carter's strategists saw Ronald Reagan as just another trigger-happy conservative, a reincarnated Barry Goldwater, and a dumb actor who needed a script just to say "good morning." All they had to do, they felt, was put Jimmy Carter between Reagan and the voters, and there was no way the Democratic majority would desert their party's candidate. Voter affiliations seemed to favor their cause, since in 1980 people identified themselves to pollsters as 46 percent Democrats, 22 percent Republicans, and 32 percent Independents.

Pat Caddell summed up the feelings in Carter's high command by pointing out the near-reverent overtones in a Presidential race: "People view a Presidential election very differently from an election for governor or senator. They take a Presidential vote much more seriously. Very few will cast a frivolous vote or a protest vote. When you look at the data on Reagan, you want to salivate. A lot of people have enormous doubts about him, his judgment, and his concern for individuals in society. He is viewed as an extremist, and there are lots of people concerned about having a seventy-year-old man as President."

Caddell's man, Carter, had the obvious problems that go with running a nation suffering from economic difficulties and reverses in foreign affairs. But, Caddell emphasized, the final choice would be between the two men. President Carter was still regarded highly on his character traits. "Overall, people feel he is a good and decent man," Caddell noted. "That is critical. In elections, we deal with choices, not absolutes."

Carter's team disregarded the advice they received from a group of Democratic Californians at the Hay-Adams Hotel in Washington. The Californians had been invited there by Carter's strategists to share their campaign experiences. At one point in the session, old pol Jesse "Big Daddy" Unruh, who lost to Reagan in the 1970 gubernatorial race, shook his finger at Hamilton Jordan when Jordan called Reagan a has-been left behind by the surging political currents of the 1970s. "Don't make the mistake every person in this room has made at one time or another," Unruh warned Jordan. "You may think Ronald Reagan is too old or too much of a right-winger, but above all else he is an excellent and effective communicator."

Jordan, Rafshoon, and the other Carter aides considered
Unruh of the same out-of-date vintage as the opponent he
tried to warn them about. Carter and his entourage had not
the slightest doubt that, when it came to a choice of whom the
American people loved more, it would be Jimmy Carter who
would come out on top—just as he always had. Carter's campaign strategy, as they saw it, was simply to make Ronald
Reagan seem a dangerous, heartless, narrow-minded, mad-
bomber bigot with no brains of his own, so that the American
electorate would reject him just as decisively as it had rejected
Barry Goldwater in 1964. As Jerry Rafshoon put it, all they had
to do was keep Reagan from becoming "a plausible candidate."

Republican Party chairman Bill Brock picked Detroit, a
troubled Democratic city of the industrial North, for his party's
convention for a good reason. The choice symbolized his party's appeal for the votes of blue-collar workers and urban
blacks, thereby challenging the Democrats for the support they
had long taken for granted, the support that might decide the
election. And for the first time in its history, the Republicans
had a candidate with a bona fide union background. Reagan
had served six years as head of the Screen Actors Guild. The
party of big business could finally promise a working class
suffering from inflation and unemployment, "We will give you
a President to look after your interests."

On the weekend of July 12 around 4,000 delegates and
alternates checked into hotels along the Detroit River and center city. They were hopelessly outnumbered by an army of
15,000 print, radio, and television people who would make the
nominating conventions of 1980 the most thoroughly covered
in political history. Despite the elaborate security and media
hype, the only real suspense surrounded the choice of Reagan's
running mate and the Republican platform on the Equal
Rights Amendment and abortion-on-demand.

This Republican convention featured special coverage. Independent candidate John Anderson was hired by NBC Television to appear in ten exclusive *Today Show* interviews in
which he analyzed maneuvers and floor demonstrations. Without a convention of his own to boost his candidacy, he enjoyed

the privilege of taking daily potshots at his opponents and appreciated the resulting national exposure for his own candidacy. Lyn Nofziger, Reagan's acting press secretary, was openly miffed: "It's a campaign contribution from NBC to John Anderson," he grumbled.

That Monday, Stu Spencer boarded the Reagan jet for the flight to Washington.

"I was a little apprehensive about flying with the Reagans," Spencer admitted. "Ron was the first person ever to call me a gun for hire. We're not social friends; we don't go over to each other's houses, for example. Reagan understands that I'm a professional and my interest in him is professional. That's what makes me valuable. He respects what I do and the way I do it. I respect him as a man and a candidate, and that's it. I didn't know how the Reagans would accept me after my doing Ford's 1976 campaign. But they were both very kind, very generous, and we got along well. They did needle me pretty well about it, though."

While the television cameras focused on the convention hoopla, Spencer went straight to the Reagan election headquarters in Arlington, Virginia. There, in a run-down, three-story concrete building that he described as "a zoo," he worked out of a desk in Bill Timmons's office, away from the limelight, organizing Reagan's state-by-state battles. Spencer knew all the pitfalls. He conferred with all Reagan's campaign divisions, helping to mold strong state organizations, recruit volunteers, and shape voter-group blocs and associated media that would convince their "coalition of 51 percent" that Ronald Reagan was the one.

The Republican convention adopted a platform tailored to Reagan's free-enterprise philosophy, which had not varied since the 1950s. The platform called for military superiority over the Soviet Union, peace through strength, an anticrime, progun policy, decentralization of the federal government, and war against a "bloated bureaucracy." The party sparked the enmity of feminists by advocating a Constitutional amendment

barring abortion on demand, but decided to stay neutral on
the ERA issue by leaving the decision to individual state
legislatures "without federal interference or pressure."

Away from the arena madcaps, Gerald Ford visited Ronald
Reagan's suite on the sixty-ninth floor of the posh Plaza Hotel.
He had come at Reagan's invitation, to discuss the possibility
of a Republican "dream ticket." After listening to Reagan's
offer, Ford spelled out his own terms. The two were on different planets when it came to the division of power.

"I don't see how we can reconcile my demands with yours,"
Ford concluded. "I won't agree to be just a figurehead."

But others from the moderate wing were determined to
force the issue. After Henry Kissinger gave his speech on the
second day of the convention, he made a midnight visit to
Ford's suite and argued until two in the morning that Jerry
should accept Reagan's offer.

"Only if I can be a co-President," Ford replied.

The next morning Kissinger, Alan Greenspan, and other
Ford aides met with Bill Casey, Ed Meese, and Bill Timmons
to present their package: Ford would join the ticket only if
promised a dominant role in the National Security Council,
budget planning, and selection of the White House staff. That
afternoon Reagan's people handed Ford a two-page memo outlining Reagan's ideas for a beefed-up Ford Vice-Presidency.
Ford studied the proposal and called it a "reasonable attempt,"
but he was still not persuaded, fearing that by the nature of
the office Vice-Presidents were doomed to modest roles. All that
night and the next day, memos passed back and forth between
the two camps. As Reagan would meet Ford's demands, they
would get stiffer, finally demanding that Henry Kissinger be
secretary of state and Alan Greenspan secretary of the treasury.

Evening arrived. With George Bush still hanging on, Reagan
had not yet decided on a choice for Vice-President. Jerry Ford
appeared on camera with Walter Cronkite and teased the nation by hinting that he would be Reagan's Veep, taking a
"meaningful role" in an unprecedented dual Presidency.
Though Cronkite could not quite pin him down, the CBS
newscaster was certain Ford would be Reagan's choice.

As the convention buzzed with this prospect, George Bush went to the podium to give his scheduled speech. He bravely delivered his talk, but his heart was heavy. Afterward Bush left the arena and went to a nearby bar for a beer with some staffers, then returned to his room at the Pontchartrain Hotel three blocks away. He was undressing for bed when just before midnight the phone rang. It was Ronald Reagan. "George," he said. "You're the one."

Bush helped Reagan where he needed it most, in the industrial states of the Northeast and Midwest. A youthful fifty-six, Bush added solid national experience to complement Reagan's regional proficiencies, moderate views to temper Reagan's conservatism, and aristocratic breeding to counterpoint Reagan's populist, maverick magnetism.

And Gerald Ford? Having embarrassed Reagan by teasing him with his "dream ticket," the score was now even. Ford had repaid Ronald Reagan for not campaigning for him in 1976. Now, according to the unwritten code of politics, Ford no longer had to be mad. He promised to work like hell on Reagan's behalf to beat Jimmy Carter in the fall.

In the early morning hours of July 18, Ronald Reagan and George Bush raised their hands in tandem while the convention roared its approval. Bush made his acceptance remarks, and Reagan completed the long day with his own acceptance speech.

"They say the United States has passed its zenith," he said. "They tell you the American people no longer have the will to cope, that the future will be one of sacrifice and few opportunities. I utterly reject that view. I will not stand by and watch this country destroy itself under mediocre leadership that drifts from one crisis to the next, eroding our national will. 'Trust me' government concentrates its hopes and dreams in one man, to trust him to do what's best for us. My view of government places trust where it belongs—in the people. Isn't it time to renew our compact of freedom, to pledge to each other all that is best in our lives, for the sake of this, our beloved and blessed land? Together, let us make a new beginning."

The campaign theme was launched that night: "Reagan and

Bush for a New Beginning." As a unified Republican image was projected through television all over the land, Reagan's poll numbers soared—from a three-point Gallup lead during the convention to a fourteen-point lead after two weeks. With the prospect of civil war at the Democratic convention still to come in August, Republicans began to believe this might be their year.

On July 14, as Republicans argued over platform planks, Billy Carter signed a paper admitting he was "a foreign agent for Libya." Behind that act lay a web of concealment, lies, and White House manipulation that earned the event the media nickname "Billygate," which underlined similarities to the Nixon administration's cover-up.

The national press reported that Billy Carter had visited Libya several times after his brother the President had instructed the National Security Council to brief Billy on the radical regime. Shortly after the hostages were seized by Iranian terrorists, Jimmy had shown Billy classified State Department cables and had commissioned him to seek the help of the Libyan dictator, Muammar Qaddafi.

Billy had profited handsomely from his Libyan connections. After first denying he had received money, he later admitted getting $2,500 in gifts and a $220,000 "loan" in cash, which Justice investigators called a payoff since no loan papers were ever signed. Additional testimony before a Senate subcommittee set up to investigate the scandal revealed that Billy got another $50,000 from the Libyans which he did not report. In return, Billy put Libya in touch with influential administration figures, through whom the Libyans pursued their real goal. They were after a shipment of military transports that had already been ordered but were being withheld as a protest against Libya's sponsorship of worldwide terrorist activities. Billy Carter was to have been Libya's key for unlocking the delivery of those planes.

For eighteen months the Justice Department had tried unsuccessfully to get Billy Carter to discuss his involvement with the Libyans. Two weeks after investigators discovered proof of the $220,000 payoff, Billy agreed to meet with them. The inescapable implication was that Billy had been tipped off by administration insiders. Billy denied he ever discussed the problem with his brother Jimmy, but eventually the White House admitted to a series of talks between the President and Billy on the subject between June 28 and July 1. Attorney General Civiletti at first denied that he had discussed Billy's problems with the President. Later, his "memory refreshed," Civiletti recalled that he advised Jimmy that Billy was "foolish" for not registering as a foreign agent, implying that Billy would escape prosecution if he did so.

The special Senate subcommittee kept the "Billygate" pot boiling with new revelations into early October, producing an ongoing irritant in Carter's campaign. It undermined Carter's most valuable political asset, his image as a decent and scrupulously honest man.

On July 24 Carter called a meeting of his campaign strategy team to assess the political fallout from Billygate and how to counter it. Hamilton Jordan, Jerry Rafshoon, and the others opted for a frontal assault. "Better now than in October," they concluded. So Carter announced he would appear personally before the subcommittee to clear up any misconceptions and turn over all his notes bearing on their investigation, though he in fact did neither. Instead, on August 4 Rafshoon scheduled a Presidential press conference in the east wing of the White House. Covered by all three television networks, it was staged by Rafshoon to dispel any rumors of a Billygate cover-up.

"Integrity has been and will continue to be a cornerstone of my administration," the President proclaimed. "Neither I nor any member of my administration has violated any law." He denied impropriety in his discussions with Civiletti, claimed to know nothing about the money Billy got from the Libyans, and pleaded guilty only to using Billy's "special influence" on Qaddafi, in the hope that Qaddafi could convince the Iranians to release the Americans. "That may have been bad judgment," he conceded.

By scheduling the Billygate press conference exactly one week before the Democratic convention, Rafshoon softened the impact of a scandal that could have damaged his candidate's reelection hopes much more than it actually did.

While Carter wrestled with Billygate, John Anderson left on an eleven-day trip to Europe and the Middle East. Besides the press exposure his travels brought him, they bolstered his weak foreign affairs image. His warm reception by the Israelis strengthened his ties to Jewish supporters.

On Anderson's return, strategist David Garth put the finishing touches to his campaign plan, a near replica of the blueprint Abraham Lincoln used to win the Presidency in 1860. It called for victory in seventeen states: seven in the Northeast including Pennsylvania, New York, New Jersey, and Massachusetts; seven in the Midwest including Illinois, Ohio, Wisconsin, and Michigan; and three in the far West—California, Oregon, and Washington. Anderson planned to campaign hard for two Southern states, Texas and Florida. The key states in Garth's equation were California, Connecticut, New York, and Massachusetts, all of which Anderson needed in order to have a mathematical chance.

Many of these target states had large liberal-to-moderate blocs—the same states that under different circumstances might have been targeted by a Ted Kennedy effort. Anderson meant it when he promised in early August to "reassess" his candidacy if "someone other than Carter was chosen" at the upcoming Democratic convention. In that event, both he and Kennedy would have been butting heads over the same voting blocs, to no one's benefit except Ronald Reagan's.

Since Garth expected to raise less than half the money available to both Reagan and Carter, he planned to campaign for those key seventeen states using an army of young volunteers, targeted advertising, and plenty of candidate exposure through free media and speaking tours. Garth hoped to extend the Anderson appeal beyond his current coalition of Easterners, Jews, liberals, college-educated professionals, and campus youth. Attacking Reagan's tax-cut proposal as a windfall for rich people, he aimed to attract blue-collar voters by calling for the "reindustrialization of America." To break Carter's stranglehold on the black bloc, Garth publicized his candidate's heroic efforts as a congressman pushing for the open-housing act of 1968.

Garth held back announcing a running mate, hinting only that it would be a prominent Democrat with appeal to dissidents unhappy with Carter as their party's nominee. Along with the Vice-Presidential choice, Garth delayed revealing a detailed plan of what an Anderson administration would do for the country. By holding back Anderson's plan and his running mate until after the Democratic convention, Garth expected to offset any momentum the Democrats would generate from wide television exposure. All through the convention period, biographical television spots played in eight major cities, raising Anderson's recognition level and neutralizing the nominating hoopla.

A month before Labor Day, Anderson's chances seemed to be improving. A Lou Harris poll taken just before Billygate broke, when voters assumed Anderson had a chance to win, showed Anderson nosing ahead of Carter 25 to 23 percent behind Reagan's 49 percent. "If we can get to Labor Day without falling off," Garth predicted, "it will end up Ronald Reagan versus John Anderson on November 4."

As Democrats prepared to convene in New York, the President's popularity continued to plummet. His job rating was the lowest ever recorded for a President since the first reading was taken in the 1930s.

Stu Spencer was hidden away at the Reagan-Bush headquarters in Arlington, still busy organizing the Reagan campaign. "We'll move out after the Democratic convention," he told me.

"Do you want Carter to take it?" I asked.

"Oh yes, yes," he replied. "But even if he doesn't, the process of taking the nomination away from him will be so bloody, it'll look good for us."

Democratic consultant Matt Reese and pollster Bill Hamilton did some research and determined that their party's traditional support from New Deal advocates and blue-collar workers was eroding badly. They voiced the fear 1980 might prove a "1932 in reverse." In 1932, not only had Franklin Roosevelt beaten incumbent Herbert Hoover, but the Democrats had won majorities in both the House and Senate, replacing hundreds of local Republican officeholders in the wake of the Roosevelt victory. Before that "realignment year," Republicans had dominated national politics since the Civil War.

Ted Kennedy and his supporters exploited realignment terror in their advocacy of an "open convention," in which delegates would be free to vote according to their conscience instead of their state's primary or caucus preference. Like Ronald Reagan, who had staged a desperate rules fight in the 1976 Republican convention, Ted Kennedy attempted to overturn his party's Rule 3-C, written by a pro-Carter Democratic National Committee in 1978. The rule bound all delegates "to vote for the Presidential candidate they were elected to support for the first ballot unless released in writing by the candidate."

In the weeks before the Democratic convention, an "open convention" was pushed by a group of party leaders, congressmen, and union heads who warned that Carter could not win the general election and might trigger a Republican landslide. Named as alternatives were Ted Kennedy, Walter Mondale, Ed Muskie, Henry Jackson, and Morris Udall. An "ABC movement" was started—"Anybody but Carter." Vice-President Mondale and Secretary of State Muskie publicly disavowed the dump-Carter sentiment while a visibly upset Jimmy Carter told a House group that he absolutely refused to release even a single delegate "as a matter of important principle to me."

Ted Kennedy was the bridge between the New Deal legacy of Roosevelt, Truman, and Lyndon Johnson and the New Politics ideal spawned by peace candidates Eugene McCarthy and George McGovern. Kennedy had family roots deep in the New Deal tradition and espoused liberal philosophies on defense and foreign policy that gained him a loyal following among New Politics leftists.

Jimmy Carter was ideologically closer to conservative Southerners than to Eastern liberals. Aside from some stands on civil rights and defense, most of his policies represented a hodgepodge of quid pro quo payoffs to union bosses, party leaders, local officeholders, and other blocs seeking favors and grants. His most reliable support, from fellow Southerners and blacks, came more from regional and ethnic loyalty than from political conviction.

Kennedy backers promised a bitter battle in Madison Square Garden, since Kennedy himself considered Carter "unworthy to be President." Though Kennedy had no practical strategy for stealing the nomination, he intended to hang on until the end. Reports from associates explained his persistence as a hope to weaken Carter badly enough to ensure his defeat in November. A Reagan victory would help dispose of Walter Mondale, clearing the way for another Kennedy Presidential try in 1984 when the social climate might be more favorable to Kennedy.

It was a hell of a way to begin a nominating celebration.

Monday, August 11. "I love New York" banners blanketed the city and New Yorkers made special efforts to be kind. But down in the corridors of the Garden on 33rd Street, the Carter muscle machine was busily cornering shaky delegates and applying pressure. Jerry Rafshoon set up a propaganda operation to counter criticisms of Jimmy Carter. Arguing that the television networks were obliged to broadcast "balanced reporting," he offered to trot out a spokesperson to voice the Carter view on any subject from black unemployment to the PLO.

"Television cameras will search for people who say the President is a son of a bitch," Jody Powell explained. "So if we want others to say he's not, we have to find them ourselves."

NBC reporter Tom Brokaw recalled how the operation worked: "Say we did a segment with somebody who favored Kennedy. Carter's media manager Greg Schneiders would come by and say, 'You've had lots of Kennedy people on camera saying they can't support Carter. Well, we've got Kennedy people who say they can support him.'"

Carter's television task force had a panel of two hundred administration officials, from Mondale to Muskie, available for interviews. Its Network Liaison group handed out typed "talking point" papers to support the interviews, so reporters

wouldn't have to resort to probing or tape transcripts. It called
the Kennedy-backed "open convention" a "misnomer invented
by a loser," alleged that Reagan "called the New Deal fascist,
wanted to repeal the minimum wage, thinks the '64 Civil
Rights bill was a mistake and that we should turn our backs on
apartheid in South Africa."

A Pat Caddell poll raised hopes inside Carter's trailer-head-
quarters, when it showed a "surprising" public perception of
Reagan as a right-wing extremist, rating him far below Carter
as a person voters believe "cares about me." This led to whoops
of joy among the President's strategists, who saw Reagan as a
helpless target made vulnerable by years of conservative
speechmaking.

The Democratic gathering was a showcase of American di-
versity—a spectrum of skin colors from Saxon pink to Latin
brown and African black, sexually balanced, rich and poor.
What was noticeably lacking was enthusiasm, optimism, or
even excitement, all of which had been abundantly visible
among the Republicans a month before.

Hidden from the television cameras, party caucuses vented
other emotions, mostly anger against Jimmy Carter. Nowhere
was the wrath more pronounced than among the group that
had been Carter's most loyal backers, the blacks. At one point,
the black caucus advocated walking out of the convention.
Using Ted Kennedy's rule challenge as a bargaining chip, they
aimed to force strong plank guarantees for black-centered job
programs and grants. At that point, Rev. Jesse L. Jackson,
who had been touting himself as an independent free of
Jimmy Carter's influence, showed his real face to his colleagues. Just before the Monday night vote on the "open convention" proposal, Jackson got up to argue, threaten, and
cajole the black caucus to destroy the walkout.

Other blacks fell victims to Carter's muscling tactics. California Congressman Ron Dellums spoke out against it: "The
candidate was chosen by force. One black delegate pledged to
Carter fully intended to vote for him but wanted to open the
convention. That man was so intimidated he was almost in
tears. They were playing plantation politics there. The Presi-

dent's got his black officeholders and he hands out goodies to them. But they don't turn out the people's votes. Carter looks at my black face, says I'm just a civil-rights type and he's got all of those he needs. But the issues I believe in have nothing to do with the color of my face. Carter thinks he can out-Reagan Reagan. Well, I saw Reagan win in California and you don't beat Reagan without a positive alternative."

When the rules change came up for a vote, it became clear that Kennedy's hopes for an "open convention" were doomed. The delegates approved 3-C by six hundred votes and Kennedy withdrew his challenge. Frustrated Kennedy backers turned their energies to battles over plank stands on the economy, which they won, and to the battle for a comprehensive national health program, which they lost.

Tuesday night, Ted Kennedy made a scheduled speech to the convention. Ironically, his last hurrah of 1980 was his crowning glory: eloquent and persuasive, he overshadowed Carter. When he congratulated Carter on his victory, Kennedy seemed conciliatory, but not wholehearted in his endorsement. Then Kennedy spoke:

"Someday, long after this convention, long after the signs come down and the crowds stop cheering and the bands stop playing, may it be said of our campaign that we kept the faith." A hush fell over the crowd as Kennedy recalled the words of Tennyson: "I am a part of all that I have met . . . though much is taken, much abides . . . that which we are, we are . . . strong in will to strive, to seek, to find and not to yield." He staked his claim for 1984: "For all those whose cares have been our concern, the work goes on, the cause endures, the hope still lives, and the dream shall never die."

As his words echoed through the amplifiers, cheers and tumult burst forth from the crowd. It was Kennedy's finest hour. For forty-five raucous minutes, Madison Square Garden rocked with passion as delegates wept openly, tears streaming down their cheeks.

Though Americans had long ago rejected the concept of a "royal family," in their heart of hearts the craving for aristocratic rule—Kennedy rule—still lived. First billed as Ted Kennedy's Presidential funeral, the convention became his resurrection, making him the odds-on favorite to be the party's 1984 nominee.

Wednesday, August 13. James Earl Carter was officially nominated the Democratic candidate for President. The last time a Democrat incumbent lost a reelection was in 1882, but Carter's task was formidable if he meant to maintain that record. The omens were not good: when Carter was officially nominated, half the celebratory balloons remained frozen in a canopy when the lever was triggered; they hung limply from the ceiling, a plethora of multicolored frustration.

August 14. Walter Mondale accepted his party's nomination for Vice-President by immediately adopting his role as campaign hatchet man. He read from a book of Reagan statements compiled by researcher Marty Franks: "I have included in my morning and evening prayers every day that the federal government will not bail out New York City." He then followed up by asking, "Now who would ever say a thing like that?" And the gleeful delegates roared back, "Ronald Reagan!"

After Mondale had fired up the crowd, Jimmy Carter came on for the main assault. He described Reagan's career as "a world of tinsel and make-believe. This election is a stark choice between two men and two parties. Between two sharply different pictures of America and the world. Reagan lives in a fantasy world in which all the complex global changes since World War II never happened, where inner-city people, farm workers, and laborers are forgotten, where women, like children, are to be seen but not heard."

Then, after praising past Democratic demigods F.D.R., Harry Truman, and John Kennedy, Carter stumbled in alluding to Hubert Humphrey, "the big-hearted man who should have been President, a man who would have been one of the greatest Presidents of all time—Hubert Horatio Hornblower!" Instead of the applause he expected, Carter was met by a stunned silence. When the echo of his own words reached him, he looked up, a sick expression on his face, and mumbled, "er, Humphrey."

Once Carter finished speaking, Ted Kennedy mounted the platform, greeted Mondale and Muskie warmly, shook Carter's hand briefly, and walked off without raising the President's hand in the traditional show of unity. It remained to be seen whether Kennedy would campaign for Carter in the weeks ahead, despite Carter's plea: "Ted, I need you and the party needs you!"

The Nielsen ratings, released a few days after the convention ended, showed that the Democrats had outscored the Republicans decisively, attracting 55 percent of the available television audience against the GOP's 49.5 percent. Gallup's postconvention ratings of the candidates showed the election a tossup—Reagan 39, Carter 38, and John Anderson 14 percent.

Concerned over his candidate's drop in the polls, Anderson campaign manager Michael McLeod blamed the low reading on the millions of dollars of free air time given the two national conventions: "We're dealing with a halo effect now. But the further you get away from the convention, the less intense that effect is." David Garth predicted that Anderson would pick up dramatically in the polls before the September 10 deadline for the debate set by the League of Women Voters. Anderson would have to score 15 percent or better in the polls to be invited.

Monday, August 26. Anderson named former Wisconsin governor Patrick J. Lucey his Vice-Presidential running mate. Bigger names—Sen. Henry Jackson, Gov. Hugh Carey, and former Congresswoman Barbara Jordan—had refused. Lucey, a liberal Democrat, had chaired Ted Kennedy's primary campaign. The hope was that Kennedy backers would prefer Anderson-Lucey to Carter-Mondale.

On Labor Day weekend Anderson released a 300-page platform book that blended liberal ideas with fiscal responsibility. He was the only one of the three candidates not to promise a tax cut. Instead, he advocated an extra fifty-cents-per-gallon tax on gasoline, and a "convocation on federalism" where state officials would meet to consider limiting federal control over tax money. His platform called for a new fund of $4 billion to revitalize inner cities; stronger support for Israel, Japan, and the NATO countries; support of the Equal Rights Amendment; opposition to the MX missile; and rejection of a Constitutional amendment banning abortion. The platform differed enough from both the Democratic and Republican planks to merit promotion as "the Anderson Difference."

A Lou Harris poll taken the last week of August gave Reagan 41 percent, Carter 37, and Anderson 17. Garth pinned his hopes for a dramatic breakthrough on upcoming debates and the national exposure they would give his long-shot candidate.

To get the jump on Jimmy Carter, the Republican high command scheduled a series of speeches to make things hot for the incumbent President. Instead, Ronald Reagan took the brunt of press criticism himself for calling the Vietnam War "a noble cause," for proposing upgraded relations with Taiwan that raised the specter of a "two-China policy," and for questioning the validity of Darwin's theory of evolution before a Dallas convocation of evangelist broadcasters so as to garner "born-again" votes. In all three instances, Reagan rejected the advice of strategists to delete the statements from his speeches. After the media fuss confirmed their worst fears, he promised to concentrate on making Carter's record, not his own words, the burning issue of the campaign.

September 1, Labor Day. The President opened his campaign in Tuscumbia, Alabama, a town whose television broadcasts reached Tennessee and Mississippi. It was also home base for the Ku Klux Klan, who burned a cross the night before the campaign opening. By launching his drive in Tuscumbia, Carter's team stressed the crucial role of the Southern base in the election. Carter invited George Wallace to sit beside him on the stage, signaling to segregationists that he remained a loyal son of the Confederacy, but by denouncing the Klan in his opening remarks, he sent out signals to black supporters that he was really on their side. Then, after returning to the White House, Carter picnicked with labor leaders and complained about "taking the heat for unpopular decisions and speaking the truth that was not always welcomed." Aiming for support from the Kennedy holdouts, he promised if reelected "to fully implement a national health program." So in a few short hours Carter had wooed the four voting blocs critical to his chances: Southerners, blacks, union people, and liberals.

Ronald Reagan opened his campaign with a speech on Ellis Island, the spot from which most immigrants first glimpsed their newly adopted country. In the background stood the Statue of Liberty and the imposing obelisks of the Manhattan skyline. There Reagan pitched hard for the votes of blue-collar America as, coatless and tieless, he addressed a crowd of two thousand, composed largely of the descendants of Catholic immigrants. The Statue of Liberty had never betrayed anyone, Reagan declared, "but this administration has betrayed the working men and women of America." A Reagan Presidency, he vowed, would cut taxes, lick inflation, create jobs, and revive the country's languishing spiritual values.

Later, at a fair outside Detroit, Reagan continued attacking the Carter economy until he spotted a youth wearing a Jimmy Carter mask. Forgetting his resolve, he could not resist a bit of ad lib needling. "I thought you were in Alabama," he told the Carter look-alike. "I like the contrast. I'm here dealing first-hand with economic problems, and he opens his campaign in the city that gave birth to and is the parent body of the Ku Klux Klan!"

Technically, the Klan was born some eighty miles away from Tuscumbia; reporters badgered press secretary Lyn Nofziger for clarifications. Reagan, Nofziger explained, was simply drawing a contrast between himself talking to working people in depressed Michigan, while "Carter opened in a safe part of the country for him." Pressured further, Nofziger finally snapped, "Why are we getting all these questions now, when nobody asked Pat Harris questions when she kicked us around?"—a reference to the black Carter cabinet member who made a fuss over a Ku Klux Klan endorsement that Reagan strongly repudiated.

In Missouri Jimmy Carter seized the opportunity to attack Reagan's Klan statement: "Anybody who resorts to slurs and innuendoes against a whole region is not doing the South or our nation a service. As a Southerner and an American, I resent that."

Although Reagan had mentioned only a small town, not a "region," reporters accepted Carter's complaint as valid. Fearing defections from his own Southern supporters, Reagan backed off. Maintaining with some justification that his remark had been misinterpreted, Reagan replied, "I intended no inference that Mr. Carter was in any way sympathetic to the Klan." He ended his statement with a counterpunch, calling on Carter to reject suggestions from his own people that linked Reagan to that same troublesome Klan.

John Anderson, campaigning in Illinois, fought vainly to attract media attention with elaborate plans to achieve wage and price balances through tax rewards and penalties. It was a well-thought-out program, but it clearly demonstrated that in politics the emotional issue always gets more attention than the rational proposal. Even though Anderson attacked Reagan as "slick, simplistic, and irrelevant," and the Carter years as ones "that may have made him wiser but us sadder," his media attention was relegated to a few paragraphs buried in the back pages of newspapers, and a twenty-second clip on the evening news. The Reagan-Carter Ku Klux Klan battle stole the show.

At the time, Joe Napolitan was characteristically blunt on the affair: "Reagan may just talk himself right out of the Presidency. He would win without any problems if he didn't fuck around so much. If he went away for two months, he might become President, but he might just campaign himself out of it." Napolitan predicted that Carter's forces would be "breaking some big foreign affairs thing to put them in the limelight. I'm sure they're planning something."

If Napolitan was critical, Reagan's strategists were shaken by the Klan affair. They knew they could lose, if Carter's record were not the issue. That was when they turned to Stu Spencer. "I had gone home for Labor Day on business," Spencer recalled. "Then I got a call from Mike Deaver about Ron's alleged gaffes. The team felt they needed a more political person on the campaign trail with Reagan, somebody with

political background who knew the candidate. Deaver wanted
to know if I'd do it. Since I had agreed to spend only 70
percent of my time on the campaign, I hesitated. I had to go to
New York soon anyway, and while there, I got another phone
call saying how badly they needed me. So I flew from New
York to Dulles Airport in Washington, boarded the Reagan
plane September 4, and didn't get off that plane until election
day. That was why I was so hard to find," he concluded, referring to a series of unreturned calls I had made to his Arlington
office.

Chosen for his "great sensitivity and quick reaction time,"
Spencer now helped Reagan stay focused on campaign goals
and limited his free-lance responses to the press. Spencer objected to my calling it "putting the muzzle" on his candidate.
"Everything you say in a Presidential race is scrutinized and
reported much more widely," he explained. "And questions are
not always asked in good faith. Because he's a decent guy, Ron
Reagan believes that when somebody asks a question, he
deserves an answer. I explained to him that the big leagues are
a lot rougher and you have to be a lot more careful. People
who hit you with questions at curbside conferences are not
asking them in good faith. You don't have to answer them.
Reagan's a smart guy with a memory like a computer. He's
tough on ideological questions and has a strong character, but
he can be very soft on certain occasions. He has a hard time
firing anybody, for instance. Once I explained curbside conferences to him, he didn't have any more problems. Nobody
put the muzzle on him."

Strategy decisions were made through conferences between
the plane and the Arlington headquarters, using telephones
and DEX machines to exchange printed material. While
Spencer was captive aboard the campaign plane, he wrestled
with a campaign hierarchy he described as "convoluted and
ludicrous." "You can't run a campaign with eight or nine deputy chairmen," he complained. "It was poorly organized in the
sense that there were many divisions and it was hard to get
decisions and answers. A smaller group had the most input on
strategy—Wirthlin, Timmons, Meese, Deaver, and myself."

Planning conferences were held in the middle of the night while in flight, using the day's appearances as a springboard for discussion. Ideas were transmitted from the plane to Arlington, where Meese and Wirthlin added their reactions, then were wired back and forth until everyone agreed. This cumbersome arrangement led Spencer to describe his situation as being "up to my ass in alligators," requiring group approval for every move. "We tried to keep a coherent strategy for one week at a time, in terms of our press and what we were going to say. It was a focus-impact concept. We went to an area, hit a theme for a period of time there, and followed up with media on the same theme after the governor left."

"I have a secret weapon in this election," President Carter boasted. "That weapon is the black people of this country." In 1976 Carter had received over 90 percent of all black votes, which he aimed to improve on this time. Early on, it seemed he might achieve his goal as even black African leaders endorsed his candidacy. Robert Mugabe, Prime Minister of Zimbabwe, visited the White House and declared that if the election were held in his country, "President Carter would be assured of victory."

The *Washington Afro-American*, a black newspaper in D.C., urged blacks to support Carter, warning, "We can't afford to go fishing." The Democratic National Committee created a thirty-nine-member special task force led by Andrew Young and Coretta King to get blacks to the polls. The group described a possible Reagan Presidency as an "awesome threat and distinct danger to black Americans." Said Aaron Henry, a Mississippi member of the task force: "When you say Reagan to the black community, you might as well say Hitler."

The NAACP committed $500,000—15 percent of its annual budget—to register the black vote, with the task force targeting big cities with large black concentrations in critical states like Alabama, California, Florida, Michigan, New York, Pennsylvania, Texas, Illinois, and Ohio. Jesse Jackson, ostensibly an independent during the convention, came out as a Carter supporter early in the general election campaign. Muhammad Ali traveled widely, campaigning and even cutting television commercials for Carter. The administration's most influential black, Andrew Young, continued to enjoy Carter's backing despite the fact that he made statements supporting the PLO and justified Iran's imprisoning American hostages "because of the Shah's record." Carter strategists felt that since Young's controversial views conflicted with official U.S. policy, Young had a great deal of "credibility" with militant blacks and white liberals. Writing frequent columns published in the nation's leading newspapers during the campaign, Young warned black Americans that they would pay dearly if they stayed home election day.

Gerald Rafshoon ran an ad in over one hundred black-oriented publications, including *Ebony* and *Jet*, featuring a photo of Carter with black appointees Justice Thurgood Marshall and Patricia Harris. "Jimmy Carter," the text read, "named thirty-seven black judges. Cracked down on job bias. And created one million jobs. That's why the Republicans are out to defeat him." By the time protests poured in from both black and white Reagan supporters, the ad had served its purpose well. Rafshoon did not have to reschedule it. The impact on his target audiences had already been achieved.

The Republicans made an honest effort to include blacks in their coalition of 51 percent. Reagan held private meetings with black leaders in New York, visited Urban League President Vernon Jordan, who was recuperating in the hospital from an assassination attempt, toured black ghettos in Brooklyn and the Bronx, and met with the publishers of *Jet* and *Ebony* in Chicago. It was not pure political expediency that fueled Reagan's overtures for black support. Long ago, back in his days as a college athlete at Eureka, he led a walkout from a restaurant that refused to serve a black teammate. Later he had helped desegregate a hotel. He really believed in the ideal of equal opportunity, but he would have to fight hard to prove it.

At midweek, Carter told a black audience at Philadelphia's Zion Baptist Church that Reagan would "destroy the Social

Security System." He then toured the city's famed Italian market with Mayor Bill Green. Later he announced the endorsement of the one-million-member government employee union.

On Wednesday of that week Carter's Mideast negotiator Sol Linowitz created news by helping Egypt and Israel to resume talks on Palestinian independence. What he did not report was how speculations about the outcome of the election affected the talks. American Jewish supporters of Carter had warned Menachem Begin that the President was climbing rapidly in the polls and would probably win in November. Begin took their advice to make concessions to Carter now or suffer the consequences for the next four years. So while Reagan was speaking before the B'nai Brith, describing Carter's Mideast policy as a "bunch of zigzags and flip-flops trying to court favor with everyone," and attacking Carter himself for refusing to brand the PLO a terrorist organization (which Reagan didn't hesitate to do), Carter interrupted a routine press conference to tell reporters he had just talked to Linowitz on the phone from Cairo. "Sadat and Begin will resume negotiations for peace in the next few weeks," he proclaimed. "And both leaders agreed to another summit conference later this year." It was a fine morsel to take before the B'nai Brith, whom Carter was scheduled to address on Thursday, the day after Reagan outlined his own strongly pro-Israel stance. Since the Jewish vote was crucial in some of the big swing states, Carter's timing of the Mideast peace talks was a stroke of good fortune.

Naturally, Carter was delighted with the endorsement of the 13.6-million-member AFL-CIO, which he received the following day. If the union put its political-action money and volunteer work where its numbers were, the Democrats would have little to worry about.

On Thursday afternoon a rumor swept Wall Street that Ronald Reagan had suffered a heart attack; panic selling ruined a booming morning until the phony story was discredited. Lyn Nofziger accused Jody Powell of spreading mischief so as to suggest to voters that for Reagan, at age sixty-nine, a heart attack was not unlikely. Nofziger told two reporters he would start a rumor of his own—"Jimmy Carter has the clap."

Ronald Reagan injected a sober note into the election battle when he accused Carter of "playing a dangerous political game with national security for a two-day headline." At issue was Reagan's charge that the Defense Department had revealed an important military secret, the Stealth Aircraft Project, which made planes invisible to enemy radar, simply to boost Carter's reelection chances. Defense Secretary Harold Brown countered on Friday, accusing Reagan of "factual errors and gross distortion." At a press conference, Jody Powell called Reagan's statements "wrong, not responsible, and far beyond the accepted bounds of political partisanship." Henry Kissinger counterpunched, telling reporters that when he was in government, "the Stealth program was one of the most sensitive secrets we possessed."

And John Anderson? Burdened by money worries and near invisibility in the media, he took solace in small victories. Buoyed by word that the Federal Election Commission would give him federal money if he won at least 5 percent of the vote, he hoped that swing loans now being denied would come through. On Saturday he won the overwhelming endorsement of New York's Liberal Party, which had backed Jimmy Carter in 1976. If its leadership delivered, 145,000 New Yorkers would land in Anderson's column and throw the normally Democratic State's forty-one electoral votes up for grabs.

In the wake of the first week's campaign bombardments, Gerald Ford—still smarting from his 1976 defeat—felt vindicated by the outbreak of a worker's strike in Poland. Reminding the public of his infamous statement that the Poles were not dominated by the Soviet Union, Ford pointed with satisfaction to events in Warsaw. "It's tragic my remarks were not understood in 1976," he told reporters. "I think I was about four years ahead of most people." A surprising conclusion to a surprising first week of campaigning.

Carter's strategists decided to exploit Ronald Reagan's first-week gaffes, using handouts and their special influence with

White House reporters. "I have to conduct the affairs of our country," Carter told reporters. "I can't take a three-month vacation to attack opponents who criticize every defect in our societal life and make irresponsible judgments."

The Latinos made news when Cesar Chavez promised votes and precinct work from his thirty-thousand-member United Farm Workers union to reelect Carter. At the same time Herman Sillas, the highest and most visible Latino in the Carter administration, resigned as U.S. Attorney in California. In the Latin community, the Chavez-UFW endorsement deadened the sting of corruption in the Carter administration. Though not so partisan or numerous as Carter's black bloc, the Latinos had given Carter his winning edge in Texas and Florida in 1976. This time, though, Reagan and his team were determined to make it more of a contest, hoping to cut deeply into Carter's 87 percent of the Latino vote.

Inside the White House, Rafshoon-staged media events bolstered Carter's weak defense image. Carter signed a bill in the East Room which awarded a sum of $53 billion for weapons research and military pay hikes—a bill he had opposed vehemently for months. The next day the President told New Jersey newspaper editors that Reagan's accusations about the Stealth Project were "absolutely false and ridiculous," and claimed that Gerald Ford, who launched the project, never classified it. Ford replied that he was "amazed and upset" by Carter's words, insisting that the records showed that Stealth was probably "the most highly classified secret weapons system in the whole Defense Department."

Then the former Chief of Naval Operations, Admiral Elmo Zumwalt joined the fray, charging that President Carter made the decision to publicize Stealth independently for political gain: "There is no doubt, based on my contacts with White House staff and Pentagon officials, that the President decided to disclose the existence of this technology. The method chosen was first to leak the information and then be forced to confirm the leak. That decision placed greater priority on the reelection of the President than on the national security of the United States."

Ronald Reagan let his surrogates carry on the dispute while
he concentrated on bread-and-butter concerns. In Philadelphia he intercepted the age issue by admitting that he identified with the older generation: "Our generation has been
blamed for much of what seems wrong today. But I will not
apologize for our generation. We have known four wars and a
Great Depression. No people who ever lived fought harder,
paid a higher price for freedom, or did more to advance the
dignity of man."

His sights were clearly set on the senior citizens, who voted
overwhelmingly Republican, and in higher percentages than
any other age group. Reagan assured them they need have no
fears about Social Security payments: "I will support and defend the integrity of the Social Security system, the foundation
of economic life for millions of Americans. That system will be
strong, reliable, and protected under a Reagan administration."

As Reagan addressed a gathering of senior citizens, Carter
operatives moved among the ranks of reporters covering the
speech, and handed out releases which quoted Reagan's past
statements, implying that he advocated making the Social Security system voluntary. But although network news shows
commented on Reagan's past statements about Social Security,
on film the message came across that Reagan was strong and
would protect the system. The pictures spoke louder than the
words.

One would not expect Republicans to campaign for office in
Kokomo, Indiana, a heavily industrial Democratic city. But in
September 1980 Ronald Reagan drew cheers from a crowd of
unemployed workers there when he proposed to cut taxes and
government spending, and thereby create jobs and cut inflation. Introduced on that occasion as a "labor leader," Reagan
was really speaking to all the besieged blue-collar people of
America. Later in Chicago he walked through a Lithuanian
neighborhood, then met with Polish-American leaders in his
bid for ethnic support.

"Our coalition targets were basically blue-collar people and rural America," Spencer pointed out. "When you talk blue-collar, you have to mention all the ethnic deviations within that category in the East. So we worked the Lithuanian, the Polish, and the Italian communities using the same basic approach—family values. We went to areas of high unemployment—Youngstown, Steubenville, Flint, Kokomo, places we wouldn't normally visit—to emphasize that problem to the whole country. We got great coverage back East."

Reagan unveiled his five-year plan in Chicago, calling for a 30-percent tax cut over three years, sharp reductions in federal spending, and depreciation advantages to spur business. He called Carter's economic record "an American tragedy" and stayed close to his written text, avoiding questions from reporters.

Throughout the campaign, Reagan read from "half sheets," 5½ × 8½ pages with speech paragraphs typed out in full caps and triple-spaced. New speeches he would read entirely. For routine speeches, half sheets were used as inserts for any local references or specific topical points. If the speeches were written by a number of different people, Reagan did substantial rewriting, putting the speech into language he felt comfortable with.

"His basic appeal is his ability to communicate," Spencer stressed. It was the same evaluation of Reagan that Jesse Unruh had offered earlier to Carter.

Later in the week Reagan taunted Carter for refusing to join the scheduled debate between himself and John Anderson, who had accepted. Reagan argued that Carter was using Anderson as an excuse to avoid appearing on the same platform with him. "Now I don't find Mr. Anderson too much to be afraid of," Reagan chided. "But then in the primaries, Carter found Ted Kennedy too much for him to debate, also."

Hamilton Jordan claimed they were passing on the first debate because appearing with John Anderson in a three-way affair would give Anderson "an aura of credibility" that would pull votes from Carter. Pat Caddell, who had strongly advocated Carter's debating Kennedy in the primaries, felt even more strongly that Carter should keep away from Reagan. "Don't debate Reagan," he advised, "if there is any honorable way to avoid it."

Meanwhile John Anderson busily recruited volunteers on college campuses to use for phone banks and canvassing. As polls showed him pulling anywhere from 15 to 18 percent nationwide support, the League of Women Voters formalized their earlier conditional invitation and asked him to join the other two candidates on September 21 in Baltimore.

David Garth announced that Anderson had already gained ballot access in thirty states with 326 electoral votes, and had met the requirements in twelve other states and the District of Columbia. Touring California, Anderson appeared on all the free media Garth could arrange—talk shows, radio call-ins, media events, and press briefings—where he continued to expound the "Anderson Difference." But in spite of Anderson's invitation to the first debate and the promise of postelection funding by the FEC, Garth still had big troubles trying to arrange bank loans for his impoverished campaign.

Peter Dailey, the Los Angeles adman credited with helping Nixon pull off the most devastating electoral- and popular-vote victory in American history, was director of Reagan's 1980 campaign. He explained why Reagan's 1980 media race was so different from Nixon's campaign in 1972:

"To develop a mass-persuasion strategy to elect a Republican, you cannot depend on your base vote. If you cater to that base vote without reaching the 10 to 15 percent of undecided Democrats and independents, you'll end up with only 40 percent of the votes, and you'll lose the election. In 1972 we pinpointed characteristics of the 15 percent who were undecided, and we concocted a strategy to reach them. Fortunately, that strategy and its execution also reinforced our base vote of 40 percent. In 1980, the strategy we needed to reach that 15 percent was not at all what the 40 percent wanted to hear. Dick Wirthlin's research defined the undecided 15 percent Democrats and independents in a phrase we heard all around the country—'I can't stand Carter, but I just don't know about Reagan.'

"It was a very aware and very cynical group. They probably voted for Nixon in '72 and felt betrayed, then they looked for another alternative and found this peanut farmer who kept saying, 'I'll never lie to you.' They gravitated to him in '76 and felt betrayed for a completely different reason—the man was incompetent, a failure. Instead of being emotionally betrayed, they were financially betrayed, their livelihoods were being eaten away. Yet, knowing all that, they were still unsure about Reagan. Research revealed that the first perception of Reagan was as a political figure. But outside California and the West, the second level of perception was Reagan the actor. Combine that with 'I can't stand Carter but don't know about Reagan,' and it was clear there was no way we were going to get those people to vote for either a politician or an actor. They didn't trust politicians and didn't think an actor could solve their problems."

So Dailey's first commercials had to convince the undecideds that Ronald Reagan was an experienced administrator with solid accomplishments behind him.

"Our basic strategy was to run a documentary showing Reagan as an effective governor of a nation-state, California. Probably 80 percent of our messages were in that documentary. It ran for six weeks, but when it comes to mass persuasion, six weeks is the wink of an eye! We know how long it takes for an idea to take root. About a third of all television messages are misunderstood. Look at television advertising, its longevity. And still it affects people. That's what we tried to do."

The five-minute documentary was played often in those six weeks. Beginning with Reagan's Screen Actors Guild work in negotiating union contracts, the scene shifted to Sacramento as the narrator dramatically intoned, "In 1966 he was elected governor of the state of California, next to the President the biggest job in the nation. What he inherited was a state in crisis. Working with volunteers, he got things back on track." As visuals showed the governor signing bills, shaking hands with judges, and striding confidently with Nancy at his side, the narration continued along the same lines that Stu Spencer had used in California fourteen years earlier: "His common-sense style and strong, creative leadership won him a second term in 1970. The *San Francisco Chronicle* said, 'We exaggerate very little when we say Governor Reagan has saved the state from bankruptcy.' When he left office, the state's $194-million deficit had been transformed into a $554-million surplus." Because of Reagan's 95-percent recognition factor, the copy and on-screen scrawls never mentioned the name "Ronald Reagan" directly. Dailey's commercials along this line were scheduled to run fully two months into the campaign.

As in the primaries, a series of spot commercials focused on "issues." They were usually filmed in an "Oval Office" library setting. From behind a desk, Ronald Reagan spoke quietly, persuasively, and effectively. On inflation Reagan proclaimed: "We do not have inflation because, as President Carter says, we lived too well. We have inflation in great measure because the federal government has lived too well." On unemployment: "We'll beat the unemployment problem by allowing America's economic system to do what it does best—produce. Expand, produce some more, expand some more, and at every step of the way create new jobs."

Another called "Peace" was designed to fight the "trigger-happy" theme that Rafshoon was exploiting. A strip of convention footage showed candidate Reagan at the podium insisting, "Of all the objectives we seek, first and foremost is the establishment of lasting world peace." This was followed by a quick cut to the "Oval Office" set where he sat in a leather chair, wearing a Presidential dark blue suit. "Nancy and I have traveled this great land of ours many times over the years and we've found that Americans everywhere yearn for peace just as we do. It is impossible to capture in words the feelings we have about peace in the world, and how desperately we want it for our four children and our children's children."

A repeating theme line, echoing Eisenhower's "Time for a change," followed every Reagan commercial: "The time is now for Reagan, Reagan for President."

These commercials were not slick, not in any way Hollywood. Though Dailey was criticized for using "the old talking head" format, he vehemently resisted the temptation to inject glamor or mood. His reasons were solid: "We found that if we presented Reagan as anything but a competent former governor offering solutions, we reinforced that level of perception we wanted to avoid—*actor*. Because our 40-percent-base voters knew and loved the governor, they enjoyed stylized associations—the Statue of Liberty, 'God Bless America,' waving wheat, farmers around the table, the governor choking up while speaking—but for the 15 percent we were targeting, the slightest hint of that kind of production would have been disastrous, invalidating everything we did. We simply showed a nice man who ran a very complex state very successfully. I was less concerned with technique than with getting him elected. Every campaign is based on situation analysis. Once you think you have a formula that applies to all situations, you're in big trouble."

Rafshoon's first wave of television commercials were gently suggestive essays on the Presidency and Jimmy Carter. The name "Reagan" was never mentioned and "Republican" appeared on only one of the nineteen spots in the initial package. There were two basic themes: the first, the complex domestic and foreign responsibilities of the Presidency; the second, the President's interaction with ordinary citizens—in a suburban backyard, in an old folks' home, at a building site.

Rafshoon used separate five-minute film essays to describe the Presidential roles of Chief of State, Commander-in-Chief, and Planner of the Nation's Future. The tone was academic, the style reminiscent of old newsreels. Rafshoon's "Commander-in-Chief" spot, aimed at dispelling Carter's weakling image, showed the President reviewing troops and inspecting missiles and aircraft carriers, while a narrator said, "When President Carter sits down at the White House with the Secretary of Defense, he brings a hard, military professionalism to the meeting. This President is an Annapolis graduate. He spent eleven years in the Navy. And he knows what he's talking about. President Carter has always worked for a strong military, knowing the importance of being strong." The final footage in this spot featured Carter, Sadat, and Begin signing their celebrated treaty, while the narrator concluded, "In the end, President Carter knows our final security lies not only in having a strong defense but in being willing to sit down and negotiate for peace." The theme line followed: "President Carter—a military man and a man of peace."

Another commercial included a selection of Democratic politicians praising Carter's "mature and sound judgment." "He's the kind of President whose hand I want on the red telephone," said one Democrat—the first hint of a war-and-peace attack about to be launched against Ronald Reagan.

The most effective of the "Chief of State" commercials was the one called "The President Alone." The film, using fast cuts and swirling action, showed Carter involved in the frenzied activity of a Presidential day. The narrator boasted of his "hammering out" an energy policy, deregulating air and trucking industries, organizing the Camp David talks, and reducing federal regulations and paperwork. Then, as daylight turned to twilight, the President climbed an outside stairway at the White House and entered a study: "The responsibility never ends. Even at the end of a long working day there is usually another cable addressed to the Chief of State from the other side of the world where the sun is shining and something is happening." As the light in the Presidential study flashed on, the voice-over concluded, "And he's not finished yet."

When Carter was not being actually quoted, all the words and narration in his commercials were the work of Harry Muheim, Jerry Rafshoon's secret weapon. Thanks to the excellent work of producer Eli Bleich, Carter's commercials were skillfully made and highly professional—even if ultimately not politically effective. Voters, polls showed, did not doubt that Carter kept long hours and worked hard. What people questioned were the results of all this activity—questions the advertising did not satisfactorily answer.

Rafshoon's "Town Meeting" spots opened with the narrator's observing, "Over the past three and a half years, in nineteen American communities, the quiet rhythm of everyday life was exploded by the same memorable event—the President came to town." The spots then showed Carter mingling with everyday Americans, emphasizing his closeness to common people.

A commercial on defense showed a crowd of black, white, and Hispanic workers in T-shirts and hardhats on a construction site. A black man opened the discussion by charging, "Everyone used to talk about how great and powerful the United States used to be. Well, we're not so powerful anymore. It seems like we're second." To which the President replied, "We're still the most powerful. In almost every kind of new weapon, the United States comes first. Politically, militarily, economically the most powerful nation on earth. And morally and ethically the most powerful nation on earth. This country is one that believes in human beings." The narrator concluded: "President Carter, for all the people."

Another commercial ended with the phrase, "He cares about peace and people," implying that his opponent didn't really care about such things. It was the "doubleback" technique, used so tellingly against Kennedy in the primaries; only now, against Reagan, Rafshoon had to tread more carefully and measure his character assaults.

"Our anti-Reagan material was put together with discretion," explained Harry Muheim. "For example, we talked about a President's having to know things himself. No matter how many aides or advisers he has, he can never escape the responsibility of understanding the issues himself. That statement can be construed as aimed at Ronald Reagan. It also happens to be true, no matter whom you're running against. I tried to maintain that tone throughout the campaign." What Muheim did not say was that Caddell's research showed that had they attacked Reagan more directly, there would have been a negative backlash against their "mean tactics."

One "Town Meeting" spot came back to haunt the Carter campaign. At a high school auditorium in Steubenville, Ohio, Carter invited the wife of a coal mine operator to meet him in Washington after she complained that unnecessary bureaucratic meddling was threatening her family business. Beaming with relief at the President's invitation, Mary Downend blew a kiss at Carter and began to weep as the commercial ended. It made very effective television. But later in the campaign Mrs. Downend appeared with Tom Brokaw on the *Today Show* to report that when she tried to see Carter in Washington, he shunted her aside to aides and nothing was ever done. The situation in the Ohio coal industry was unchanged. Now, a year later, her family was one step away from bankruptcy. Although she had voted for Carter in 1976, this time she would back another candidate. "President Carter deals in symbols," she lamented. "And I was just another symbol. I feel used now, and even though I'm in a Carter commercial, I'm going to vote for Ronald Reagan."

As for John Anderson, so little money had been raised that David Garth decided to conserve resources for the final weeks, hoping to keep close enough with free media to preserve his slim hopes. The few television buys made that first month were simply replays of what had been running during the summer—Anderson talking about issues, saying, "I don't believe in the easy solution, the glib panacea." Inside Anderson's strategy offices, the talk was all about the debate and how they would use it to pull out from behind.

After the first two weeks of campaigning, the national polls showed the race closing up: Gallup found Reagan ahead, 40 percent to Carter's 38 and Anderson's 15. CBS and the *New York Times* had Carter leading 38 to 35 percent, with Anderson at 14 percent. Any way you looked at it, it was still a horse race for win and place; the "show" spot seemed inevitable.

Carter's hopes of keeping media attacks focused on Reagan suffered a setback when Carter campaign manager Tim Kraft resigned to face charges of cocaine possession. At a special Sunday session the strategy group discussed the possible fallout over Kraft's departure, and released a statement assuring America that their departed comrade "would be exonerated completely."

The President visited Texas, a critical state in his game plan, and told a town meeting that the latest events in Iran "might very well lead to a resolution of this problem." He denounced Reagan for making the hostages a campaign issue, and needled him for using monitors to control his off-the-cuff remarks.

While Carter tried to regain momentum by waving the hostage banner out West, his opponent was busy in the President's own backyard playing statesman. Reagan and Bush stood together on the steps of the U.S. Capitol building in Washington, where they hoped to return on Inauguration Day, 1981. There they promised an audience of 250 Republican congressmen and candidates that by September of 1981 the Reagan-Bush administration would have achieved five important goals: cuts in the Congressional budget, cuts in other federal programs by cracking down on waste and fraud, an across-the-board tax cut for working Americans, a crusade to produce more jobs in private industry, and a crash program to strengthen the nation's military forces.

The next day Reagan flew to Texas on the heels of his Democratic rival and visited towns with large Mexican-American populations. With Texas Governor Bill Clements at his side, he came out strongly for a guest-worker plan advocated by Clements and the governors of New Mexico, Arizona, California, and six Mexican border states, which would grant Mexican nationals labor visas for up to a year. It was clear that Reagan craved Latino support.

"We really worked the Mexican-Americans in Texas," Stu Spencer recalled. "They're very family-oriented, so we kept talking family values. We knew our best chance was with the middle-class entrepreneur Mexicans, people who own restaurants and little shops, who are affected by the same things as other middle-class Americans—the economy, mostly. On our first trip to Texas we went deep into the Valley—Harlington —which is unheard-of for a Republican. On our first California trip we went to East Los Angeles. The signal was clear. The Mexican community knew this guy was serious about seeking their support. He talked about promoting jobs and licking inflation, though he backed off on bilingual education."

Although the numbers of Mexicans who attended those

Texas rallies were much smaller than would have probably gathered for a Kennedy appearance, Reagan's people were heartened. "For a Republican running in Texas, the Mexican turnout was surprising," said Jim Baker.

By Tuesday, Carter had modulated his enthusiasm over a hostage deal, telling reporters in Atlanta, "We have no prospect of an early resolution." Meanwhile the State Department was putting the finishing touches on a five-hundred-page review ordered by the President, detailing U.S. involvement in Iran since 1940. Iran had requested the report as a precondition for releasing the prisoners. Carter promised to present it to an "international tribunal."

In Iran various officials were quoted, ranging from advocates of early release to hardliners urging spy trials. John Anderson tried to find his "difference" on the hostage issue by criticizing Ronald Reagan's public acceptance of some of the Ayatollah's conditions: "The extent to which Governor Reagan sought to leap in and get the drop on President Carter is an indication of the strong temptation to politicize that issue. I am trying very hard not to make the hostages part of this campaign."

Revealing that he had now fulfilled ballot requirements in all fifty states, Anderson stressed he was running a "positive campaign." He then used the early part of the week to attack Reagan as "irrelevant" and "too old" to understand the modern world. "Those in the older generation fear change," he told a Portland audience. "They darkly predict the end, the demise of the family, and they've always been wrong." Later, in Seattle, he continued to berate the "old man": "Chronological age does affect our thinking. And Reagan represents a kind of vintage thinking that says we can go back to some previous period in our history and find answers to problems that face American families today."

Anderson expected the upcoming debate to vault him into a competitive position. To offset criticism that his candidate appealed only to "bridge-table suburbanites," Garth announced that two prominent blacks were endorsing Anderson—actor Paul Winfield and San Francisco minister Cecil Williams, both former supporters of Jimmy Carter.

A bitter fight developed over a memo leaked to the press by Carter's people. It described the legal troubles any bank would have to face if it loaned money to John Anderson. Prepared by the President's staff, the memo was made public just as David Garth was preparing to approach a "consortium of banks" for desperately needed loans. "It's another sleazy attempt at intimidation, aimed at the American banks," Garth noted bitterly.

Jimmy Carter was in his element that Wednesday, speaking to black supporters in the Ebenezer Baptist Church in Atlanta. He accused Ronald Reagan of creating "stirrings of hate between blacks and whites, using code words like 'states rights,' and relating the Ku Klux Klan to the South."

Ironically, at that moment Reagan was accepting the endorsement of Eldridge Cleaver, ex–Black Panther leader and now a born-again Christian who had seen the free-enterprise light. After listening to a Texas reporter read Carter's comments about injecting "racism and hatred" into the campaign, Reagan shook his head and grimaced. "I don't know how much further he'll go," he said, "to divert attention from the fact that if he agreed to debate, he could say all these things to a nationwide audience." Clearly, he was trying to goad Carter into showing up in Baltimore on Sunday.

Thursday, September 18. Rafshoon scheduled a nationally televised press conference in the White House three days before the first debate, a clever move designed to steal the thunder from Carter's two opponents. But the best laid plans sometimes backfire. Carter opened proceedings with a five-minute recital of his accomplishments as President, reeling off a list that put him into contention with Franklin Roosevelt as our most productive leader. By the time he finished with the phrase, "And the progress of America goes on," the normally supportive White House press corps had been transformed into a pack of inquisitors. During the question session they focused on his "racism" charges.

"Do you really believe Governor Reagan is running a campaign of hatred and racism?" one asked. "There are people who say that in political campaigns you get mean and try to savage your opponents," another suggested. "Do you regret

using such words as 'racism,' 'hatred,' and 'racist' in referring
to Governor Reagan?'" probed a third.

Replying to each with growing uncertainty and irritation,
Carter tried to end the matter by saying he didn't think Reagan was a racist. "The press seems to be obsessed with this
issue. Now I believe we ought to drop it."

But Lisa Myers of the *Washington Star* would not drop it,
signaling a radical change in a press corps that for years had
acted as virtual publicists for the Carter communication network. "It was your own cabinet secretary, Patricia Harris, who
first interjected the KKK into the Presidential race," Myers
said. "So how can you now blame Governor Reagan?"

Carter stared hard at Myers, but she did not avert her eyes.
In a shaky voice he replied, "I am not blaming Governor
Reagan," then cued his press aide to say, "No more ques-
tions," and walked off the podium.

Adding insult to the injury, both the Reagan and the Anderson camps filed formal protests with the three television
networks, demanding equal time to compensate for the President's opening statement—an "obvious campaign commercial
on free time." Though they were turned down, they kept the
news pot boiling to remind voters of Carter's self-serving performance.

On Saturday, hoping to lay an awkward situation to rest,
Carter released a letter to a Congressional panel denying he or
his staff leaked the secret Stealth information. He made it
clear he would not debate anywhere with John Anderson,
"who is a creation of the press." He offered instead to debate
Reagan head to head after Sunday's matchup—an idea rejected the same day by Reagan, Anderson, and the League of
Women Voters.

Opinions were divided over how much Carter suffered from
his decision to stay away. Carter's own strategists felt they were
in a "no-win situation," finally agreeing to abide by Pat Caddell's contention that to appear side by side with Anderson
would only give Anderson more credibility. September polls
showed Anderson pulling slightly more votes from the President than from Reagan. In a two-way race Carter would have

led Reagan by several points, but with Anderson added to the equation, Reagan pulled slightly ahead. Anderson ran best in those very states that Carter needed desperately to win— New York, Pennsylvania, Illinois, Ohio, Michigan, New Jersey, Massachusetts, Wisconsin, and Connecticut, which carried a total of 190 electoral votes. For Carter to win those states, Caddell argued, Anderson's candidacy would have to fade away. If he debated Anderson, that would make Anderson's demise less likely. Jordan and Strauss bought Caddell's thesis, but Rafshoon, Eizenstat, and Powell were less convinced. In the end they went with Caddell, a move that delighted the Reagan people.

"It was a mistake," Stu Spencer declared. "It just looked like Carter was avoiding the whole political process, and by referring so negatively to John Anderson, he looked mean and ornery. There was no way he could have gotten hurt in a three-man debate. If the two others had ganged up on him, it would have made him a martyr. He kept out for one reason: he didn't want to help Anderson pull his vote. But John Anderson is too harsh. You can give him all the exposure in the world and he's just going to hurt himself. We didn't want Anderson's demise to come too early. We wanted to keep him alive if we could, because it helped us, particularly in the states with many electoral votes. He hurt us more than Carter only in Illinois."

The League of Women Voters, according to their policy for debate no-shows, planned to set up an "empty chair" between the other two candidates to signify that the President had been invited but chose not to appear. There was instant backlash from the White House. Jody Powell reported that Carter was "fuming" over the empty-chair prop and threatened to find other sponsors for future debates as a way of punishing the League. A few days before the debate, the League conceded, announcing that no empty chair would be placed on the stage.

Political reporter Bill Moyers was chosen to moderate. The six journalists picked for the questioning panel were selected solely by the League. Both Reagan and Anderson asked to play a role in the process, but when that request was denied, they agreed to abide by the League's judgments. Panelists included Charles Corddry (*Baltimore Sun*), Soma Golden (*New York Times*), syndicated columnist Daniel Greeneberg, Carol Loomis (*Fortune*), Lee May (*Los Angeles Times*), and Jane Quinn (*Newsweek*). CBS and NBC carried the event live over their networks, as did the Public Broadcasting System and National Public Radio; ABC was the only network which did not screen the affair. At the candidates' request, television camera crews were forbidden to shoot audience-reaction shots.

On the weekend of the debate, Anderson huddled with David Garth in Washington to prepare for the ordeal. He had high expectations that the contrast between him and Reagan would be to his advantage. "You see us on the evening news a minute a day, read about us in newspapers, and you are bombarded with paid political ads," he explained. "In the debates, however, you can see us side by side for several hours. We are not reading prepared texts, we do not know what the questions are going to be. You get to see our minds at work and can judge for yourself which of us most effectively communicates his ideas and inspires his audience." Anderson studied videotapes of himself during the primary debates and watched a film of the 1976 Carter-Ford debates. Admitting he may have seemed "too preacherlike" in the primary debates, he vowed to soften his intensity and relax his coiled-spring body stance.

Ronald Reagan retreated with his advisers to the estate in Atoka, Virginia, that he had leased from Texas Governor Bill Clements. Built by John and Jackie Kennedy, the estate is in the heart of hunting country, overlooking the Blue Ridge Mountains from a twenty-six-acre ridge. The twelve-room ranch-style house sits back from the main road on the grounds that Jackie named "Wexford," to honor Kennedy's forebears from County Wexford, Ireland. Spencer, Wirthlin, and Nofziger set up a studio in the rear of the house, where they screened tapes of past debates. Then they brought in outsiders, tough political veterans, to fire hard questions at their man. One of these inquisitors was a former Anderson aide,

Representative David Stockman of Michigan. Once a fierce anti–Vietnam War activist, the now conservative thirty-four-year-old Stockman played the role of Anderson brilliantly in the mock sessions.

"We worked with Ron on the points we felt we should make in the debate," Stu Spencer explained. "To hell with the question they asked, what point did we need to make? One goal was to keep Anderson as a viable candidate and not destroy him. Another was to reach 50 million people, particularly on domestic issues. We wanted to underline the fact that Carter was not there. And finally we wanted to show the country that Ron didn't have horns on his head."

The Sunday before the debate, newspaper headlines read: "U.S. ILL-PREPARED FOR WAR, LAIRD DECLARES . . . IRAN MOBILIZES FOR IRAQ WAR . . . WHITE HOUSE DENIES ANDERSON CHARGES." This last was particularly harmful for Carter's hopes. Carter was quoted as saying, "Jack Anderson's latest column alleging that the U.S. plans to attack Iran is false, grotesque, and irresponsible . . . a complete invention which can only damage efforts to obtain safe release of the American hostages." The denial only helped fan speculation about a pending "October Surprise."

At 10:00 p.m. eastern daylight time, Anderson and Reagan climbed to the stage of the Convention Center and faced the panel of reporters. According to the ground rules, the debate would last one hour; panelists would ask one question each, and each candidate would have two and a half minutes to reply plus an extra ninety seconds to answer a follow-up question from his opponent. Striding to center stage, the contestants shook hands and then went behind their podiums to wait. Reagan seemed relaxed and confident, Anderson stiffly intense.

During the debate, Anderson continually referred to his opponent as "Governor Reagan" or "Sir," while Reagan called the Congressman "John" with easy familiarity. Both referred often to the President and both assailed his policies, but they reserved most of their remarks for defining their own differences. Reagan said he would solve the energy crisis by pulling government off the backs of the oil industry; Anderson insisted it was necessary to ban gas-guzzlers, use car pools and mass transit, and levy an extra fifty-cent-per-gallon gas tax to force conservation. Both candidates ducked a question asking if they favored a military draft; instead, they criticized Carter for allowing military pay and benefits to fall so low that the best-qualified volunteers dropped out.

After Reagan praised his own fiscal achievements as governor of California, Anderson challenged his arithmetic, insisting that during Reagan's eight-year term, state spending in California rose from $4.6 billion to $10.2 billion. Reagan listened with an expression of pained disbelief and then replied with a tried-and-true rejoinder that had been part of "the Speech" for years. "Some people look up figures and some people make up figures," he said, smiling. "And John here just made up some very interesting figures."

An audience of twenty-five hundred sat in the dark portion of the auditorium, keeping silent most of the evening as Moderator Moyers had requested, stifling applause, cheers, and hisses. But on two occasions discipline was breached when murmurs rippled through the crowd: first, when Reagan proposed rehabilitating condemned houses and selling them to needy families for one dollar (a program that host city Baltimore had run successfully for many years); and second, when Reagan remarked about abortion, "I notice that everyone who is for abortion is somebody who has already been born."

Reagan concluded his remarks fervently and eloquently, calling America "a nation which is for all mankind a shining city on a hill." One celebrated Democratic consultant admiringly commented: "A hell of a closing. That was 180 seconds of the best television there is."

When the debate ended, Nancy Reagan was the first to climb onstage. She gave her husband a congratulatory kiss while a galaxy of Anderson family members, led by his wife Keke, surrounded the Congressman. As photographers took pictures, Anderson crossed the stage to shake hands with Reagan and both sides finally exited.

The winner?

"John Anderson was too much the insider, the technician, to get people genuinely enthusiastic," offered Democratic pollster Peter Hart. "Reagan spent most of his time addressing people who were already for him," noted his ex-strategist John Sears. "The only loser was Carter," observed Stu Spencer. "A guy already upset about the way Carter's handled the economy will be even more upset, because Carter won't even debate that economy with the other candidates."

Both candidates gained from exposure to the estimated 55 million Americans who watched the debate. Lou Harris, polling immediately following the encounter, found that both Anderson and Reagan scored three points higher among people who saw them than among those who had not watched the debate. Gallup showed a three-point drop for Carter in the days following the debate, as did the NBC/AP poll. As Stu Spencer pointed out, for those who participated in the debate, there were only winners.

After viewing the debate, President Carter said he felt comfortable with his decision not to join the "two Republicans." Despite Carter's insistence that he had not lost ground, Jody Powell announced a stepped-up travel schedule for the week ahead, including stops in New York, Michigan, Illinois, and California.

In Chicago an obviously pleased John Anderson said the debate established him as a "clear alternative" to Reagan and Carter. He predicted Carter would change his mind and join the next debate, scheduled for mid-October. Asked what would change the President's mind, Anderson quipped, "Sagging polls, sagging polls."

Meanwhile Pete Dailey of Reagan's media unit produced a universally admired commercial. Called "Empty Podium," it was aired the week following the debate, and contained only one prop, an empty podium on a stage. A disembodied female voice made the point: "The League of Women Voters invited President Carter to join in the 1980 debates. He refused the invitation. Maybe it's because, during his administration, inflation has gone as high as 18 percent, the number of Americans out of work has reached 8 million, housing starts have hit a new low, while interest rates have hit a new high."

At a town meeting in Torrance, California, Jimmy Carter warned that this election was a choice between "war and peace." Later in Los Angeles, where Ted Kennedy joined him onstage at the Beverly Hilton to lend lukewarm support to his candidacy, the President again charged that a Ronald Reagan Presidency would endanger the peace.

Meanwhile Reagan was busy in Tennessee trying to bolster a weak spot uncovered by his pollster—poor female support. Pledging to enforce laws protecting women from discrimination, he explained that he opposed the Equal Rights Amendment not because he was against women, but because he was unwilling to put more power in the hands of already-too-powerful courts. "Who knows what decisions will be made there?" he asked.

The next morning Reagan called Carter's "war and peace" attack "unforgivable and beneath decency." At an airport rally in Pensacola, Florida, he reiterated his desire for peace: "I have two sons, a grandson, I've known four wars in my lifetime, and I think world peace must be the principal aim of this nation." Later in the day, while visiting the campus of Louisiana State University, he emphasized that Carter favored draft registration and he opposed it. The students cheered enthusiastically.

In Washington Jody Powell desperately tried to soften the backlash on the "warmongering" attacks. "I talked to the President last night," Powell said. "He realized as soon as he said it that he had overstated his case. But we have no apologies to make for raising that issue and asking Governor Reagan to explain the numerous occasions on which he has advocated the use of military force in international disputes."

Carter staffers then gave reporters a list of statements by Reagan that ostensibly urged military involvement in various parts of the world. In Los Angeles the President appeared in a television interview to specify instances when Reagan had advised military moves into Cuba, Lebanon, and South America.

"The record's there," Carter concluded. "What he would do in the Oval Office I hope will never be observed by the American people." When told of Reagan's indignation over the warmonger charge, aides accompanying Carter in Oregon were gleeful. "That's great," one said. "He's rising to the bait."

The "war and peace" gambit was based on polls by Caddell and others showing that most Americans believed Jimmy Carter would be better at avoiding war than Ronald Reagan, by a 2½-to-1 margin. As the war between Iran and Iraq escalated, Caddell carefully monitored public reactions, hoping that the conflict would drive voters to back the President, as war traditionally does.

Meanwhile leaders in Iran were calling the Iraqi invasion a "U.S. plot that would impact on the destiny of the hostages." President Carter called for a negotiated settlement, while emphasizing that the Persian Gulf must be kept open to international shipping. In Texas Reagan called the outbreak "tragic. What is happening in Iran and Iraq is the consequence of policies this administration has followed for the last three and a half years. A vacillating foreign policy and a weakened defense capability are largely to blame."

At the end of the week Reagan rejected an invitation from the League of Women Voters to meet Carter in a debate that would exclude John Anderson. "I have always believed any series of debates should include every viable candidate," he said at a Portland airport runway, proving he had learned his lesson well in the New Hampshire primary. "Jim Baker, my negotiator, has informed the League I cannot agree to a series of debates which preclude John Anderson from debating President Carter in the same way I debated Mr. Anderson."

Bob Strauss conceded that the first debate had helped Anderson, who threatened to take enough votes from Carter to give Reagan an edge in some key states—New York, Connecticut, New Jersey, and California. "That's a real concern to us," he admitted.

Anderson aides protested the League's offer to bypass their man, branding it "an effort to appease President Carter," while Anderson himself, campaigning in Cleveland, asked the public to pressure the League with "cards and letters from all over the country, suggesting a three-man debate in October."

George Bush accused the League of "carrying water for the White House." Behind the furor lay a carefully considered Reagan debate strategy: "Carter's people thought we were afraid because of our attitude, that we were using Anderson as a crutch to avoid Carter. They thought Carter would chew Reagan up, nail him with twenty years of speeches and all those extrapolations they had researched to make Reagan look bad. All we wanted to do was keep our cards close to the vest until we felt we needed a debate. Then, if that time ever came, they were already committed. The option was ours, not theirs."

After the first four weeks of the campaign, Gallup showed Reagan ahead 39 to 35 percent, while Anderson fell to 14 percent. Curiously, the amount of undecided voters had risen to 12 percent, whereas normally it decreases as a campaign develops.

Jimmy Carter reminded a group of New York business and union leaders that Ronald Reagan would soon visit their city —the same Reagan who had prayed that "the federal government would not bail out New York City." At a Manhattan dress factory Carter gladly accepted the endorsement of the Ladies Garment Workers Union and used the occasion to blast his opponent's stand on the ERA. Then, hoping to patch things up with the Jews, he told the workers that he vehemently rejected an Arab threat to throw Israel out of the United Nations. In New York, those Jews he boasted he "didn't need" in 1976 were very important to him now.

Jordan knew that if Carter couldn't carry the New York Jews, he couldn't win New York, and chances for reelection would be dim indeed. Jews traditionally are Democrats (60 percent). Only 8 percent at the time were Republicans, and 32 percent were independents. In 1968 Humphrey took 80 percent of the Jewish vote. George McGovern scored an all-time low in Jewish popularity when he received 64 percent in 1972. In 1976 Jimmy Carter had 75 percent of their votes and won New York by nearly 300,000 votes. In 1980 a mid-August Lou Harris poll showed an unprecedented disaster in the making with Anderson pulling 36 percent and Carter only 30 percent of the Jewish vote. Even more surprising, Republican Ronald Reagan had a solid 25 percent of Jewish support. According to Harris, the U.N. snafu was not the only reason for the defections.

"There's a deep emotional thing working here," he explained. "Jews feel that if it came to a choice, Carter would come down against Israel and against the Jews."

"We've got more trouble with the Jews than with any other constituency," admitted Carter's special-interest emissary, Elaine Karmarck.

"The Jewish vote is up for grabs," claimed Max Hugel, Reagan's director of voter groups.

In spite of money problems, Anderson hired well-known Jewish activist Aaron Rosenbaum to work the Jewish lode. All three candidates went to the national B'nai Brith convention and pitched their causes, but there was no consensus of support for any of them. Middle-income Jews with more conservative views were attracted to Reagan. Anderson pulled best from the upper-middle-class segments, the professionals and suburbanites. Carter's support came from loyal working-class and union Jews.

In an oblique appeal to Jews and liberals, Anderson began the week by warning a group of evangelist broadcasters to stop "their medieval meddling in American politics." "The political marriage of the Moral Majority and the New Right is not ordained in heaven," he told the stony religious broadcasters' convention, which represented a radio and television audience estimated at 130 million a week. His remarks were obviously not geared to earn him many born-again votes.

Reagan, meanwhile, started his week with a bang. Former Watergate prosecutor Leon Jaworski announced he would lead a Democrats-for-Reagan group, citing his "deep disappointment in President Carter's lack of leadership, his vacillation, and his lack of consistent goals," as well as in Carter's responsibility for "casting a cloud of suspicion over the Presidency in the Billy Carter–Libya fiasco."

In a swing from Iowa to New York, Reagan courted votes by changing his mind on two issues—the Russian grain embargo and federal aid to New York City. He told a crowd of farmers outside Des Moines he now opposed the grain embargo, because it didn't really hurt the Russians and was "mere grandstanding for the American people." Then, at a fund-raising banquet in New York City, he proclaimed his change of heart on the aid question because "Mayor Ed Koch began straightening the city out." Clearly, the Reagan strategists were conceding nothing to Carter.

In a highly publicized development, the Parliament of Iran finally agreed to set up a special commission to "study the hostage question." Rumors of an impending release began circulating and political observers speculated that the October Surprise was brewing. At Reagan-Bush headquarters in Arlington, Virginia, Dick Wirthlin scheduled "tracking studies" to begin October 2, designed to measure the possible impact of a hostage release on voters. "We felt if the hostages were released and went to Wiesbaden, Germany, prior to the twentieth of October, the President had a chance," Wirthlin explained. "But it was our judgment that the closer we got to the election, the more skeptically the American voter would look at their release." By constantly referring to the October Surprise from the start of the campaign, Reagan and his surrogates introduced that note of skepticism, preempting any potential national jubilation over the event. And just in case, they had a batch of television commercials waiting, specially designed to blunt the political impact of such a surprise.

As Carter ballyhooed a plan to help the steel industry through tax breaks and protection against imports, Congress voted to extend unemployment benefits. Republicans charged that the bill, providing an extra thirteen weeks of unemployment payments, had been rushed through the House to help Carter's reelection. "It will be known as the Jimmy Carter Reelection Act of 1980," quipped Congressman John Rousselot of California.

Campaigning in Pittsburgh for Catholic votes, Reagan promised to promote tax credits for families with children in parochial schools, in a bid to break up another strong Democratic bloc. In Wilkes-Barre he invoked the names of John Kennedy and Harry Truman and attacked Carter's credentials as a Democrat, accusing him of "deliberately using unemployment to curb inflation. We can't afford one more year, let alone four more years of Carter's cruel policies."

October 1, Detroit. Reporters sang "Happy Birthday" to President Carter, which evoked a grin and a birthday wish from Carter for "four more years." Speaking to auto workers outside the Flint Ford factory, Carter told a cheering crowd he would not rest "until every man and woman in the auto industry is back on the job full time." UAW president Douglas Fraser, at Carter's side, claimed that auto workers who had flirted with John Anderson were flocking back to the Democratic fold.

Meanwhile Anderson told a Denver audience how Carter was using foul tactics to keep him off the ballot in many states, freezing him out of the debates, and drafting a memo "leaked into print so bankers would read it and not lend us money." Citing Carter ads running in half a dozen big industrial states that read, "A vote for Anderson is a vote for Reagan," he assailed the President's "meanness of spirit," charging him with being "desperate, hysterical, and undemocratic."

Carter refused to allow aide David Aaron to testify before a Congressional committee about leaks on the Stealth aircraft, amid reports that Aaron had leaked information on instructions from Carter himself.

As Carter defended his flanks, Ronald Reagan visited Illinois and at a rally of senior citizens spoke a familiar refrain: "No senior citizen will ever miss a Social Security payment in a Reagan administration." He labeled Carter's charge that he wanted to make the system voluntary "not only inaccurate and incredible, but a smoke screen to hide the fact that this President, with his high inflation and low-growth policies, had done more damage to the Social Security system than any President in recent history."

At a town meeting in Dayton, Ohio, the President counter-attacked, hitting Reagan where he hurt most—on the war-and-peace issue. "If the American people get the mistaken idea a nuclear arms race from our side is going to cause the Soviets to quit building nuclear weapons on their side, they are silly." Later in Lansdowne, Pennsylvania, Carter expounded on the subject: "For a Presidential candidate to advocate a nuclear arms race is shocking." Mondale got on the news as he joined the assault, accusing Reagan of risking nuclear war by "reckless, irresponsible, and dangerous" opposition to SALT II, encouraging "the final madness" of a nuclear holocaust.

On Thursday the House expelled Democratic Congressman Ozzie Myers of Pennsylvania, on the heels of the Abscam bribery scandal. It was the first expulsion of any member of Congress in 119 years.

On Friday Reagan visited the National Religious Broadcasters group at Lynchburg, Virginia, where host Jerry Falwell, the television evangelist, headed a drive to mold the electronic born-again church into a pro-Reagan faction. "I don't think we ever should have expelled God from the classroom," Reagan said, promising to work for voluntary school prayers. Stating that he favored the separation of church and state, he emphasized his belief that God hears the prayers of Jews as well as Christians. "Since both religions are based on the God of Moses, I'm sure those prayers are heard," he noted —an ecumenical sentiment that could not offend anyone except Buddhists and nonbelievers.

With an estimated 40 million evangelical Christians now in the country, the support of Falwell and other television preachers was no small matter. A Gallup survey found that evangelicals were concentrated in the South, in rural areas, and among women, blacks, the less educated, and the less well-off. In early September Carter led Reagan in born-again support, mostly because the majority of his black followers were evangelicals. Gallup showed Carter with 52 percent backing, Reagan 31, and Anderson 6. Among white evangelicals who watched television preachers, however, the situation was reversed: a *Los Angeles Times* poll found Reagan had 50 percent of this group to Carter's 29 and Anderson's 12 percent. Though Jimmy Carter had the born-again vote in his pocket four years before, it looked like he would be hard pressed to win it this time.

In 1976 the Catholic vote was Carter's, 57 to 41 percent, but that was the lowest Catholic margin for a winning Democratic President since Harry Truman's 56 percent in 1948. Making up 25 percent of all Americans, Catholics are concentrated in the Northeast and Midwest; almost half are registered Democrats. They are predominantly blue-collar workers who go to the polls in higher percentages than any other religious group except Jews. That was why Reagan's support for parochial schools and his antiabortion stand were trumpeted so loudly and emphatically whenever he visited areas densely populated by Catholics.

On Friday David Garth released new polls showing Anderson gaining ground in six states—Massachusetts, New Jersey, Connecticut, Wisconsin, Oregon, and Washington. In Connecticut he claimed 27 percent of the vote and in Massachusetts, 24 percent. Garth hoped these revelations would help spur lagging contributions and support.

At the end of the week, Richard Nixon attracted media attention by telling a *Parade* magazine interviewer: "Ronald Reagan values my foreign policy advice and may call on me as a counselor or negotiator," if elected. A Reagan strategist, requesting anonymity, reacted to Nixon's claim bluntly: "He's hallucinating."

A quotation never published in the *Parade* interview emphasized Nixon's high regard for Reagan the communicator. "I have never underestimated Jimmy Carter, and in certain forums, particularly small groups, he can be very persuasive," Nixon said. "But in terms of being able to communicate to great masses of people, it's a little leaguer against a big leaguer. Speaking from the Oval Office quietly and affirmatively as he does on television, I think Reagan would mobilize the people. He has the style to go over the heads of Congress, the media, and the bureaucracy in Washington—straight to the people."

While the television networks, because of their coverage of the Anderson candidacy, did not assign back-up units to travel

with the Vice-Presidential campaigners or other important
surrogates, they did include frequent footage of such Carter
cabinet members as Harold Brown, Patricia Harris, and Walter Mondale. Almost invisible on the network news were
George Bush and Jerry Ford, who were as busy as anyone else
in either camp. Shut out of the national news, they made up
for it with regular interviews in local papers and television
interviews wherever they traveled.

For Jerry Ford, the issue was deeper than simple politics. He
honestly didn't like Jimmy Carter as a person. "No man of
either party in my thirty years in Washington ever did what
he did," Ford explained. "He went too far using the government in the campaign, in personal attacks on Reagan and
Anderson—he crossed a line that men wanting to be President
should not cross." So Ford signed on to travel fifty-three of the
sixty-four days between Labor Day and election day, scheduled to cover sixty thousand miles and thirty states to raise
money and beat Jimmy Carter. Written into his speeches was
a stock paragraph that summed up his true feelings: "When
Betty and I talked about what has happened to our country
since Jimmy Carter became President, we decided our con-
sciences would bother us the rest of our lives if we did nothing
and Carter was reelected. So we are going to do all in our
power to get Ronald Reagan elected. Under Carter, our allies
no longer trust us, our adversaries no longer respect us. He
was handed the economy on a silver platter and he blew it."

Invariably, he would cite Carter's invention of the "misery
index," the sum of the inflation and unemployment rates. "It
was 15.8 percent when I left office," Ford noted. "As a matter
of curiosity, I looked it up now. It came to 21 percent. If 15
percent was a good reason to defeat Jerry Ford, then 21 percent is a better reason for throwing Jimmy Carter out of the
White House."

As the sixth week began, Ronald Reagan got his first major
newspaper endorsement. The Scripps-Howard chain, with seventeen papers under its umbrella, backed his candidacy with

the statement, "Reagan couldn't be a worse President than Carter if he tried. And he won't try."

In New Jersey the Californian was angrily accusing Carter of juggling official government statistics to make inflation look less drastic than it really was. The Labor Department had included car and truck discounts in its producers' price index for the first time, thereby showing a 0.2 percent decrease instead of the 0.4 percent increase obtained by traditional arithmetic. "He has changed the rules to make the wholesale price index go down," Reagan charged, as several thousand cheered him on at a supermarket rally. "Given the way this administration has used the imperial incumbency over the past year, I am not surprised by this *jimmying* of official government statistics." It would not be the last time he would accuse the President of "jimmying" numbers for political advantage.

Reacting to polls that showed he was not making up ground as quickly as his planners had hoped, Carter flew to the Midwest for appearances in the Chicago area. At a Democratic National Committee fund-raiser, he told his supporters that the country was threatened with nothing less than civil war if Ronald Reagan became President. "You will determine whether America will be unified," he warned. "Or, if I lose the election, whether America might be separated—blacks from whites, Jews from Christians, North from South, rural from urban." Carter aides Strauss and Powell, insisting that voters "do not know the real Ronald Reagan," promised to continue the attacks when the President went south at the end of the week.

Campaigning in Pennsylvania, Reagan called Carter "a badly misinformed and prejudiced man" for suggesting that he, Reagan, would divide the country across racial, religious, and regional lines. "He's reached a point of hysteria that's hard to understand." Refusing to be distracted by the attack, Reagan continued to hammer away on the economy—"the highest interest rates since the Civil War, and prices which have turned simple shopping trips into an oppressive burden." He told a Polish-American audience in western Pennsylvania that he was no "warmonger," but that he knew that peace comes only from a strong defense that discourages any potential attackers.

On Tuesday Anderson won his last battle to be on the ballots of all fifty states, when Georgia dropped its month-long fight against him. "I have just begun to fight," he told a group of newspaper editors in Massachusetts.

The next day Reagan picked up the surprise endorsement of the 2.3 million members of the Teamsters Union, the nation's largest. Though they had backed Nixon in 1972, the Teamsters had stayed neutral in 1976. Their candidate, touring an idle steel plant in Youngstown, Ohio, proposed that the Clean Air Act of 1970 be rewritten, blaming its overzealous provisions for causing many factories to close and lay off workers. "There is new evidence that air pollution has been substantially controlled," he said. The comment came at a time when Los Angeles was choking under its worst smog attack ever, although Reagan did not know that. The unfortunately timed statement made big news, not only in California, but on national television.

Meanwhile Carter kept a low profile, admitting he had made a mistake in saying that Reagan would divide the country. Promising to do his best to avoid name-calling, he signed a mental health bill and praised his wife Rosalynn for inspiring it. Stu Spencer charged that the "Jew from Christian, black from white" statement was premeditated—and that it was successful in picking up some ground for Carter. Bob Strauss, on the other hand, apologized for the President's remarks, blaming it on Presidential overwork. "He's trying to run government too much," Strauss explained. "The President has not hit his stride, so we're going to put him on the road more."

On Monday night, out of the sight of the media, Jody Powell called Barbara Walters to tell her that a long-deferred interview could now be granted. Walters, busy working on a special in California, suggested the following week for the taping, but Powell insisted it had to be that week. "The President wants to talk about the tone of the campaign," he said. Walters made a few quick phone calls to New York, and at

3:30 p.m. Wednesday she and her film crew were ushered into
the Oval Office. At 6:00 p.m. that evening, on ABC television,
Carter was denying that he was running a "mean campaign";
"The focus of this campaign," he told Walters, "may have been
obscured by my own rhetoric." But as Hamilton Jordan noted,
the "retraction" was merely a ploy to neutralize Carter's
"mean" image. "I am not sure he really felt that way," Hamilton later wrote in *Life* about the apology. "Or if any of us
[insiders] really believed it." The interview with Walters was
a prime example of Presidential media manipulation.

Shortly thereafter both Carter and Reagan received more
endorsements: Reagan from the National Maritime Union,
and Carter from Tom Hayden's 10,000-member Campaign
for Economic Democracy. "We would have preferred Governor Brown or Ted Kennedy," Hayden said. "But we're not
neutral between Carter and Reagan."

Press reports painted a picture of leisurely optimism in the
Reagan high command from Ed Meese, Wirthlin, and Nancy
down to the volunteers. The cocky attitude was supposedly
based on Wirthlin's research that showed his candidate with a
comfortable hold on more than the 270 electoral votes needed
for victory. The upbeat mood prompted one veteran reporter
covering the Reagan camp to dub it "the Dewey Campaign,
1980." Lyn Nofziger vehemently denied they were overconfident: "We're simply pacing ourselves for a hard finish." The
press didn't believe him but, according to the game plan,
that's exactly what the Reagan strategy called for—peaking in
the last ten days with a blitz of television commercials and
media events, outspending the Carter forces 2½ to 1.

On Thursday the President slashed away on the war-and-
peace theme in Tennessee, North Carolina, and Florida. "My
opponent said he would withdraw SALT II, launch a nuclear
arms race, and play a trump card against the Soviet Union,"
he repeated in all his stops. "I've watched the awesome power
of nuclear weapons grow all my adult life, and I'm not about
to do anything that would risk raining death on any American
city."

Hoping to firm up wavering support in Florida—the result

of a backlash against the thousands of Cuban and Haitian refugees flooding Miami and Key West—Carter signed a bill on Friday to reimburse the state for $80 million that was spent to feed, house, and process the refugees. In Texas, Carter aides complained they were being outspent 4 to 1, but they said they were optimistic nevertheless. "We're like a speedboat going against the *Nimitz*," said Texas coordinator Bob Beckel. "We'll sneak up behind them and strip their propeller."

Returning home to Los Angeles, Reagan ended the week with friends at an enthusiastic rally in Northridge, where he said he had no intention of lowering the requirements for pure air. "I think this smog situation here is tragic and everyone has my sympathy," he told a cheering crowd of six thousand. Reagan then used his standard recession line to pull applause: "Recession is when your neighbor loses his job, a depression is when you lose yours, and a recovery will be when Jimmy Carter loses his job." As I was covering that rally myself, I was sensitive to the reports in the *Los Angeles Times* that played up three hecklers and omitted mentioning the spirited enthusiasm there, which had been lacking at both the Carter rallies I attended. If the establishment media of the nation could pick the President, Carter would have won hands down.

According to the *Los Angeles Times*, Reagan led in the West while Carter retained the Northeast and the Deep South. The battleground was in the industrial Midwest, the states ringing the Great Lakes—Pennsylvania, Ohio, Indiana, Illinois, Michigan, Wisconsin, and possibly even Mondale's home state, Minnesota. "That's where the hunting is this season," agreed Stu Spencer, who was home for the weekend.

Though Gerald Rafshoon had eagerly invited reporters to preview his first wave of commercials, he refused all requests to look at his second series—the tougher "Empty Oval Office" spots that he began airing the end of September. These commercials featured a repeating visual—an empty chair in front of an Oval Office desk—while a voice-over began with the question, "When it comes down to it, what kind of a man should occupy the Oval Office?" Then variations on the theme criticized Reagan statements on Social Security, unemployment, SALT II, defense, and foreign policy. The intention was to capitalize on a pet theory Carter had about his political appeal: "I seem to do better running against another human being than when I run against perfection or myself." Rafshoon reasoned that once American voters visualized Reagan sitting in that empty chair, they would rush in droves to return the familiar, comforting figure of President Carter to his rightful place.

Typical of the arguments used in "Empty Oval Office" spots was the one on economics, where following the opening the narrator said: "Ronald Reagan has proposed an economic plan that *Business Week* magazine called a completely irresponsible approach that would touch off an inflationary explosion that would wreck the country, a plan his own running mate George Bush called 'voodoo economics.' Or should a more prudent, realistic, and experienced man sit here? Figure it out for yourself."

A batch of new anti-Reagan "man-in-the-street" commercials were produced for Stage Two, using fast cuts to typical Americans saying: "I think he makes a lot of people uneasy; I know he makes me uneasy" . . . "The kind of guy who shoots from the hip" . . . "As governor it didn't make much difference because California doesn't have a foreign policy, but as President, it's scary." A variation on the "hip-shooter" theme was Rafshoon's "Keep Cool" spot, where people on the street said: "To be President today you've got to have your wits totally about you" . . . "Reagan doesn't stop to think about things before he acts" . . . "That scares me about Ronald Reagan, it really does" . . . "President Carter, without even a hesitation."

It was the war-and-peace theme out of the mouths of selected advocates, the fear tactics that Caddell's research had shown were Carter's most effective weapon. This second wave of Rafshoon advertising was characterized by a focus on Reagan negatives instead of Carter accomplishments. Even the "Looking Ahead" piece, a five-minute essay about the future delivered by President Carter, carried the threat of doom and gloom: Carter, looking grimly into the camera, warned of "the 6 billion people who will live on the planet by century's end," the complex problems to be faced; now that he had been in office three and a half years, he emphasized, he had learned from his experience how to deal with such a monumental challenge. This commercial was the result of Caddell's theories of a "national malaise." It positioned Carter between the American people and their hopes and fears.

On October 2 Rafshoon began scheduling his first "roadblock" of five-minute commercials at 10:55 p.m. on all three networks. By buying that same time slot on all three, he was guaranteed a tremendous audience. Because of the highly negative character of his past advertising, he was particularly anxious for the more positive "futures" spots to be widely seen, so as to offset the growing perception of a "mean Jimmy Carter."

Desperation breeds strange tactics. During the sixth week of the campaign, ads began running in smaller newspapers around the country, pleading: "John Anderson, we don't need you now, we need you in 1984. Get out before it's too late! We don't need a 9-to-5 ex-star of B-grade movies, a graduate of General Electric U. surrounded by far-right conservatives." The disclaimer indicated that these ads were part of a "Citizen Campaign for Carter" and asked for money. Reportedly, they were funded by the Carter-Mondale Reelection Committee and were placed through the local organizations.

Reagan's "Campaign '80" still held fast to its media plan. The plan called for bringing on the campaign late, hitting hard the last three weeks after the advertising in the first six weeks had done its job—letting Americans know and feel that Ronald Reagan was a serious politician. Showing him as a strong administrator of a major state helped to eradicate the "actor" image. Though Reagan was "champing at the bit" to attack, the plan held him back. Reagan's first negative commercial would not hit the airwaves until October 10.

"We took those first six weeks to stress the positives," noted Dick Wirthlin. "A lot of people were not aware of the credibility and knowledge Ronald Reagan had. About 40 percent of the voters said they knew very little about him or what he stood for. So we attempted to familiarize the electorate with him. Once that was established, we could go on to the thematic element of leadership, especially the economy, and take Jimmy Carter on very directly with some of the rhetorical questions we asked about whether it was easier for people to buy a home and so on."

Time-buys concentrated on the "Governor in Action" spots and five-minute pieces, designed to familiarize Americans with the politician they didn't know and to expunge memories of the actor they did know. Visuals repeatedly showed Reagan being sworn in as governor, saving a "state in crisis," and discussing complex questions about economics and the art of governing. In a very important sense, the first debate helped reinforce what the commercials were selling.

Meanwhile Garth's media on behalf of John Anderson never varied at any point. With only a few million dollars to spend up until the last few weeks of the race, Garth substituted logic and verbiage for the more extended time-buys he would have preferred, appealing to an unhappy electorate in what constituted the biggest batch of undecided voters Caddell had ever seen so late in a campaign.

The basic Anderson pitch featured five-minute lectures and a few shorter spots pulled from them. A talking head of Anderson argued, "Multibillion-dollar tax cuts proposed by my opponents sound good. I can't support them. The solutions to our problems are going to be difficult—that shouldn't come as a surprise to anyone. But if saying so jeopardizes my election, so be it. A hundred-billion-dollar MX missile sounds tough. I am against it. ERA? Absolutely. And I'm repelled by those television preachers who call themselves the Moral Majority. How would it feel if your vote on November 4 made possible not a lesser evil but a greater good? A new chance for our country—you can make it happen." Wearing a Presidential blue suit and red club tie, Anderson sat behind a desk backed by "Oval Office" bookshelves to expound his "difference."

During the first week of October I asked Tony Schwartz for his evaluation of the television war to date. As usual, his comments were concise and instructive.

"Rafshoon doesn't understand resonance," he pointed out. "He tries to sell things rather than connect with what's inside people. It's like trying to plant seeds on a wooden floor— there's no soil for them to grow. He's trying to tell people Carter's handled the country beautifully, when they know he hasn't done a good job. Take the ads where he discusses Carter's foreign policy. He ends with the Egypt-Israel peace thing and says, 'He's a military man and a man of peace.' All he's really saying is, 'If you want a war we can give you a good one, and if it's peace you want, we can give you that, too.' He doesn't understand research or how to convince people. The writing on the Carter commercials is excellent. So is the production. But the thinking is not. Harry Muheim does the writing and is superb. Eli Bleich does the film production and does it beautifully. The writing is exquisite, the production is exquisite, and the commercials stink."

Schwartz, who did some of Ted Kennedy's primaries commercials, felt that Pete Dailey's work for Reagan was more effective than Rafshoon's work. "Telling people what he did as governor of California is something they need to know. What he did with the empty chair was good. The best ads in this whole election are those from the Republican National Committee, showing a truck driver outside his truck and a guy in his TV repair shop saying they've always voted Democratic, but they're going to vote Republican for a change. Those ads speak directly to what people feel in terms of the economy. They are so convincing that even though they're done by actors, they come across as real."

Schwartz pointed out that David Garth was hampered severely by lack of money, because of the kind of campaign he runs. "His strength is not in any one part of the campaign but in the fact that his whole campaign has consistency. His television is nothing special, his radio is nothing special. It's the fact he has total control that works for him. David Garth is supersmart politically, an insightful strategist, but his commercials are artless. His assumption is: since the ads run so often, let's put a lot into them, and if the people get a little out each time they see them, they won't get bored. If it were up to me, I'd do simpler ads."

With a little over three weeks to go, a third of all Americans were still undecided. "People just aren't paying attention," complained political commentators.

Reagan was a regular visitor to working-class neighborhoods, where he expounded his "blue woo" themes. To offset the guilt feelings that blue-collar Democrats suffer when they contemplate "betraying their party," Reagan assured them that party labels no longer mattered. Having been a lifelong Democrat himself until he saw the light, he understood what ideals prompted a voter to leave his party. "Those who have traditionally voted Democratic," he told them, "are now asking themselves an important question: 'Shall I vote the old label or shall I vote for the values the label used to stand for before Mr. Carter became President?' "

Reagan emphasized that Carter was not from the same mold as "such great Democrats as John F. Kennedy and Harry Truman." Reagan suggested that he, Reagan, was closer to that ideal than his opponent. He himself was once a "bleeding-heart liberal" who almost supported Henry Wallace in 1948, before voting for the more conservative Harry Truman. Reagan also reminded them that he was elected head of his Screen Actors Guild six successive terms. "I am the first person to run for President who could say that," he told blue-collar listeners, and then recited a litany of Carter economic disasters he called "an American tragedy."

"Research showed there were lots of blue-collar Democrats Ronald Reagan could reach," Stu Spencer disclosed. "Early on it also showed we had a problem with moderate suburban Republicans. This was virtually the identical situation to his governor's race in 1966. The governor sensed this. Lyn Nofziger, the only other person who had been with us back then, saw the similarities and we discussed them often. But most of the other people in the campaign were not around in 1966. Both the research and the events confirmed what we already knew in terms of those repeating patterns. That helped us in our planning."

Polls showed that the strategy was working. A nationwide *Los Angeles Times* survey found that one out of every four blue-collar workers who voted for Carter in 1976 now supported Ronald Reagan. In the big industrial states this kind of margin could be the winning difference.

Hoping to counter these raids into normally Democratic blue-collar ranks, Carter pitched hard for the traditionally Republican white suburbs, working the outskirts of Philadelphia, New York, Cleveland, and Detroit. "The suburbs are the key," Pat Caddell said, pointing to the big increase in better-educated white-collar people forming the bulk of suburbia. The barrier blocking the President's path was the public's perception of him as a weak leader. Noted David Keene of George Bush's staff: "The key thing suburbanites look for in a President is competence, and Carter just hasn't filled the bill."

Carter aimed to change that image with the first of three weekly radio talks from the White House, proclaiming a revitalized economy: "The economic outlook has now brightened. We see the beginnings of recovery, a reduction in inflation. The number of jobs is increasing and unemployment is declining." He based these claims on advance copies of encouraging GNP figures that the Department of Commerce would share with the nation at the end of the week. Carter's economic "good news" strategy borrowed a page from Richard Nixon on how to deal with economic matters. Nixon had pointed out that actual results are not the key to success: "All that really matters is whether the voters perceive the trend as favorable when they go to the polls."

Warning against the "simplistic solutions" advocated by Reagan, the President ended his talk with a gloomy scenario: "The election three weeks away presents a choice for the nation. Are we mature enough and strong enough to accept the realities of the 1980s and to take the difficult but rewarding steps that are needed? Or will we close our eyes and dream of earlier times, simpler problems, and painless solutions?" Echoes of the Anderson Difference.

In Los Angeles, Reagan cut and broadcast a five-minute

television commercial replying directly to Carter's rosy fore-
cast: "I wish I could believe things were getting better, but it
just isn't so. Things aren't getting better. We can't live on a
dream that it's just going to happen overnight."

On Monday Carter courted ethnics in New York. First he
marched up Fifth Avenue with Italians in the Columbus Day
parade, trailed by John Anderson a quarter mile back, and
George Bush. Later the President wooed a crowd at a Jewish
community center in Queens, bolstered by two staunch supporters of Israeli at his side, Senators Henry Jackson and
Daniel Patrick Moynihan. He proclaimed, "This President
will never turn his back on Israel—I never have and I never
will," while a bunch of Orthodox Jews shouted, "Liar, liar,
liar!" Later Carter's feelings were soothed by polls showing
Jewish voters returning to the fold and pushing him into a
more comfortable lead for New York's crucial forty-one electoral votes.

A California conservation group, the Sierra Club, endorsed
Carter, but meanwhile the Los Angeles news media revealed
that Democrats were paying a dollar for every new name that
volunteers could register, spurring overzealous efforts that
brought dead people and rock-ribbed Republicans into the
Democratic voting pool.

Even Fidel Castro got into the act when the head of Cuba's
diplomatic mission in Washington reported that his government would release all thirty-seven Americans currently held
in Cuban prisons, without a quid pro quo attached. Castro
openly feared a Reagan victory, stating just after the Republican convention that the nomination of Ronald Reagan reminded him of "the times that preceded the election of
Adolf Hitler in Germany."

At Los Angeles rallies Reagan began to stress his support of
women's rights. He told how, as governor, he had helped abolish fourteen state laws that discriminated against women, and
he vowed to do the same on a federal level, if elected. Reagan
insisted that he was a dedicated advocate of equal rights for
women, but not of "the simple-sounding amendment" that
carried that name.

His women's crusade was a planned response to a growing

weakness. "The research showed that Reagan had a real problem with women," Spencer pointed out. "There were particular negatives there in terms of war and peace. That came from
his rhetoric over the years, things he'd said about tuna boats
off Chile, the *Pueblo* incident, and Cuba. It showed up in our
opponents' polls, too, and was probably the root of Carter's
'war and peace, black-white, Christian-Jew' statement."

A *Los Angeles Times* poll conducted during the second
week of October revealed that men gave Reagan his lead and
that women were keeping Carter in the ball game. Men saw
Reagan as an activist—a "strong leader" who "speaks his
mind," "can get things done," and would "stand up to the
Russians." Women were more skeptical: they worried about
Reagan's getting the country into war, and were not convinced that he "cares about people like me."

"Reagan is not a good print candidate," Spencer explained.
"When he says things in person or on television, it doesn't
sound that harsh. But when you read it in print, it sometimes
has a harsh effect. Since we did have this problem with
women, I made a suggestion—that he recommend a qualified
woman for a seat on the Supreme Court. Ron had no problem
with the idea. Not that he would pick a woman just to have a
woman in there, but he would get the best qualified person
who also happened to be a woman. That gave all those women
turned off by the platform plank on ERA a chance to stop
and give Ron a second look."

Reagan's vow to put a woman on the Supreme Court inspired lead stories on Tuesday when, just before leaving for
the industrial Northeast, he told a Los Angeles press conference, "It is time for a woman to sit among our highest jurists."
Carter called in an NBC television interviewer to brand Reagan's move a political disgrace: "It was a mistake to promise
that a Supreme Court appointment would be a particular
kind of American. I'll consider them all and continue to treat
women fairly." But Carter's response was a mere footnote on
television newscasts and the back pages of newspapers.

Meanwhile John Anderson promised a Chicago business
group that he could balance the budget, distributing a forty-

eight-page analysis that showed a balanced budget by 1983 and a $129-billion tax cut by 1985. His economic proposals earned him a six-second segment on the evening news.

In a week full of Reagan surprises, Wednesday saw Rev. Ralph Abernathy, Martin Luther King's lieutenant, stun a meeting of fifty black ministers in Detroit when he told them, "President Carter has not kept his campaign promises. Poor black people cannot make it under this system for another six months. We as patients are getting sicker and we need to change doctors." Abernathy, who had switched his allegiance from Carter to Ted Kennedy during the 1980 primaries, concluded by promising to work to elect Ronald Reagan. On hand to second his endorsement was another former associate of Dr. King, Rev. Hosea Williams, who added, "Ronald Reagan did a whole lot more for black people and poor people in California than Jimmy Carter did in Georgia."

Black activists were shocked by the first important defections from Carter's "secret weapon" coalition. Coretta King hinted darkly of "other forces operating there," and Rev. Darneau Stewart, the head of Detroit's Board of Education, called Abernathy a "traitor." Dr. Claud Young of SCLC wondered aloud "how Ralph ever got involved with Reagan."

Stu Spencer clarified the mystery. "We just made an honest attempt to win the blacks," he told me. "We got Abernathy, Hosea Williams, and Charles Evers—blacks that Coretta King and Andrew Young had thrown out of the system. We just moved over and made room for them." That "room" included assurances that Reagan would appoint a black justice if Thurgood Marshall left the Supreme Court, along with strong efforts to bring black people into the mainstream. Ignored by the Carter White House, these black leaders wanted a ground-floor position in the event of a Reagan Presidency.

Meanwhile Carter was having problems with Andrew Young. The President dissociated himself from statements that Young made at Ohio State University on behalf of the Carter-Mondale campaign. In a prepared speech, Young "decoded" Reagan's reference to "states rights" earlier in the race. "Black folks will catch hell for the rest of this century because 'states rights' is a code word that it's going to be all right to kill niggers when he's elected," Young said with his usual circumspection.

In Newark the President challenged Reagan to debate him man-to-man, citing polls showing Anderson well below the minimum 15-percent-support needed for inclusion. Mimicking the tactics of professional boxers, he offered to meet Reagan "any place, under any format." Reagan replied guardedly in Lima, Ohio: "This is something we watch. We'll wait and see if the ladies of the League have made a decision about Anderson, then we'll make a decision."

On Wednesday Anderson abandoned efforts to borrow $10 million from banks, blaming his failure on President Carter. At a Milwaukee press conference he repeated his charge that Carter had intimidated bankers by publishing a memo questioning the legality of his loan requests. Unlike Carter and Reagan, who each had nearly $30 million of federal funds to spend on the campaign, Anderson had to rely on private contributions. Three weeks before election day he had raised about $9 million and owed $1.5 million to supporters.

Thursday, October 16. As the League of Women Voters were deciding whether to include Anderson in a second debate, Reagan's advisers had to decide whether to take part at all. Carter had already agreed to participate in the match, though only because research showed that four out of five Americans regarded him as "the candidate who refuses to debate." The Reagan camp expressed hesitancy to reporters, but there was no question inside the campaign about what they would do. "The hesitancy was a ploy," Spencer admitted. "Why should we tip our hand? We just held our options open."

On Thursday afternoon, October 16, Reagan's research team made a presentation to the campaign's directors, summarizing the results of their tracking polls. The numbers showed a clear Reagan lead of six points in the popular vote and, more important, 320 solid electoral votes. "The directors wanted to believe," recalled DMI's Vince Breglio. "But they weren't convinced because of what the national polls were saying then." At that point Gallup was calling it 45 to 42 percent for Carter, while the CBS/*New York Times* poll had it 39 to 38 percent for Carter. Among the national pollsters, only ABC's Lou Harris showed Reagan in front, 45 to 42 percent.

Anderson, still hoping to be included in a debate, taped a television interview for the CBS affiliates, calling Reagan "a kindly man whose views are irrelevant for the 1980s," and branding Carter "despicable for trying to make Reagan look like the mad bomber." Looking ahead to the upcoming debate, he pleaded with the League "not to knuckle in to Jimmy Carter and deprive Americans of hearing all three candidates."

The President visited New York for the annual Al Smith Dinner and met Reagan face to face for the first time since the campaign had begun. Both men wore tuxedos, Carter stiffly and Reagan with easy elegance. On that occasion, when election barbs are traditionally softened by humor, Reagan got laughs by making fun of himself. "President Carter asked me why I looked younger whenever he saw pictures of me at the ranch riding a horse," he said, imitating Carter's Southern drawl. "So I told him I just keep riding older horses." But when Carter spoke, he ridiculed Reagan's flip-flop about aid for New York City. "The paint on the governor's i love new york button is still wet," the President teased, and the crowd groaned. Jody Powell sighed despairingly about his boss's lack of a light touch: "You give him a funny line, and somehow he'll change it so it comes out hard."

The Iranian U.N. representative changed the campaign focus when he reported that Iran's premier would visit New York on Friday. He hinted that Ali Rajai might want to discuss the fate of the hostages while he was in the United States. President Carter immediately broadcast his willingness to meet and talk with Rajai, once again sparking widespread speculation about an October Surprise.

The campaign really came to life on Friday, when Reagan agreed to debate Carter head to head in Cleveland on October 28. Stu Spencer explained how the announcement "really froze the power of the incumbency and everything else for ten

days: it was the most important single thing that happened
in the campaign.

"Before that I felt we were dead in the water, stalled. Others felt that, too, so we decided to debate. A few people were opposed—they thought we could win by three yards and a cloud of dust, just plowing into states and bringing Reagan in to make points. But I had problems with that logic, because there is just too much power in the incumbency."

Having exhausted their surprises with the female Supreme Court appointment and Ralph Abernathy's endorsement, Reagan's team was just playing out the last few weeks and waiting for the other side to make a move. "When you've got just a three-point lead, your opponents can destroy you overnight with something," Spencer pointed out. "We need something to give us a shot in the arm and freeze Carter. The debate challenge froze him. We were rolling a lot of dice on that debate. But I had never seen Reagan do a bad job in that set of circumstances and I thought the odds of bombing out were very small."

Henry Kissinger told a crowded Los Angeles press conference that he thought the hostages would soon be released. Emphasizing his support for the administration's negotiations, he nonetheless hoped they would act "with sufficient majesty" to avoid encouraging other nations to seize hostages for gain. The Reagan "October Surprise" strategy was being set in motion, paving the way for later assaults on what was a very sensitive political issue. Then on Friday night Iranian Prime Minister Rajai held a news conference at the United Nations, where he flung his right leg on a table, bared the calf, and displayed what he claimed were torture scars inflicted by the Shah's musclemen. He told reporters that his Parliament would "very soon" announce conditions for freeing the hostages, triggering wide speculation that a deal was in the works.

The Commerce Department released third-quarter figures showing a rebound in GNP growth. The headlines that resulted —"SLUMP MAY BE OVER"—were very helpful to the administration.

When the League of Women Voters decided to exclude

John Anderson from the Cleveland matchup, Anderson lashed out at the League, President Carter, and the polls. Vowing to stay in the race to the end, he accused Carter of manipulating the debate decision: "With Jimmy Carter, winning isn't the only thing—it's everything!"

The seventh week ended with Reagan's demanding that the U.S. government apologize to the hostages for leaving them languishing. "Our government owes them an apology for letting them stay there that long," he charged on Saturday in Illinois. By reminding voters how badly the affair had been handled and how long these Americans had suffered, Reagan hoped to preempt any political gain that Carter might glean from an impending release. And the Reagan camp had more such ammunition stored in the armory for the battles ahead.

In the second of his Oval Office radio talks, the President concentrated on the one theme his researchers told him was making points—portraying his opponent as "the Mad Bomber." "Peace is my passion," Carter proclaimed, contrasting his position on nuclear arms with Reagan's. "He believes that by abandoning the SALT agreement and suggesting an all-out nuclear arms race, we would frighten the Soviets into negotiating a new agreement based on American nuclear superiority. I've had four years of sobering experience in this life-and-death field. In my considered judgment, this would be a very risky gamble. I do not propose to turn away from the duty to bring the terrible weapons of nuclear annihilation under some kind of rational control."

But the other side was just as determined to dispel the "bomber" image. Within ten hours, Reagan appeared in the first of his half-hour paid television talks to calm voters panicked by Carter's "warmonger" charges. Seated in a look-alike Oval Office, backed by books and wearing a simple dark suit and tie, the candidate promised that if he were elected President he would immediately open talks with the Soviets to control atomic weapons.

"But the way to avoid an arms race is not simply to let the Soviets race ahead," he argued. "We need to remove their incentives to race ahead by making it clear we can and will compete, if need be. At the same time we should tell them we prefer to halt this competition and reduce nuclear arsenals by patient negotiation." Taking on the "Mad Bomber" charge directly, he explained: "My own views have been distorted in an effort to scare people through innuendos and misstatements of my positions. Possibly Mr. Carter is gambling that his long litany of fear will influence enough voters to save him from the inevitable consequences of his policies, which have brought so much human misery."

Pushing hard to exploit the hostage break, on Monday Carter pledged to release frozen Iranian assets and restore trade for "a strong and united" Iran. Made during a televised question-and-answer session in Youngstown, Ohio, his offer coincided with news that the influential Ayatollah Rafsaujani had announced that Iran's Parliament would set conditions for the hostage release in a few days.

Campaigning in Kentucky, Reagan took time off from rips at the "Carter economy" to comment on the developing hostage situation. "I don't understand why fifty-two Americans have been held hostage almost a year now," he grumbled. Henry Kissinger made news in St. Louis by telling reporters there: "Judging from the plethora of statements and the rapidity, there are some negotiations going on." The Reagan campaign was moving in to preempt any political gains. Kissinger joined Reagan's campaign plane in Kentucky and flew with him to Cincinnati, discussing how to handle the October Surprise and who was to say what. When Reagan landed in Ohio, he continued to reassure voters about war and peace. "The President seems determined to have me start a nuclear war," he smilingly told an airport rally. "Well, I'm just as determined I'm not going to." The cheers were heartening.

Tuesday, October 21. Negotiators for the two candidates ratified the debate in Cleveland exactly one week away—one week before voters would choose. The ninety-minute debate would begin at 9:30 p.m. EST and would be arranged like the Ford-Carter debate of 1976, with a moderator and four panelists. The debate would be divided into two forty-five minute segments, the first consisting of questions from the panelists with followups and rebuttals. The second segment would give each candidate the chance to rebut and counter-rebut, with time reserved for closing statements.

Looking ahead to what promised to be the decisive event of the campaign, Carter tried to belittle what he saw as his opponent's chief advantage. "Governor Reagan is good at making speeches," he admitted in Miami. "But when you're sitting across a negotiating table from President Brezhnev in a time of crisis when every word and thought counts, you can't rely on 3 × 5 cards and you can't read a teleprompter."

The governor told an Illinois crowd that Carter had done too little to free the hostages: "The fact they've been there this long is a humiliation and a disgrace to this country. I certainly wouldn't stand by and do nothing." Asked what he would do, Reagan replied, "I've had ideas but you don't talk about them. That's been one of his problems—he's done all his ne-gotiating through the press."

Countering at a town meeting in Miami, Carter insisted that the Iran-Iraq war had not created new dangers for the hostages: "I believe the hostages will come home safely. But their fate should not be used as a political football." Pledging to abide by his own promise not to make them a campaign issue, he "regretted" that Reagan had "broken his pledge" to do the same. Later that day Reagan denied he had broken any pledge: "If President Carter thought the hostages were too important to be a political football, then why did he use it himself to defeat Ted Kennedy in the primaries?"

Lost in the shuffle was John Anderson, fighting to hold wan-ing support in Illinois and New York. Small but enthusiastic gatherings cheered his advocacy of arms control overseas, gun control at home, strong support for Israel, and the conserva-tion of fuel. "My task in the next two weeks is to convince voters to vote their conscience and not their fears," he said, emphasizing that a vote for him was not a vote for anybody else. As usual, he refused to comment on the latest furor over the hostages.

In Iran the prime minister conferred with Khomeini, then dismissed Carter's overtures. "They're just a fresh design to fill the ballot boxes in the U.S. election," he said, echoing the

Republicans. The White House replied that there were, nonetheless, signs indicating that the Iranian Parliament might decide Thursday on conditions for the hostage release.

On Wednesday Carter held a pair of cowboy boots up before a crowd in Waco, Texas, and called them "stomping boots." "Republicans have a habit of spreading a lot of horse manure around right before an election," he cried. "It's getting pretty deep, so I can use these on the campaign trail and then stomp the hell out of those Republicans November 4." As most of his Texan supporters looked on dumbfounded, he ridiculed Reagan's "secret plan" to free the hostages, comparing it to Nixon's "secret plan" to end the Vietnam War in 1968.

In Louisiana Reagan said he planned to drop the hostage issue and focus once again on Carter's "record of failure" to regain momentum. He admitted Carter's "racist-warmonger" theme hurt him some in the polls: "He's been effective in creating this stereotype of me."

Stu Spencer explained their opponent's tactics: "Carter's statements about blacks and whites, Jews and Christians, and so on was premeditated. They knew their man would take some flak over it, but they also figured they'd end up with 15 percent favorable fallout, which they got for a while. But it didn't have lasting effects—it faded away because people just didn't believe the charges. One thing it did do, it hurt Carter's decency perception badly. It was just a vicious thing to say about anyone."

At Carter-Mondale headquarters in Washington, the mood was sheer frustration. The campaign "dirt-digger," Marty Franks, complained about the backlash against Carter's attacks. "Mean? What's mean about telling the truth?" he asked. "All we're doing is quoting the guy." He tried to explain the rebounding effects. "With Nixon, it was easy to whip people up. But Reagan's not evil. It's just hard for people to believe that somebody who smiles that nicely, looks so grandfatherly, and has that 'aw, shucks' manner could do anything to hurt people."

Tony Dolan, Franks's counterpart for the Republicans, was gleeful over the mud-slinging's failure: "Carter's committed

the greatest political blunder of all time. His record is a disaster and all he had going for him was this odd perception
that he's somehow a nice guy. Well, Carter's never been a nice
guy. In every campaign he's always engaged in vicious distortion and character assassination, fear and falsehood all the
way. Now he's made the case against himself with his mean
streak. You should never underestimate the basic decency of
the American people."

Anderson complained to the National Press Club in Washington that both Reagan and Carter should be embarrassed to
debate without him. "But I don't know what I can do about
it, other than speak out as frankly and caustically as I can," he
concluded ruefully.

On Wednesday Iranian Prime Minister Rajai again raised
hopes that the hostages might soon be freed, when he told
reporters that the United States was prepared to accept
Khomeini's four demands. The U.S. State Department fed the
flames of anticipatory jubilation, as spokesman David Nalls
said knowingly, "We've said all along we've been in indirect
contact with the Iranian authorities, but we're just not going
to discuss the substance of those contacts."

Reagan regained the offensive on Thursday by challenging
Carter's competence and ability to govern. He predicted the
next Consumer Price Index would show that "Mr. Carter has
given us an economic record of misery and despair unparalleled
in recent history," adding that Carter might "jimmy" the figures
to make them look better. The Republicans sprang a surprise
when ex-Sen. Eugene McCarthy, who challenged Lyndon Johnson in 1968 as a peace candidate, announced he was backing
Reagan because "he has run a more dignified and becoming
campaign."

At the White House, Carter countered with his own endorsement from SCLC's head Joseph Lowery, who said, "I am
frightened that the forces of insensitivity to human suffering,
racism, and negativism are gravitating toward the candidacy of
Governor Reagan." As 150 black ministers applauded, the
President pledged to "root out the criminals" attacking blacks
across the country.

The President ended the week with a two-day blitz of New

Jersey, Michigan, and Ohio—swing states of the crucial industrial North. At the Wyoming, Michigan, public library he said
he had not yet received a "clear signal" from Iran, so Americans should be "very cautious about building up expectations." But Iran's U.N. ambassador revealed that the United
States had already accepted "in general terms" the conditions
that his Parliament would formally demand on Sunday at
their scheduled meeting. He hinted at the possible use of
"third-party negotiations" to hammer out fine points. Lead
stories on television news and daily papers trumpeted, "WAR
PRESSURES MOVE IRAN TO END HOSTAGE CRISIS." With the election twelve days away, the October Surprise seemed more
certain than astonishing.

After using part of Friday to tape a half-hour television
speech on the economy, Reagan returned to his Virginia hideaway and began preparing for the following Tuesday's debate.
While he studied briefing books, John Anderson stumped
New England, where polls showed he had his best chances for
victory in Connecticut and Massachusetts. Anderson berated
Carter for his economic policies and his exploitation of the
hostages.

Friday night, on prime-time television, Ronald Reagan did
what he does best. He spoke heart to heart about the economy
with an estimated 12 million Americans. After he pointed
out that the average American now had 8.5 percent less buying power than when Gerald Ford left office, he described the
appalling rise in the Consumer Price Index over the last four
months and outlined his own program to fight it, including a
7-percent cut in federal spending and a 30-percent cut in
income taxes phased over the next three years. But the real
impact came not from his figures, but from his figures of
speech.

"Mr. Carter has blamed OPEC for inflation, he has blamed
the American people for inflation, he's blamed the Federal
Reserve Board for inflation. The symbol of this administration is a finger pointing at someone else. Mr. Carter went on
to misrepresent my economic program. Now it's one thing
when his administration jimmies its own figures to make its

record look good; but when he starts jimmying my figures, that's going too far! The President says my proposed reduction of tax rates would be inflationary. Let me ask him a simple question in economics. Why is it inflationary if you keep more of your earnings and spend them the way you want to, but it isn't inflationary if he takes them and spends them the way he wants to?"

It was vintage Reagan, real give-'em-hell-Harry stuff that made the challenger look more like an incumbent, more in control, and more on the attack.

Entering the last full week, the national media saw Reagan within striking distance of the White House but Jimmy Carter in an improved position, since from being the underdog of the summer months he had become a possible winner, matching Reagan in the polls. And movement in the hostage deadlock seemed to promise Carter an extra edge.

Harry Muheim, Rafshoon's resident television expert, was holed up at Camp David, where Carter busily crammed for the debate. The feeling around the President's men, he told me, was "affirmative but qualified. Fact is, it's going to be a very close election."

"Why do you say that?" I asked.

"As you come to the wire, people's perceptions of the enormity of the job and the energy needed to do it come to the fore. If you look at those two considerations, the tendency would be to vote for the President even if you substantially disagreed with what he's done."

Enormity and energy—two code words indicting Reagan. Carter's people hoped voters would think Reagan too simple-minded to deal with the "enormity" of the Presidency, and too old to put out the required "energy." The "helpless target" image Hamilton Jordan and Jerry Rafshoon had gloated over during the convention still strongly influenced late-campaign strategy.

The debate, Muheim predicted, would decide the outcome: "I was just talking to Sam Popkin, one of Pat Caddell's peo-ple. He told me this is the largest number of undecided voters this close to an election that's ever been recorded. It's up in the 20-percent range. The debate may help decide many of those."

The October Surprise, Muheim noted, could cut one of two ways. The happier scenario would see the hostages return before election day to win the contest for Carter. But if their return were seen as a media event, it could backfire. "People might think it was a remarkable coming together of events," he suggested. The wild card was still wild. Even inside Camp David, Carter had cautioned Muheim, "Don't take this too seriously," when alluding to media speculation over the progress of secret negotiations. "It reminds me of the time they sent in the rescue team, which was a disaster, of course," Muheim recalled. "I was with Jerry Rafshoon at the time and I told him, 'Boy, could we ever use a sixty-second spot to handle this!'"

While Carter and Reagan prepared for the debate, the news media were preoccupied with hostage stories. Trivial details mushroomed into profound significance, beginning Sunday with "HOSTAGE DEBATE IN IRAN . . . PARLIAMENT TO SET TERMS" to Monday's "HOSTAGES' FATE STILL UNRESOLVED." The Iranian Parliament adjourned after its two closed sessions produced much yelling but no agreement, and so their decision was postponed until Wednesday. Meanwhile rumors circulated that the Iranians planned to free some but not all of their prisoners. The adjournment triggered predictions that a Tuesday speech by Ayatollah Khomeini would cut through the Parliamentary haggling. A high-ranking Iranian U.N. official was widely quoted as saying there was a 99-percent chance that forty of the fifty-two Americans would be released Thursday provided the United States met at least some of Khomeini's conditions: unfreezing Iranian assets, including military equipment paid for but not delivered; returning the dead Shah's wealth and property; pledging to drop all legal claims against Iran; and pledging never again to interfere in Iranian affairs.

On Monday Bob Strauss hinted that the Carter campaign

would close out in California. He released a poll showing that Reagan's lead in his home state had dwindled to a mere 4.5 percent, down from over 12 percent a few weeks before. "We've said all along Reagan can be beaten here," boasted Democratic California director Mickey Kantor.

In Washington the black civil-rights leader Clarence Mitchell, once an NAACP lobbyist, called Reagan a racist. "I don't apologize for saying it," he told a civil-rights conference. "Governor Reagan is, although a sophisticated one, a racist."

While the Reagan camp remained conspicuously silent, John Anderson publicized his suspicions about Carter's handling of the hostage developments. "Everyone still remembers Kissinger's 'peace is at hand' statement in 1972," he said. Inside Anderson's headquarters, however, all hopes of victory had disappeared. Discussing his chances, the congressman said he would "not be disheartened no matter how few votes I get. I cannot believe this will not in some way bear fruit."

The White House mood was one of grim determination. From the start Jimmy Carter had dared Reagan to debate him with no other candidates onstage to protect him. Now that he was to get his wish, Carter was set on exposing his opponent as a shallow memorizer of other people's words who had no grasp of the real world. He hoped to provoke Reagan into losing his cool and saying something stupid. The President spent the weekend at Camp David, reading briefing books put together by Stu Eizenstat on domestic issues and by Zbigniew Brzezinski on foreign affairs, loading his mental computer with ideas, facts, and telling phrases. A strategy memo from Pat Caddell laid out the tactics.

"Our strategy was simple," Hamilton Jordan explained. "He could not be passive nor could he allow ninety minutes of focus solely on the economy. Carter had to be Presidential, but he also had to press the attack on Reagan and make his points strongly."

On Sunday, Jerry Rafshoon outfitted Hickory Lodge with cameras, lights, and podiums. Sam Popkin of Caddell's staff played Ronald Reagan, impersonating the governor with quotes from Reagan's political past and replying to challenges with Reagan-like syntax. Jordan noted "the look of dismay" which crossed Carter's face while the President listened to Popkin's words: "The rhetoric was so slippery, so attractive in its simplicity, and so hard to get a grip on."

The President's job was to stall Reagan's glibness, to nail him with incriminating quotes, and to discredit him in full view of the entire nation. Carter would reserve his heaviest guns for war-and-peace questions, eager to prove that Reagan was prone to hasty, oversimplified, and dangerous solutions to complex world problems, confirming the worst fears of women voters. Jody Powell described the predebate feeling at Camp David: "There's a good deal of anxiety, as you'd expect. But we're confident the President's mastery of detail and unflappable if boring manner will carry him through."

At the back of Reagan's rented house in Virginia, Michigan Representative David Stockman impersonated Jimmy Carter in mock debate sessions. His grasp of detail and eloquent assaults were not lost on an appreciative opponent. "I think I beat Anderson," Reagan remarked to associates. "And I may beat Carter. But I know I never beat Stockman."

More important than any points he was advised to make on the economy, defense, and federal bureaucracy, Reagan's main goal on Tuesday was to demonstrate that he was a warm, decent man and not the "Mad Bomber" portrayed by Carter's strategists. His performance would be directed at the undecided, at skeptical women, not at backslapping men. "Our goal was simply to show what kind of human being Ron is," Spencer explained. "That he's a very decent person and not a threat. That one perception was our whole ball game."

While the antagonists were rehearsing, the League of Women Voters busily assembled a panel of journalists acceptable to both sides. Taking suggestions from a score of news organizations, the League pared a master list of one hundred names down to twenty-one, which they sent to the contending camps. Each side returned a list of nine names acceptable to them, and four reporters common to both lists comprised the final panel. Barbara Walters was a last-minute substitute for the *Washington Post*'s Meg Greenfield, who declined the honor—a replacement which again had to be approved by both sides. The rejected names were journalists that the Carter and Reagan advisers felt would be the toughest for their cause. Lee Hanna, a former television news executive who produced both Presidential debates, refused to identify the excluded news people.

What Hanna found most incredible was the complete lack of curiosity or interest by reporters investigating the debate: "Not one reporter in all the United States asked me how the reporters were chosen." He regarded predebate reporting as "slipshod, studded with inaccuracies, a dismal performance." Hanna disclosed that neither side was allowed to have prepared notes on the podium. Suspicious Reagan aides insisted that the units be swept before the debate in case Carter had crib sheets stashed somewhere, since the lecterns would be supplied by the White House.

Details were hammered out in over eight hours of direct meetings and forty phone talks between the Carter, Reagan, and League negotiators. "The major decision in Cleveland," Hanna said, "was the color of the cloth background." He described with a straight face how a squad of Reagan aides "crawled across the stage with a light meter." More than two hundred network television reporters, producers, and technicians were assigned to cover the event, along with fifteen hundred newspaper and radio reporters.

On Monday, Carter told an airport rally that he didn't know "which Ronald Reagan" he would face the next night. "I don't know if I'll be debating a man who lately professes to be almost the image of Franklin Roosevelt, or one who a little earlier said the foundation of the New Deal was fascism." Meanwhile his opponent, after watching videotapes of past Carter debates, lunched with Jerry Ford and discussed the best ways to attack the President's record and reply to anticipated assaults. Ford emerged from the meeting to tell reporters that he expected Carter to be "mean and vindictive" in the confrontation.

On Tuesday, as the combatants, their staffs, and media observers gathered in Cleveland, the election played out in other forums. Ladbrokes, the leading British bookmaker, listed Jimmy Carter as a 2-to-1 favorite. Ted Kennedy urged blacks in Watts to stay loyal to the Democratic Party on election day. In Chicago Jerry Ford accused Carter of manipulating the hostage situation against Reagan as he had done against Kennedy in the primaries.

Ayatollah Khomeini in an hour-long speech criticized Carter but made no comments on the hostages. His only political reference involved the war with Iraq, which he used as a springboard to taunt Carter's record as an armchair soldier. "In which wars has Mr. Carter gone to battlefronts?" he asked. "He sits in the White House, causing other people to fight and be killed." Meanwhile Israeli Prime Minister Begin expressed "deep regrets" over his former Defense Minister Ezer Weizman's endorsement of Carter, concerned that if Reagan won he might hold this against Israel, while the U.S. general responsible for contingency planning expressed fears that America could not match the Soviets in any Persian Gulf showdown.

Completing a downbeat news day, the Ford Motor Company reported a third-quarter deficit of $595 million, exceeding the record $567-million loss set Monday by General Motors. With Chrysler expected to announce equally disastrous sales in a few days, the prospect seemed certain that this marked the worst three-month period in history for American auto makers.

Polls published the day of the debate found the Presidency "up for grabs." Weekend surveys by *Time* and *Newsweek* scored it an absolute tie. *Newsweek* had it 41 to 40 percent for Carter, with Anderson at 10 percent and the momentum going for Carter. *Time* showed 42 to 41 percent for Reagan, with 12 percent for Anderson and the undecideds breaking 7 to 4 for Carter.

Inside the downtown Cleveland Convention Center, the 3,000-seat Music Hall had cut its seating capacity to 750 at the request of the candidates. The adjacent 10,000-seat Public Hall had been converted into a giant press room for the national media, where reporters would watch developments on a 9 × 12-foot screen. Only 200 seats in the debating room were set aside for the press. Another 200 tickets were divided between the rival camps, and the remaining 350 were distributed by the League.

Reagan slept until 8:30 a.m., breakfasted with Nancy at their leased Virginia home, and spent an hour scanning briefing papers. Then he watched videotapes of Carter news conferences and television interviews, familiarizing himself with the President's style and mannerisms. After packing for their last week of campaign travels, the Reagans took the limousine to the airport to catch the flight to Ohio.

Carter began his day at 6:30, jogging three miles in a cold drizzle on the running track of Cleveland's Cuyahoga Community College. After showering at his downtown hotel, he had breakfast with Rosalynn, studied briefing books, and remained in seclusion until it was time to make the block-long trip to the Music Hall with Rosalynn.

The debate moderator was veteran broadcaster Howard K. Smith; the panel included ABC's Barbara Walters, Harry Ellis of the *Christian Science Monitor*, William Hilliard of the *Portland Oregonian*, and Marvin Stone, editor of *U.S. News and World Report*. The two candidates entered the stage just before the 9:30 p.m. starting time. Carter wore a navy blue suit, a white shirt, and a tie clasp binding a dark blue tie with pencil-line red and white stripes. Reagan wore a navy blue suit, a white shirt with a slightly spread collar, a blue tie with subtle white polka dots, and no tie clasp. Both were dressed for high authority, though Carter's outfit was somewhat more corporate than Reagan's.

The Californian got the jump on the Georgian with his entrance. While Carter marched resolutely straight to his assigned lectern at stage right and turned to grin at the audience, Reagan bypassed his stage-left lectern, crossed right, and surprised Carter by extending his hand. Though the crowd had been cautioned not to react to anything onstage, they broke out laughing at the unscheduled contact. The sportsmanlike crossover gave the crowd and television cameras a chance to note the obvious height difference between the two men.

Carter stared grimly ahead while Reagan smiled at Nancy and others in the crowd. Though the contestants were forbidden to bring notes to the podium, they were allowed to jot down ideas once the debate began. Carter listened rigidly and rarely changed expression. Reagan, on the other hand, took notes almost every time Carter spoke, occasionally mugging when off camera, and gripping the sides of the lectern as Ford had done four years earlier. Carter glared at Reagan, trying to unnerve him, as the Californian answered questions.

There were few surprises. Both candidates mostly rehashed the positions and themes on which they had been elaborating for almost two months. Unexpectedly, it was Reagan who played better on his feet, relying much less than the President on stock phrases borrowed from campaign rhetoric. Though there were a few minor gaffes, no major mistakes erupted to settle the issue.

Carter went on the attack from the beginning, calling his opponent "dangerous" and diverting the focus from his own record to historical Reagan quotes. When the President assailed Reagan's proposed tax cuts, quoting George Bush's term "voodoo economics," Reagan glanced at Nancy and mugged an expression of mock horror. Then in his reply Reagan played off the "voodoo" theme, describing Jimmy Carter as "the witch doctor who gets mad when a good doctor comes along with a cure that will work." He reminded viewers of Carter's 1976 campaign invention of the "misery index," which under Ford was 15.8 percent: "At that time, Carter said no man with that size misery index had a right to seek reelection to the Presidency. Today the misery index is in excess of 20 percent. I think this must suggest something."

When Carter accused Reagan of wanting to make Social Security voluntary and of being opposed to Medicare, Reagan could not contain himself: "There you go again," he said, referring to being misquoted as he glanced at Carter and smiled good-naturedly. The President attacked Reagan's call for "nuclear superiority," charging that his proposal to scrap SALT II was "extremely dangerous and belligerent in tone, though said with a quiet voice." The governor protested that this "just was not true," but he seemed somewhat defensive.

Reagan regained the offensive with a surprise call for a complete Congressional investigation of how the hostage crisis was handled once the Americans were safely home. He insisted that the probe should cover not only diplomatic and military efforts to free the hostages, but the very origins of the crisis.

The President, as planned, hit hard on war and peace at every opportunity: "A President in the Oval Office has to make a judgment on almost a daily basis how to exercise the enormous power of our country for peace—he can do it diplomatically, or carelessly, belligerently." In an attempt to evoke Tony Schwartz's "Daisy Girl" commercial, Carter said, "Amy and I talk frequently about her concern for nuclear weaponry and the control of nuclear arms." The statement was greeted with shocked silence.

Replying to one charge that he aimed to destroy the minimum wage, Reagan accused Carter of distorting his position again. He had no wish to abolish the protective minimum but only to add a special minimum for teen-agers, he said, arguing that the high general minimum deprived black youths of jobs. The Republican told of visiting a group of blacks in a section of the Bronx that looked like "bombed-out London during the war" and being asked, "Governor, is there any hope for people like us?" He was so moved, he said, that he couldn't find words to express his feelings. Reagan also said that when he was growing up in Illinois, he was never aware of race problems—a remark that made his supporters wince.

In his closing, Carter said, "I want to thank the people of Cleveland and Ohio for being such hospitable hosts during these last few hours of my life," thus betraying a certain anxiety over his performance.

When the debate was over, Reagan unhooked his lapel mike, crossed the stage, and shook hands with the President again, smiling easily. Afterward, reporters asked both men how they felt they did. "Very good," Carter offered, and later told a crowd of supporters back at his hotel, "I have no doubt we'll have a tremendous victory November 4." Reagan replied, "I've examined myself and I can't find any wounds."

Who won? The President recited facts and figures humorlessly, without wit, anecdotes, or imagery. Reagan loosened up more quickly than Carter, showed a basic grasp of the issues, and spoke more movingly, more simply, so that people could understand. Carter used the words "Oval Office" all evening, reminding everyone who was and who wasn't President. Reagan, however, successfully softened his "Mad Bomber" image.

The first attempt to name the winner came from ABC, from a telephone call-in poll. Nearly 700,000 people responded and named Reagan the winner 2 to 1 in what ABC disclaimed as a "strictly unscientific survey." The next day most newspaper columnists called Reagan the winner, except for David Broder of the *Washington Post*, who thought Carter won "on points." The *New York Post* claimed the voice-stress analyzer revealed that Carter was lying throughout the debate. A CBS poll found it 44 to 36 percent in favor of Reagan, with 14 percent calling it a tie. ABC/Lou Harris showed a bigger spread: 44 to 26 percent for Reagan, while 30 percent called it even. Despite early widespread criticism of the ABC telephone poll, it actually proved closer to the mark than the journalists' prediction that Carter won because of his detailed elaboration of facts, figures, and dates.

The only obvious loser was John Anderson. Through Cable Network News he reached an audience estimated at a maximum 3.5 million, compared to the 120 million who watched Carter and Reagan on the national networks. Before a studio audience of twenty-five hundred at Washington's Constitution Hall, Anderson attacked both rivals for their evasive answers. "I feel somewhat inadequate to compete with either Little Amy or the witch doctor," he joked bitterly.

As of October 15, the Carter campaign had used up $24 million of its $29.4-million legal limit, whereas the Reagan side had used only $16.6 million. For this reason Carter campaign manager Bob Strauss, despite even-up poll readings, told reporters just before the debate, "I'm afraid we may have peaked too early." Spending heavily on media to discredit Reagan early and make him "an implausible candidate" had succeeded in closing the ratings gap, but left Carter weakened in the final week of the campaign.

On the other side, Richard Wirthlin and Pete Dailey calmly played out their hand. "From the beginning, we felt that to beat Jimmy Carter we had to peak the campaign very strongly in the last ten days," Wirthlin explained. "As a result, we spent about $6 million in media during that period alone." A full 40 percent of their $15-million advertising budget was reserved for the last 16 percent of the campaign's time span. During those last ten days, Dailey was able to outspend Rafshoon by about 2½ to 1. Dailey's anti-Carter commercials weren't aired until October 10, and the really heavy assaults came only in the final days of the campaign.

"The debate conditioned the environment for 'peak week,'" Wirthlin observed. "First we needed to establish Reagan's positive credentials, then we needed to have the public see him close to Jimmy Carter. Then we could go into our attack mode, comparing the kind of leadership that Carter's given us in the last four years with what Reagan offered."

Pete Dailey translated the broad strategy into specifics: "Wirthlin's research in the beginning told us 40 percent of the people didn't know enough about Reagan to vote for him. By the time we reached the last week, that figure had dropped to 26 percent. So the last week's strategy was to rally the troops. By the last week we felt we had communicated as much as we could about Reagan, so we launched an all-out attack on Carter, with more production values, more wheat-waving things. It concluded with an election-eve speech by the governor. That was a blatant appeal to his own people.

"People who write about politics in the press tend to define political advertising in terms of *solutions*. They say, senator so-and-so ran a terrific campaign down in Texas and here's what he did to win. As a mass persuader, the most important single thing is to define the problem. It's a difference of situation analysis, unique for every campaign."

One thirty-second Dailey spot called "Flip-flop" dramatized the perception of inconsistent Carter leadership. Jerry Rafshoon had blundered by not copyrighting his 1976 Carter commercials. The oversight allowed Dailey to use film cuts of Carter making campaign promises four years ago, then comparing them to present realities. The effect was to ridicule the President and damage his credibility—his strongest trait.

Visuals featured blowups of Carter's face grinning as the narrator quoted a campaign promise, then quickly cutting to Carter grimacing in a frozen frame as his actual performance was contrasted with it: "He promised to create more jobs (*grin*), and now there are 8 million Americans out of work (*grimace*). He promised to balance the budget (*grin*); what he gave us was a $61-billion deficit (*grimace*). Can we afford four more years? The time is now for strong leadership."

Using statistics and charts, an "Economy" commercial proclaimed the business expertise the Reagan administration promised to bring to the Oval Office. A satiric slide trombone accompanied a rising graph line as a narrator told the story: "Food prices UP over 35 percent (*vroooom*); auto prices UP over 31 percent (*vroooom*); home prices UP over 46 percent (*vroooom*); clothing prices UP over 20 percent (*vroooom*); transportation UP over 50 percent (*vroooom*). The Carter record speaks for itself. The time is now for Reagan."

The most effective advertising featured Ronald Reagan himself, and was shown in the final week in a variety of paid material. Typical of this advertising was a five-minute inflation commercial that showed Reagan and his wife walking through a crowd of well-wishers:

"He believes in America, and the strong creative leadership that can restore our faith in the future. He calls not for retreat into the past, but for a confident advance into the future." Reagan's talking head then appeared: "Record inflation has robbed the purchasing power of your dollar. And for three and a half years this administration has been unable to control it. I'm very worried, as all Americans are, and I'm prepared to do something about it." He then described a six-point program and said: "Now these are not simple solutions, but they all make sense. We can turn this country around and we can turn this economy around. And the time to do it is now."

Added to the onslaught were commercials developed independently by a $4-million Republican National Committee war chest. These commercials urged Americans to "vote Republican for a change." A classic on inflation showed a blowup of a one-dollar bill in the fingers of a workingman's hand. As the narrator recited the list of Democratic sins, the dollar shrank to postage-stamp size: "A shrinking dollar commemorates five years of reckless spending. Since the Democrats got control of Congress, spending has increased 700 percent, taxes have increased 700 percent. And what is that dollar worth today? Thirty-six cents. Vote Republican for a change."

Another independent Republican group, Americans for an Effective Presidency, produced a batch of spots using Reagan endorsers to promote their cause. No Reagan cheerleader was more effective than Jerry Ford, who added his ex-Presidential status to a hard-hitting attack on the same Jimmy Carter who he felt had "dirty-tricked" his way into the White House four years earlier. The Ford spot simply had him look into the camera and say: "People say they wish they had voted for me last election. Now they realize they made a mistake. But '76 is behind us. This nation will be better served by a Reagan Presidency than a continuation of the weak and politically expedient policies of Jimmy Carter. For the future of our country, cast your vote for Ronald Reagan."

Other endorsers included distinguished admirals and generals making points on defense, economists on the economy, and George Bush on Reagan's character. One inadvertent endorser of Reagan was Ted Kennedy, whose primary commercials blasting Carter had become available as public-domain material and played a key role in the New England and Northern states. In one of those commercials, Kennedy was shown at the podium urging: "If we want to get rid of inflation, if we want to get rid of unemployment, if we want to get rid of high interest rates, then we've got to get rid of Jimmy Carter!" The frame was frozen, the legend "Vote for a new beginning, Reagan for President" was inserted, followed by a disclaimer, and that was it. Run heavily in Kennedy country, the spot was devastating.

Some fringe groups backing Reagan aired less savory fare. The Christian Voice, a fundamentalist organization, spent

$50,000 to run a "homosexual rights" spot in local markets.
Created by the same agency that did Anita Bryant's 1977 anti-
gay crusade, Long Advertising of Miami, the narration began
by accusing Carter of "advocating acceptance of homosexuality." A woman came on camera, identifying herself as a
"Christian mother opposed to my children being taught that
abortion and homosexuality are perfectly all right." Pointing
out that Jimmy Carter disagreed with her on these issues, she
concluded, "I am duty-bound as a Christian and a mother to
vote for Ronald Reagan, a man who will protect my family
values."

A national committee was formed by the other side to
counter such appeals. Under the direction of film maker Norman Lear, Carter supporters created commercials selling the
separation of Church and State while attacking the evangelists
who favored Reagan. A typical effort featured an attractive
housewife with a Southern drawl, who looked up from her
vacuum cleaner to explain that even though she came from
the Bible Belt, she was not proud of some misunderstandings
circulating about her people: "Jesus didn't imply anything
about how we ought to vote, or how we ought to build more
weapons. Some television preachers would have everyone believe all us folks feel that way. Well, it ain't true. If my
preacher and I don't tell anyone how to vote, then nobody
will try to tell me how to worship. After all, that's the American way, isn't it?"

Jerry Rafshoon's last wave of advertising was desperation
material. One series of radio spots used Reagan quotes to
make him seem simple-minded and reckless: "Recently Ronald Reagan said air pollution is substantially under control.
He made this statement when people in Los Angeles were
gasping for breath, many being hospitalized for respiratory
ailments. Ronald Reagan makes lots of statements like this
because, as usual, Ronald Reagan was shooting from the hip."

Harry Muheim, teaming up with film maker Eli Bleich, did
a batch of "mini-doc" commercials, elaborations of their "man-
on-the-street" series. Intended as "highly affirmative one-
minute little movies," they were designed to counter the growing perception that Carter had failed to do anything good and

was not an effective leader—two powerful themes in Reagan's campaign.

Film crews spent time shooting ordinary folks across the country—a nurse in Atlanta, an old couple in Maine, an Akron rubberworker, a black Chicago schoolteacher. Explained Muheim: "'Each person talked about how he felt, about life generally, and about the President specifically. Naturally, these were all people in favor of Jimmy Carter. The guy in Maine said Jimmy Carter could sit right down with him now and they'd get along. A farmer said the grain embargo didn't get us a war, and that's a fairly cheap price to pay for freedom, so he was going to vote for Carter. They were interviews, but you could tell that the people believed what they were saying. The spots had a quiet impact, in keeping with the President's personality."

Jimmy Carter cut talking-head spots urging voters to come out to the polls, reminding them that Hubert Humphrey would have won the White House in 1968, "if only a few hundred thousand more Democrats had voted." This was a direct response to research showing that a low turnout was equivalent to defeat. Meanwhile another batch of television and radio spots beseeched Anderson supporters not to waste their votes. The spots criticized the congressman for "voting against key civil rights legislation," hoping to persuade defecting liberals and young voters to return to the Democratic fold.

Rafshoon produced his own version of "Flip-flop" spots, using film cuts of old Reagan speeches spliced to on-camera commentary from Carter. The narrator began:

"On nuclear proliferation, a candidate must remember what he has said."

(Carter at the podium during the debate)

"Ronald Reagan has made the disturbing comment that nonproliferation of the control of nuclear weapons is none of our business."

(Cut to Reagan at the podium during debate)

"I have never made the statement he suggested about nuclear proliferation."

(Cut to earlier Reagan speech)

"I just don't think it's any of our business. Unilaterally the United States seems to be the only nation in the world . . ."

The narrator concluded, "Which Ronald Reagan should we believe?" as a running scroll crossed the screen: "ELECT PRESIDENT CARTER."

Another in the series showed a blowup of the California state seal as the voice-over said: "When Ronald Reagan speaks of the good old days when he was governor of California, there are some things he does not mention. He increased state spending by 120 percent and brought three tax increases to the state. He added 34,000 to the state payroll . . ."

Then the California seal dissolved into the Presidential seal, and a running scroll explained point by point that Reagan didn't accomplish as governor what he claimed to accomplish.

The voice-over concluded: "Can we trust the nation's future to a man who refuses to remember his own past? Reelect President Carter."

After being virtually begged by the President, Ted Kennedy finally agreed to do commercials endorsing Carter on one condition—that Jerry Rafshoon have nothing to do with it. Kennedy still harbored bad feelings against Rafshoon for what he felt were dirty tactics in Rafshoon's primaries advertising. So he cut commercials written by ex–Carter speech writer Bob Shrum and produced by David Sawyer, more anti-Reagan than pro-Carter in tone. Typical of the three spots was one where he addressed the camera, "I am convinced: to prevent a Reagan victory and preserve our hope for an America of progress and fairness, vote for President Carter."

Even in the final days, Rafshoon continued playing his "peacemaker" spot, promoting the single Carter achievement for which many Americans would agree he deserved praise. But after the debate Reagan no longer seemed a real threat to peace, and after so many plays earlier the commercial seemed a feeble reply to the omnipresent Reagan media blitz.

The Carter cause got help from "invisible" pop culture supporters who tried to sway the electorate their own way. Gary Trudeau, the *Doonesbury* cartoonist, prepared a last-week round of strips featuring "The Brain of Ronald Reagan." The series described a trip through the skull of the Republican hopeful, noting that "the brain of Ronald Reagan has been shrinking ever since 1931," with "severe perceptual disorder within the cortex that has plagued the candidate's vision for years. Instead of looking forward through clear eyes, Reagan is only able to see backwards through a rose-colored mist. The hypothalamus, the deep dark coils of human aggression, is the source of Reagan's impulses to send U.S. forces to Angola, Iran, Korea, Cyprus, Cuba, Lebanon, and countless other hot spots. Tragically, his condition is thought to be inoperable."

In a single week of four-panel strips, Trudeau replayed the most damaging perceptions that Jerry Rafshoon and the Carter campaign had been working to imprint on the electorate for months—the warmonger, Mad-Bomber, hip-shooting dumbactor stereotype—reinforcing negatives in the disguise of innocent satire. A few newspapers refused to run the cartoons in the ordinary day-by-day manner. Instead, the *Indianapolis Star* and the *Salt Lake City Desert News* published the series on a single day opposite the editorial pages, while the *San Bernadino Sun-Telegram* did the same on its news pages. The major dailies, including the *Los Angeles Times* and the *Washington Post*, played Trudeau's partisan game the way he intended.

A week before the vote, a film called *The Trials of Alger Hiss* opened in major cities around the country. Suggesting a government conspiracy to frame Hiss, it starred Richard Nixon as principal villain, recalling the release of *All the President's Men* during the Ford-Carter 1976 campaign.

Dick Tuck, the political prankster who dogged Nixon's Presidency, popped up the last week of the campaign on a nationwide tour of radio and television talk shows, playing "never before heard" Watergate tapes starring the inevitable Richard Nixon—a potent reminder of what Republicans could do, once ensconced in the Oval Office.

As for John Anderson, he managed to become more visible in the last days through a package of five-minute and sixty-second commercials produced by David Garth. The long pieces were variations of the harangues the candidate had delivered in his stump speeches, while the one-minute versions repeated selected excerpts. All the spots featured Anderson's head talking:

"Personal attacks, easy promises, easy answers—and none of it feels true. What does it mean for a great democracy, when two major candidates for our highest office refuse to face up to the issues? The people know it, and feel they can do nothing about it. It means we're in serious trouble. It's led me to take a very different approach in my own campaign—to break through the frustration and paralysis to create a new sense of possibility. I start with some hard facts—the solutions to our problems are going to be difficult. That shouldn't come as a surprise to anyone. But if saying so jeopardizes my election, so be it.

"We must reject proposals that feel good but fail to get at the root of our difficulties. Multibillion-dollar tax cuts proposed by my opponents sound good. I can't support them. A hundred-billion-dollar MX missile sounds tough. I am against it. Aid to our cities? We can't survive without it. How would it feel if your vote November 4 made possible not a lesser evil, but a greater good? A new chance for our country? You can make it happen."

There was one thing to be said about Garth's campaign for Anderson: it was consistent. In fact, it stayed virtually unchanged from start to finish.

The day after the debate, the media were dominated by rumors from Iran that a deal was in the works and the hostages would soon be flown to Germany. "Many members of Parliament want to free the hostages before the election," Ayatollah Khalkali told Radio Sweden.

While the October Surprise developed, Ronald Reagan started a final ten-state tour that his people felt would ensure victory. His first stop was Texas, where he launched his toughest attack on Carter's economy by asking, "Are you really better off than you were four years ago?"

The Reagan team behind Stu Spencer had totally outcampaigned Carter's people in the Lone Star State, with a state-wide organization first put together for Bill Clements two years earlier by Spencer. "Clements did a tremendous job," Spencer noted. "He took what organization we'd built for his governor's race and added to it. There was only one state I bet money we'd win—Texas. We really worked the Mexican-Americans hard there." In 1976 Carter took 87 percent of the Mexican vote and won the state by 150,000 votes. This time, if Wirthlin's readings were right, it looked like Reagan would cut at least 10 percent off Carter's Mexican base and maybe more. But that alone would guarantee Spencer's collecting on his wager.

Before it was all over, Reagan was scheduled to stump in Arkansas, Louisiana, New Jersey, Pennsylvania, Illinois, Michigan, and Oregon before returning home to California on election eve. He would bypass New York, virtually conceding it rather than be burned as Ford was in 1976.

The media were still arguing over who had won the debate. Dick Wirthlin released his figures, showing Reagan victorious by 45 to 34 percent, while Pat Caddell dug up a two-hundred-member panel who scored Carter 76 percent positive to Reagan's mere 50 percent. Spencer and the others on the plane felt good about the encounter, confident they had forced the issues and made Carter admit he could not defend his record.

Reagan was helped by the business news on Wednesday when three stories broke: "CARTER BUDGET $59 BILLION IN RED . . . CHRYSLER LOSES $497 MILLION IN THIRD QUARTER . . . PRIME RATE UP TO 14½ PERCENT." But Carter got a boost when the *Wall Street Journal* accused Richard Allen, Reagan's foreign-policy adviser, of having used his position in the Nixon administration to make some private deals for himself.

When the President campaigned in New York on Thursday, he went to the garment center where in 1976 thousands of workers cheered him like a conquering hero. This time, though, the response from the ten thousand onlookers was tepid. When Polish-American and Jewish audiences in Philadelphia showed the same lack of enthusiasm, Carter's brain trust grew worried.

In St. Louis, in Michigan, and then in South Carolina Carter harangued Democrats with the warning that a small turnout would elect Reagan by default. Quoting old Reagan speeches, he reminded senior citizens that his opponent was "a traveling salesman for the anti-Medicare lobby." To prove his charges, aides gave reporters a specially produced record that anthologized Reagan quotes from radio and television tapes going back up to twenty years. One of the bands came from a 1962 speech to an American Medical Association convention, where the Republican spoke of the problems with "socialized medicine."

To stem massive defections in the evangelical bloc that had been another Carter "secret weapon" in 1976, he appeared in Memphis with Rev. Jim Bakker, the host of the popular "Praise the Lord Club" television show, who praised the President as "a fine born-again Christian." Then, even as a Justice Department report was leaked to the press accusing Carter of being "remarkably uncooperative" in its investigation of Billygate and warning that the President might be subpoenaed, Richard Allen resigned from the Reagan campaign "so as not to be an issue."

As expected, on Friday the Commerce Department revealed that the Consumer Price Index for September had reached a 12.7-percent annual rate. Carter commented that while inflation was still a serious problem, under Reagan's "economic voodoo" things would be much worse. But Reagan told Washington reporters that the Index said one thing loud and clear: "Carter's economic medicine . . . is going to put the patient on the critical list if it isn't stopped." Aide Ed Gray confirmed that Carter had "jimmied" the figures. Had the CPI included the normally reckoned FHA mortgage rates, it would have read 13.9 percent—a full 1.2 percent had been "jimmied away"!

The last week ended with the news that Iranian hardliners had postponed Parliamentary debate until Sunday, leaving hopes of a preelection return up in the air. Campaigning in New York, Carter couldn't estimate the chances that the hostages would come home soon: "It's out of our control." While

Iran's mullahs and Parliament feuded, Americans held their breath to see how the hostage wild card would affect their choice of a leader.

In the battle for endorsements, Reagan won the raw numbers while President Carter was the overwhelming favorite of the powerful establishment papers. Carter had the blessing of the *New York Times, Chicago Sun-Times, Washington Post, Philadelphia Inquirer, St. Louis Post-Dispatch,* and *Baltimore Sun.* Reagan's only major prizes included the *New York Post, Boston Herald, Dallas News,* and *Seattle Times*—papers not nearly so influential. The outcome would help prove how important such backing was.

More tellingly, Pete Dailey's "Campaign '80" began running a series of full-page ads in major city newspapers during the last few days of the race, which in consecutive banner heads asked Americans: "CAN YOU AFFORD FOUR MORE YEARS OF JIMMY CARTER? . . . CAN WE AFFORD FOUR MORE YEARS OF JIMMY CARTER?" The text detailed facts and figures indicating that the obvious answer was no. These ads were conditioning Americans for the candidate's election-eve speech, designed to be the centerpiece and crowning event of the campaign. On election day the ads would ask, "ARE YOU BETTER OFF NOW THAN YOU WERE FOUR YEARS AGO?"—exactly as candidate Reagan would have done on television.

Saturday's big stories were headlined: "SWEDISH AIRLINE READY FOR HOSTAGES . . . IRAN REVEALS JUST METHOD TO FREE HOSTAGES." ABC reported that Iranian newspapers urged, "Now is the best time to trade the hostages, before the election, because if Reagan wins, the options will narrow." With the hostages overwhelming the election itself, the growing question was whether a year-long media event from Iran could save Carter from almost certain defeat. Bob Strauss admitted that Carter's drive had suffered a "pause in momentum" since the debate, but Caddell showed it was coming their way again. Campaigning fifteen hours a day across four television markets, Carter planned to wrap up the race with a coast-to-coast "death march" from Philadelphia through Cali-

fornia, Oregon, and Washington and back to Georgia where
he would vote and rest, then return to the White House on
election day.

Reagan, who had soft-pedaled his rhetoric during the predebate period, now slashed away at the President. In Illinois,
Wisconsin, and New Jersey he added new punch lines to his
standard ones: "In 1976 he promised to give us a government
as good as the people, but he gave us one that was as good as
Jimmy Carter, and we know that's not good enough. . . . I
know they say he's doing his best—that's our problem. . . . The
reason he's so obsessed with poverty is because he never had
any as a kid."

The crowds, big and enthusiastic, laughed heartily. He
really broke them up with a reference to the debate: "When
the President said he talked about nuclear proliferation with
thirteen-year-old Amy, he touched our hearts. I remember
when Patti and Ron were little kids and we used to talk about
nuclear power."

In Texas Carter tried to bring home Democrats with his
agenda for a second term—"security at home and peace
abroad." He promised to push for nuclear arms control and an
end to the horrendous atomic competition. His voice hoarse
and his hand sore from shaking, Carter warned Texans of the
threat imposed by "a Republican in the Oval Office the next
four years. There is no one here," he told Mexican-American
supporters in Brownsville, "who can't reach several hundred
people between now and election day. Some of you have
enough influence to reach a thousand or ten thousand."

Richard Wirthlin's private tracking studies showed Reagan's lead growing in the home stretch. On Thursday, October
30, it showed a seven-point margin and 380 electoral votes; on
October 31 a nine-point lead; and on Saturday, November 1, a
ten-point popular lead. But they never dared show those figures to Ronald Reagan. "We were too conservative," admitted
pollster Vince Breglio.

Sunday, November 2. Headlines dominated: "HOSTAGES ON
CENTER STAGE AS ANNIVERSARY NEARS . . . SUPPORT GROWS FOR
HOSTAGE RELEASE . . . HARDLINERS FAVOR RELEASE BEFORE

ELECTIONS . . . MUSKIE DENIES DEAL IS MADE." Naturally, Muskie's denial triggered widespread speculation that a deal had in fact been made. Frequent network news breaks reported that the Iranian parliament was meeting for zero-hour discussion, while planes at Teheran airport stood by to fly the Americans to Wiesbaden, Germany, for debriefing on release.

Launching their hostage-release contingency, Reagan surrogates used free media to preempt the expected national euphoria. Henry Kissinger appeared on ABC's *Issues and Answers* to counter any surge toward Carter. "I'm not accusing the administration of doing this on political grounds," he told the panel and viewing Americans. "But I am accusing the Iranian government, which has tormented us for a year now, of trying to tell the American public how to vote."

On *Meet the Press* George Bush said: "Gotsbadegh is the man who talked about the election of Ronald Reagan adversely affecting the hostage problem, clearly trying to intervene in the election. I don't think Ronald Reagan would be very tolerant of the U.S.' being held hostage a year." And Lyn Nofziger told CBS News: "For now the plan is to say as little as possible. There is a contingency plan if the hostages are actually released, including speeches and television commercials questioning Carter's handling of the whole thing."

Waiting in Pete Dailey's files at Campaign '80 was a special version of the "Flip-flop" commercial. Having rerecorded the Carter "Grin/Frown" track, new quotes were inserted from things he had said about Iran and foreign affairs before the hostages were imprisoned, compared to statements he made afterward. The juxtaposition was a convincing indictment of how the President had exploited the hostages for political gain; it ended with the comment, "And it's taken him a full year to get them out."

Another hard-hitting hostage-release spot waiting on hold featured film of people suffering in the Middle East, bloody and dead war victims, and scenes of Afghans being slaughtered by Russian troops, while a narrator itemized Carter's failures of foreign policy all around the world. The commercial concluded with the President's inability to gain the hostages' release until the last days of the campaign, urging voters not to allow Iranian terrorists to choose our President for us.

Pollster Burns Roper judged the hostage furor a net neutral for Carter: "It casts doubts on his ability to handle foreign affairs. But that's neutralized by people who think it might be worse—they might be dead if Reagan were in there."

At 6:25 EST on Sunday evening, CBS broke in on its National Football League telecast in the third quarter of a close game. "We interrupt the program in progress to bring you a special message from the President of the United States," said an off-camera announcer. Carter, looking grim and harried, walked into the East Room of the White House and was introduced. Wearing a red, white, and blue striped tie, he read a prepared statement:

"The Iranian Parliament has finally taken a position on the release of our hostages. This is a significant development. We are pursuing the matter through diplomatic channels. We are within two days of an important national election. Let me assure you my decisions on this crucial matter will not be affected by the calendar. I wish I could predict when the hostages will return. I cannot. But whether before or after the election, and regardless of the outcome, the Iranian government will find our country, its people and leaders united in desiring the early and safe return of the hostages to their homes. But only on a basis that preserves our national honor and our national integrity. Thank you very much."

As he left the East Room, the President refused to answer any questions. The news media and most Americans were left dangling as they speculated on what effect the "significant developments" would have on the election. Would it trigger an outpouring of last-minute support for Carter, enabling the man aide Hamilton Jordan called "the luckiest politician I know" to turn certain defeat into victory on the eve of election? For many political observers, the answer to that question posed nothing less than a crucial test of American democracy. If an electorate could be turned on its head by an obvious emotional event that had little to do with the major questions of the election, it would be to them final proof the nation was just as vulnerable to propaganda ploys as some of the totalitarian societies it so loudly condemned.

While ordinary citizens held their breath, the mood inside both political camps was hopeful. Pat Caddell outlined his reasons for optimism: "When the debate ended, there was a bump-up for Governor Reagan Thursday and Friday lasting until Saturday morning. By Saturday night to early Sunday morning, our surveys indicated that instead of a four-point loss President Carter was back even, maybe even a slight point ahead."

Caddell had taken six national polls between Friday and Sunday, with the last three showing it a dead-even race. But the mood was even more sanguine on the other side. "I felt good about things," Stu Spencer recalled. "We knew if Carter hadn't pulled off a release by then, he was in trouble. Wirthlin had been tracking the whole time and the research showed that if they negotiated something at that late date, the voters wouldn't go for it. They would see it strictly as a political move. He had been to the well with this thing too many times."

Wirthlin's national surveys showed a ten-point margin for Reagan on Saturday and Sunday, a bulge that had built steadily following the debate and was now holding firm. "Carter should have reacted five days earlier, when the Iran flurry first started," Spencer noted. "He should have come out and said, 'Nothing's going to happen with the hostages until after the election, the Iranians are not going to dictate our election.' He's the one who should have taken the hard line but he didn't, he just futzed around with it."

On Sunday evening, thirty-six hours before the polls opened, Mike Wallace ran a lead story on 60 Minutes about Teamster Union racketeering in Thousand Oaks, California. It was a story that the top-rated CBS show had been holding in the can for months, showering muck and negative attention on the only major union endorsing Ronald Reagan a day before voters would have to make up their minds.

Monday morning's media reports were dominated by speculation about how the Iranian wild card would affect the election. While many experts hedged their bets, both sides continued to argue over who won last week's debate. Wirthlin acknowledged there had been no "knockout blow," but claimed that the fallout had widened Reagan's support. Hamilton Jordan disagreed. "Ten days from now," he prophesied, "people will say the debate was a small plus for Reagan and a significant plus for Carter. Reagan reassured his people but Carter reassured Democrats—and there are a lot more of those."

Everyone agreed that a key to the outcome would be how many of these abundant Democrats would reach the polls to vote. Lou Harris pointed out that when Carter beat Ford, the turnout was 54.4 percent of the voting-age population. "If it goes above that, it will help Carter," Harris predicted. "If it drops to 52 percent or less, it will help Reagan."

Caddell reported that his readings showed that most of the "undecideds and soft Anderson voters were Democrats." So Carter spent the last day of the campaign hustling for those Democratic defectors. Pointing out that his views and Anderson's were "very close," he beseeched those voters to "come home or be responsible for electing Reagan." He echoed the same message at stops in Ohio, Michigan, Missouri, Oregon, and Washington before boarding *Air Force One* for the flight back to Washington.

Reagan used the last day to work crowds in Michigan and Illinois. He was scheduled to tape an election-eve speech in Illinois, designed to crown his four-year effort. As Pete Dailey tells it, it almost didn't get on the air. "It was the last day of the campaign and we were in Peoria," he told me. "Reagan had traveled more that last week than at any other time in the entire campaign. When he got to the studio and we started to tape the speech, it was early Monday morning and he looked very, very tired. We had to stop taping and were even thinking of canceling it. But he rested a little and then he came on very strong. It was his best speech, even though it was a blatant appeal to his own people." After the taping, Reagan flew to Oregon for a last-hour appeal, then returned to California to vote and await the verdict.

Anderson ended his campaign bathed by cheers from students at his alma mater, the University of Illinois. "I will celebrate tomorrow, whatever the outcome," he told supporters.

Election eve. While network newscasts commemorated the first anniversary of the hostage seizure with filmed historical narratives, the three Presidential candidates completed their formal campaigning with network television films. Because his treasury had so little money left, President Carter was limited to a twenty-minute presentation shown on only one network. Moderated by actor Henry Fonda and put together by Harry Muheim and Eli Bleich under Rafshoon's direction, it typically moved fast, featured quick cuts, and crammed lots of faces saying nice things about Jimmy Carter into its limited time span. Overall, it left an impression of being just another well-produced piece of political propaganda with little emotional clout. Meanwhile Anderson's last exposure was an extension of his earlier Garth material, a fifteen-minute discussion of his "differences" on the issues.

Campaign '80 had held back $400,000 to buy time on all three networks for their thirty-minute election-eve speech. First the governor introduced George Bush, who lauded him with a three-minute character reference. Then Reagan came on for twenty-six minutes doing what he does best—communicating.

"The election will be over soon," he said softly. "Autumn will become winter, this year will become next." He made a passing reference to the hostages and the shared wish for their safe return. Then he went on to paint a picture of America under a Reagan administration—"A vision of a better America . . . of a society that frees the energies and ingenuity of our people while it extends compassion to the lonely, the desperate, and the forgotten."

Many Americans, he said, were asking: "Does history still have a place for America? For her people and her great ideals? There are some who answer no—our energy is spent, our days of greatness at an end . . . we must tell our children not to dream as once we dreamed. Last year I lost a friend who was more than a symbol of the Hollywood dream industry. To millions he was a symbol of our country itself. Duke Wayne did not believe our country was ready for the dustbin of history. Just before his death, he said in his own blunt way, 'Just give the American people a good cause and there's nothing they can't lick.'"

After asking the rhetorical questions about Carter's performance—"Are you more secure in your life? Is your family more secure? Is our nation more capable of leading the world toward peace and freedom?"—his closing evoked the poetry and feelings last heard when John Kennedy led the nation twenty years before:

"It is autumn now in Washington. Residents there say that, more than ever the last few years, Americans are coming to visit their capital. In a time when our place in history is so seriously questioned, they say Americans want their sons and daughters to see what is still for them, and for so many millions of others around the world, a city offering the last best hope of man on earth. These visitors to that city on the Potomac do not come as white or black, red or yellow. They are not Jews or Christians, conservatives or liberals or Democrats or Republicans. They are Americans, awed by what has gone before, proud of what to them is still a shining city on a hill.

"Let us resolve tonight that young Americans will always see those Potomac lights, that they will always find there a city of hope in a country that is free. And let us resolve they will say of our day and of our generation, we did keep the faith with our God, that we did act worthy of ourselves, that we did protect and pass on lovingly that shining city on a hill. Thank you and good night."

It was a masterful performance, holding high the torch of his vision to a nation united.

On Monday night CBS broadcast a special election-eve report. "Most national polls show the two campaigns almost even," noted Bruce Norton. "What movement there is is toward Reagan. The last CBS/*New York Times* poll out yesterday had Reagan one point ahead. Gallup showed a three-point Reagan lead. Only the ABC/Harris poll, with a five-point Reagan margin, had a lead bigger than the margin of error. The polls suggest a very close race."

When the President returned to Washington that evening, he was tired but optimistic as *Air Force One* was greeted by a thousand cheering partisans. When staffers played his 1976 theme song over the loudspeakers, Carter's eyes filled with tears and he believed victory possible. But Pat Caddell was tormented by another scenario—the building of a Reagan landslide. "The Iranian development was our final undoing," he moaned. "It was during the Sunday-night to Monday-night period that we showed massive erosion from a point of equality—five points down the first night and ten points down the second."

It was only after the President was a full hour in the air flying to Georgia, mellowed by a double martini, that Jody Powell, himself braced by a stiff drink, was able to collar his boss alone. He told him that Caddell's latest numbers showed Reagan with an insurmountable lead. Unable to believe it, Carter broke the news to Rosalynn when she met his helicopter at Plains and both spent the rest of the early morning hours fighting their emotions. Reportedly it was not until after they voted and boarded the plane back to Washington that they broke down and wept.

At the White House they napped to prepare for the tough night they knew faced them. At 5:30 p.m. on Tuesday Carter called his loyal disciples for a meeting in the Oval Office and listened to Pat Caddell explain how the race had "exploded" on them in the final days. Carter exhorted them to be "proud and gracious" in defeat, then they stood and filed by for a final handshake and a kiss from Rosalynn.

When Jerry Rafshoon, who had been unusually quiet through the entire meeting, accepted his handshake with downcast eyes, Carter asked, "Are you all right?" Rafshoon nodded and mumbled, "yes." The image-shaper who had vowed to "save the President's ass" had accepted the failure as his own, despite the absurdity of such feelings. It was an emotion shared in some degree by all the President's men. Hamilton Jordan described the wakelike atmosphere in the room:

"When my turn came, I gritted my teeth, shook his hand, and tried to avoid direct eye contact. I just wanted to get the hell out of there."

Americans going to the polls the morning of November 4 were greeted by these headlines: "ORDEAL IN IRAN, ONE YEAR IN CAPTIVITY . . . VIGIL MARKS FULL YEAR FOR HOSTAGES . . . U.S. STUDYING IRAN DEMANDS."

About 86 million Americans voted, almost 5 million more than in 1976. But because of the increase in eligible voting-age citizens, that represented just under 54 percent of the potential turnout, compared to the 54.4 percent of four years ago. It was nowhere near the "massive stay-away" predicted by most experts.

Unlike recent elections when Americans had to stay up until the wee hours of the morning watching the electronic tote boards declare a winner, this verdict was decided before many people had even left work to go cast their ballots. At 6:25 p.m. EST, based on exit polls taken of people leaving their voting places, NBC News called Ronald Reagan the winner. During the next forty-five minutes the other networks joined in to project a Republican victory building to a landslide in the electoral vote.

While many Westerners were still in the process of voting, with the polls open for yet another hour and ten minutes, President Carter arrived with his entourage of Georgians at election headquarters in Washington, climbed the stage of the hotel ballroom, and threw in the towel, anxious to get the ordeal over with as quickly as possible. At 9:50 p.m.—6:50 in the West—Bob Strauss introduced Carter for his concession speech.

"I promised you four years ago I would never lie to you," he said in an emotion-choked voice. "So I can't stand here tonight and say it doesn't hurt. The people of the United States have made their choice and of course I accept their decision. But, I have to admit, not with the same enthusiasm that I accepted their decision four years ago."

Network cameras captured tearful faces and weeping followers all across the ballroom. Even field reporter Judy Wood-ruff of NBC looked as if she had on a death mask. It was all over but the final counting, and the howls of Western politicians who felt betrayed by an untimely concession that they blamed for keeping Democrats from the polls, resulting in narrow defeats for scores of congressmen, legislators, and local officials who were denied their rightful votes.

As the night progressed, the defeat took on humiliating proportions for the President, Ham Jordan, Jerry Rafshoon, and the other Democratic strategists. When all the votes were tallied, Reagan had defeated incumbent Carter by more than 8 million votes, 43.3 million to 35 million. John Anderson found 6 million Americans to opt for his difference.

In percentage points it was Reagan 51, Carter 41, Anderson 7. Had Carter come away with all of Anderson's votes, he still would have lost by a plurality of more than 2 million. But the fact emerged that Anderson had borrowed just as much from Reagan as from the Democrats. Anderson had actually provided a measure of disaffection from the two-party choices—considerable, but nowhere near the amount pulled by George Wallace in 1968.

Reagan's popular vote total was the second largest in history, surpassed only by Nixon's 47 million in 1972. His electoral sweep—forty-four states for 489 votes against Carter's six states and the District of Columbia for 49 electoral votes—marked the third largest landslide ever, surpassed only by Franklin Roosevelt's 1936 thrashing of Alf Landon (523 to 8) and Nixon's 1972 trouncing of McGovern (520 to 17).

A television audience estimated at 150 million saw Ronald Reagan enter the ballroom of the Century Plaza Hotel in Los Angeles at 8:55 p.m. local time, climb the stage with Nancy, and smile at the cameras in full view of his delirious followers crammed into the room. Smiling shyly, he spoke with a voice that was hoarse from campaigning:

"You know, here we are. There has never been a more humbling moment in my life. . . . I consider the trust that you have placed in me sacred and I give you my sacred oath I will do my utmost to justify your faith. . . . I am not frightened by what lies ahead and I don't think the American people are frightened by what lies ahead. Together, we are going to do what has to be done."

In giving thanks to those who helped bring about his moment of triumph, President-elect Reagan referred to the people "meeting tonight in our national headquarters in Arlington, Virginia, the dedicated professionals who made the campaign run. . . ." Unnamed, they knew who they were, and so did the insiders following the campaign and its ebb and flow. As professionals, it was the highest public tribute they could ever hope to expect. Their greatest reward was in seeing their candidate climb that stage and accept the moment of triumph they had all worked to accomplish.

Reagan had in fact attained his "coalition of 51 percent," much of it drawn from Carter's 1976 ranks. A fourth of normally Democratic votes went to Reagan, and he captured a majority of independents from Carter (52 to 30 percent). He sliced 14 percent of the Catholic vote from the Democrats and won this heavily Democratic bloc 51 to 42 percent. He got the most Jewish support of any Republican in history (40 percent) and won among women 47 to 42 percent, among blue-collar workers 46 to 44 percent, and even in Carter's own South, which gave him 54 percent of their votes. Taking from his Democratic opponent, he managed to hold on to 87 percent of the Republican vote, shared a bit with John Anderson.

Of those who voted for Carter in 1976, barely half repeated in 1980. Many of those disgruntled people turned to Ronald Reagan. The "born-again" Christians deserted Jimmy Carter in droves. Moral Majority's Jerry Falwell claimed credit for registering 4 million electronic followers alone for the Reagan cause.

Only among blacks and Latinos did the Democratic ties still bind, but even in these rockbound ranks there was some erosion. Carter took about 85 percent of the black vote nationwide, down from 1976's 92 percent; and since 5 percent fewer blacks even registered, the numbers were down even more than the percentages. Reagan took 14 percent of the black vote and a surprising 36 percent of Hispanics—extra leverage that helped him win such swing states as Texas, Illinois, and Florida.

It was a stunning victory for Reagan and his strategists, who ran a well-conceived, consistent campaign that made good use of "the greatest television candidate in history," as Stu Spencer tabbed him.

Harry Muheim saw that "television candidacy" in a somewhat different light, from the perspective of the other side: "Reagan emerges as a comfortable figure. If you tune in *The Waltons*, Reagan shows up all the time. There are a lot of people on television like Reagan. The concerned man really trying to explain something in intense detail, as Carter did, is not a figure you're accustomed to seeing on American television. The uncle who assures you everything is going to be all right, that Reagan-like figure, is an historic figure in American theater and film. Since politics has become so intensely theatricalized, it couldn't help but work to his advantage."

As for most of the national pollsters, it was a campaign that caused lots of head-scratching and excuse-making. Where had they gone wrong? With the notable exception of Lou Harris— who published a consistent five-point Reagan lead during the entire final week and confidently predicted the victory— Gallup, Roper, Yankelovich, and Mitofsky, along with house pollsters for major newspapers and broadcasting organizations, all had it "too close to call" or "within the range of sampling error" right up to election day. Only Dick Wirthlin's readings, which proved uncannily accurate, foresaw the landslide victory well in advance. Pat Caddell, on the other hand, blamed an "explosion" in the final two days for breaking what he was seeing as a virtual tie. Why didn't Caddell see what Wirthlin saw?

One highly respected pollster who was not directly involved in the race thought he knew the reason: "There were a lot of closet Reagan voters. They might not tell an interviewer they were for Reagan, but they sure as hell would punch a ballot for him." Another pollster explained that Pat Caddell is known in the industry as a researcher who puts forward a thesis, then uses his polls to prove it. In the case of the 1980

campaign, Caddell theorized after the Reagan-Carter debate
that there would be a surge toward Reagan in the next sev-
enty-two hours, but then the pendulum would begin to swing
back in Carter's direction. Perhaps what he expected to see
influenced the data he got back from the field.

Polling is still an art, not a science. The way questions are
asked and even who asks them can affect the findings. When
Caddell's interviewers made their phone calls, their voices may
have betrayed their loyalties, and they got back what they and
their boss hoped to hear. In every pollster's career, such a
moment of truth is bound to arrive. But the glory goes to the
victor and Wirthlin got some when the advertising Bible *Ad
Age* named him their "Advertising Man of the Year."

In a post-mortem, Hamilton Jordan reported spending several hours closeted with his campaign teammates, trying to
understand their humiliating defeat. In the end, they
couldn't figure it out. "We ran a good technical campaign
and lost," Jordan concluded. "There was not a single thing we
could have done in the campaign that would have brought
about a different result."

Not so, insisted Stu Spencer: "Carter's people just did not
know how to run as incumbents. They had never run such a
campaign and it showed. I was surprised they did such a terrible job. There wasn't any consistency in their campaign. They
played hatchet ball one week and high road the next. One
problem they had was that Carter couldn't govern very well
and there's not much you can do about that. I would have
tried to make his record seem more positive and I would have
handled the hostage thing differently. Rafshoon's media was
overproduced and not very good."

I asked Spencer a final question. Did this election, as many
political writers had suggested, portend "a massive ideological
shift in American politics? An end of the New Deal era?"

"No," Spencer replied, "I don't think there's been that big a
shift. The country generally has become more conservative,
but not as conservative as a lot of people in the New Right
would like to think. If things aren't going well in a conservative administration, the voters will throw it out, too."

After the election, the strategists who helped Ronald Reagan into the Oval Office were rewarded by the new President. Richard Wirthlin was named political adviser to the Reagan administration. William Casey became head of the CIA; Ed Meese, Chief of White House Staff; and Mike Deaver, Meese's Deputy Chief. Lyn Nofziger, hired as Presidential manager of political affairs, was assigned a suite in the Old Executive Office Building next door to the White House—ironically, the identical office so recently vacated by Gerald Rafshoon.

Instead of living in the reflected glory of Washington, D.C., the "city on a hill," Stu Spencer returned to Irvine, California, where a new batch of campaigns cried for his attention—new challenges, new polls, new candidates, and new "coalitions of 51 percent" to dominate his life over the next two years. It was the fate of the professional campaign consultant; and Stu Spencer had no complaints.

9

Hal Evry, Enemy of the Party

At most, only ten campaign consultants from each generation get the chance to run a Presidential general-election extravaganza. For those consultants who miss out, the reason is not necessarily lack of ability. Some top professionals are considered too specialized—heavy on media skills, and weak on organization. Charles Guggenheim has that reputation. Some, like Matt Reese, are celebrated for their organizational abilities but enjoy less prestige as media experts. Others, like Doug Bailey and John Deardourff, have built their reputations on management genius, but are regarded less highly for their media prowess and their ability to organize precincts.

Then there are the iconoclasts. Hal Evry is the *enfant terrible* of the consultancy world. For more than twenty years he has outraged news people, citizens, and fellow professionals with his pronouncements on talk shows and in interviews. Evry has won gubernatorial races for George Wallace in Alabama, William Scranton and Raymond Shafer in Pennsylvania, David Hall in Oklahoma, and Winthrop Rockefeller in Arkansas. The closest he came to a Presidential campaign was his losing effort for Bill Scranton in the 1964 Republican primaries. But as an innovator and educator, Evry has influenced campaigns all over America, in Canada, and even in Japan.

I first saw Hal Evry on a local Los Angeles television talk show. Cohosts Mort Sahl and George Putnam asked him about various state and city races. I was about to tune out, anticipating the traditional half-lies and evasions, but I suddenly realized that Evry was not replying in the manner of old politicians. Instead, I heard a brilliant man clinically assess the candidates, not in terms of party, ideology, or right/left jingoism, but strictly on their chances of winning.

"In any election, the special golden rule applies," Evry told Putnam. "He who has the gold, rules. The more money a candidate spends, the more likely he is to win."

"Do you think voters have a distaste for poorer candidates?" Sahl asked. "Maybe it reminds them too much of home."

"Not at all," Evry said. "It's just a question of visibility. When you see the same commercial for a Lever Brothers detergent over and over, it's not because the ad agency or the client particularly loves that commercial. The fact is that great masses of people need to be told something many times before the message will take. Now it just takes common sense to understand that someone with plenty of money to spend can repeat his message more times than someone who hasn't got very much money. That's why rich people have the odds going their way long before the ballots are ever cast. Studies show that the candidate who outspends his opponent wins four out of five times. Understand, I'm speaking professionally and not personally. Personally, I couldn't care less whether someone is rich or poor, unless I'm going to do business with him. Being rich is not just an advantage, it's virtually a prerequisite for most offices today."

Before the show ended, I made a note on my telephone pad: "Contact Hal Evry to interview." Our first discussion took place a few months later at his Wilshire Boulevard office suite near downtown Los Angeles. The sign on the glass doors read, "Public Relations Center," and below that, "Western Research Inc." The walls of the four-room complex were filled with framed mementos of past glories: newspaper headlines proclaiming record victory margins, photos of Evry and Dwight D. Eisenhower, Evry shaking hands with Winthrop Rockefeller, Evry with his arm on the shoulder of a grinning, robust George Wallace, fliers from old campaigns, and voter mailgrams blown up to double size. A pretty receptionist led me through an open door into a large office with a teak desk in the far corner and a circular coffee table ringed with chairs just inside the entrance. Evry came over to greet me with a hearty handshake, and we sat down to talk.

Physically, Hal Evry fits the stereotype of the campaign consultant, with his stocky body and prominent jowls. Unlike the stereotype, he speaks softly, with just a hint of his native Kentucky accent. Evry has been masterminding elections since 1955. He is not well liked by his peers, who resent his media posturing, taste for gimmickry, and disdain for protocol. Evry's colleagues aim for the cool touch and responsible dialogue; he enjoys teaching through shock.

"Every year half a million people run for public office," he proclaimed on that first visit. "They spend a billion dollars but don't have the slightest idea of what they're doing. They see flags flying, bands playing, people applauding. To find out what's happening, they read stories by reporters making two hundred dollars a week. But they miss the whole point. People really don't want to vote—it's an abnormal act. If the media didn't get on their backs the week before an election and say, 'Be sure to vote,' hardly anybody would show up. As it is, most candidates are elected by less than a quarter of those eligible to vote. Since people don't want to vote, you have to make things simple for them.

"Pure emotion is what works. The higher the emotion, the less the reason—and the things that impel people most are self-preservation, sex, and money, in that order. Textbooks call it *security*, but I like the word *money* because it's more blunt.

"We made a rule that anybody walking into our office had to have half a million dollars in assets before we would even talk to him—because 95 percent of the people who run for office don't have the money to run and win. When a poor man stops by, I always tell him to give his money to the Cancer Society, where a small amount might do some good. I firmly believe that poor people should not be allowed to run for public office. When poor people enter politics, they get in hock, spend everything they have, sell their cars, see their wives once a month, go out and give speeches to a dozen people, shake hands at doorsteps, end up losers, and it's a disaster. At least when a rich man runs and loses, all he's lost is money and a little ego.

"The only good reason for a man to run for office is because there's lots of money to be made. If he didn't have that reason, I'd advise him to forget it. People who approach us are usually very rich and introverted. We prefer that type. We tell our candidates the best person to get money from is yourself. Then you go to your relatives. The third source is, obviously, rich people—whether they like you or not. Poor people who like you can't do anything for you, but rich people who hate you can help you. It's conceivable that you can change a rich person's mind and make him see things your way."

Candidates that get Hal Evry as their consultant sign an agreement to follow his orders and strategy for the duration of the campaign. Evry designs the advertising, printed material, publicity, television commercials, and special events. He runs regular polls to see how well the candidate is meeting preset goals and how well the voters understand and support the candidate's aims. Evry charges $6,000 a month for gubernatorial and U.S. Senate races, $3,500 a month for Congressional elections, and $2,000 a month for lesser offices, except in big cities where large concentrations of voters require more time and effort. Today he handles only one major campaign a year but acts as part-time consultant to three or four others.

Overall he claims a 93-percent win average. Even reducing that by 10 percent to account for self-promotional hype leaves an impressive record, particularly since Evry works totally without the support of political parties—Democratic, Republican, or otherwise. He makes a point of showing his contempt for them.

"Party chieftains want to perpetuate the mystique that makes a candidate come to them and ask, 'May I run for President, please?' Lots of candidates believe they have to ask permission. Ridiculous! If a man came here and told me he had party support, we wouldn't represent him. What does a party do, anyhow? There's no evidence a party gets out even one vote. People affiliated with either party are totally inept anyway. Most of them are hacks and hangers-on, housewives, students, lawyers, retired people, and other time-wasters whose chief objective is to obstruct the candidate's view of the only people that really count—the voters. The myth of party influence is perpetuated by unsophisticated media who dignify these ward heelers by calling them party leaders. Party *support* is a mirage. *Organization* is a lot of crap. What has the real effect today is television, not party support.

"Candidates have to make the public like them. If people like a candidate, they will vote for him, it's as simple as that. If you're a fairly decent guy, half the people will like you and half won't. If you're a person like me, eight out of ten will dislike you. But if you appear to be all things to all people, get on television and don't say anything but make it sound good, you can get three out of four to like what they read into you. That's why any extra money I have goes into television ads."

Since the early years when pioneer consultants Clem Whitaker and Leona Baxter bypassed the party hierarchy and appealed directly to the voters on behalf of their corporate clients, guerrilla warfare has been the norm between the two groups. Party power faded with the emergence of electronic media during the 1950s, when consultants became dominant. While most professional strategists maintain a polite relationship with the vestigial party organizations, Hal Evry is unique in his unabashed hostility.

Professionals like Stu Spencer and Sandy Weiner learned their politics working as volunteers for their party, hitting the precincts and pounding in lawn signs, so they still have a warm spot for that structure. Those who came out of advertising, like Gerald Rafshoon and Bob Squier, treat party people with the sort of surface respect due a client's wife or father, just to be on the safe side. But Evry learned his early lessons in research, free of all restraints but his own judgment of truth and power. He worships at the shrine of Gallup, for whom he once worked, and over the years has developed complete disdain for news media and reporters. He told me how a World War II experience shaped his attitude.

"I was on a communications ship," he explained. "We were

caught in a battle with the Japanese off the Subic Bay. It was nightfall, and you couldn't see the enemy, only their superstructure from time to time. When you spotted them you fired, and when they saw you they fired back. All you could see were the flashes of cannon, bombs going off, and once in a while a hit which caused a big blaze. Of course the Japanese were seeing and doing the same thing.

"After four hours of this, the skipper said, 'Hal, we hit three destroyers, crippled a light cruiser, and devastated an aircraft carrier. The Japanese lost 875 men and had 3,120 wounded while we took minimal casualties.' I was a young intelligence officer then who figured the skipper knew what was going on. So I encoded it all, took it to the radio room, and told the radio operator to get the message back to Commander, Southwestern Sea Front. He sent it out to the media, and some guy wrote up the story for AP and UPI. It went out over the wires, and was picked up by every paper in the country and repeated in front-page banner headlines: 'U.S. FORCES IN PACIFIC WIN GREAT VICTORY IN SUBIC BAY, CASUALTIES LIGHT.' You know, it took me ten years before I asked myself, 'How the hell did the skipper know we killed 875 Japanese sailors and wounded 3,120?' That was when I got wise about media."

Evry now insists the news media couldn't care less about truth and fair play, and they completely violate their public trust: "The press is totally manipulative. So I make sure I use the media and the media never uses me. Every special event we do is contrived. Every event in a campaign is contrived, only some get pious and deny it. A candidate will go to Modesto and give a talk, just so he can get a plug in the local paper. He contrived that talk, that's the only reason he went there. So I figure it's easier not to go there and still get the plug."

Evry uses ploys and gimmickry whenever possible to get media coverage for his clients. He has used facsimile hundred-dollar bills with the face and name of his candidate, has filed legal actions with great fanfare, mailed out football schedules with the candidate's name and picture prominently displayed, and sponsored patriotic essay contests on behalf of clients. In the 1960s he managed Ivy Baker Priest's campaign for state treasurer of California. The day before Washington's Birthday he suggested she take a trip to the Sacramento River and throw a silver dollar across its narrowest point.

"But that's undignified," Priest protested.

"Don't be silly," Evry argued. "Everyone knows George Washington threw a silver dollar across the Potomac and nobody thought he was undignified."

His logic persuaded her and his assistant drove her to the river narrows at Miller's Landing where the press, alerted by his memo, waited dutifully. Priest made the ceremonial toss across the four feet of water and spoke the line Evry had scripted for her: "See? A dollar doesn't go as far today as it used to!" That bit of contrived news made every newspaper in America. Even *Sports Illustrated* did a write-up, despite their policy against doing political stories.

A few years later Evry dressed a candidate in a colonial costume, sent him to Miller's Landing, and had him throw tea bags into the river on the three-hundredth anniversary of the Boston Tea Party. The man was elected controller.

"People get upset about gimmickry," Evry noted. " 'Gimmick' is a Hollywood term with sinister implications. I suggest that 'gimmick' usually means a new twist, a novel approach, an unusual angle. The word deserves better public relations.

"The media are pretty dumb, generally. And the political media are very dumb. We send out stories on our letterhead or the candidate's letterhead to newspapers and magazines, saying our candidate is going to buy the San Francisco Giants or climb a mountain barefoot. The editor looks at that and says, 'That's interesting, that's news—go to the press conference and cover it.' And reporters show up because they're told to.

"I have no background in journalism," he admitted. "That's one of the best things I have going for me. I just realize old news is new news so I pick up today's paper and read the headlines. Whatever that headline says, that's the news of the day to whomever wrote it. Everything I do will relate in some way to that news item—that's how simple it is.

"Young newspaper people never understand this. They're
fresh out of journalism school feeling half priest, half FBI
agent, guardian of the public morals, and they won't let anybody put anything over on them. But they don't make the
decisions—they just get sent out to cover stories. They may
slant it a little one way or the other if they like or dislike me,
but as long as they cover me, I don't care."

Evry was heir apparent to the original PR rulers of the
consultancy business, Whitaker & Baxter. Founded in 1934,
the husband-and-wife team developed a style that paved the
way for today's media manipulators. Using the available tools
of mass persuasion—mostly newspapers, and increasingly
radio—they pushed the interests of oil companies, railroads,
the AMA, and any other client who could pay their hefty
fees and expenses. Whitaker & Baxter managed seventy-five
major political campaigns and won 90 percent of them, beating Upton Sinclair when he ran for governor and electing Earl
Warren on his first try for the same office. When the Democrats took over California in 1958, the team retired from the
political arena.

Evry had studied their techniques and made pilgrimages
to their office in San Francisco's Flood Building. From them he
learned the art of simplification, as well as how to "ladle it on
thick," Clem Whitaker style, when aiming for a dramatic
slogan.

Before his stint in the navy, Evry had earned a degree in
business from Columbia University. When he came out of
the service, he taught research at Woodbury University,
worked for opinion researcher Paul Stewart, and then for the
Gallup organization. He taught political science at Los Angeles City College and then, in 1955, opened his Public Relations Center to serve corporate clients.

Evry's first political client, Charles Latimer, was a millionaire who lived in Ontario, California. He asked Evry whether
a candidate for mayor should give talks at veterans' clubs. As
brash then as now, the consultant suggested that Latimer
enjoy a trip to Bermuda while he ran the campaign for him.
Latimer took him up on the challenge. Evry developed a few

direct-mail pieces, placed newspaper ads, featuring photos of the candidate and his little daughter in a supermarket, and made sure he kept it all simple. Out of a field of eleven candidates, including the incumbent mayor, Latimer took twenty of twenty-one precincts. When he returned from vacation, tanned and rested, he found himself the new mayor of Ontario.

"Give me a candidate with lots of money and an IQ of 120," Evry proclaimed on dozens of appearances on national talk shows. "If he promises to keep his mouth shut, I'll elect him to Congress."

When asked about that ideal candidate, he explained that the IQ test he insists they take is not intended to measure the stringent skills required of public officials. "The only reason we ask for the 120 IQ is so he's smart enough to understand the good reasons for shutting up and will do it. We run the new campaigns nice and easy. No speeches, no debates. He faces the people only on television, in the newspapers, and by direct mail."

One of Evry's famous slogans sent an obscure young lawyer from Pasadena to the state legislature with a minimum of effort. The candidate, Pat Milligan, was completely unknown, so Evry conjured up a five-word battle cry: "Three cheers for Pat Milligan!"

"We splashed those words on billboards, in full-page newspaper ads, and in direct-mail pieces. By the time the election came around, voters knew his name better than their own and he won big. After the campaign we took a poll to find out why people had voted for him, since he'd never once spoken about anything of substance. They reported things like, 'We thought he'd already won because the ads said "three cheers," so we voted for him.' Others said, 'It sounded so American!' Most of them reasoned, 'He must have been the best man, that's why you were giving him three cheers.' Voters don't understand anything complicated, so we make sure we keep it simple."

Evry enjoys assaulting convention and attracting attention in nontraditional ways. In the 1960s he outraged fellow mem-

bers of the professional consultants' association by running ads
in newspapers and political journals that read: "WANTED:
CANDIDATES FOR U.S. CONGRESS." He dutifully interviewed
everyone who replied, gave them the promised Stanford-Binet
IQ test, and evaluated their financial standing. In the end,
his mail-order clients did as well as those who came to him
through referral—more than 90 percent won.

The advertising was good promotion for the PR Center and
even better fun for Evry. He regards campaigns as a kind of
idea-and-image contact sport, no holds barred and no quarter
asked or given. The democratic ideal views the People as a
pool of collective wisdom, with an inherent instinct for justice
and a genius for "choosing right when the chips are down."
Evry rejects this notion as so much journalistic hogwash. He
regards the People as a mob of bewildered consumers whose
desires and emotions are easily stirred and used to the advantage of anyone who knows how to manipulate them.

In 1970 Evry managed David Hall into the governorship of
Oklahoma. Two years later, Hall ran into problems. The
state's most influential newspaper, the *Oklahoman,* had
launched a crusade to bring him down. In Evry's view it was
hardball politics—dirty, unfair, and not particularly surprising.

"Hall had unseated a popular Republican named Dewey
Bartlett," Evry recalled. "So the paper's publisher, who was a
friend of Bartlett's, went after David Hall. For two years he
was on the front page three times a week: 'HALL'S SECRETARY
SEQUESTERED' . . . 'HALL'S FUNDS QUESTIONED' . . . 'HALL'S BOOKS
GARNISHEED'—a thousand stories like that. It was the worst
journalism I'd ever seen against a governor. As the incumbent,
Hall could have cut them to pieces. But like most people
who run for office, he was scared stiff of the media. I don't
know why—those people barely earn a living, they have no
power. It finally dawned on Hall that things were getting bad
when his kids complained how hard it was for them when the
other kids called them names at school. Finally Hall asked me
for help.

"I created a series of television scripts, 'A Report from Your
Governor.' These were five-minute pieces starting with letters

from constituents. For example, one began: 'Dear Governor,
why is that paper saying such naughty things about you?
Signed, Kathy, age 8.' And Hall was to come on and say,
'Kathy, you're too young to know anything about power politics and newspaper people. Now this Oklahoma publisher is a
hundred years old and his favorite person lost to me in the last
election, so this is how he tries to get back at me.' We went to
great lengths and spent lots of money designing those commercials. But Hall wouldn't use them. 'Why don't you use them?' I
asked. 'I can't antagonize the press,' he said. 'Antagonize?
They're bludgeoning you to death—what more can they do
to you? Tell me one more thing they can do!' 'You're right,'
he said. 'I've got to do those commercials.'

"But he never used even one. The reason he didn't was
because his press secretary, who was an ex-newspaperman, advised him, 'Don't antagonize the media.' And that one
medium was killing him. We were coming close to the end of
the reelection campaign and our polls showed Hall losing by
fifteen points. Since he never fought back, voters undoubtedly
thought, if he doesn't explain those charges, maybe they're all
true.

"So at the last minute I said, 'David, there's only one thing
you can do. You got all the renown and notoriety you want;
99 percent of voters in Oklahoma know you now. All we've got
to do is give you some Holy Water.' So we designed the greatest billboard ever made, done like a sampler, a very traditional design. It read: GOD BLESS OUR GOVERNOR, REELECT DAVID
HALL. Did he use it? No.

"'They laughed at it,' he told me. 'Who laughed at it?' I
asked. 'The newspapers, at the press preview.' 'But those are
the people who hate you,' I told him. And that was the crux
of the problem. Hall never got over his fear of attacking the
media. No matter what they were doing to him. Proof of that
was another candidate we had in the same state. Thanks to
that same newspaper's efforts, he was indicted, but we immediately subpoenaed Mitchell and Kleindienst of Watergate
fame, they dropped their case, and he was elected. The point
is, you have to fight back."

While David Hall refused to fight back, his opponent David

Boren ran a campaign based on a simple symbol—a big broom, showcased on billboards and commercials and all campaign literature, which he would use to "sweep corruption out of Oklahoma." He ran around giving speeches headlined by the *Oklahoman*, promising reforms but committing himself to nothing specific. Boren and his broom beat David Hall in the primary, so that Boren became governor and served two terms.

"Hall should have run those five-minute spots and the billboards," Evry concluded. "As it was, he didn't lose by much, but he lost. And in campaigns you have to come in first— nothing else counts."

Hall lost more than the election. After leaving office he was convicted of bribery and extortion. He served fourteen months in prison and was on probation before evidence turned up by columnist Jack Anderson proved that the tape transcripts used to convict him were full of "errors" that made him appear guilty of accepting bribes. In fact, the tapes clearly showed that he had repudiated the offer through an assistant. Hall was exonerated and his record cleared, but his career in politics was ruined by the newspaper publisher who hated him.

"That's why I have so much contempt for the media," Evry explained. "The American people are fully manipulated by the media, by the people who run them. If a newspaper reporter is honest and digs too deeply, he's thrown out. One day when I was in Philadelphia, two reporters who used to write for the *Inquirer* came over and complained how bad that newspaper stank. 'The publisher told us what to write,' they admitted to me. Most reporters are married, with a couple of kids, so it's pretty hard for them to find a new line of work. They end up going along for the ride and by the time they learn the truth, it's too late.

"My wife and neighbors watch the network news religiously. They listen hard, study what is said, and never realize that those anchormen are basically Ted Baxters. They walk into the studio, pick up their scripts, and read what others have written. One of our colleagues was the managing editor of a big city paper. Over the years he grew to understand what I'm talking about, but there he was. He had to create news and teach journalism, until one day he came to me and said, 'Hal, they're going to kick me out because I'm telling the truth.' Most reporters hate to admit that to an outsider. But more and more people are waking up and becoming critical of the media. Now they're saying: 'The Media watch the world, but who watches the Media? You answer that one for me.'"

Evry publishes a monthly newsletter called the *Campaign Letter*, in which he airs his iconoclastic ideas and examines the inside world of elective politics. His mailing list covers the biggest political names in the world, including Presidents past, present, and future. Despite his self-proclaimed cynicism—which he calls "realism"—behind the tough, worldly-wise political scientist one senses the deeply buried cry of a moralist begging to be proved wrong.

"I've never ever voted in my life," he boasts. "And I never intend to vote. It doesn't make any difference to the system who gets elected. The society runs its own way, with or without the politicians."

Apartheid U.S.A.

10

To the new breed of political consultant, research is the heart of any campaign. Yet fewer than 15 percent of all campaigns use any kind of scientific polling. The rest depend instead on casual telephone interviews and "seat of the pants" intuition that misleads more often than it enlightens. Most of the newspaper and television polls are notoriously poor in producing reliable information, which accounts for many "upset victories" and "campaign surprises."

Hal Evry approaches elections the same way General Foods goes about launching a new product. "It's simply a marketing job," he explained. "Research is the tool that lets us find out what's on the consumer's mind—in this case, the voter's mind."

He concentrates on those who voted in the last primary or special election, since they are the people most likely to vote this time around. "I save money studying those people because they have something very strong and personal at stake. What that is we don't know, but we want to find out. We poll them, using indirect questions, codes, questions asking for animal associations—does this man remind you of a horse, a snake, a rabbit, a lion, or a jackass? People like games like that, and their answers reveal a lot about the candidates. We use good random sampling and find out what's bothering people."

Ethnic, racial, and religious bigotry turn up again and again. Evry makes no apologies for taking advantage of it.

"Reactions to black faces or foreign names can be used in a campaign. So we go out and ask the people about it. We don't ask outright whether they would vote for a black. Instead, we ask what kind of neighborhood they live in, if they would like to see minority groups moving in, and step by step lead them along until they indicate their feelings. You know, 90 percent of the black voters in Los Angeles cast their ballots for Thomas Bradley as mayor. If you think they voted for him because of what he stands for, think again. They voted for him for the same reason whites vote for white people. Maybe you want to dress it up a little so you call it 'affinity groups.' All things being equal, a man named Delgado is likely to vote for a man named Pintero.

"All this talk about the American Melting Pot and democracy is just a lot of words, as far as actual voting is concerned. In New York City they always run an Italian, a Jew, and a Protestant on the ticket—or an Irishman. They do that to span the ethnic groups. Nowadays they use blacks and Puerto Ricans in their spans. Critically I understand that—the object is to get votes. You must realize that I speak not from a moral framework but from a critical one.

"When a man runs for Congress, he gets a questionnaire from a group called PRO-LIFE. They are against abortion and they can give a candidate hell. It's a Catholic organization, but they don't say they're Catholic. The same man is pressured by Jewish groups about Israel. I tell my clients to keep quiet and be noncommittal. We fill out those questionnaires for them, so we're sure there'll be no problems."

One afternoon in late February 1970, Evry made an appearance on the Art Linkletter television show. As in his other frequent guest spots he chose his statements for their shock value, and had a great time laughing with Linkletter over the foibles of American politicking. Describing the arduous route most candidates take, he emphasized that his clients did best when they took long vacations during the heat of the campaign so he could use pure communications to do the job and not risk the candidate's sticking his foot in his mouth.

That night, Evry and his wife Mary Ruth were having a cup

of tea in the living room of their Palm Desert home, reliving the Linkletter show, when the telephone rang. Evry noted the time: 10:15. The voice at the other end of the line had a distinctly Southern accent and was vaguely familiar.

"Mistuh Evry?" the caller asked.

"Speaking."

"Mistuh Evry, do you judge a man befoh you meet him?"

Evry thought a while. "I'm a researcher and therefore I'm supposed to be totally objective," he replied. "But I have to admit that sometimes I forget that. Generally, though, I don't make prejudgments. Unfortunately, I usually don't have the chance to do pioneer research on everyone I've heard about. But as soon as I know I'm prejudging, I stop doing it."

"That's a good and honest ansuh, Mistuh Evry," the caller said. "This is Jowge Wallace in Montgomery. Mah election is coming up, Ah'm running twenty-one points behind in the polls, and Ah'm in the fight of mah life. Can you help me, Mistuh Evry?"

It was a summons to battle Evry could not ignore. He asked his research director, Dr. Arnold Ismach, who is Dean of Communications at the University of Minnesota, to meet with Governor Wallace that week and gather the details of his campaign efforts to date. Then he familiarized himself with the political history of his new client.

George Corley Wallace gained prominence in 1958 when, as a circuit court judge, he refused to open his files to civil rights investigators from Washington. That gave him credibility and a chance to run for higher office.

To understand the Southern mentality, a bit of history helps. Even during our Revolutionary years, the Southern colonists were not very concerned with "freedom." They felt quite comfortable serving under the crown of England. The institution of slavery gave them wealth, a gracious life style, and automatic superiority based on race. What the Civil War changed most dramatically was the style by which Southern apartheid views could be expressed. Instead of openly asserting racial superiority, Southerners learned to be sly when dealing with outsiders. Language became the chief weapon against

Yankees and their notions of equality. The most successful politicians were those who could twist language cleverly enough to accommodate the conquering "feds" and maintain credibility with their own constituencies.

After George Wallace leaped into the news, he ran for governor but lost in the primary to John Patterson. Patterson pulled most of the rural vote and the blue-collar rednecks with Klan sympathies by using the code of segregation. Wallace had run on a populist plank. As Wallace himself observed after that election, he had been "outnigged." He vowed never to let that happen to him again.

In 1962 he tried again, promising "segregation forever." This time he forced a primary runoff that brought him eventual victory and the governor's office in November. In 1966 an Alabama law, later changed by Wallace, prohibited his running for a second consecutive term as governor. So he put up his wife Lurleen as his surrogate, added protégé Albert Brewer to the slate as his preferred lieutenant governor, and elected both to office by a quarter million votes. Wallace then ran the state as Lurleen's "special assistant" until her death from cancer in 1968, when Albert Brewer became governor. Wallace played an important role in the Presidential election that year by taking the normally Democratic "solid South" and allowing Richard Nixon to squeak into office.

As governor, Brewer inherited a system of kickbacks and bribery that has characterized most Southern states for half a century. Liquor companies who do business in Alabama pay one or two dollars per case of their wares to "agents" who then distribute the revenue to higher officials. They have to ante up another dollar per case for advertising placed by the governor's office in the newspapers of their choice, thus assuring an enthusiastic press. Road builders make the same kind of arrangements for state contracts, as do sellers of asphalt, legal services, and so on. This is an old Southern tradition that has spread to places like California and New Jersey.

In 1970 Wallace assumed that his drive to win back the governorship would be a shoo-in. His national popularity had never been higher, and conservatives all over America were contributing millions to a Wallace war chest solicited by direct-mail expert Richard Vigurie. During the winter months Wallace and his aide of thirty years, Gen. Taylor Hardin, along with an army of hangers-on, stumped the state railing against "pointy-headed intellectuals," "bleeding-heart liberals," and a federal government that had taken "public schools away from the people." He demanded "freedom of choice," the updated code word for "segregation forever," but somehow it wasn't working the same magic as it had during the 1960s.

An exhaustive poll by a Dallas researcher showed Wallace trailing Albert Brewer badly in a field of three major candidates. Brewer, the incumbent, was well liked by Alabamans, who saw no reason to make a change. Brewer had carried on the segregationist tradition quietly, without hollering "nigger." Business was good, unemployment low, and some people resented Wallace for getting too involved in national concerns. The raw numbers were depressing. Brewer had 53 percent of the vote, Wallace 32, and an obscure businessman from Dothan 11, with the remainder dribbling to also-rans. Hal Evry studied the research and knew he was in for a tough haul. When he arrived in Birmingham, he went to the Parliament Hotel for his first meeting with the candidate.

"I saw this tiny little man," Evry recalled. "Soft-spoken, extremely courteous, and very alert. All our dealings were carried on in this very courteous tone, totally different from his popular image. He had been a bantamweight prizefighter before going to law school, so you get some idea of how small he is. He was unlike his press reports in other ways, too.

"I remember one evening at the Holiday Inn in Montgomery. Wallace was putting on a tie before going out to a rally, when I suggested we might use a photo of his wife Lurleen as background to a commercial we were setting up. He turned and frowned. 'Mistuh Evry,' he said. 'I will nevuh, nevuh unduh any suhcumstances use mah deahly depahted to fuhthuh mah po-litical ambitions.' That was typical of the man. He was not at all the ruthless, Huey Long demagogue the press always painted him."

Demagogue or not, unless Evry could alter the balance of popularity over the next five weeks before the election, Brewer would win the nomination. Evry's first goal was to force a runoff, pulling some of Brewer's support over to Wallace's column so the incumbent could not win a majority the first time around. That would not be easy.

"Brewer was running a smart campaign," Evry explained. "He was not going out to give speeches, and he kept his mouth shut to the press. Meanwhile George was making two or three speeches a day, giving statements all over the place, some of which were hurting him. So I told him to cut down and stop pushing himself. He didn't need exposure—everyone knew who George Wallace was."

Evry set two goals. The first was to soften his candidate's image as a tough demagogue. The second, more urgent, was to smoke Brewer out into the open, goad him into making statements that could be attacked. Though Brewer had furthered the kickback and payoff system that was a tradition in Alabama, Wallace couldn't very well accuse Brewer of corruption when he himself had handpicked Brewer for public life.

Instead, Wallace began blasting his opponent as a "do-nothing governor who had never been elected." He blamed him for ignoring the scandalous smog problem in Birmingham and accused him of cowardice, charging that he was "scared to come out in the open and debate the issues." The press picked up the rhetoric, and the constant attacks got on Brewer's nerves to the point where he began replying to reporters' goads. Brewer made speeches charging Wallace with being antiblack and with encouraging payoffs from liquor companies. Brewer was as much a part of the apartheid/kickback system as Wallace, of course, so to most Alabama voters it was a case of the pot calling the kettle black. The "antiblack" label was a badge of honor to rural rednecks. Evry's ploy was working.

"We had Brewer out in the open at last," Evry recalled. "He was losing ground. Every time he spoke he dropped a point in the polls, down to seventeen, then sixteen. With only three weeks to go, we put nearly a million dollars into adver-

tising, most of it television commercials. We attacked Brewer
as a do-nothing governor and used the slogan, 'George Is Your
Kind of Man for Your Kind of Alabama.' We showed Wallace
with his little daughter, put an American flag behind him, and
lambasted Washington.

"Brewer was not liked by blacks but neither, of course, was
George. The only difference between them was that Brewer
was quieter about it. George complained to me, 'Hal, more
blacks like me than don't like me. The Eastern press keeps
writing how I hate blacks and they hate me, which is not true
at all.' Now I can't vouch for that, but whenever we'd be in
hotels or out somewhere and he'd see a black, he would make
a point of going over to him and shaking hands."

Evry flew to Nashville to hire the entire *Hee Haw* show. He
rented the Civic Auditorium in Birmingham, flew in the *Hee
Haw* band and regulars, and crammed in twenty thousand
screaming Wallace supporters for a series of televised shows.
The format was arranged so Wallace would come onstage during the telecast no less than ten times, taking part in skits or
being called up by an actor who would introduce "our good
buddy George Wallace" to lots of backslapping, foot-stomp-
ing hillbilly hilarity.

"Those Hee Hawers made George seem like the nice, fun-
loving guy he really is," Evry said. "And right after those shows,
George really spurted in the polls. How much was attributable
to *Hee Haw* and how much to our attacks, I couldn't say.
Anyway, we got down to the last two weeks before the primary
with only a seven point difference between Wallace and
Brewer. Then the Republicans entered the act."

Aiming for a Nixon reelection in 1972, the GOP had made
a "Southern strategy" integral to its plans. To stop those
electoral votes from going to Wallace as in 1968, Nixon's postmaster general, Winton Blount, flew down to Alabama and
campaigned for Brewer. New money found its way into the
incumbent's campaign treasury, buying more time for television commercials. If they stopped Wallace now, he was
through.

Evry fought back with paid media, using Wallace's bottom-

less campaign treasury. TV commercials showed Wallace looking into the camera and shaking his fist while wondering
aloud, "Why did Nixon send down a Republican to support a
Democrat? Why do these Eastern folks want me beaten so
badly?"

"We made it a race against Nixon," Evry explained. "And
we planted seeds of doubt in the minds of white people there
about Brewer. But we still had our problem with the minority
groups. Brewer was just as apartheid in his politics as George,
only blander. So we badgered him to state his position on
blacks in government. He said that while whites still held all
the important posts in his administration, blacks were welcome to take the jobs, if they could win them through their
own talent and efforts. He would have been hurt no matter
how he answered that question. It was poor strategy to reply,
but he did, and we used that."

George Wallace never referred to black people as blacks,
negroes, or any other term of color. Instead he insisted that
everyone around him, including Evry and his staff, use the
code words "minority" or "low-income" groups. Whenever that
protocol was disregarded, Wallace became very upset and severely corrected the offender.

With ten days to go, the gap was now only five points. It
looked as though Evry had a fighting chance to keep Brewer
from getting the 50 percent he needed to win the primary outright and prevent a runoff.

"Our problem was in Birmingham with the minority
groups," Evry recalled. "The press down there had heated up
a big anti-Wallace campaign. We had to neutralize that anger.
So I sent Bob Dresser to South Carolina on a buying trip."

Evry's partner arranged to buy a half million cloth potholders, decorated with a smiling picture of their candidate
and the inscription, "FROM YOUR FRIEND GEORGE WALLACE."
Evry knew that the potholders, a useful kitchen aid, would be
kept by those to whom they were sent. In this case they were
mailed to every "low-income" and "minority" family in
Birmingham, identified by lists purchased from the registrar of
voters.

"We got feedback from black people at hotels and restaurants," Evry explained. "They were saying, 'Did you see what we got from Ole George?' When you hear that in the South, it means there's friendly feelings behind it, so we knew our little gift was working. That potholder diluted those negative feelings and kept many blacks from casting an anti-Wallace vote. They really didn't care for Brewer and now that 'Ole George' had sent them a nice gift, why bother?"

Evry is convinced that the fifty thousand dollars spent for potholders and postage saved the election for Wallace. On May 6, when Alabamans voted in the primary, 43 percent went for Brewer, 41 percent for Wallace, and a surprising 15 percent for Dothan businessman Charles Woods. Since no candidate had an absolute majority, it came down to a runoff between the two top vote-getters. Although 68.5 percent of registered white voters showed up at the polls that day, only 61.5 percent of the blacks voted. In Birmingham, where potholders had flooded all the black precincts, the black stay-away percentages were even larger.

It came down to hard combat for four weeks, no holds barred. In such a contest soft-spoken, fair-playing Brewer stood little chance. Both Brewer and Wallace visited Charles Woods in Dothan and asked for his backing, hoping to attract the 135,000 churchgoing, working-class votes that Wood had won in the primary. But Woods held back his endorsement, demanding stiff idealistic terms that neither could accept. Lacking formal support, Wallace adopted most of Woods's twelve-point reform platform, including its tax breaks for the little people of Alabama. Brewer retaliated by dealing for the "bloc vote," a euphemism for paying money to black power brokers in return for solid minority backing. In the kind of machine in-fighting that dominated the runoff, Evry was relegated to a minor role.

"No need for brainstorming this time around," a Wallace aide noted. "We all knew what we had to do—promise them the moon and holler 'nigger.'"

Instead of referring coyly to the "bloc vote" as he had done in the primary, Wallace called it the "black bloc vote" and

charged Brewer with buying it outright. In a talk to factory
workers covered by television cameras, he complained that
"three hundred thousand nigger votes is mighty hard to overcome," appealing for widespread redneck support in the language they understood.

In Alabama papers, Wallace's Klan supporters placed ads
that showed a little blonde girl surrounded by grinning black
boys on a beach, captioned: "This could be Alabama in four
years—do you want it?" Unsigned circulars accused Brewer of
being homosexual, rumors spread that Brewer's wife was
an alcoholic, and a radio spot attacked a black group supporting Brewer and pushing for integrated state police: "Suppose
your wife is driving home one night and is stopped by a highway patrolman," a narrator intoned to the sound of squealing
brakes. "The patrolman turns out to be black. Think about it.
Elect George C. Wallace!" Though most of the newspapers in
the state endorsed Brewer, Evry countered by running a heavy
schedule of paid ads and commercials that repeated themes
from the primary—"Your Kind of Governor," "Freedom of
Choice," and "Get Washington Off Our Backs."

Brewer's strategy was to play "Mr. Clean," charging Wallace
with embracing race and hate in the dirtiest campaign he had
ever seen. He argued that Wallace would be a part-time governor who would be seeking the Presidency in a few months,
that Wallace's "political hacks wanted to get back inside the
voters' pockets." He foolishly answered Wallace's attacks with
"Good grief, Mr. Wallace." In Alabama, "good grief" sounds
effeminate. Wallace replied by calling Brewer "sissy britches"
and raised the specter of a solid "black bloc vote that would
control Alabama politics for the next fifty years" if he lost.

On June 2 Alabamans made their choice. Wallace got 51.5
percent of the votes in the runoff, Brewer 48.5 percent. The
Wallace plurality was only 32,000 out of over one million
votes cast. Though black voters went overwhelmingly for
Brewer, the turnout was light: again, just 61 percent. Yet for
Wallace it was a short reign of joy: two years later a would-be
assassin's bullet in Maryland put him in a wheelchair for the
rest of his life and ended his chances for national office.

As for Hal Evry, he left Birmingham a week before the runoff vote to concentrate on the other campaigns he had going. He didn't expect to work in Alabama again soon, but he was wrong. A few months later, he got a call from Dothan. Charles Woods, the man who lost in the primary, wanted to run again. Heartened by the fact he had pulled 15 percent of the vote with little organization or professional help, he was aiming for a go in 1974. He had been impressed with the job Evry had done for the embattled Wallace and wanted him to do the same for him.

Evry had never met the enigmatic Mr. Woods, though in Alabama he had heard something about him. Woods was a self-made millionaire who owned a television station, several radio stations, and a big property investment firm. He had been injured in a war accident. He was a believing Christian and a dedicated idealist, which Evry reminded him could interfere with his getting elected. Undeterred, Woods said he would take his chances, so Evry invited him to Palm Desert where they could meet and talk.

It was early December and Evry drove over to the Hilton Riviera in Palm Springs where Woods had registered. He called him on the house phone and waited in the lobby until the elevator doors opened and a man came out to greet him. Evry's first reaction was shock: Woods had a face that looked as if a stocking had been pulled over it—just skin and scars. One eye was covered with a black patch and the other with a tinted lens. His lips had been burned away, so that his teeth showed in a perpetual grin. Most of his ears were gone and his head was totally bald. The hand that reached out to shake his had only two fingers, like a pair of talons. But the spirit that shone through the mutilation was gentle and full of resolve.

Over dinner, Evry heard his story. In World War II Charles Woods had been a pilot of a plane loaded with fuel that exploded on takeoff. The only survivor of the five-man crew, he had crawled through 2,500-degree flames and persevered through five years of hospitals, pain, and reconstructive surgery whose most valiant efforts left him a featureless mask for

a face. Others might have fled from society or committed sui-
cide, but Charles Woods borrowed a sum of $5,000, added that
to his severance pay, and contracted to build a house. He sold
it for a solid profit, did it again, and in a few years owned a
construction empire.

From 1959 through 1963 he served on the Alabama Board of
Corrections and was appointed its chairman in 1963. Adding
television and radio stations to his holdings, he now felt the
need to do something for the people of Alabama and so entered the governor's race. After his showing against Wallace
and Brewer and his uncompromising attitude, he was a
marked man in Alabama. If he insisted on his reform platform, he would be opposed at every turn by the machine. The
obstacles were so great that Evry tried to dissuade Woods from
running. "But he was determined to serve Alabama," Evry
said, shaking his head. "I had never met such an idealistic,
determined man in politics. He just laughed at my warnings
and wouldn't let me say no."

So they laid plans for 1974, still almost three years off. As
owner of the CBS affiliate for southeast Alabama, WTVY-TV,
Woods had a natural platform to get better known. But he
would have to spread the word. So Evry set up a letterhead
organization, Citizens for Alabama, headed by Woods, which
Woods used as a sounding board to issue press releases detailing reforms he planned to initiate. As Evry had foreseen,
Woods locked horns with the system from the start.

In Alabama, as in the other one-party states, newspapers are
married to politics through the advertising they carry. In Alabama the liquor ads give the politicians leverage. When a
paper dares displease the Man in the capitol, the Man cuts
off their funds. The *Birmingham News* had once made George
Wallace unhappy over some nitpicking story, so he "jerked
their whiskey ads and cost them $400,000," as Governor Wal-
lace had once bragged to Charles Woods in a moment of
candor. The publisher of the *News* had read the riot act to
his managing editor; the paper recanted, and the flow of
liquor advertising resumed.

As a man against the machine, Woods was cut off from

traditional forms of expression and support. Unlike other victims, his enormous wealth made him far from helpless, and owning his own television station gave him a voice that could not be stilled. Evry did polling that found some Alabamans, particularly women, were turned off by his candidate's disfigurement. So he counseled Woods to stay off television entirely. But Woods had other ideas and in this case the special golden rule applied—he who had the gold, ruled.

"I didn't consider my appearance a political drawback," Woods told me. "In fact it's an asset because, once someone sees me, they remember me. People like to vote for somebody they know. Even in business, looking this way can be an advantage. It makes me look stupid and when you look stupid, the opposition has a tendency to underestimate you. You wind up with all the marbles."

If he were bound and determined to get on television, Evry suggested he use shadows and romantic backgrounds to shroud his features. Again, Woods refused to hide. He appeared in full lighting when he was interviewed on his own station and others across the state, hitting hard on the theme that would be the cornerstone of his 1974 campaign.

"Ninety percent of Alabama officials are corrupt," he charged. "The political machine is well organized, well financed, and the only way you can fight it is with the truth. Truth is a devastating weapon. We have a situation down at the state docks that is unbelievable. The law says no state employee can belong to a union. Yet we have a state agency that makes dock workers sign cards to join a union in a state where it's illegal to do that. Then state officials deduct ten dollars a week from each man's pay check.

"Now when you ask the governor about this or about the liquor payoffs, he just looks up at the ceiling and says, 'What's wrong with that?' Why do the good people of Alabama let this happen over and over? Because most of them don't know it's going on. Machine candidates have lots of money to campaign with and they pass it around to help each other. But the honest candidate can't get any money, and people will not get out to work day and night for good government the way these crooks get out and work because they know easy money will come their way once they get themselves and their friends into office."

Despite his open attacks, Woods had still not declared for office. In the autumn of 1973, Evry flew to Dothan for a strategy meeting. Since Wallace was sure to run for reelection as governor, it would be foolhardy to challenge him with the resources at his disposal. But Jere Beasley, the incumbent lieutenant governor, was a horse of another color. Beasley had worked at cross-purposes with the Wallace people on tax cuts and some local improvement bills. Though young and good-looking, polls showed that people were irritated by him because of his "noncooperative" and "corrupt" image. Several newspapers had leveled charges of payoffs by business to Beasley's personal account and he hadn't fought back, so the voters tended to believe the stories and center their anger against him.

Evry decided to announce Charles Woods as a candidate for lieutenant governor, running him as an independent reformer with a feeling for the common man. The tactics were simple and clear-cut. Billboards identified Woods with the image he had built in his previous campaign: "Honest Government for Alabama, Woods for Lt. Governor," and "Clean Up Alabama, Elect Charles Woods."

Direct mail spelled out his reforms, and radio spots used the candidate's soft, compelling voice to good effect. Compared to the convoluted efforts required in ordinary campaigns, doing publicity for an idealist in the post-Watergate climate was simplicity itself—except that Woods insisted on showing his marred face at every opportunity and had a tendency to talk off the cuff. But the man's obvious sincerity overshadowed the negatives.

In the off-year election 700,000 voters went to the polls that May to choose among five candidates. Woods led the pack, beating Beasley by several thousand votes. Since the incumbent pulls his strength in the first round and 70 percent of the voters had shown their displeasure by supporting Woods or one of the other challengers, the runoff between Woods and Beasley seemed a shoo-in for the Dothan tycoon.

"Just before the runoff in June, Beasley was taking polls and so were we," Woods explained. "His poll by Oliver Quayle showed him losing 54 to 46 percent. Ours showed it 57 to 43, and the last poll we did on Sunday before election Tuesday showed the same thing—57 to 43, my favor."

On the morning of June 5, after the votes were counted, the numbers showed a remarkable turnaround. Jere Beasley, who had done no campaigning and little advertising, had buried Charles Woods by a margin of over 100,000 votes. Woods was shocked. A few days later he bumped into Bill Kimmelman, a professor from the University of Alabama who had done some of the polling work for the Quayle organization.

"I still can't believe it," Woods told him.

"No need to," Kimmelman replied. "You know, they bought the black vote on you. I wanted you to know that."

"It's one thing losing an election," Woods noted. "But it's another thing to have it stolen from you."

So he decided to contest it. He went to the State Democratic Committee, who heard his protest and gave him thirty days to produce his evidence of fraud. Thus began a month of frantic efforts, working against the clock to overturn the results. First, Woods and his people tried to get voting records from the sixty-seven counties, applying to probate judges, sheriffs, and county Democratic leaders.

"We didn't get a solitary one voluntarily," Woods explained. "We had to use subpoenas for the few we did manage to get. Most of them fought the subpoenas or quoted outlandish prices to copy the documents—fifteen cents a word. It would have cost millions just to copy the records, had they let me, which they didn't. We checked signature sheets we got from the polls. Many of them showed every signature in the same handwriting. I collected as many of those fake signature sheets as I could lay my hands on and gave them to an agent in the Vote Fraud division of the FBI—and never heard a further word."

In all one-party states, the system for controlling the black vote is identical. County Democratic chairmen maintain contact with "approved black leaders"—ministers, doctors, teachers, and other professionals who have demonstrated their reliability over the years. These leaders recommend loyal friends to be appointed as poll workers. These poll workers get a day's pay plus a bonus of thirty dollars to "render service"— which includes forging signatures and voting for dead people and those who don't show up, pulling the "preferred handle" for old and illiterate blacks, and making false counts at the end of the day. Candidates without the backing of the Democratic machine in Dixie are dead. Even the approved candidates must spend about $250,000 for the black vote. The money comes from each candidate's pocket, but after they are elected, "donations" from the liquor, construction, and gambling interests more than make up the outlay.

In Alabama, black voters are pressured by the Alabama Democratic Conference, which tells the black community whom to vote for. Five days before election day, the Conference prints sample ballots that are distributed to every black in the state by ministers, teachers, and other power brokers. Invariably, the marked ballots mimic the choices of the official (white) state Democratic Party.

"Jere Beasley borrowed a quarter million dollars from the bank at Childersburg," Woods pointed out. "We documented that. The bank's president is part of the state machine and Beasley used that money to pay for the black vote. Another machine lackey, the Farm Bureau Insurance Company, guaranteed that loan. We know how it was done and who did it, but it was like hitting your head against a brick wall."

H. Dohn Williams, a Florida state attorney, was called in to investigate the election, and he agreed that Beasley had indeed bought the black vote. "My investigation showed that predominantly black precincts voted 60 percent of their registered voters" he wrote me, "while predominantly white precincts voted 30 to 35 of theirs. In the black precincts the blacks voted in overwhelming numbers for an incumbent who had been linked to the Ku Klux Klan."

A black delegate from a southern county had sat in on that meeting of the Alabama Democratic Conference in May 1974. The issue to be decided was whether to back Beasley or Woods for lieutenant governor. The witness reported seeing Beasley people pass out stacks of hundred-dollar bills for their candidate. Beasley was then announced as the officially endorsed candidate.

Black mayor Johnny Ford of Tuskegee confirmed the practice of merchandising the black vote in Alabama. "They do it through people who are supposed to be black leaders but who have sold out," he told me. "These are mostly teachers, preachers, and old-time political leaders. There is a crying need in Alabama for a voting rights act."

In contested elections, voting machine handles "jam" so voters can't pull the handle down for certain names. In 1974, Charles Woods was one of those names. "Somehow the mechanic couldn't get down there all day long to fix those boxes," a disgusted Alabaman reported.

The chairman of the registrar board in Mobile acknowledged the absolute power of Southern state machines: "The one in favor with the state party always wins the count. As for the black vote, if my political opponent takes money to a few black leaders, he gets all the black votes. The closest thing to a leader of blacks in the Southern states is the chairman of the white Democratic party."

Finally disheartened by the process, Charles Woods withdrew from politics a disillusioned man.

"There's no practical way to fight back," he said. "They pad ballots, falsify them, and lock them away so nobody can get their hands on them. When Northern liberals came down South to help register black voters, I was real glad at the time. But it has turned around now to make a corrupt power structure even more powerful. There's no way to beat it. If you expose this black vote mess, they label you a Ku Kluxer or antiblack. Some of the younger blacks see the truth about what their 'leaders' are doing to them. I got 15 percent of the registered black votes, which means over half the black people who actually went to the polls voted for me. But the only way this will ever be cleaned up is by federal intervention. We need federal marshals at every polling place."

Buying minority votes is not restricted to the Old Confederacy. In Jimmy Carter's 1976 Presidential campaign, his people were caught passing out money to black ministers in the

San Francisco Bay area. The Reverend J. L. Richards admitted getting $2,000 from Carter's treasury, and three other black clergymen got $1,000 apiece for pledging support. In Carter's last three primaries that year, similar payoffs were made to black, Chicano, and other minority vote brokers.

Hal Evry is unperturbed about these machinations. "One day I was on my way to lunch with a client," he explained. "He's a legendary sheriff in St. Louis, well respected in every way. Suddenly he pulled over to the curb and parked."

"Can you hold off a minute, Hal?" the sheriff asked. "I forgot to deliver this $10,000 for the black vote. I'll only be a minute."

"What do you want to do that for?" Hal asked. "Don't you think we could win without it?"

"I guess we could," the sheriff replied. "But you see, Hal, it's kind of a tradition we have down here."

As Evry quickly reminds you, he's not in the crusading business. "I don't want to educate the world. I don't even want to upgrade it. I just want to understand it. And one of the realities of American elections is street money. When Charles Woods told me about it, I advised him to pay it if he wanted to win. But he refused and he lost. Like the sheriff said, it's kind of a tradition."

11

The Electronic Ward Heeler

The United States Constitution makes no reference to political parties. The men who set up America hoped to avoid the divisive party intrigues that plagued England. Their intent was to elect leaders whose only allegiance lay with the new Republic—but the experiment was soon abandoned. By George Washington's second term, two major parties—the Federalists and the Antifederalists—battled for the loyalties of Americans. Today those same philosophies war against each other in modern dress: the Democrats campaigning for stronger central government, the Republicans preaching free trade and less government control.

When party power reached its zenith in the early decades of the twentieth century, its tentacles reached into every ward, precinct, block, and home in the land through a web of payoffs, favors, threats, and bribes. Today, particularly in the Deep South and in some big cities elsewhere, the party machines still operate, but social changes have doomed them. Today's party ward heelers are relics of the past. As political parties lost power, professionals skilled in the arts of communication rushed in to fill the void. A few campaign consultants imitate the old political machines, concentrating on personal contact by phone and at the doorstep.

Few experts specializing in "instant organization" can match the relentless precision of Matt Reese. Since 1960, when he organized a massive volunteer army that helped John Kennedy pull an upset in Reese's native West Virginia primary, he has been a power in the Democratic Party. Appointed Deputy Chairman of the Democratic National Committee, he directed Lyndon Johnson's get-out-the-vote drives in 1964, registered 2 million new voters, and contributed mightily to Johnson's runaway win over Goldwater.

Throughout the 1960s Matt Reese was devoted to the Kennedys. "I worked for both John and Bobby Kennedy and would have jumped off the top of this building for either one of them," he recalled. "Only for Bobby I'd have shouted hooray as I came down. The difference is, he had passion. Bobby was a very impressive man. He exuded a warmth and caring that attracted people, and I loved him."

The building whose roof would have been Reese's launching pad is located on Massachusetts Avenue in Washington, D.C. Reese's first-floor suite is tastefully outfitted with comfortable sofas, antique furnishings, and Impressionist watercolors. The walls of the reception room are covered with photos of Reese with John, Bobby, and Ted Kennedy, Hubert Humphrey, and other legendary Democrats.

Reese's specialty is "organization on demand." Where media strategists use images, symbols, and subliminal persuasion, organizational geniuses like Reese go right for the voter's lapels like high-powered salesmen. Using phone banks, volunteer armies, and doorstep visits, Reese mingles persistence, intimidation, and simple West Virginia charm to work his magic. When a campaign begins, Reese packs his bag and moves into his client's state. He assembles voter lists, runs computer analyses of special "predispositions," isolates those voters who are convertible, uses research to find out how to convince them his man is best, and then orchestrates a series of mailings, phone calls, and home visits.

When a candidate calls his Washington, D.C., office and laments, "I have lots of money, I want to be a senator, but I don't know a soul in either party to help me," Reese goes straight to work. He has condensed political campaigns into a logical sequence of events as reliable as the hole punches in a computer card. "The purpose of any campaign is to get the voter into a booth to cast his ballot for you," Reese explained. "There is a 'want-to' line down the middle of the electorate. People on the right side of this line *want to* vote for you enough to actually vote for you; those on the wrong side *don't want to* vote for you. Most people are bunched closely around the 'want-to' line. Our job is to pull enough people to our side of the line to win, not from the hard cases but from the ones closest to the line. Let me show you what I mean."

Reese took a pad and pencil from the oval coffee table. He is an imposing man—six-foot two and nearly 300 pounds— with the resonant voice of a stage actor. Yet there is an appealing vulnerability in his watchful blue eyes. There is no mistaking his intelligence: his words are quickly spoken but well chosen.

"Take a typical Congressional race in Ohio. There are 465,000 people in the district, 310,000 of whom are adults. About 100,000 will not be registered to vote. That means 210,000 *are* registered. Of those, 70,000 will not vote, so 140,000 people do the voting for everyone else. Of that 140,000, 45,000 are ours and 40,000 theirs—it's my chart so I may as well have the advantage. That means 55,000 are undecided. We win that election right here, with the undecided voters," he said, pointing at the marked pad.

"I wish God gave green noses to undecided voters, because between now and election eve, I'd work only the green noses. I wish God gave purple ears to nonvoters for my candidate on election eve, because on election day I'd work only the purple ears. The ones we go after are nonvoters who are for us and the undecided voters. When we target, we measure concentrations of green noses and purple ears, and then we rank the precincts twice: once from best to worst according to the concentrations of green noses, the undecideds; and a second time from best to worst for concentrations of purple ears, nonvoters who are for us.

"But knowing who the purple ears and green noses are is not enough. I have a third political target, the precinct itself. I study the past and predict what will happen in the future. Say a precinct is strongly liberal. In 1962, 1968, and 1976 they voted heavily for a liberal Democrat by a margin of 62 to 38 percent or 60 to 40 percent. Chances are, this time they'll vote the same way, unless my candidate gets caught making love to a goat on the courthouse steps and the local paper runs a front-page photo of the event.

"I look at past elections—the turnouts, the ticket-splitting, the party-registration switches between elections. If we find a precinct where a Democratic President gets 62 percent of the vote but the Democratic governor gets only 54 percent, that split indicates independence or indecisiveness. It pinpoints the undecideds. A precinct that is highly liberal but low in turnout is where the purple ears live, favorable but not likely to vote. Another precinct high in independence and turnout is where the green noses live, the undecideds.

"These are the historical voting patterns. We hope they vote the same way this time, but we can't be sure. That's why I always do canvassing. We study voter registration cards and go after those most likely to vote because they've always voted before. We knock on their doors and ask how they feel about our candidate, and if they say, 'I hate him,' it's a throwaway. Only when they love my man and have a poor voting record will we spend our resources to get them to the polls on election day. You get them there by making them *want to* enough through mass media, mail, phone, and in-person contact. Again and again, one-on-one contact through those four channels. Why the repetition? Because they're not listening. Elections aren't very important to most people. The fact that their fifteen-year-old daughter was out after midnight or that heating oil is expensive is more important to them than whether you, I, or anybody else is their governor. So I've got to repeat my message over and over again to get them to do what I want."

In Missouri in 1978, Reese and some research colleagues developed a sophisticated technique for pinpointing voter blocs favorable to their cause. Called "Geo-Demographic Targeting," the system uses U.S. Census information, attitude polls, life-style analyses, and computers to isolate names and addresses of the people most susceptible to certain ideas, issues, or candidates. Early in 1978, legislators in Missouri had proposed a "right to work" amendment to the state constitution, outlawing union shop contracts. The AFL-CIO sponsored a poll of Missourians and found to their dismay that Missourians favored the "antilabor" proposition by more than 2 to 1—63 percent for, 30 against, 7 undecided. Worried labor leaders picked up the phone and sent out an emergency call for Matt Reese.

For the past one hundred years it has been common political practice to root out clusters of potential support for a particular issue and concentrate efforts in those areas of potential support—"working the Irish, or Italian, or Jewish wards." Reese, in collaboration with research expert Jonathan Robbin, took that concept and refined it into a computer operation.

Robbin, head of Claritas Research in Virginia, specializes in matching human personality traits with the way people buy products, travel, and vote. He has found that people with similar personal habits, life-style stages, income, and education tend to buy the same products and the same brands of those products. Isolating forty specific types he calls "clusters," Robbin analyzes people and the neighborhoods in which they live. Cluster Twenty-Seven, for example, is "upper-class mobile managers with older children." Cluster Thirty-Seven is "middle-class young mobile suburban families." "Educated young business professionals/clericals in similar areas" make up Cluster Twenty-Nine. "Low-income widows and elderly, South and Southwest," make up Cluster Two. After analyzing a billion pieces of mail every year, Robbin could accurately predict how many units of a certain mail-order product would be bought by Cluster Two or Cluster Twenty-Eight, when a targeted sales pitch was used.

Reese called in Jonathan Robbin to help him in Missouri. "The problem was clear," Reese explained. "There were more people against us in Missouri than for us. So we had to let the opposition's sleeping dogs lie and get out our vote without disturbing theirs. We couldn't use television, which contacts everyone indiscriminately. The campaign had to be done by mail, by phone, and in person—the hard way."

Robbin's research found that just eighteen of his forty

"demographic clusters" favored the pro-union position. By matching those eighteen desirable clusters to the 6,000 Missouri census bloc groups, he isolated 2,300 favorable bloc groups. These 2,300 blocs became the targets for Matt Reese's "invisible campaign." Reese cross-matched a computer tape of all phones and homes in the state with his 2,300 blocs, and emerged with a list of 595,000 households—all of them inhabited by people whose life styles predicted support for his client.

"Those were my fair-minded voters," Reese noted. "In one county I had 618 malleable voters whom I could contact without touching the other 575 unfavorable voters. My job was to approach friendly folks without waking up the others."

He hired telephone interviewers to call every one of the targeted homes. First, the interviewer asked the voter to be a volunteer for their cause. Most refused. Then the interviewer asked straight out whether the person was for or against "right to work." Those who answered "for" were discarded because they were for the other side. If someone was unsure, his card was set aside for future contact. These undecideds required delicate handling, since they were just as likely to help the other side as the union. Only when a person replied that he was strongly against "right to work" did he get the full Matt Reese treatment.

Reese's polls uncovered three fears among Missourians that favored his cause. First, though these people had no great love for labor unions, they were worried that state interference would hurt them in the pocketbook. Second, they felt that big business, labor, and government were in a power balance, and they didn't want to disturb the status quo. Lastly, since unions are democratic institutions, these people believed that the majority-rule principle was in jeopardy.

Using these research findings, Reese produced eighteen different versions of a letter to voters. Depending on its cluster number, each targeted home received the appropriate appeal. For example, suburban voters were told that "right to work" laws constitute government interference in the free-enterprise system. In low-income neighborhoods where people welcome government subsidies and grants, "sweat-shops" were prophesied.

All targeted households were contacted ten times during the month before election day. Reese sent out two mailings of his letter the first few weeks. Ten days before the election, volunteer block captains called on each favorable home. They knocked on the front door, chatted with neighbors they already knew about the upcoming election, and left a piece of literature that focused on the fears uncovered by polling. Then a week before election day, each block captain phoned the homes he had visited, to apply some psychological pressure:

"Mrs. Smith, when you go to vote next week we hope you can do it early, when we need it most. Can you vote by ten o'clock? By eleven? By noon?"

The captains negotiated the time until the voters committed themselves. On the Saturday before the election, union representatives visited the homes, spoke briefly about the working person's stake in the election, and left a richly produced eight-page magazine behind. The magazine featured quotes from Harry Truman about how awful "right to work" was, a horror story by an Arkansas woman who worked in a factory under "right to work" laws, a piece about a farmer who had suffered the evils of nonunion labor.

Meanwhile, union leaders were getting jittery. They had seen the opposition's slick commercials on television night and day, while their own cause was nowhere in sight. "The labor people kept calling me, all upset," Reese laughed. "They wanted to know when the hell our campaign was going to begin!" Though only $300,000 of his $2.2-million budget went for television, Reese was confident.

Monday morning before election Tuesday, every favorable voter received a card showing a photo of the ballot with its thirteen items. Copy explained that a "No" vote was a pro-labor vote, clearing up the usual confusion caused by tricky wording. The card also clearly identified the local polling stations.

Tuesday morning, election day. Each volunteer election

captain received a stack of cards listing prolabor voters and
the times they promised to vote. The captains phoned tardy
cases and knocked on their doors, renegotiating their voting
times. Late that afternoon, labor-union captains were left with
a small list of no-shows. In the few hours remaining, the captains visited these homes and personally drove willing people
to the election centers.

The targeted efforts paid off: the vote was 60 to 40 percent
against "right to work." Of the 900,000 Missourians who defeated the initiative, 600,000 were rounded up by Reese's invisible campaign. A clear victory for Matt Reese's Geo-Demographic Targeting.

Reese, fifty-one, is a confessed news addict: he reads eight
daily papers, religiously watches television-network news, and
listens to all-news radio.

"I came out of the lower middle class—intellectually and
culturally, if not financially. I always wanted something more.
I was raised in a little box in West Virginia and somehow—I
don't know how—managed to escape. My people are Republicans through and through; I'm not sure they believe in labor
unions yet. I was the only one I knew who was interested in
politics. When I got back from the army in Korea, I got a call
from a guy I'd played football with. He was county president
of the Young Democrats and he needed help decorating the
hall. So I went over and found my place in life. I discovered
the level of competence in political circles is so low you don't
need much to succeed."

In 1966 Reese rented a small office and started Matt Reese &
Associates. He took on all comers and won eleven straight
campaigns. "You smart son-of-a-bitch, you've found the secret," he told himself. Then he lost one. "And I didn't know
why," he recalled. "I'd done everything just the way I always
did and we lost. I'm still trying to figure out why."

Officially Reese lists a 73-percent win record, but he puts no
great stock in such numbers. "I've lied so much about it I
don't know what it really is," he confessed. "I have a reputation for winning and I keep it because I win lots of elections
I'm not supposed to win. In 1972 Claiborne Pell, the senator

from Rhode Island, was behind 59 to 22 percent and everybody in town knew it. Well, we won that election 54 to 46
percent. I didn't do it all but, hell, I have to take the blame
when we lose, so I guess I can claim credit if we win.

"One thing a consultant does is free everybody in the campaign from arguments and indecision. I've got a strong personality, so I come in with my campaign plan on a stone tablet
and say, 'See? God wrote that,' and they usually do what I tell
them. Sometimes, though, things get so messed up that it's too
much trouble to fix, so I surrender.

"Some consultants work on an all-or-nothing basis. Either
you do things their way or they won't help you. I tend to
adjust and carve out an area of the campaign that is too
complex for anybody else to do well. My style is not to play
God. Once in a great while I'll have a big row with a candidate. Maybe I should do that more often.

"I work scared all the time. I do what the research calls for
and I'm still afraid I'm not making the right moves. I check
things over forty-three times and rewrite again and again because it's never good enough. When I take somebody's money
I don't want to con him, so I do everything I can to win.
When I get frustrated, I eat a hamburger—that's why I weigh
a ton."

Reese reacts strongly against the charge that consultants
have trivialized campaigns into a media circus; the rap, he
feels, has been placed unfairly on the heads of political professionals. "The press causes the problem," he argues. "You can't
get their attention unless you do something kooky or unspeak-
able. Sure, you can drop your drawers on the courthouse steps
so they'll run a picture on page one—but what do you do for
an encore? What they want is for my candidate to call the
other guy bad names—then they'll cover me. Or if I have
someone jump off a building with an umbrella, they'll send
photographers. What we have to do to get coverage is de-
grading.

"Advertising and the press feed the public sugar kernels.
They give them only exciting bits of detail and define things
on the basis of simple answers. But there are no more simple

answers. All our simple problems have been solved. We've got nothing left but complex problems."

Reese plays the game hard and to win, accepting the ground rules as he sees them and not as he would like them to be. He keeps things objective by holding "truth sessions." A typical Reese truth session involves a dozen people—Reese, his staff, and the candidate's advisers—and is held in closed quarters over a weekend. They bash ideas around in frank, informal meetings, sustained by coffee and sandwiches. From the argument and observations, Reese drafts a report summarizing the facts about the campaign and circulates it among the others, who revise and edit until a final outline evolves.

The outline describes the "geo-politics" of the state or district; breakdowns of voting blocs; potential opponents; important popular and political concerns; strengths and weaknesses of the candidate, and how to exploit the one and minimize the other; and the resources—money, people, and time—available to the campaign. From this information Reese extracts a list of reasons why their candidate should be elected. Once the case has been made, the rest of the campaign is dedicated to making it over and over again—repetition in simplified form to voters who make the final judgment.

Glamor plays a large part in politics, and television makes it mandatory that aspiring politicians have it in good supply. You can create *image* by media, Reese points out, but *charisma* is a God-given blessing that can be invaluable to the smart candidate.

"It's possible to win office without charisma, but not many people do," he noted. "If charisma is there, it attracts all the good things—money, people, talent. If Ted Kennedy wants the answer to a question on the economy, he can pick up a phone and summon John Kenneth Galbraith. When Congressman Snork needs the same information, he has to ask the clerk at the Congressional Library.

"Sometimes there's charisma and nothing else. If I have such a candidate, I try to hide it. I've sent political science professors on tour with my candidate to drill him, to tell him how the Commerce Department or Justice Department works. Why should he have to know these things, anyway? If voters wanted substance, we'd have all our governors coming out of college or the civil service. If the caring is there, substance can be learned later. If neither is there, that's when I wish I weren't involved in the campaign."

Reese recalled a recent race in Rhode Island where Claiborne Pell was returned to the Senate because of inverse snobbery. "Pell proudly wears the same kind of clothes today that he wore as a Princeton undergraduate thirty-five years ago. Everybody said I should get him out of those awful clothes. What they didn't understand was that the old-fashioned look is part of the man's attraction. You see, all these Portuguese and Italian second- and third-generation immigrants in Rhode Island admire Claiborne Pell precisely because he's from a rich, privileged background. That makes him extraordinary. They don't want a guy from the shops like themselves dressed in a doubleknit suit. They don't want a sharpie. They want someone extraordinary whom they can trust. So they sent Pell back to the Senate.

"Basic prejudices are paramount in the way people vote. The most basic prejudice of all is whether a candidate really cares for the voter. That is simply a perception which may or may not be accurate. Ethnic splits are still very important, but geography doesn't mean much anymore—except that New Yorkers are more jaded than people in other cities. Age has become a crucial factor. Older people vote in heavier concentrations and are more conservative. Under-thirties vote lightly —they make up 40 percent of those eligible to vote and 20 percent of the total vote. The biggest biases come from wealth. The rich are Republicans. The Democrats are the poor and the well-to-do, bypassing the upper middle class."

Reese explains today's voter cynicism as a simple lack of passion. "The passions that fueled political fever are gone. The Civil War gave us passion for fifty years, the Depression gave passion for thirty years, and the Vietnam War for five years. Without passion, people get cynical. That makes my job harder to do. My job is to make voters know my candidate and his opponents. But they won't listen, they're not interested. So

I have to sugarcoat it, say 'Hey, listen to me real quick now and let me tell you what a great guy he is.' I've got to say his name fast three times before they're gone."

The system is fine, Reese insists. It's not the way we elect our leaders that causes problems, it's the quality of information on which voters base their choices. "We're trained to listen with a tolerant ear to advertising. When the commercial croons, 'Brush with our toothpaste and you're gonna get laid,' nobody really believes that. But we buy it anyway. When Mobil says, 'We'll put an oil well in your backyard and it'll make things beautiful like these clouds and trees here,' we don't believe that crap. But the way we've been trained, Mobil cannot say, 'Let's put an oil well here—we need oil and it won't screw things up too badly.' We won't go for it.

"But in a political campaign you can't use that kind of overstatement. Toothpaste techniques won't sell candidates today—it's got to be subtle. You can't say, 'Honest John Reese needs your vote.' Voters today are less impressed with flashy production. Because of Watergate, in 1974 we used a plain blue background in our commercials. Now we're getting a little sophisticated, but still no baloney-slicing like we used to do."

In 1978 Reese got to handle a campaign for a man many fellow Democrats claim will be a future President of the United States. The battleground was Kentucky, the candidate John Y. Brown.

12

The Kentucky Fried Prince

A new kind of personality now dominates American politics —the candidate from central casting. John Kennedy was the model that launched this new breed of politician. These men are rich or they project the impression of wealth. They wear the right clothes, speak with assurance and an educated manner, and boast full heads of hair and athletic stances even into middle age. They are moderate social adventurers who stretch the limits of acceptable political behavior only slightly, never beyond the borders of good sense, i.e., survival. They boast attractive families and glamorous wives who take an active role in campaigning. They possess an inordinate ambition for political power. They see politics as a form of competitive sport and know how elections are won and lost. They are telegenic, stage-wise, crafty. For better or worse, these spiritual sons of the New Frontier represent the leadership pool of the 1980s.

John Y. Brown is straight from the mold. He is forty-six years old and blessed with "the look": six feet tall with blue eyes, graying blond hair, and a handsome, full-faced boyishness. His suits are from Brooks Brothers, his ties quietly correct. The only visible signs of mortality are his slender, fidgeting hands and his heavy smoking of Kent cigarettes.

A Kentuckian, Brown spread the fame of bluegrass country with his Kentucky Fried Chicken and Lum's drive-in restaurants, amassing a few hundred million dollars on the way. His father, John Y., Sr., is a lawyer and longtime political maverick who rose to power in the state Democratic Party. He failed to win his race for governor, unwilling to burden his conscience with political favors that called for repayment somewhere down the line.

In a state where fried chicken and basketball are equally sacred, John Y., Jr., came to prominence through his wealth and gained popularity through sports. His ownership of the Colonel Sanders franchises brought worldwide recognition to the special country recipe Kentuckians had long enjoyed exclusively. When he brought professional basketball to the state, launching the Kentucky Colonels team of the old American Basketball Association, he gladdened the hearts of Kentuckians and boosted their regional pride.

Brown didn't set out to win political office. He was content to see others gain power—specifically, Democrats and Kennedys. After the national Democratic Party had been steamrollered by the McGovern defeat in 1972, the Democrats had not only lost forty-eight of the fifty states and come in 18 million votes behind, but were left with $12 million in bills they couldn't pay. So Brown put up a million dollars of his own to bankroll telethons that pulled in $19 million and gained him the lasting friendship of Democratic Party stalwarts Larry O'Brien, Ted Kennedy, and Matt Reese.

Still, Brown considered himself a businessman, not a politician. He had toyed with running for office in 1976, but dropped the idea when his advisers told him he would probably lose because of ongoing divorce proceedings against his wife Elly. In 1978 he met Phyllis George, television star and former Miss America. They fell in love, and were married on March 17, 1979, in New York City. The place was a Fifth Avenue church, the minister the famous positive-thinker Norman Vincent Peale. It was Peale who triggered Brown's political ambitions when he linked an addendum to the traditional "I now pronounce you man and wife": "You're a team now—go out and serve mankind."

The Browns spent their honeymoon talking about the upcoming governor's race in Kentucky. There were lots of good reasons not to run. If they got into it now, they would have only weeks to campaign. Still, Kentucky had a corrupt state government from the governor's office on down, and as top man Brown could help light candles instead of just cursing the political darkness. On the other hand, he knew nothing about Kentucky politics. His father had run for governor in 1940 and lost; the defeat still rankled. Finally, Phyllis and his own spirit of adventure decided the question.

They had to move fast, since April 4 was the last filing day for the state primaries. Brown took his first step toward the capitol dome when he called Matt Reese in Washington.

"I want you to do my campaign," he said.

"This year's election?" Reese asked.

"Yes."

"I was afraid of that," Reese said. "You sure didn't leave any stretching room."

The primary was sixty days away and nobody knew John Y. was running except the candidate's wife; Larry Townsend, a top aide from the corporate world; and now Matt Reese. Back in Kentucky, meanwhile, the strongest field of Democratic candidates in years had been bashing heads for a good twelve months.

Terry McBrayer was the choice of outgoing Governor Julian Carroll, who had won office by a record 192,000 votes in 1975. In Kentucky a governor cannot succeed himself, so Carroll willed his personal popularity, patronage, machine support, and money to longtime legislator McBrayer, a personal friend. Harvey Sloane, a well-liked former mayor of Louisville, had scored points with a highly publicized walk across Kentucky and currently led all polls. State Auditor George Atkins and U.S. Congressman Carroll Hubbard radiated their candidacies from solid centers of political office, and Lieutenant Governor Thelma Stovall had the backing of feminists to go with her high title and visibility. The weakest candidate was Ralph Ed Graves, former state commissioner, who wielded heavy influence in the western part of the state, where he published two weekly newspapers.

As his friends are quick to tell you, John Y., Jr., is a man who likes to run things himself. He insists on control and is only comfortable when he gives the orders. Like many who have built great businesses, Brown has a problem taking advice, particularly when it conflicts with his own notions. Such a candidate is far from a consultant's dream, but Reese perceived in Brown an untamed spark that, properly directed, would be more precious than blind obedience.

In that first telephone conversation, Reese suggested they hire Robert Squier, a Washington-based media expert, to join the team. Brown took that opportunity to step in and assume executive control: "I know Bob Squier," he replied. "I'll call him myself and fix things up." Reese was given responsibility for choosing strategy, drafting the campaign plan, doing print material, and coordinating his organizational magic. He and Brown agreed to meet in Louisville a few days later.

Brown's next call was to Bob Squier. Four years before, Brown had sent Larry Townsend to Washington to lunch with Squier and talk about Brown's running for governor. The odds had seemed too long then, so he hadn't filed. This time, though, he was committed.

"I'm running, Bob," he told Squier the moment he came on the line. "I want you to do my campaign."

"Have you announced yet?" Squier asked.

"No. I'm in New York with Phyllis."

"Congratulations. When do you expect to file?"

"I want to talk to you first. When can we meet?"

The next day he and Phyllis were in Squier's office. They talked about the field of candidates, Brown's ideas about Kentuckians, and the approach they should take.

"Who's doing your research?" Squier asked.

"Nobody. Who's good, fast, and smart?"

Squier named Hugh Schwartz, a San Francisco pollster who had left a career in marketing research to serve California politicos like ex-Senator John Tunney, legislator Bob Moretti, and scores of initiative sponsors. Schwartz had never worked with Matt Reese before, so Reese checked out Schwartz through Bob Keefe of the Democratic National Committee. Keefe's report came back glowing, and on April 2, Hugh Schwartz was hired.

Schwartz recalled those first moments: "We had three things going for us right off the bat. We knew none of the primary opponents had staked a claim; they were all vulnerable. We knew we could spend lots of money without worrying where it would come from, since Brown was funding the whole thing himself. We were going to use a technique in the primary never before used in Kentucky."

The secret weapon was Matt Reese's Geo-Demographic Targeting, first used to crush the "right to work" initiative in Missouri. Primary opponent Thelma Stovall unwittingly helped Reese score bull's-eyes by her zeal in compiling state statistics. As lieutenant governor, Stovall had put together a computer tape identifying Kentucky voters by age, race, income, and the date they registered, showing in which elections, general or primary, each had cast ballots. Available for a bargain three-hundred dollars, the voter tape became a cornerstone of Reese's phone, mail, and in-person assault.

"We classified the whole Democratic voting population," Schwartz explained. "We matched our polling to hard-core voters, soft-core voters, and even had a double-X category for newly registered people with no voting history at all. Once we analyzed it, we saw where we were doing well and where we needed to work harder."

The first research Schwartz put out in the field found John Y. Brown generally popular, with no serious negatives among the natives. They knew about Phyllis George and liked her. They didn't care much for Brown's divorce from his first wife, Elly, a well-known personality in her own right, but they were not losing any sleep over the split. The one big question in the minds of Kentuckians was whether Brown knew enough to be a governor, since he had never held any public office.

Polls showed Brown fourth in a field of seven—twenty-five percentage points behind front runner Harvey Sloane. That did not trouble the pros, who were long accustomed to turning impossible leads around. The big news from the early surveys was the burning resentment people had against the old politicians, from Governor Julian Carroll's regime on back. It was common knowledge that a system of corruption fostered by Kentucky business interests helped elected politicians leave

office a lot richer than when they entered. Everyone—Reese,
Squier, Schwartz, Townsend, Phyllis, and last-word John Y.—
agreed they had to attack Julian Carroll and Carroll's hand-
picked heir apparent, Terry McBrayer. The primary campaign was stalemated, so emotional heat could only help their
cause.

Bob Squier recalled the confused situation eight weeks before the election: "So many candidates were saying so many
different things, the voters were split into slivers. George
Atkins almost had the right approach. George was attacking
Governor Carroll because his polls told him people were disgusted with corruption in state government. Because we had
more sophisticated polling, we discovered that even though
Kentuckians were upset about corruption, they didn't necessarily connect Carroll to it."

So Squier's media spots attacked corruption without mentioning Carroll, the ranking Democrat. In a state where Democrats outnumber Republicans 2½ to 1, you try not to antagonize party machinery that can punish you in the general
election. This way, Brown came to be seen as a reformer, but
not as an enemy of Julian Carroll.

Brown's great wealth, even as it energized his hand-picked
team of voter technologists, became a source of controversy.
Since Brown was one of the richest men in Kentucky, shrill
cries of foul play and "buying the election" were raised from
the day he announced—charges that the local reporters and
newscasters eagerly publicized. Soon the polls showed Brown's
image was as a free-spending millionaire playboy rising fast.

Squier countered with a series of television commercials portraying his candidate as a hard-working leader of industry.
Clips showed Brown in his office, jacket off, handling people
and making tough decisions. Other spots talked about the need
for fresh leadership, for an honest man who was tough but
compassionate. One clever commercial covered two goals in
its thirty-second span.

The scene: a political meeting. The moderator is about to
introduce speaker John Y. Brown when a man in the audience
stands up. The camera zooms in for a close-up. "I'll tell you

something," the citizen-actor volunteers. "I'd rather have a rich one going in than a rich one coming out. When they're rich coming out, it's our money. I know how John Y. Brown made his money."

The spot covered corruption without naming Carroll, and simultaneously converted Brown's great wealth from a potential problem into an instant asset. The "too rich to steal" theme perked up many an ear weary of institutionalized corruption, and the word was out that John Y. was a good man to clean it up.

Then there was the question of Phyllis George. From day one all the pros agonized over how Kentuckians would respond to the glamorous Miss America star of CBS Sports, a woman who married local boy Brown less than a year after he had divorced one of the most popular women in the state. Would they see her as a home-wrecker by association? Should they keep her under wraps?

Matt Reese felt Phyllis would be best used campaigning on her own, visiting ladies' clubs while John stormed factories and farms. Reese was concerned that Phyllis was *too* good. Her stage sparkle and rapport with crowds could overshadow Brown, a basically shy man. Brown showed no great enthusiasm for campaigning. He would much rather hang around Louisville sitting in on strategy sessions than be flying off to Ashland for a speech to coal miners. Like most businessmen, he felt more potent and comfortable with small groups than with mobs. Some of such crowd fear is primal: if three or four disagree with you, they might change their minds; if five hundred or a thousand find fault, they can rip you to shreds before you can calm them down. Most candidates find public appearances threatening, even when the crowds are reasonably friendly.

"John didn't like campaigning," Reese said. "He was scared of it, even if he wouldn't say so."

Brown himself decided what role Phyllis would play: "No way I'm going to hide Phyllis. Wherever I go, she goes beside me."

Since they couldn't hide her, the professionals used her to the hilt. Early film clips featured Phyllis talking to people, accompanying John Y., getting off planes. The moment she hit the TV screens, news analysts misinterpreted the motives behind the media. "They thought we wanted to cash in on her fame," Squier noted. "That wasn't it at all. John had plenty of fame on his own. All that early media with Phyllis was to let Kentuckians know there was nothing wrong; people get divorced and remarried, and in this case there were no victims, so everything was fine."

Reese gave out the same message with computer letters and literature. "Here she is, Kentucky," the theme ran. "She's a Miss America and a terrific lady, not threatening at all. She's from Denton, Texas, which is very much like Lexington, Kentucky. Take a good look, get comfortable with her." They had taken the play away from the opposition by meeting any negatives head on before the others could attack. Though there would be later charges of swinging life styles and frivolity, the sting had been removed.

Reese sent John and Phyllis out on a "helicopter safari," accompanied by film crews and reporters from local and national news organizations. The stunt was cooked up by Reese to get the candidate out where he was weak, in the small towns and the countryside, and at the same time get free press attention to validate his candidacy. The gimmick did both jobs admirably, but Reese quickly gave credit for the idea to a foreigner.

"An African politician used a helicopter to campaign in the boondocks," he explained. "When the natives saw the metal whirlybird descending from heaven, they were convinced the candidate was a god, so they voted for him. People in Kentucky may not have thought Brown was God, but in those small towns it had to be impressive."

Brown found the safari at times a frustrating experience. In the first weeks before his campaign developed momentum, he would whirl out of Louisville and, after a jerky two-hour ride, descend on a small mining town where a crowd of ten people waited for him to speak, two of the ten his own staff. On such occasions he would blow his cool, grow agitated, and scream at his aides for not delivering more bodies to the rally. Since these were people from Brown's own corporate world, he felt free to ease his humiliation by blowing off steam in the traditional bosslike way.

The advertising, applied research, and phone banks began to pay off. The crowds got larger and more enthusiastic, and the press began taking his candidacy more seriously. Brown fully understood the power of advertising from his days of selling chicken. While Matt Reese looked for voters with green ears and purple noses, and Hugh Schwartz put Kentuckians through his bag of research tricks, Bob Squier shot miles of film and played psychologist to get the most from his candidate.

"John has built his career around being successful," Squier pointed out. "One day I took him to an empty factory and had him walk around inside that useless, wasted space. I thought the forlorn atmosphere of a failed business would hit him hard and it did. We got some good emotional footage and edited that into a spot."

Brown's clean business record was an excellent asset. He had never been sued and had never declared bankruptcy. The worst that could be said was that he made more money from the old Colonel's original recipe and bearded-image value than Harlan Sanders himself.

In an era when all politicians are suspect and Kentucky pols anathema, Brown was positioned firmly as a businessman. He had no knowledge of government, which resulted in a few embarrassing moments in the campaign. For one thing, his positions were philosophically inconsistent. "He's a liberal man, but not a liberal," Reese offered. "He just wants to do good things for Kentucky."

"I'm a free enterprise man," Brown told reporters. "I think you'll find me a two-fisted governor!"

Reese hired an "issues man" to travel with the candidate and brief him on the people he was to meet. But Brown is an impatient man who doesn't take advice graciously. Often he left his adviser behind at the airport. On one trip it cost him dearly. A black questioner asked for his stand on affirmative action and he quickly shot back, "What's affirmative action?" The national press and television picked up the story, publicizing Brown's ignorance of civil rights laws. This faux pas even caught the attention of Gary Trudeau, who devoted a series of *Doonesbury* comic strips to caricaturing Brown's uninformed exchanges.

Another handicap was Brown's discomfort among common people. In a state where being downhome comes with the territory, Brown was awkward and uptight. Off stage and off camera, he chain-smoked, fidgeted, and exploded in bursts of anger. Research showed that ordinary Kentuckians feared his great wealth would make it hard for him to appreciate their problems. Though he tried to offset that feeling, his campaigning often worked against his own ends.

One day he visited a United Mine Workers' meeting to ask for their support. A UMW boss, in the oblique language of politics, continued to hint for a meeting of minds, a quid pro quo to trade union support for the candidate's accessibility. "June Carroll always kept his door open to us," the man said in ten different ways. "We want to know if your door will be open, too." According to the formula, Brown was required to say, "If you want to call me, you can." But he never got out those magic words. He had taken a personal dislike to the union leader and was damned if he would promise that man anything—in short, he was what the pros call a "difficult candidate." In the end, it cost him a personal goal in this election.

While John and Phyllis flew around making press copy, Matt Reese's targeted mail and phone banks reached into the nooks and crannies of the state. By the May 29 primary day, Reese had managed to organize an army of 14,000 block captains to get out the Brown vote. These were hard-core voters, volunteers eager for action whom Reese turned loose a week before the event to call people, ring doorbells, hand out literature, and drive bodies to the polling places where they could vote for John Y. Brown. Television screens were loaded with John-and-Phyllis commercials, newspapers ran full-page ads and stories, and the polls now showed Brown as the favorite. It had cost him $1.6 million of his own money.

When the votes were counted May 30, Brown had beaten his nearest rival Harvey Sloane by twenty-five percentage points, despite the fact that Sloane and third-place finisher McBrayer had each spent a million dollars on the campaign. They had been outgunned by Brown's heavy-hitting professionals.

The real fight was over. Now the Democratic state machine and its local bosses joined hands in traditional post-primary unity to back their new champion. With the massive advantage the Democrats enjoyed in voter registration, the question became not if Brown would be governor, but by how much he would win. Brown set a goal: he would try to win office by a record popular vote. Outgoing Julian Carroll had amassed a 192,000 plurality, so Brown set his sights on 200,000.

If primaries are beauty contests, general elections are boxing matches. The kid gloves are off because it's not your own party you're fighting, but the enemy's. Republican nominee Louie Nunn was a figure from the 1960s, an oldtime Goldwater-Nixon conservative who won the 1967 gubernatorial race with a plank that excluded blacks and poor people. Since 1971, Kentuckians had consistently elected Democrats to both Senate seats and the governorship. Nunn, fifty-five and heavy-jowled, was an old pol lawyer and landowner. He faced an uphill battle. In 1971 his hand-picked heir apparent for the governor's throne had lost badly to a Democrat. Most of the bad feeling toward Nunn came from an unpopular sales-tax increase he had pushed through soon after taking office. The tax, known as "Nickels for Nunn," was a 5-percent levy on food. It had been 3 percent before he took office, and he had been elected on a promise to lower taxes. Instead, to save the state from bankruptcy, he raised the food tax, a fact that the people of Kentucky had not forgotten.

Brown's campaign strategy was changed for the general election. When you have a twenty-five-point lead and the other guy is chasing you, traditional wisdom says to make no waves and stay clear of name-calling contests, media arguments, and debates—in short, to avoid any situation where you might put your foot in your mouth with a testy answer or factual error. But John Y., craving action and confrontation, had a difficult

time adjusting to the new strategy. When his consultants recommended a low-key campaign against Louie Nunn, he resisted. This became a big problem in August, when Nunn
launched his "candor campaign."

Robert Goodman, a Baltimore media director who would
later handle George Bush's 1980 Presidential campaign, did
the film work for Louie Nunn. When your man is chasing a
twenty-five-point lead with eleven weeks to go, strategy dic-
tates one of two actions: belly up and admit defeat, or attack
hard until the gap closes. So Goodman produced a series of
radio and television spots asking the question, "What do we
really know about John Y. Brown?" The copy charged Brown
with high-stakes gambling, jet-set carousing in "jelly beds at
Florida motels," "proabortion swinging," and having "pot-
smoking associates."

One television commercial showed a man in a business suit
who resembled Brown. The camera shot across the back of his
shoulder as he rolled dice on a craps table. A voice-over said,
"We don't think a high-stakes gambler ought to be gambling
with our money in state government." Brown had reportedly
bet $25,000 at the race-track the year before. Another commer-
cial showed a locked file cabinet, while a narrator charged
Brown with corruption because he had refused to make his tax
return public. The voice-over asked, "What do we really know
about John Y. Brown?"

Brown's blood began to boil. All set to "go after the bastards," he wanted to counter every charge with paid media
and television appearances. His advisers had their hands full
holding him to their game plan. In the end, it was Brown's
wife who tamed him. "Phyllis gave John some of the best
advice he got in the campaign," Bob Squier noted. "You don't
get to win the fifty-candidate primary of the Miss America
contest, work for Allen Funt and David Susskind—the two
toughest guys on television—and climb to the top of CBS
Sports without knowing something about human nature and
politics. Phillis saw what was happening and said, 'Hold your
fire, John—he's just trying to get you mad.'"

Squier's media spots were not scheduled to run until the

third week in September. By Labor Day the "candor campaign" was showing up in the polls. The twenty-five-point lead was now fourteen points. Schwartz's research showed that Kentuckians were beginning to believe the charges. "There was a sharp increase in Brown's negatives and a jump in his image as a gambler," he recalled. "And more people were undecided about him now."

The Brown campaign looked to their candidate's glamorous friends for endorsements. Muhammad Ali joined Brown's helicopter safari one day and praised him for his $2-million gift to the Louisville YMCA and a geriatric hospital. "John Y. Brown is the only white man I know who tells the truth," Ali raved, adding, "sometimes." Ted Kennedy attended a Brown rally in Louisville, to help capture the city's heavy black and labor vote.

Nunn countered with heavy hitters from the Republican Party: Ronald Reagan, John Connally, and Gerald Ford rushed in to bolster the beleaguered campaigner. Then Squier's media hit, with its accent on the positive. Brown would make Kentucky as prosperous as his own business. His clean record was set beside Nunn's despised "nickel" tax. The copy avoided specifics—a classic front-runner stance.

Two weeks before the election, a television debate decided it all. Nunn, jowly and scowling, with his thick drawl and country-lawyer manner, growled a replay of his media charges. He attacked Brown's high living, gambling, shady friends, and sharp dealings. He hurled a challenge to Kentucky voters: "You've got to decide if you want a man with a plan or a boy with a toy." The effect was scatter-gun, petty, reminiscent of old-time precinct politics.

Brown kept his cool, trying to look more statesmanlike and gubernatorial than his desperate opponent. In broad, good-mannered terms he described Nunn as a relic of the old corrupt Kentucky, reminding viewers that Nunn had been on the receiving end of $100,000 of Watergate-tainted money. He questioned Nunn's honesty, citing the false charges he had been throwing around so recklessly.

The deciding factor, however, was simply the way the two

candidates looked side by side. Don Edwards, city editor of the *Lexington Leader*, summed it up: "Brown was nervous and smoked endless cigarettes off camera. But when the red light was on him he appeared open, alert, and positive. Nunn came off as sarcastic, menacing, and negative. Brown won the television battle." Kentuckians began to believe Brown and doubt Nunn. The point spread widened, and newspapers that had been headlining every new Nunn attack now came out to endorse Brown for governor. The election was over. The only remaining question was how big the final margin would be.

When the outcome seems certain, voters who favor the leader often stay home in the belief that their one vote will not be missed. Matt Reese knew better than anyone that upsets can happen this way. So he launched his army of 14,000 block captains, union captains, phone banks, letters, and volunteer home visitors. Repetition, follow-up—the old Reese magic.

On November 6 Kentuckians voted. When the count was in, Brown was elected governor by twenty points—60 to 40 percent. His winning margin was 185,000 popular votes, 7,000 shy of the record. "Some races just aren't races," Bob Goodman concluded. "Nunn is not as photogenic as John Y. Brown. He doesn't have the same star quality. I think Nunn could have beaten an ordinary Democrat, but it's hard to beat Paul Newman."

Goodman gave high marks to his opponent's media strategy: "Bob Squier really understands the *present tense*. He must have done forty Brown spots, each with a life of just one or two showings. We put lots of production values into our work, trying to make a spot very dramatic so that we would have a longer life with it. But Squier's strategy was brilliant. When forty spots come at you over three or four weeks, they create quite an impression."

Brown was disappointed that he didn't break the record. He looked for chinks in his battle plan, and thought he found one in Squier's media. "If you ask him today, John will say the stuff I did in the primary was terrific," Squier noted. "Then he'll tell you the stuff I did in the general election was dull and awful." Squier attributes Brown's evaluation to Brown's business experience. "He used lots of product advertising to build his companies, and he sees political advertising the same way. He liked only those spots that had pizzazz. The primary commercials were done that way because we started out behind and had to go for the whole thing. In the general election we started ahead, so we had to solidify our gains and hold Nunn off."

Matt Reese believes some votes may have been lost when Brown insisted on answering Nunn's charges, even in general terms; to answer a charge usually gives it credence. "He said a lot more about those charges than I'd have liked," Reese explained. "But it turned out okay."

"Okay" means another win notched in Reese's ample victory belt and more trials, errors, and triumphs to file in his memory bank. The good people of Kentucky have the next few years to find out just how okay John Y. Brown will be for them, while the rest of America has the 1980s to see whether his Presidential star will rise—or sputter and go out.

13

Paving the Way for Ronald Reagan

Until the early 1960s, no Hollywood star had ever been elected to high public office. At that time Ronald Reagan was doing a radio show and hoping for a movie comeback, John Wayne was endorsing candidates, and Bob Hope was entertaining troops. No one dreamed that a movie actor could translate celluloid affection into votes at the polls. The feeling was widespread that actors were simply not very bright.

In 1963 George Murphy, who had danced his way through a series of hit films in the 1930s and 1940s, was working as a public relations executive for Technicolor Corporation. Murphy was well known in Republican circles for his willingness to entertain at party fund-raising affairs. On one such occasion he ran into the young Republican consultant, Sandy Weiner. "Whenever they threw a Republican event, a banquet, rally, or whatever, George would always be there," Weiner told me. "He'd show up for free, do his bit, and charm the eyeballs out of everybody."

Weiner had been in the consulting business only a few years, had a few clients, and was looking for extra income to support a growing family. George Murphy suggested a business partnership selling a liniment invented by his father, the first track coach of an American Olympic team. Weiner jumped at the chance. "We called it Mike Murphy's Liniment," Weiner recalled. "We bottled it, packaged it, and went out to peddle it. But the stuff didn't sell. It burned. One night, after the liniment business died, we got to talking about the chances of a movie star running for office."

Weiner did not think the idea so farfetched. Murphy was a celebrity and had acquired new fans from the *Late Late Show*, which featured the old musicals he made with Judy Garland, Lucille Ball, Gene Kelly, Ginger Rogers, and Fred Astaire. He had served as president of the Screen Actors Guild, knew most of the big spenders in Hollywood, and had close political ties from many years of volunteer work for the Republican Party.

The next morning Weiner and Murphy visited Ed Ettenger, Murphy's boss at Technicolor, to ask what he thought about the idea of George Murphy, politician. "Great idea," Ettenger said, and backed his enthusiasm with a $1,000 check.

On Christmas Day 1963, Weiner told the media that George Murphy was declaring candidacy for the U.S. Senate. Murphy flew to San Diego, Los Angeles, and San Francisco that same day, called press conferences in each of these cities, and told reporters the same thing.

"Everybody laughed," Weiner recalled. Democratic Sen. Clair Engel had held the post for years and was considered unbeatable by the Republican hierarchy. No one of any stature wanted to run and get beaten by him, so when Murphy stepped forward, party regulars were glad to offer him up as a sacrificial lamb. But he had the last laugh: in April 1964, two months before the primary election, Senator Engel died. By that time every Republican who would have been glad to fill the void had already signed intent papers of support for Murphy. So, for good or ill, Murphy would be their candidate.

In March, Pierre Salinger resigned as President Johnson's press secretary. That night he flew to San Francisco, took a room at the Fairmont Hotel, and "established residence." The next morning he got sixty-five friends to sign nominating petitions and, two hours before the deadline, declared himself a Democratic candidate for the Senate, competing for the nomination against State Controller Alan Cranston. Sandy Weiner gathered ammunition for the fall election by compiling Cranston's verbal attacks on Salinger. When the primary smoke cleared in June, Salinger was the Democratic candidate.

June polls showed Salinger leading Murphy by twenty-eight percentage points. Las Vegas bookmakers quoted Murphy's chances as 20 to 1. "Then fate took over again," Weiner noted. "Murphy somehow convinced Walt Disney to endorse him. This was the first time Disney had ever done such a thing. In those years Disney stood for motherhood, apple pie, and the American family all rolled into one. So our newspaper ads, television, and radio all played off of that: 'Walt Disney urges you to vote for George Murphy.'"

Despite Disney's support, Murphy's chances were poor. A month before the election, the gap had closed—he now trailed Salinger by a dozen points—but his campaign had stalled. "Anybody who had any sense was betting big on Salinger," Weiner explained. "Our only chance was to get Salinger to debate. But Salinger cleverly refused. So I turned to a good friend, Bill Ames, who was then news director of the CBS station in Los Angeles, KNXT-TV. Bill's the guy who designed the first instant election projection for television, using key precincts to get results on the air five minutes after the polls closed. Bill kept challenging Salinger to debate and Salinger kept saying no. One afternoon, Ames called Salinger with an ultimatum. He warned him if he wouldn't debate Murphy, Walter Cronkite was going to blast him over the whole network for being a coward. It was all a bluff, but it worked."

In early October, Murphy and Salinger met in an hour-long, free-wheeling debate aired by CBS affiliates across the state. Weiner had insisted on a "standing debate," with the contenders side by side facing KNXT cameras in Hollywood. He had good reasons.

"Here's tall, twinkly-eyed, gray-haired Murphy—and next to him is short, pudgy Pierre," Weiner related, smiling at the memory. "Pierre did the in-depth thing on all the issues, spouting facts and figures like a wire-service ticker. Murphy just smiled and talked about the desalinization of water. It was no match. The voters fell in love with Murphy.

"The last four weeks we did television and newspaper ads across the state. All our material said Disney and Murphy,

Murphy and Disney. That year Goldwater was running a losing effort against Johnson for President, so we hid from Goldwater throughout the campaign. Whenever he was in the
north we were down south, and vice versa."

Weiner attacked Salinger on the carpetbagger issue, using
Pierre's own line to newspaper reporters—"I arrived in San
Francisco at one-thirty a.m., took a room at the Fairmont
Hotel, and signed up to run for the Senate the next afternoon." He borrowed a slogan from Alan Cranston's primary
campaign against Salinger: "Why vote for a man who can't
vote for himself?" On election day, even as Lyndon Johnson
blitzed Barry Goldwater by a 1.3-million plurality, Republican George Murphy licked Pierre Salinger by 216,000 ticket-
splitting votes. Weiner had turned more than 1.5 million ballots around.

The movie-star embargo had been broken and Senator
Murphy went to Washington. Over the next two years,
Murphy convinced his friend Ronald Reagan that he could
become governor of California. In 1966 Reagan won his race
by a landslide.

A year later, Sandy Weiner got his chance to prove that it
isn't necessarily the film star who guarantees victory, but the
strategist who runs his campaign. It was 1967. The Vietnam
War was raging and Shirley Temple Black, urged on by Sen-
ator Murphy and Governor Reagan, set her sights on a vacant
Congressional seat in San Mateo County, ten miles south of
San Francisco. Temple had the backing of the Republican
Party organization and all its fat-cat contributors.

A pack of no-names challenged her in the primary campaign, virtually assuring her success. Among them was a Menlo
Park lawyer who had never run for public office and whose
only political experience came from volunteer efforts in en-
vironmental battles. But Paul "Pete" McCloskey was smart
enough to get Sandy Weiner as his campaign consultant. In
addition to an ideological compatibility and their mutual
detestation of the Vietnam War, the two men simply liked each
other.

Polls showed a majority of Republicans supported the war.
But this Congressional race was a special election, which

meant voters could cross party lines and cast ballots for anyone they chose. In the end, that made the difference. "At that
time, Shirley Temple meant motherhood and God," Weiner
recalled. "The moment she announced she was running, reporters came here from all over the world and stayed the
entire six weeks writing stories. There was no doubt in anyone's mind that Shirley would win—except Pete's and mine."

Weiner's first move was to call a press conference and have
his candidate declare himself violently opposed to the Vietnam War, making that the key issue of the campaign. Gasps of
dismay arose from Republican regulars who felt McCloskey
had blown any future chances he may have had.

"That one move separated Pete from the mob," Weiner
explained. "And it brought in the strongest volunteer organization I have ever seen, then or since. People against the war
poured in from Stanford University—college professors, Democrats, students, you name it.

"The key was television. This was the first time anyone used
television for a local campaign in northern California. To buy
San Francisco air time for a campaign in San Mateo County
meant you were paying a price for covering five other counties
that could not vote for you. But Pete is terrific on the tube
and his looks turned it around. We cut the spots ourselves
over at KQED in San Francisco. Nothing fancy, just simple
pieces with McCloskey looking into the camera and speaking
straight. The entire media campaign consisted of five thirty-
second spots with Pete telling people why he was against the
war. The experts had predicted Temple would win by twenty
points. McCloskey won by twelve."

"Not every star can make it in politics," Weiner observed.
"Movie stars need to combat the feeling among voters that
they don't have the background or intelligence to hold public
office. People remembered Shirley Temple dancing and singing
'On the Good Ship Lollipop' and then they saw this neat,
well-dressed matron who was a mite too stuffy. She came off on
television as too cold and well-rehearsed. With George Murphy and Ronald Reagan, people were charmed and went away
saying 'Wow!' With Shirley, they just went away."

Those early "upsets" made Sandy Weiner an important

name in campaigning, and new business flowed in. In the 1970s, he took over the reins for San Francisco's Mayor Joe Alioto, under attack by national magazines as a *mafioso*, and beat the odds by getting him reelected. He managed the first black man into statewide office with California's Superintendent of Education Wilson Riles, and elected the first woman, Asian-American March Fong Eu, to be California's secretary of state.

Weiner is proud of his 87-percent-win record for over two hundred races. "Like football coaches, we're judged on our records," he points out. "Our standing may not be published in the *New York Times*, but the inner fraternity of political circles watches me and my peers. They know who is winning and losing over a period of time. Nobody wants to go with a loser, so if you're offered a candidate with no chance to win, why the hell do it? You have to balance what you gain in money against what you lose in reputation. Your reputation is the only thing that keeps people walking in that door."

The door he mentioned is to a second-floor suite on Jackson Street, a cobbled lane just off Chinatown, in downtown San Francisco. The neighborhood is filled with art galleries and antique stores. A glass door at street level has two neatly painted legends in small black letters: "John A. Hutton, Designs—Interiors" and below that "Weiner & Company." Wooden stairs lead to Weiner's two-room suite. His secretary sits behind a simple, polished desk in the reception room. A water cooler, a coffee machine, and metal files complete the Spartan furnishings. Two Uncle Sam "I Want You" recruiting posters point patriotic fingers at the new arrival.

Sandy Weiner's private office is no more impressive. He makes a point of being store-front and folksy. Bare bulbs hang from the ceiling. The message is that Weiner sells expertise, not glamor. On the wall to the right of his desk is a painting of the peace symbol of the 1960s. Behind Weiner, two posters of an Alaskan brown bear stare down at the visitor.

"Why the bears?" I asked.

"I just like them. Bears make me feel good." He lit his pipe and smiled enigmatically.

Weiner has a secret weapon—"overworry": "I'm a good enough professional to feel that if I lose, it's my fault. Any election should be won, if you do it right. I play every campaign as if I'm going to lose. I overworry problems to make sure I compensate for them. I know the other side will probably not do everything I've planned for them, but if they do, I've accounted for it. I'm rarely surprised."

Like most consultants, Weiner is a loner. He belongs to no religious group or social club. A McLuhanite, he believes in the power of television, uses it every chance he gets, and subjects all new clients to a screen test.

"We take a new candidate, sit him in front of a video-tape machine, and see how he and the camera interact. People look one way across my desk and another way on film. Most new people move their heads a lot or shift their eyes, which registers on camera as dishonesty. Eyes are the most important element. Whether someone is good-looking or homely, the public first looks at the eyes—how direct they are, how strong.

"When the public says 'I like that person' or 'I don't like him,' it's usually a question of trust. When you get a candidate with good eyes, you've got something going for you. Bad eyes, and you have a problem. Scoop Jackson is the perfect example. Scoop is a very credible human being, but he has a nervous twitch in both eyes which he can't help. When you see him on television, those eyes are always moving. It presents a terrible image problem for him. People think, 'Gee, that's a creepy fellow.' "

"What would you do if he were your client?" I asked.

"I'd have his eyes operated on," Weiner replied without hesitation.

Campaigners today resign themselves to the fact that Americans cannot be stirred up by "issues" as they once could. After Vietnam, Watergate, and Carter, campaign promises are looked on with more cynicism than in any other period of modern American history. Voters today are deaf to political oratory and vote largely out of anger and frustration.

"It's sad, like the end of adolescence," Weiner observed. "But it's realistic, it fits the country's diminished view of itself.

Today the most believable person wins, even if he says 'Sorry but there's not much I can do for you' or 'Don't expect too much.' The public would like to have a Churchill or an FDR, sure, but they're willing to settle for anyone who will do an honest job. But the honesty has to be real. People today can spot the guy whose language has been programmed."

In 1974 an obscure Chinese-American woman asked for Weiner's help. March Fong Eu had served in the state assembly with little distinction and now, at forty-seven, she sought the third highest office in California—secretary of state, the post that launched Jerry Brown into the governorship. Weiner figured Fong had little chance of winning. She was Oriental and a woman, and lacked the recognition necessary for a statewide race. Though she and her husband had money from business ventures and investments, they did not intend to spend much of it. On the other hand, Weiner admired March Fong's independent mind and the tough spirit that took her from a family laundry shop to a Stanford Ph.D. in education and a small personal fortune.

Running against her in the primary were some of the best-financed candidates in the state: Assemblyman Walter Karabian, feminist Cathy O'Neill (who had the backing of women's-rights groups), and Chicano activist Herman Sillas (who had the backing of liberals).

While Karabian and O'Neill had over $500,000 each to spend, Fong had set aside only $75,000 of her own savings for the primary battle. But after analyzing the challenge, Weiner thought he saw a way Fong could win. "It's hard to find an issue these days," he explained. "When candidates say 'I'm going to cure unemployment, cut taxes, and reduce crime,' voters say 'Sure you will!' and turn away. They just won't go for it. Everybody says that. So you look around for something besides tired issues like crime in the streets to focus on and ride with. When March Fong was an assemblywoman, she introduced a bill to eliminate the dime charge for public rest rooms. It never passed and nobody paid much attention to it. But I happened to be doing a statewide poll for somebody else at the time and I threw the idea of free toilets into the poll to see how people would react—and, boom! Tremendous."

With only $75,000 to spend, Weiner decided to put it all into daytime television. Research showed the biggest support for free toilets came from women over thirty-five, most of whom were home busily raising families. Women over thirty-five also vote more heavily than younger people. So Weiner bought time adjacent to daytime soap operas and game shows, watched by many of his target women and available at cheap local rates on small stations. He avoided the expensive markets in San Diego and Los Angeles, buying only from Bakersfield north through San Francisco.

"The strategy was to write off the south, where rates are highest and our two chief opponents had their strength. We did nothing down there and let our rivals spend their money fighting it out between them. There are enough votes in northern California to win any election, which everybody seems to forget."

The whole campaign centered on a single commercial, filmed in the ladies' room of San Francisco's international airport. It showed Fong, a tiny, middle-aged Chinese woman, standing next to a booth, saying, "While everybody talks about inflation, cutting budgets, and saving you millions of dollars, I'm going to talk to you about just one thing—saving you a dime to go to the toilet."

While Weiner's simple spot played repeatedly all through TV's soap-opera land, fellow professionals kept asking him, "Where's your campaign? You don't have any campaign!" His reply was a mysterious smile and a pull on his ever-present pipe.

Before the commercial, Fong polled a poor fourth in a field of five. After seven weeks of screening the pay-toilet spot, the June vote gave Walter Karabian 27 percent and feminist O'Neill 25 percent, whereas March Fong Eu surprised everybody except her strategist by winning 29 percent. In the general election she spent only $110,000, mostly to show the toilet commercial to southern Californians. This time she ran away with the race, amassing 3.4 million votes—a half million more than Jerry Brown's plurality in the governor's battle. In 1978 Fong, now renowned throughout California as the "Toilet Lady," was reelected secretary of state, again without spending much money.

"Which shows that if you give voters something they can believe, they'll buy it," Weiner concludes. "They can't swallow the lofty promises and high-faluting crap most candidates give them. Promise something small you can accomplish and they'll understand. Today, that's the meaningful issue."

The underdog challenge is what turns Weiner on most. He has a soft spot for minorities—racial, ethnic, or social—even though they are a threat to his 87-percent-win average. "There's still lots of prejudice in this country," he admits. "You have plenty of Archie Bunkerism to fight against. It's a big negative to run a black candidate, a Mexican-American, or a Jewish candidate in most places. In parts of northern California, the Southern states, and many big cities around the country, women are a very unpopular item. A woman candidate today will get from 12 to 15 percent more women voting for her than for a male candidate, but more men tend to vote against her, too. The country's come a long way, but biases are still strong.

"A few years back we elected the first black man as California's superintendent of education. Wilson Riles is a good-looking, intelligent, and gentle guy. But we knew it would be tough. Even the press was saying it couldn't be done. Up to then, if you had a black candidate you never put his face on a poster or brochure. You hid him or quietly hinted at the fact he was black and promoted his name instead. You kept him off television completely, did a lot in print and radio, and made him the invisible man. We changed all that with Wilson.

"We had his photo and face on everything—posters, billboards, literature, and particularly on television. We did dozens of commercials, put him into everybody's living room and dared people to look at him. Our narrator said, 'Study this man. Listen to what he has to say and the way he says it, then if you like him, vote for him.' We thought that would appeal to their sense of fairness and it did. It set a new trend for black candidates in California."

California, home of the initiative and referendum process, is exporting citizen power through Proposition 13–type lawmaking. As faith in professional politicians wavered, the California idea of grass-roots action has spread across the country and even into Europe. Because the initiative process has been a mainstay of California politics for over sixty years, the California consultant is often called to ply his talents elsewhere. In the spring of 1976 a group of New Jersey investors phoned Weiner and asked him to fly east. There he was to join forces with Joe Napolitan to try to bring Las Vegas to Atlantic City in the form of a proposed casino gambling initiative. Napolitan was to handle the polling and consult with Weiner. Since the two strategists were old friends and had worked together before with devastating efficiency, it promised to be an interesting time. Weiner was to be paid $10,000 a month for his efforts.

"With an initiative, you sell an idea instead of a person," Weiner notes. "Since an initiative has no true personality, you use different techniques." Two years earlier, the same casino gambling referendum had been rejected by a half million vote margin, despite the half million dollars spent by its sponsors. This time the sponsors brought in heavy-hitting professionals and gave them a budget of $1.2 million to do the job. Napolitan's research found tremendous fear in the citizens of New Jersey regarding the gambling question. Besides a small minority of churchgoers who saw it as a moral issue, the great majority were more worried about the people who would run it—"the mafia, bad men, crooks, and the Syndicate." Four months before the November election, 36 percent of the voters strongly opposed casino gambling, 29 percent favored it, and a third were undecided. Those undecideds, as in any political race, were the chief targets of the media campaign.

Going for the Weiner-Napolitan side was the sad fact that New Jersey had the highest unemployment rate in the nation, and Atlantic City the highest in the state. But those had also been the conditions two years before, when the proposition had lost badly. One peculiarity uncovered by research, however, was that New Jersey voters did not favor a "local option," by which any city or town in the state could choose to open its own casino when it liked. In fact, Jerseyites wanted no part of legalized gambling near their homes. But they might support it if it were confined to Atlantic City. That stipulation became the soul of the media message. Weiner created a slogan, "Help yourself, help New Jersey, help Atlantic City," while a shorter version reassured voters about quarantining the gambling: "Vote *yes* for casinos, Atlantic City only." The slogan was headlined in all campaign materials from posters and bumper stickers to billboards and television. Approximately $700,000 was spent for media, another $500,000 on get-out-the-vote drives.

The initiative won by 300,000 votes, mostly by taking two-thirds of the undecideds from the church-sponsored opposition. Weiner did not feel morally compromised in bringing gambling to New Jersey. He felt it was a question of personal choice, and that the extra employment and income was better in the hands of up-front legal operations than left to untaxable mob networks.

Unlike most professional consultants, however, Weiner feels responsible for people he helps elect to high positions: "I am very much responsible. My efforts help put them there."

During his twenty years in the business, he has watched a steady deterioration in the quality of candidates running for public office. He blames the press for this development: "All voters know about a candidate is what they see on television, hear on radio, or read in the paper. In that kind of system, the volunteer movement is less important and fewer people get to know the candidates. Things will get worse in the years ahead. Americans are terribly manipulated by the media. The most powerful people in the country are not the President or congressmen but the people who own the three national networks —ABC, CBS, and NBC. If you want to study power and influence, that is where you begin. On any given night Americans sit watching the news, and that is where they get their perceptions. Those perceptions are engineered totally by so-called 'news values,' somebody making a judgment that this is a good story and that is not.

"We even advise the decent person who thinks about running for office not to—'you take so much crap if you're elected.' Every reporter in this country is a junior Woodward or Bernstein who really doesn't care whether an official is doing a good job or bad job. All he's looking for is scandal. Reporters literally hide in the bushes in Washington and Sacramento, spying on people's nighttime activities. Which doesn't have a damn thing to do with job performance. Between federal disclosure laws, state laws, and pressure and scrutiny on the family, the right to privacy goes right out the window. This discourages good people from running. There are fewer issues these days, so most elections are a choice between the lesser of two evils. That's sad for the country.

"Somewhere along the line, the press and the media are going to have to realize they have a responsibility to produce something more than sensationalism. They have an obligation to project what's right about our system, instead of just blowing up what's wrong. Until that happens, the public is going to believe every politician is a crook and that there's no use in caring. The country is cynical."

A recent study supports Weiner's charges. Syracuse University political scientist Thomas Patterson analyzed how television campaign coverage affected voters in the 1976 Presidential campaign, then compared these voters to those in a pretelevision 1948 survey. In 1948 over half the news coverage concerned issues and leadership skills. Only 35 percent of the coverage described tactics and campaigning. In 1976 Dr. Patterson found these figures reversed, with half the news reports devoted to electioneering and only a third to issues.

When voters discussed the election without prompting, in 1948 two-thirds of the comments centered on the candidates' stands and qualifications, only a quarter on who was likely to win. In 1976, talk of odds dominated two-thirds of the spontaneous chatter. Patterson blamed television—and newspapers, to a lesser degree—for not focusing public attention on important campaign issues. His preliminary analysis of the

1980 race found "the same general pattern of providing the most coverage to the maneuvering of candidates."

ABC Television executive Hal Bruno, the network's director of political coverage, points the finger of blame at our extended primary system: "The party leaders have created a monster with the primaries. It's a monster in which organizational skill and the ability to manipulate the media and imagery have become more important qualifications in a candidate than wisdom, experience, and judgment. We do not always get the best man."

Sanford Weiner worries about the future of American democracy: "Media has become the whole ball game in campaigns, as opposed to organization, volunteers, and people stirring things up on the streets. Consultants are part of that process. If I'm representing a candidate, I'm only going to show his good side and have him say things on television geared to winning votes. That's manipulation which is necessary to win elections. The public is cynical and apathetic because of it. I'm enough a part of the system to know that the networks are not held morally accountable," he concludes. "It's up to them. I respect power, but I also fear it. In this case, I fear it more than I respect it."

The Fraternity
of Heavy Hitters

14

In December 1978 forty-two men and women gathered in the conference room of the Hyde Park Hotel in Knightsbridge, an elegant district in London just south of the famous park. They were there for the annual three-day meeting of the International Association of Political Consultants, an elite club with representatives from five continents.

Among those seated at the tables were Peter Radunski, strategist for West Germany's Christian Democratic Party; José Sanchis, adviser to Spain's Prime Minister Adolfo Suarez; Gordon Reece, a television producer from England then handling media for future Tory Prime Minister Margaret Thatcher; and Michel Bongrand of France, who managed Prime Minister Raymond Barre's return to power in 1978 and who, together with America's Joe Napolitan, cofounded the IAPC in 1968.

On the agenda for discussion were the upcoming British and European parliamentary elections later in the year, the 1980 Presidential election in the United States, Latin American campaigns in 1978, the new French election laws on political strategies in that country, and as always, the latest developments in public opinion polling and media techniques. The keynote speaker was U.S. Senator George McGovern, who flew in from Angola the night before to talk about the political practices of the African nations he had just visited.

The International Association was created a few months

before its American counterpart; Joe Napolitan was responsible for both. In the late 1960s, political consultants had bad
press in the United States and England, though they had a
more respectable reputation in other Western European countries. The Anglo-Saxon temperament publicly condemns political manipulation, but privately extols its most adept practi-
tioners. Joe Napolitan and his partner F. Clifton White
decided to fight back against the ugly "image maker" label
pinned on their industry by the popular press. Immediately
after the Humphrey/Nixon race of 1968, the International
Association convened its charter members and held the first
meeting. Every year the three-day convention meets at a
different site in Europe, and every fourth year in the United
States to coincide with the Presidential election.

In January 1969, a few months after the Paris get-together,
Napolitan invited the top American campaign consultants to
the Plaza Hotel in New York, to form the American Association of Political Consultants. About fifty people showed up.

After some heated argument, they agreed on strict qualifications for membership. Only full-time professionals who managed campaigns for a living would be eligible for full membership, but those who provide specialized services to campaigns
—pollsters, film makers, mail firms, and academic analysts—
could become associates. Later, some would be accepted as full
members.

By the end of the first year, there were sixty full members.
By 1980, that number had grown to about two hundred plus
an equal number of associates. The group now publishes a
bimonthly newsletter and organizes two seminars a year, attended by both politicians and consultants. Presentations concentrate on fund raising, polling, computer innovations, and
trends in political television.

Although there are more than one thousand people around
the country selling their skills to candidates for public office,
the Association limits its recruiting to those who have won
their spurs in battle—the "comers" and big-name "heavy hitters," as Napolitan calls them. "The good people in this industry are bright, politically aware individuals with the

ability to make decisions," he explains. "They work long hours, travel constantly, understand the media, and most of all know how to find top-flight specialists and use them in all facets of political communications."

Some consultant superstars belong to both the American and International Associations, often working campaigns in languages they don't understand. Joe Napolitan may be even better known abroad than in the United States. One afternoon in 1972, he got a call from the representative of Carlos Andrés Pérez of Venezuela. Pérez, who was minister of the interior during the 1960s, had gained a "tough cop" reputation by putting down guerrilla uprisings bankrolled by Fidel Castro. Now the Accion Democratica Party candidate for president, Pérez feared he had an image problem and hoped Napolitan and his associate Clif White could solve it. The challenge was intriguing, so Napolitan and White agreed to help. They opened an office in Caracas, hired local talent and translators, then ran polls to see where their candidate stood. The research confirmed that Pérez was known as a harsh guerrilla fighter.

To soften the public myth, Napolitan and White suggested that Pérez make contact with ordinary Venezuelans and talk to them. Their recommendation was that Pérez "walk the villages"—literally cross the country on a walking tour to meet with common people so as to dispel his dark reputation and promote the image of a vigorous young man suited to lead a vigorous young nation. His campaign theme "The Man Who Walked," was used in posters, literature, and television commercials. Starting from a losing position, out of a field of fourteen candidates Pérez ended up winning almost 50 percent of the votes, and the presidency.

Napolitan feels the only difference between doing campaigns in America and overseas, apart from language, is the restrictions on the media in some foreign countries, particularly in Europe. "Television and radio are state-controlled in some places," he notes. "The state limits the time you can be on the air and makes stringent conditions on how that time can be used. In France, for example, a candidate has to sit at a desk, and the only prop allowed is a bowl of flowers. So you can't go out and hire a top-flight producer to make glamorous television or radio spots.

"Your sense of pace is dictated by the government, not by your own strategy. In lots of campaigns we've been able to start television in spurts six months before the election; in others we've had to wait until ten or twelve days before the voting to run our television. In those countries you put a lot more emphasis on visual materials—posters, signs, pamphlets, brochures.

"You don't have the instant media access in Europe that you have in the United States, although in most of those countries political broadcasts are watched more attentively than they are here. In Great Britain, if Margaret Thatcher were going to speak, people would make a special effort to watch her ten-minute talk. Here they would complain because *Mork and Mindy* was canceled."

In 1974 Napolitan helped elect Valéry Giscard d'Estaing president of France, and has worked numerous campaigns in the European Economic Community elections. He has had to swear secrecy, since there is great public sensitivity toward candidates who import top American consultants. In Venezuela President Pérez was prohibited by law from succeeding himself, so in 1978 his Democratic Action Party chose Luis Piñúera Ordaz as his successor and hired Joe Napolitan and Clif White to run the campaign. Piñúera's chief challenger, Luis Herrera Campins, called in David Garth from New York to plot his moves. As is typical in such contests, where the obvious is neutralized by the skills of both sides, small things made the big difference.

Piñúera, as "heir apparent," suffered terminal overconfidence when Napolitan's early polls showed him comfortably ahead. "He acted as though the campaign was just something to be endured en route to his coronation," Napolitan recalled. "He didn't understand that a campaign ends on election day and refused to let us do what we needed to do—go after our opponent. The good campaign Garth ran had something to do with the outcome, too. Our television theme for Piñúera—*Correcto*—means not only 'That's correct' but also 'Okay.' So

Garth picked up on it, pointed out little problems with our candidate and party, then played off our theme in their television commercials by saying *No esta correcto*. He picked up a lot of points that way."

Just one of those points determined the outcome. Garth and Campins beat Napolitan and Piñúera by 45 to 44 percent of the vote. For Garth, it was a *correcto* campaign. But little competitive rancor exists between professional consultants: back in New York a few weeks later, Garth called Napolitan and asked if he could come by and talk.

Napolitan had set up a communications program for the Pérez regime, doing periodic polling to find out how the government was perceived, which policies were working, which were not, and which information techniques were most effectively getting the Pérez message across to Venezuelans. In brief, he was fine-tuning a government to its people. Now Garth had been asked to do the same job for the victorious Luis Campins. Would Napolitan fill him in on the old program? "Sure," Napolitan replied. He spent the next three hours with David Garth that night going over old research reports, explaining what worked, what didn't, and why. "We're all good friends in this business," Napolitan observes. "The guy you're fighting against today may be the guy you're working with tomorrow. And there are no real secrets in consulting, anyway."

New members are added to the Association every year, reflecting the increasing importance of consultants in every level of political campaigning. Some are protégés of the consultant superstars; others appear on the scene as if from nowhere, bypassing the usual apprenticeship process.

In the past few years, a score of firms established in the 1970s have made it big on the campaign front. Two California firms illustrate the different ways the new consultants acquire power. In 1971 Woodward, McDowell & Larson in San Francisco was born, the brainchild of two men trained in the Spencer-Roberts organization. Jack McDowell, the senior member, had received a Pulitzer Prize in journalism. He worked for fourteen years as a Sacramento political editor and learned the inner workings of government and the way media interacts with it. In 1969 Stu Spencer hired him as Ronald Reagan's press spokesman in his reelection campaign for governor of California. Dick Woodward had worked for Spencer since 1964 and was sent north to manage the firm's San Francisco office. There he and McDowell met and decided to form a partnership.

The first few years were lean ones. Woodward and Mc-Dowell handled minor assignments for the state Republican Party and worked a few corporate accounts. They lost several small races, won some, and then took on a long-shot in 1976 when they agreed to manage Sam Hayakawa's U.S. Senate try against incumbent John Tunney. Tunney's campaign was being managed by New York's David Garth, who had first come west a few years earlier to elect Tom Bradley the first black mayor in Los Angeles history. With Garth as their adversary, the fledgling Woodward & McDowell team, along with their aging candidate, was given little chance of winning.

But in 1976 America elected a peanut wholesaler President. Californians and most other Americans were mad as hell at the whole Washington establishment, which included John Tunney, the laid-back, Eastern-educated son of a famous boxing champion. Woodward hired another Stu Spencer alumnus, Dick Wirthlin of DMI in Santa Ana, to do his research. Polls found that Californians strongly linked Tunney to Washington and a federal bureaucracy seen as out of control and antagonistic to the people it was intended to serve. Tunney himself was perceived as "indecisive," with no clear pattern in his voting record. His easy manner was interpreted as a lack of caring, even laziness, by many people.

The upstart consultants matched this image against that of their feisty little semantics professor, who had defied campus radicals as president of San Francisco State University, and on that rock they based their strategy and media. The campaign hit hard at Tunney's ties to the Washington establishment, promising to bring "common sense to government." Since Tunney was seen as "indecisive," the challenger branded him "Senator Flip-Flop," and commercials attacked Tunney's lack of concern for home-state constituents.

"One thing was clear from the research," Dick Woodward said. "People were totally alienated from government. They felt nobody was listening to them." So Hayakawa's campaign offered people a willing ear. Hal Larson, who writes political ads for the firm, produced a series of radio commercials which invited listeners to write Hayakawa and tell him what they wanted him to do when he got to Washington. Over 4,000 people took him up on it, many of them enclosing unsolicited checks. "We were establishing a dialogue with the electorate," Woodward explained. "Hayakawa had a good image going in, and we wanted to enhance that—what they call the 'halo effect' in advertising."

Equally effective were attacks against Tunney, the traditional tactic of a challenger trying to soften the power of incumbency. Television spots accused Tunney of "not caring about the people of California" and praised Hayakawa as a "caring, concerned, strong leader who knows where he stands and is not afraid to speak out." One particularly effective series criticized Tunney's record of "absenteeism" in Senate activity.

Tunney complained bitterly about the charges: "They picked a thirty-day period to use in their ads, and portrayed that as representing my entire six-year term. In fact, I had one of the best attendance records in the entire Senate. They ran an exceedingly clever campaign, giving people what they want —a stress on negatives and a little bloodletting. Only in California could you get away with that, because only here do you need such enormous amounts of money to counteract such deceptive claims."

Woodward and McDowell spent over $600,000 for television and radio alone, earning a modest $80,000 in fees for managing both the primary and general-election campaigns. Garth spent an equal amount on Tunney's behalf.

Early in their planning, Woodward and McDowell considered making commercials using news footage of Hayakawa ripping out the sound system of the radical students at San Francisco State, but they had second thoughts and held back. McDowell's understanding of media prevailed. "The public had a fragile impression of that event," Woodward explained. "We felt if we played too much on it, it could backfire. We also expected the television stations would run some of that footage on their own the last few weeks of the campaign—which they did."

Going into the last week, Hayakawa enjoyed a twelve-point lead in the polls. It looked like the new consultancy team would pull off a big one. Then, on October 27, their inexperienced candidate participated in a debate. In reply to a question on South Africa, the impetuous Hayakawa waved a war banner. He suggested sending American soldiers overseas to prevent a potential bloodbath. Tunney played it smart and safe, talking about moral persuasion and diplomacy to moderate the crisis.

Immediately following the taped debate, Hayakawa compounded his error by telling a news conference more about his views on foreign policy: "I would hope to encourage insurrection in Hungary, Poland, Latvia, Lithuania, Estonia, or Tibet, for that matter—those poor crushed nations that have been under Communist tyranny all these years!" For a nation recuperating from a disastrous decade of fighting in Southeast Asia, the effect was like throwing a soggy sponge on a barbecue. Wirthlin's polls found an instant decline in Hayakawa's ratings. From a twelve-point lead on Thursday, he fell to a nine-point deficit on Friday. By Saturday, Tunney led by 12 percent.

Woodward and McDowell decided on a desperation move: they would juggle their poll results to show their man still ahead. The firm sent out a press release indicating Hayakawa leading Tunney by 3 percent, a figure dutifully reported by the daily press and TV news shows. Later they justified the release by explaining that the 3-percent margin came from averaging the daily ratings for the entire week of October 24–29; they didn't lie, they just didn't tell the whole truth.

Woodward defended the tactic: "The trend was in the wrong direction. We were all set to run away with the goddam thing, and all of a sudden here comes Africa. Our first concern was to put a tourniquet on that issue and get back to normalcy."

They instructed Hayakawa to stop adlibbing foreign policy and get back to hitting on Tunney. Their poll report showing Hayakawa a winner offset the momentum of the other readings reporting the Tunney surge correctly. Finally, the heavy schedule of Hayakawa TV and radio commercials began to heal the damage and close the gap. The day before the election, Wirthlin's surveys found Hayakawa behind by 2 percent, and with momentum moving his way.

The final poll—the only one that counted: election day, November 2—found that 7.2 million Californians had voted. Tunney got 48.4 percent of them and Hayakawa 51.6 percent. At seventy the outspoken college professor had become a U.S. senator. Woodward, McDowell & Larson were a "hot" firm.

In 1978 they scored another upset, in New Hampshire, dislodging long-term incumbent Sen. Tom McIntyre with the right-wing Republican Gordon Humphrey, an airplane pilot. They won in Texas that same year, replacing Congressman Bob Gammage with the low-rated physician Ron Paul, using their time-tested theme of "big bad government" combined with assaults on the opponent's "absenteeism and flip-flop voting record."

The firm's most interesting battle was a 1978 California smoking referendum, matching enormous cigarette money against a meagerly funded "clean air" group with Hollywood stars as spokespeople. The issue was Proposition 5 on the ballot: "The Clean Indoor Air Initiative." The proposition aimed to regulate smoking in enclosed public buildings. In work places, special smoking lounges would be required. Outright smoking bans would be in effect at jazz concerts and in airplanes, but not at rock concerts or in bars.

A full year before the vote, Woodward, McDowell & Larson were contacted by the Tobacco Institute and asked to defeat the measure. The price was right and the challenge interesting. Their first move was to hire a research firm called The Public Sector, specialists in motivational analysis, who did focus group interviews with several batches of representative Californians. The psychologists encouraged people to speak freely about smoking, government regulation in general, and

California government specifically. The dialogue was taped and the researchers analyzed the words participants used to discuss issues, the degree of emotion involved, and which arguments seemed most effective in persuading people to one point of view or the other. Their report formed the basis of campaign strategy, advertising, and even the language used in literature and copy. It was determined that Californians were bothered over growing government power, influence, and intrusion into their daily lives. There was a widespread belief that politicians were getting out of control.

The consultants gave Proposition 5 a new name—the "antismoking" initiative. Not only was it shorter, easier to say, and easier to understand, but it also "changed the battleground," according to Woodward. By calling the proposition an "antismoking" instead of a "clean indoor air" initiative, the consultants switched the premise from positive benefit (clean air) to negative authority (antismoking). Broadening their own tobacco-financed campaign by calling it "Californians for Common Sense," the firm created a letterhead organization and used it to issue press releases and solicit outside contributions.

Drawing on the study findings, Hal Larson produced scripts using words directly out of the mouths of the participants. Because this initiative was seen as relatively unimportant among the other issues on the ballot, Larson used humor to make his points. The advertising campaign ran in three stages over four months. The theme of the first wave of commercials was "They're at it again," focusing attention on how government bureaucrats meddle in the lives of ordinary people. Stage two advertising asked, "What will they regulate next?" It spelled out the initiative in more detail, using actors to dramatize the hardships people would face if the measure passed. In one spot a policeman complained how he would have to spend all his time arresting smokers, in another a city editor was shown on the telephone explaining problems with the legislation as written. During the final weeks, phase-three advertising urged voters to "read the fine print." Copy analyzed the actual language of the proposition and asked people to write in for a free copy of the ballot measure; over

100,000 did. The firm also enlisted the support of organized labor and business, and both the Republican and Democratic parties. All provided lists and manpower for direct-mail efforts to defeat the measure.

The opposition "Clean Air Coalition"—made up of educational, health, and environment groups including the state PTA, the Cancer Society, and the Lung Association—recruited film stars as spokespeople. Charlton Heston, Gregory Peck, Ted Knight, Cornel Wilde, and Lena Horne were among the dozens of celebrities who cut radio and television spots urging a "yes" vote on Proposition 5.

In the end, the special golden rule prevailed. Woodward, McDowell & Larson had the money to saturate the airwaves, but their opponents did not. The "Common Sense" committee spent $6.2 million, setting a California record for an initiative. The money came almost exclusively from four cigarette manufacturers—$2.4 million from R. J. Reynolds, $1.9 million from Phillip Morris, $1.2 million from Brown & Williamson, and $650,000 from Lorillard. The "Clean Air" campaign raised only $650,000 and was able to air their star-studded commercials only during the last two weeks. By that time, the damage had been done.

Polls conducted in August by the *Los Angeles Times* showed Proposition 5 winning 53 to 41 percent. By the end of September it had turned around; it was 53 to 43 percent against. The final vote was 54 to 46 percent against. Not only had Woodward, McDowell & Larson confirmed its place in the big time, it had also earned $500,000 in profits from the fight.

A year later, in 1979, the tobacco people asked them to repeat the job in Dade County, Florida. They got a $1-million budget against another poorly financed rival, but the results were much closer. Out of 192,000 ballots cast, the antismoking referendum lost by just 822 votes. The golden rule need not necessarily apply, and unless Woodward, McDowell & Larson can pull some new magic out of their hats for the 1980s, it appears the Clean Air proponents will one day come out on top.

Another consulting organization of the 1970s, the Butcher &

Forde combine, was hatched further south in Newport Beach, California. Specializing in computerized mail blitzes, the consultancy is considered "tough and hard-hitting" by its supporters, "factually misleading" by opponents. One fact is not disputed: when they take on a campaign, they almost always win.

Arnold Forde, age forty-three, is an ex-realtor who did volunteer jobs for the Orange County Democrats to prepare himself for a career as a politician, dreaming of Congress and higher positions. Along the way he began running successful campaigns for others and getting paid for it.

One of the young professionals he encountered was Bill Butcher, a thirty-eight-year-old direct-mail expert whose explosive copy and innovative style had helped beat some of Forde's best candidates. Butcher was a political prodigy who worked his first campaign as a fourteen-year-old volunteer and when he was seventeen managed a candidate. The candidate lost, but politics won his heart. After getting a degree in geography from California State University at Long Beach, he opened his own business featuring computerized telegrams, letters, and mailers.

Forde set up a meeting with Butcher and suggested they join forces. Butcher's first reaction was negative—"Arnold and I fervently disliked each other," he explained—but his loathing turned to respect. In 1970 he disbanded his own operation to launch Butcher & Forde.

Like any new consultancy, they were unknown outside the small circle of southern California politicos. They took whatever work they could get, mostly low-budget campaigns for city council or state assembly, supplemented by business accounts. Soon they had a reputation for running tough campaigns that sometimes hit below the belt. They were charged with "distortion" by the state Fair Political Practices Commission, as well as with using "ringers" in primary races to benefit their candidates by pulling away votes from opponents. Such accusations didn't hurt their standing. In politics, winning excuses a multitude of sins.

As their win record approached 90 percent, inquiries came

in from better-known politicians. In 1978 they managed successful efforts for California Assemblyman Ross Johnson and State Senator John Schmitz, an abrasive member of the John Birch Society who made a short-lived Presidential bid in 1976. They had losing campaigns for Democratic hopeful Penny Raven, running for lieutenant governor, and Republican gubernatorial aspirant John Briggs. But their coup, the campaign that brought them not only national stature but several hundred thousand dollars in fees and commissions, was a one-hundred-day television, radio, and direct-mail blitz they conducted on behalf of the now legendary Howard Jarvis and his Proposition 13 taxpayers' revolt.

The real story of Proposition 13 dates from the early 1960s. Howard Jarvis, a sixty-year-old retired publisher and manufacturer, had lots of money and a passionate distaste for government tax burdens. In 1962 he ran for the U.S. Senate, driving around southern California in a converted bread truck and preaching tax cuts. Ridiculed by occasional *Los Angeles Times* stories, Jarvis was taken lightly by almost everyone. When he lost badly in the primary, he announced plans to retire to the Bahamas. Instead, he got involved in a small tax-reform movement which he soon headed.

Called the United Organization of Taxpayers, the group consisted of several dozen hard-core believers determined to use California's initiative process to bypass politicians and install their own tax-limitation laws. But the attention Jarvis and his band of followers generated consisted mainly of contemptuous two-paragraph jokes in the *Times* metropolitan section, and handfuls of listeners at the lectures they gave in church basements and retirement homes. Jarvis did, however, get the attention of George Putnam, a respected television and radio news commentator, who frequently invited him to air his cantankerous views on Putnam's top-rated ten o'clock television news show.

Jarvis, battling tough odds, was indomitable. Since 1911, when Governor Hiram Johnson established the initiative process for Californians to pass their own laws, only 148 initiatives had ever been proposed of which only 26 got on the

ballot and a scant 7 were ultimately approved by a majority of
voters. Most of the difficulty came from the stipulation that to
qualify a proposal, petitioners needed to get signatures from 8
percent of the total vote in the past governor's election; in
modern years, that has averaged 6 million ballots, requiring
half a million valid signatures. In 1968 Jarvis made his first
try, but managed to get only 100,000 endorsements. In 1971 a
second attempt did much better, but still lacked 100,000 names.
Frequent appearances on the Putnam show were making him
a cult figure in southern California, so when he made his third
try in 1976, he fell only 10,000 signatures short. Feeling victory
in his grasp, he launched his fourth drive in October 1976.

The Los Angeles mayoralty race was scheduled for April
1977. Jarvis paid his filing fee, announced he was a candidate,
and used the campaign to stump for his tax-reform beliefs.
While the *Times* continued its policy of ridicule and damna-
tion by silence, George Putnam made his daily radio show on
KIEV a forum for the Jarvis crusade. Putnam's show updates
the news, interviews politicians and newsmakers across the
country, and features a "talk back" segment that encourages
listeners to participate in a no-holds-barred "town meeting" on
the air. With the rambunctious Jarvis firing unpredictable
verbal blasts at all callers, his fame grew along with the credibility he acquired from the on-air endorsements of George
Putnam.

In April his petitions were counted. Jarvis had gathered
498,500 signatures—1,400 shy of victory. As he noted, "We
were so discouraged we didn't start another petition drive
until the next day." Linking forces with Paul Gann in northern California, Jarvis began circulating petitions by mail in
July 1977. This time, he had an estimated 30,000 volunteers
haunting supermarket parking lots for support. By the December 2 deadline, over 1.2 million signatures had been
counted, with another 300,000 still in the mail pouches.

The moment Proposition 13 became an issue, the forces of
government and media closed ranks to kill it. The only major
newspaper in the state that supported it was the upstart *Los
Angeles Herald Examiner*. Teachers' organizations recruited
youngsters to picket against predicted educational cutbacks.

The Los Angeles School Board mailed notices to 21,000 teachers warning that if Proposition 13 passed, they might be fired. Gov. Jerry Brown immediately signed a law to phase out a business inventory tax, which would go into effect only if Proposition 13 were defeated.

The governor's father, Pat Brown, wrote a letter to define the issue which was reprinted in every newspaper in California. One line read: "If I were a Communist who wanted to destroy this country, I would support the Jarvis amendment." Willie Brown, chairman of the state Assembly Revenue and Taxation Committee, threatened to reward or punish California cities on the basis of how they voted on the initiative. Even the UCLA Graduate School of Management got into the act, releasing a "study" that showed how passage of Proposition 13 would double the unemployment rate and throw half a million workers on the breadline.

The *Los Angeles Times* maintained that if Jarvis-Gann succeeded, "Los Angeles County would eliminate all fire department paramedic units and close half its fire stations. It would close half the county's 93 libraries; 30,000 county employees would be laid off; 2,152 police officers would be dismissed, and 6 stations closed; 1,000 firefighters would be cut, and 56 stations shut down. More than 18,000 teachers would be laid off, class sizes would increase, and many pupils would go on half-day sessions."

Despite the post-Watergate anger of the electorate, the massive organized opposition and the amateurish campaigning of Jarvis and Gann made the passage of Proposition 13 doubtful. Three months before the June 6 election, polls showed a third of the voters in favor, a third against, and a third undecided. The undecideds would be won by the side with the best media. That was when Arnold Forde and Bill Butcher heard that Jarvis had no professional help. They visited him at his Los Angeles storefront, and offered their services. Since the funds to pay them would come from money that the consultants themselves would raise through direct mail, it was an offer that businessman Howard Jarvis was smart enough to grab.

Butcher & Forde's first move was to create a direct-mail

piece, housed in an official-looking envelope with red print reading: "Your 1978 Property Tax Increase Statement Enclosed —Response Required." A computer letter inside urged the recipient to contribute to the "Yes on 13" campaign, giving as a return address only the name Howard Jarvis. Almost $2 million poured in—money the consultants would spend on television and radio commercials aimed at the large block of "undecideds."

Their biggest problem was that many organized groups were against the initiative—unions, teachers, government, media, business.

"We didn't have one single group to count on," Butcher recalled. "So we realized early on that it would be a battle of fear against anger. If the fear was too great—that police, fire, and school services would be cut—we'd lose. But if we could get them going on anger—taxes skyrocketing, politicians holding back information—then we'd win."

Howard Jarvis wanted to stay in the background, sharing his spokesperson role with Paul Gann and others. His consultants insisted that the best strategy was to identify the cause with Jarvis. People needed a focus: Jarvis and Proposition 13 should be indistinguishable. One problem with such an identification was the kooky image that the *Los Angeles Times* and other media had given Jarvis by constant ridicule and frivolous coverage. A large number of people perceived Howard Jarvis as an irascible curmudgeon, irresponsible and totally unqualified to sponsor such an important tax measure.

Butcher & Forde produced a thirty-second commercial to offset that image. It showed Jarvis seated at his desk with books behind him, explaining in a straightforward manner what Proposition 13 was, what it would do, and why it was needed. The spot closed on two main points that formed the tag lines for all Proposition 13 advertising: "Cut property taxes two-thirds!" and "Show the politicians who's boss!" This first effort did two things: it stimulated contributions from ongoing mail appeals, and it began nudging the poll numbers their way.

A second commercial capitalized on the one big break they solicited—endorsement by a credible tax expert. At that moment, no one in California was as credible as Stanford University's professor Milton Friedman, who had just won a Nobel Prize in economics. Butcher badgered Friedman about Proposition 13 and finally persuaded him to help. They cut a spot showing a full head shot of the economist's gentle, round face with a legend reading, "Nobel Prizewinning Economist." The copy consisted of Friedman's own words, edited for time needs, explaining in calm, dispassionate terms exactly what the initiative would and would not do for the people of California. His endorsement gave Jarvis respectability and gave the campaign an enormous boost among well-educated upper-middle-class voters.

Polls showed an instant surge after the commercial ran, pulled mostly from the shrinking undecided column. With momentum coming their way, the strategists decided it was time to move from a position of patching up negatives to emphasizing strong points. "Our strengths focused on two ideas," Butcher explained. "One, everyone wanted to cut taxes. Two, everyone wanted to kick politicians in the slats."

A pair of television commercials was created to dramatize these goals. The first featured world-famous tourist attractions from the Eiffel Tower to the balmy beaches of Waikiki while a voice-over droned: "Each year California politicians go on expensive junkets all over the world, spending your money and having good times. Show the politicians who's boss, vote yes on 13."

As their paid media provoked support, Butcher & Forde's imaginative campaigning produced an unexpected coup. They called and wrote county assessors' offices all over California, demanding estimates of property tax assessments for the coming year. They assumed there would be no replies and intended to charge the government bureaucrats with hiding information from the people, but the Los Angeles assessor sent back his predictions, showing large property tax increases. "It turned out better than our wildest dreams," Forde enthused. "Survey results showed the worry over 13 went way down."

On June 6, 1978—what Jarvis termed the "Second D-Day" —California voters gave Proposition 13 its enormous victory. Out of 6.6 million votes cast, 4.3 million voted yes on 13—almost two-thirds of the electorate. Butcher & Forde had won a sensational victory and, in the process, helped turn Howard Jarvis into an international legend.

But the full members of the Association of Political Consultants are not the only successful members. The associate members are often direct-mail men, whose firms effectively promote candidates and raise money through targeted mailings to people identified by research as particularly vulnerable. The two biggest men in this business are Morris Dees of Montgomery, Alabama, and Richard Vigurie of Falls Church, Virginia. Dees works exclusively for liberals, Vigurie for conservatives. Both compile lists of Americans predisposed toward ideological extremes, culling "their people" from magazine circulation inventories, charity rolls, union memberships, church groups, and mail-order houses. "There are only two mail-donating segments in our society," Dees notes. "The right fringe and the left fringe."

Dees acquired his wealth by building his own mail-order sales empire. Involved in civil rights causes in the 1960s, he came to political fame by turning $3 million of George McGovern's 1972 Presidential war chest into $20 million through mail blitzes. In 1974 Jimmy Carter recruited Dees to raise funds for his 1976 Presidential race. In the process, both discovered that when it came to raising money, Southern pride was not nearly so lucrative as McGovern's antiwar liberalism. Carter had to borrow money from family and friends before the nomination. Afterward, for campaigning he could use taxpayer money instead of his own.

That same year, Richard Vigurie raised much more money for George Wallace's quixotic candidacy, proving that persistence in the pursuit of direct-mail dollars guarantees success. In 1974 and 1975 Vigurie needed only eighteen months to raise $2 million, which matched what he had spent on postage and production. In the language of his specialty, he was "prospecting"—testing lists, copy, and formats, identifying reliable givers, and weaning out the fainthearted to create a master list of 600,000 names.

With this refined roster he raised another $7 million for

Wallace and earned an estimated $2 million for his own pains. Using a technique borrowed from evangelist fund raising, Vigurie sent out monthly newsletters full of items reporting the bantam Alabaman's latest forays against the "pointy heads" and "bleeding heart liberals" ruining the nation. Collection envelopes carried a date when the faithful's tithes would be "urgently needed," and a fastidious computer kept watch, recording names, dates, and sums received. In today's political campaigns, direct-mail solicitations are crucial because of laws governing federal matching funds.

Simple gimmicks, determined by computer analysis, assure Vigurie higher returns for his dollar. His envelopes always carry "live postage," pasted stamps instead of metered print. When the stamp is glued on crooked, returns are greater than when straight. Even when a signature is obviously printed, it always raises more money in blue ink than black. Pages using postcripts enjoy a richer harvest, so Vigurie uses two or three PSs in a single letter.

Vigurie, a mild-looking man in his forties, is thoughtful, brainy, and dedicated to his beliefs. He dresses conservatively, has thinning hair and a diffident manner. He traces his conservative politics clear back to childhood, when, as an eight-year-old growing up in a Houston suburb, he dreamed of becoming powerful enough to "help the Indians." When asked about this apparent contradiction with the conservative image, he quickly points out that "compassion is not the exclusive domain of liberals even if they would have you believe that."

Stored in his files are some thirty-five hundred computer tapes containing the names and characteristics of over 20 million Americans likely to contribute to conservative Christian evangelical causes. Last year he mailed off more than 110 million postal pitches for his clients. These included several gun lobbies, among them the Sacramento-based Gun Owners of America and the Washington, D.C.–based National Rifle Association. Vigurie is heavy on "New Right" evangelists, boasting among his clients Rev. Robert Schuller of Garden Grove, California, Norman Vincent Peale of New York, and Jerry Falwell of Lynchburg, Virginia, of *Old Time Gospel*

Hour fame. His work in mobilizing evangelicals and other single-issue groups is credited with helping Ronald Reagan win the Presidency, and other conservatives win Congressional seats in 1980.

Recently Vigurie was instrumental in raising $3 million for the Christian Voice Group of Pasadena. This organization lobbies out of its Washington, D.C., office against abortion, television sex and violence, homosexual rights, and antidiscrimination laws aimed at Christian schools. It works to elect conservative Christian candidates and to defeat liberal incumbents, using the electronic church—the cable, satellite, and UHF television networks that feature such shows as the *700 Club* and *Praise the Lord*—and with literature regularly sent to the Vigurie-maintained lists of the faithful.

Direct-mail emotions that work best for political causes are anger, fear, or a guilty conscience. Letters that pull the most generous returns are those that identify the enemy in human terms: "raving radicals," "long-haired rapists," and "flag-waving reactionaries." Women are the best targets for fund-raising appeals, particularly on antiabortion and religious issues. Men respond most to gun lobbies and militant political messages. In both cases, people that give once are likely to give twice, three times, ten times. The reservoir of guilt and suppressed emotion that has triggered a payoff the first time is vulnerable to the same appeals over and over again.

Vigurie explains that he became a direct-mail specialist after realizing that the establishment media effectively blocked off any fair hearing for conservative ideas and spokespeople, either ignoring them or showering them with abuse and ridicule. So in 1965, after a three-year apprenticeship with Marvin Liebman's PR firm in New York as an account executive to the Young Americans for Freedom organization, Vigurie opened up his own shop with four hundred dollars and a determination to bypass mass media with direct mail targeted to likeminded Americans.

Vigurie, Dees, and the other mail experts have zeroed in on the single-issue groups that have blossomed in the last few years to fill the vacuum created by the erosion of political parties. Vigurie's focus on emotion-packed causes has prompted his liberal opposition to nickname his company the "fear-of-the-month-club." Robert Strauss, Jimmy Carter's political adviser, noted that the Left had only one weapon it could use to combat the fear tactics of the other side—namely, "fear of the Right."

The battle lines are drawn, and it promises to be a fight to the finish. According to Richard Vigurie, the final Armageddon between the Left and the Right will take place in 1984.

15

The Future of American Democracy

Approaching the twenty-first century, America will come to grips with political trends set in motion over the past twenty years. The way we respond to the political situation is crucial to our democracy.

America will grow older and more conservative. The biggest earners and spenders, aged twenty-five to fifty, will surge to 38 percent of the population. The percentage of older people will also increase. The big decline will be in young people, particularly teen-agers. That means crime will decline dramatically, since juveniles commit most of it. There will be cutbacks in tax monies spent for education.

In the 1980s there will be a resurrection of American military power. On the international scene, terrorism will intensify as have-not nations plot new horrors, helped by malcontent American rebels in the name of "oppressed peoples." The Communist movement will grow more aggressive. Pressures on capitalist countries will increase until "dealing with communism" becomes an important means of defining candidates for national office.

Inexpensive home computers and cable-television grids will connect many of us to central studios where two-way communications will let us shop and order films, news files, and research material over the air. American homes will be linked to electronic town meetings simply by pressing a few buttons on the television console.

As parties yield to single-issue groups and richly funded

lobbies, voters will become more sophisticated, wary, splintered—and politically mature. For that reason, consultants will be even more powerful in future campaigns than they are today. Candidates will be chosen and trained for television. Targeted messages monitored by computer simulations will determine how the candidates are presented to the public.

Most consultants see the 1980s as a decade when political strategy will be tuned into a single message orchestrated by every means of communication. Matt Reese ascribes the unifying trend to cable television: "During the sixties and seventies, television was treated as a separate problem. Creative television specialists went off to the woods where they dreamed up biographies, spots, and issues commercials unconnected to the targets for mail and phone efforts. Cable television changes all that. Now the network audience is too large and the shows too similar, so it's harder to target. We'll be connecting targets more, tying targets for television, radio, and newspapers to targets for phone, mail, and in-person, into a single package.

"We'll have a single message aimed at identical targets but reached in various ways. We'll have more precise campaigns, better-controlled campaigns. Understanding how people react to information, finding out what sort of information is important to certain demographic groups, listing those groups by computer, and reaching them—that is the new politics. The people who understand computers, targeting, and the forces that move people will be the new powers in American politics."

Joe Napolitan predicts that in the next ten years there will be an increase in polling during the entire span of a campaign, more sophisticated use of electronic media, and the application of computers and other instruments for fine-tuned targeting. One political tool he considers highly important is computer simulation, a technique long used in engineering and resource planning. "In theory," he notes, "you establish a model on a computer representing the attitudes and habits of voters. By feeding into the computer various positions advocated by your candidate, you can tell how voters will react."

In 1980 Richard Wirthlin used simulation testing for Ronald Reagan's campaign, predicting how Americans would react to moves made by Jimmy Carter's strategists, as well as anticipating responses to events affecting the economy and foreign affairs. He correctly predicted voter skepticism about a last-hour flurry of activity for negotiating the release of the American hostages in Iran, which was a key element in Reagan's campaign planning. There is no doubt that, in upcoming national elections, simulation testing will be widely used by both parties.

Napolitan feels that the problem with the new technology is the quality of communications, not its form: "The goal is to elect people with ability who can cope with the unexpected. Now how do you evaluate that? The more exposure candidates get and the more penetrating questions they are asked to respond to spontaneously, the better off we are. A good, solid, objective interviewer like Bill Moyers can ask these kinds of questions. If the decision were mine, I'd abolish television debates between Presidential candidates and let a man like Moyers interview each man for a full hour, three times during the last month of the campaign. That's a lot more effective than so-called 'debates' where candidates stand and answer in thirty seconds how they would solve the problem of international terrorism."

Overall, Napolitan views democracy much as Sir Winston Churchill did: it's the worst possible form of government except for all the rest. "I don't think the system is all that bad," he says. "I'm not even terribly concerned when one candidate has more money than another, because the wealthiest guy doesn't always win. I've been in campaigns where my candidate had all the money and lost, and other campaigns where my opponent had all the money and we beat him. If a man can go out and raise money for a campaign, it might be an indication of his competence and leadership ability. In a Presidential election, I'd like to see a direct primary. We should hold a series of primaries a week apart in four sections of the country—east, south, midwest, and far west—rather than state by state."

The only major reform Napolitan advocates is a change in the winner-take-all electoral college. As things stand, a Presidential candidate could win the support of most voters and still lose the election because those votes came from the "wrong" places. Losing in New York or California by merely 100,000 votes, he then could conceivably steamroller his opponent by 5 million popular votes in ten other states and yet lag far behind in the electoral-vote count. "I would abolish conventions and nominate candidates by direct vote," Napolitan suggests. "I'd abolish the electoral college and elect the President by direct vote."

Hal Evry disagrees. He does not believe everybody is qualified to vote or serve in office, arguing that debased standards for candidates and voters produce debased government: "There are virtually no standards for public office. And there are no standards for voting. If you want reforms, that's the place to start. People who run for office use poor people as ballot fodder. That's how welfare is perpetuated, and that's why we get lousy leaders. Most people don't want to vote, so why pressure them? Do you think people should be begged to vote, picked up in cars, and dragged to the polls? Should each vote count the same? Should the vote of a motivated person who reads Congressional records and who studies national and world problems count no more than that of some welfare person who can't read and really doesn't care about government?

"I would set standards for voting. One, college graduates only. Two, voters must know the issues—who's running, and why. And three, they must have a vested interest as our early forebears demanded. The Constitution held you couldn't vote unless you owned property. I agree with that. You might own lots of property and pay heavy taxes while another man owns nothing, yet his vote counts the same as yours. My tax money supports the system, his idle hours contribute nothing, but his vote just cancels me out. That's not right. The right to vote should be earned."

Sandy Weiner blames the decline of politics on an irresponsible press: "The public reflects its media. When the media say every day that all politicians stink, what's the public supposed to think? I hold it's an honor to serve in public office, something you train and work for. Plato suggested you start training leaders at an early age. If we aim to create a perfect society, we must train young people for leadership—

the same way we evaluate and train managers for corporations. Test them by IQ, interview them, convince them that politics is a noble calling. Today we elect amateurs and say, 'Okay, now run the goddam government!' "

Stu Spencer agrees that the obstacle to making things better lies with the media: "We're at the mercy of a communications system. In terms of covering national government in Washington, it's the media managers—not the field reporters—who are making a terrible mistake. They assign their White House correspondents to hang around Pennsylvania Avenue all day, watch what goes on, and then write stories. The White House can do whatever it wants—it controls the media. From a news standpoint, the bottom line is, if the guy gets shot, they want to be sure it's covered. Well, all they need to do is assign one camera pool for that eventuality. The rest of the White House reporters should be walking all over town, hanging around the Treasury and other government departments, so when they come back to the White House they can ask the tough questions. That's a structural thing media decision makers can change overnight. The best reporting is done by columnists like Broder and Novak, guys who aren't even near the White House most of the time."

Despite its shortcomings, Spencer is satisfied with the current evolution of American democracy: "What I look for is openness and access. Our system is not perfect, but it's open. I personally favor the parliamentary systems of Britain and Japan, where there is more immediate response to public opinion. There you can bring a leader down quickly, call a special election, and have a referendum on any vital issue. In a civilized nation with a high level of education, that's a definite advance in democracy, a healthy response. We're too set and rigid."

Spencer advocates limited terms for politicians. "A President should serve one six-year term so he's never thinking about running for reelection. We should limit the terms for congressmen and senators, too. Former Presidents should be given a platform in the Senate so they can share their experience. Now I know, because I've been there, that Carter's people called Ford after the election and they talked. Nixon talked to Johnson, out of the public eye. But those people should also have a public platform so the country can benefit from their vast knowledge and experience."

Unlike his colleagues, who see the 1980s as an explosion of electronic campaigning, Spencer envisions a different scenario. "You'll see a return to the volunteer. We will be coming back to organizational clout because of the tremendous costs of media. And that includes direct mail. The successful candidate will be the one who starts putting the organization back together through sheer personal magnetism and good issue selection. It will be an economic necessity. There's a whole electorate out there which was turned off by Watergate, and they're not part of the electoral process now. But if anybody turns them on, we'll see changes. It could be one person who does it, someone with style and rhetoric. And when that someone comes along to turn on the unwashed generation, then you'll see changes."

The technology web of the 1980s already functions, launched by young pioneers from the 1970s. One of them is Michael Rowan, a thirty-seven-year-old protégé of Joe Napolitan, who now heads Media Group of Mill Valley, California. Late in 1979 Rowan ran a series of video town meetings across Alaska, using telephone panels and a device called a "co-sensor" for instant measurement of citizen feedback. He visited major Alaskan television towns and organized home seminars with local politicians. Journalist Daniel Schorr moderated sessions featuring mayors of each city in the studio with the governor. Rowan chose a representative sample of residents to take part from their homes. Each citizen watched the program on his television set, telephone to his ear. During question sessions between Schorr and the officials, the at-home participants spoke up whenever they felt moved. Schorr, the mayor, and the governor all asked questions of the public to draw them out. After some lively give and take, the public was polled. Using a computer link—the co-sensor—Rowan was able to display all responses in graph form, a virtually instant reading of public opinion.

The information formed the basis for government planning

and set the stage for future sessions of these televised town meetings. Rowan later took the concept to Puerto Rico, where he designed a citizen feedback system. From his background of managing political campaigns, Rowan now creates similar government information systems in the United States, Latin America, and Africa.

"You use the same resources and media skills as in a political campaign, but you don't keep repeating things," he explains. "Instead of tuning a candidate in to voters, you tune a whole government in to its people. Almost everybody who plugs into a participation system helps control it. The only role I play is in facilitating that conversation. Getting ideas applied, getting electronic potentialities recognized and realized—that's what I'll be doing in the next twenty years."

The future is rooted in the present. In the years ahead, political consultants will continue to shape our political choices with greater skill and sophistication. The question arises whether these professionals have created a "crisis of leadership" by their manipulation. Significantly, this charge usually comes from the professionals of the popular press. Today, we do not "know" our political leaders in the same sense our forebears did. For a hundred years now the political process has been conducted by remote control. Consultants have usurped the power of the press—hence the press's rancor against them. In the years before television, when political parties dominated and bosses ruled the precincts, big newspaper publishers made or broke anyone who aspired to public office. There was no outcry about "image makers" and "string pullers" then. Now that the balance of power has passed to the Napolitans and Spencers, those same publications loudly prophesy the death of democracy.

One thing is certain. The new politics will not fade away and the old days will not return. The process is as irreversible as the introduction of electric lights, telephones, computers, television sets, and communications satellites.

The question remains—what will we make of it? As the television generation matures, it grows more sensitive to nuances, more adept at picking up subtle signals that define a candidate's character, intelligence, and grace under stress. Television is the arena where today's campaigns are won and lost. The challenge will be to enlarge the political sophistication and insight of voting viewers.

All new technologies experience cultural lag, a period when society's mass mind assimilates change and learns to project its needs and yearnings through the new mode. It happened with radio. It is now happening with television. Increasing numbers of Americans are beginning to understand the new politics, growing comfortable with its style and demands. They are learning to read past the symbolism of campaigning. The new kingmakers will steer our democracy through the uncharted seas of instant communications with confidence, skill, and, it is fervently hoped, with wisdom. Today's research-wise consultants are certainly no worse than the pompous party bosses and powerful newspaper publishers they have replaced. In many respects, they are a distinct improvement.

The campaign consultant's independent, extra-party stance has opened our political system to outsiders and mavericks, and at the same time leaves room for more conservative, traditional candidates. The paid media messages created by the new kingmakers do battle with monolithic television networks to influence mass political opinion. The nonideological philosophy of campaign consultants anticipates developing social trends long before they are recognized by entrenched social institutions.

In a society that prides itself on openness and competition, the hired guns of politics are bastions of individual enterprise, enabling any candidate who can afford their fees the right to bypass party authority and take their message straight to the people. Dragging politics out of smoke-filled back rooms, the new kingmakers offer citizens a chance to judge present and would-be leaders under the klieg lights of television, where warts and wonders are displayed in the most effective ways that human ingenuity can devise.

These are the Merlins of the electronic age, the Vince Lombardis of modern electioneering. And, like it or not, they are here to stay.

Index